Bridge Of Hope

Also by Anne Douglas

Catherine's Land
As The Years Go By

Bridge Of Hope

Anne Douglas

PIATKUS

For more information on other books
published by Piatkus, visit our website
at www.piatkus.co.uk

Copyright © 2000 by Anne Douglas

First published in Great Britain in 2000 by
Judy Piatkus (Publishers) Ltd of
5 Windmill Street, London W1P 1HF
email: info@piatkus.co.uk

The moral right of the author has been asserted

A catalogue record for this book is available from the British Library

ISBN 0 7499 0545 X

Set in Times by
Action Publishing Technology Ltd, Gloucester

Printed and bound in Great Britain by
Mackays of Chatham plc, Chatham, Kent

For Amy, with gratitude

Author's Note

Although this novel is set in real places and concerns real bridges, the characters and events themselves are fictitious. The Ardmore Boarding House and the Queen Margaret Café in South Queensferry, the Mer-Civic engineering firm and the 1954 maintenance operation for the Forth Rail Bridge are all imaginary.

Once again, I am indebted to Edinburgh librarians for all their help, and this time I should also like to thank the staff of the library at South Queensferry.

Of the many works consulted for reference, I found the following particularly useful:

Queensferry: A Guided Walk (Published by the Queensferry Association, 1996)
A Tale Of Two Bridges by Albert Mackie (Commercial Enterprises Edinburgh, 1964)
The Forth Road Bridge Official Story (Published by The Forth Road Bridge Joint Board, 1964)
Glasgow: The Forming Of The City edited by Peter Reed (Edinburgh University Press, 1993)
The files of the *Edinburgh Evening News*

Part One

Chapter One

A ferry was coming over from the north shore. Josie Morrow could see the cars lined on the deck, the passengers looking towards the pier. She stood for a while with those waiting to take the next crossing, but she wasn't going anywhere. Only the café to have a cup of tea and maybe a word with Lina. Afterwards, she'd do the messages, as promised.

That June afternoon in 1954 was sunless, the Forth at South Queensferry a study in grey. Even the famous red of the railway bridge spanning the mile of water to Fife seemed dimmed. As the expected rain began to fall, Josie tied a scarf over her rich, mahogany-brown hair.

Lovely hair. Everyone said so. Such colour, such thickness! 'My only beauty,' said Josie, though she knew it wasn't true. There was a distinction about her face which had a beauty of its own. Not so instantly recognisable, perhaps, as her friend Lina's blonde prettiness but there all the same. And recognised by Lina's brother, Angus. He and Josie had had an understanding since he'd returned from National Service. Josie had been seventeen.

Now she was nineteen and still here. Hadn't done anything, hadn't gone anywhere. Hitching her shopping bag to her shoulder, she pushed her hands into the pockets of her raincoat and stared at the ferry now docking at the Hawes Pier. Men were jumping off, making the ropes fast.

Soon the foot passengers would be streaming away and the cars driven off. Going where? Edinburgh. The south. Did it matter? Somewhere different.

Angus was now working in an Edinburgh chemist's shop, travelling to the city every day by train from Dalmeny station. He had passed his pharmacy exams and one day would have a shop of his own. When they were married, Josie would work in the shop, too, selling cosmetics and bath salts and that sort of thing. Which would be at least as interesting as helping her mother run Ardmore, her boarding house in the Queensferry High Street. Sorry, guest-house. That was what her mother liked to call it.

Watching the cars rolling away, Josie chewed her underlip and wondered what it would be like to drive off into the blue. Not just to Edinburgh, nine miles away. Not just to Angus, putting up pills and cough mixture, writing out labels in a careful hand: 'Take Three Times A Day After Meals'. What would it be like to keep going? Keep going, driving south?

Josie had only once been over the border and that was just to the Roman Wall on a school trip. She had never been to London, never been abroad. But who had? She didn't know anyone who had been out of the country except Callum Robb, Lina's young man, and he worked in a travel agent's. But it was Callum who had told them that in only a few years' time everybody would be able to afford holidays abroad. They would buy a package and go in a group, Josie couldn't believe it, but her eyes sparkled at the idea. She'd go anywhere – in a package, in a parcel, any old way – just so that she got to see something new.

Yet she was fond enough of Queensferry, the ancient township where she'd lived all her life. The waters of the Forth, the ferries, the wide arc of the sky ... these were part of her. So was the bridge. With its viaduct and three massive cantilevered sections, it had dominated the town since it was finished in 1890, and even before, in the long years of its making. But for the Morrows it held a special

4

significance. One terrible day in 1938, Josie's father John, while working on painting maintenance, had fallen through the girders and injured his back. He had never worked again except for light duties during the war at the Rosyth naval base across the water in Fife. Though he had accepted the accident as the Lord's will, his wife, Ellie, had never forgiven the amazing structure that was the gateway to the north.

'Eighth wonder of the world, they call it,' she would cry. 'All it's done is take away our livelihood!' Yet she knew as well as anyone that it was the bridge that had put the two Queensferrys, North and South, back on the map. And the compensation John Morrow had received, if it had not gone very far, had at least helped to equip the house they had rented to run as a boarding house. So they had a new livelihood, or Ellie had, while John filled in his time with odd jobs and paperwork for the local kirk, of which he was an elder. But Ellie still would not look out of the back windows of Ardmore if she could help it. From those windows, if you twisted your head to the right, you could see the bridge.

There was a train crossing now, and Josie strained her eyes through the curtain of rain to see if she could see folk throwing out pennies for luck, as they liked to do. Och, she could see nothing and was getting soaked! She shook herself and laughed. Better get across to the café, then, before Lina saw her from the windows and thought she'd gone crazy.

It was said that Queen Margaret, wife of King Malcolm III, had founded the original ferry back in the eleventh century when she'd crossed to Fife to see some holy man. Whether that was true or not, she'd given her name to the two Queensferrys that faced each other across the Forth. And also to this little teashop close to the old Hawes Inn, where Lina Braid worked as a waitress. The Braids and the Morrows lived next door to one another. Josie and Lina had been friends as long as they could remember, had started

5

school together, though only Josie had gone on to take the leaving examinations. Lina, who'd had a variety of jobs, had never wanted further education, or a career. While Josie – she had her plans.

'Looking for Lina, Josie?' asked Mrs Tassie, the large, plump owner of the café, hurrying through her crowded tables. 'Och, we're that busy – everybody's come in out of the rain. Lina, Josie's here!' As Lina bounced out of the back room, carrying a tray, Mrs Tassie added kindly, 'Nae bother, Josie, we'll fit you in somewhere. Your mam and dad OK, then?'

'Fine, thanks, Mrs Tassie. Just out for the messages.'

'Aye, and to have a bit of a break, eh? You'll be kept on the hop, this time of year.'

'We're no' doing too badly,' Josie agreed. And thought: Makes a change.

'Look at you, you're wet through!' cried Lina, who had set down a customer's pot of tea and fancies and was now grasping Josie's arm. 'Come away to the back, I'll hang your coat up, and that scarf. You'll have to dry your hair.'

'Only summer rain,' said Josie, allowing herself to be led into the back room where the tea urn was hissing in the warmth and there was the delicious smell of fresh baking. Now that things were easier and rationing ended, Mrs Tassie made all her own scones and cakes, which was one of the attractions of the Queen Margaret for Josie. Apart from seeing Lina and being fussed over. Everyone here was a friend.

'Wets you just the same!' laughed Lina. 'Sit yourself down. Mrs Tassie'll no' mind you coming in here.'

Lina's creamy skin was flushed with the heat, her flaxen hair damp and clinging in tendrils to her brow. The only sister to three brothers, she had always been a little spoiled, especially by her father, but he had died in the war at Arnhem and Lina had then grown closer to her mother, Kitty. Of the three brothers, Angus, George and Bernie, Angus, the eldest, was her favourite; she'd been thrilled

6

when he and Josie formed their 'understanding'.

'Can't wait to be your bridesmaid,' she told Josie, her large golden-brown eyes glowing.

But Josie's response was swift. 'Come on, there's plenty of time for that. No one's talking about weddings yet.'

'Not even me!' Lina agreed.

'Och, you've got Callum on a string.'

'Must like it or he'd cut himself off, wouldn't he?'

Is it that easy? Josie wondered.

Patty MacAndrew, another waitress, another girl Josie had known all her life, came flying in with an order for toasted teacakes, and Mrs Tassie followed, to begin splitting the buns and heating the grill.

'I'll give you a hand,' volunteered Josie, but they all pushed her back in her chair, giving her tea and buttered scones, ladling out the strawberry jam.

'You've enough to do back home,' Mrs Tassie said sympathetically. 'Bright girl like you should be away, studying or something. Patty, Patty, here's the teacakes! Now have you thought about teaching, Josie? I think you'd make a wonderful teacher. You talk it over with your mam.'

'Och, you know how it is, Mrs Tassie,' she replied uneasily. 'I did do that typing course, but Mum's got nobody but me. Dad can't do much.'

'It's mebbe no' for me to say, but your mam could surely get somebody in. Doesn't have to be you.'

'I suppose it's easier.' Josie bit into her richly buttered scone. 'If it's me.'

'See you in a minute,' Lina murmured, resting her hand on Josie's shoulder before hurrying back for orders, and Mrs Tassie said no more.

There was little time to talk, everyone was so busy, but the break had been very pleasant and now the rain had stopped and the sun was struggling through. Josie, putting on her dry raincoat, said she'd better be on her way.

'I'll come round tonight, shall I?' asked Lina. 'We could go out, if you don't mind me playing gooseberry to you and Angus. Callum's away.'

'Away? Where?'

'In Spain. Looking at hotels.'

Josie's mouth twisted a little. 'Lucky devil.'

'Och, he calls it work! Well, shall I come round? With Angus?'

'Yes, fine. Make it the usual time, when we've done the dishes.'

'When *you've* done the dishes,' Lina said smartly.

Chapter Two

Outside the café, in the sunshine, it was a new world. Like a black and white film turning into Technicolor, thought Josie, watching the tourists hurrying to snap the bridge in case the clouds came back. But the only clouds were small and white, in a washed blue sky. Everything was standing out in relief – the great bridge, craft bobbing vividly, the distant shores of Fife. And now another ferry-boat was churning towards the pier, painted sides starkly black and white, cars gleaming in the sun, passengers putting up their hands to shield their eyes.

'Lord, I'd better go!' cried Josie. Her mother was cooking fish that night, Josie had to get potatoes for chips. But her spirits were soaring as she ran down the long straight road that led to the High Street of the Royal Burgh of Queensferry. Like most people, she always felt better in the sun.

The township that had grown up around Queen Margaret's ferry had had a chequered history. At one time it had been a thriving port. Trade had been good, money had been made, and merchants and sea-captains had built fine houses in the terraces that rose above the main street. But though the houses had lasted, the trade had not. Queensferry had dwindled in status, in spite of having become a Royal Burgh. It wasn't until the coming of the Forth Bridge that it took on new life again. Some of that life still lingered, though the boom building time had long gone and the busy war years, when the town was filled with soldiers and sailors, were pretty well forgotten too. There wasn't a great deal of money around in 1954. Certainly not coming the way of Ardmore.

The house was one of a pair built in the late nineteenth century in the centre of the High Street, its name from Islay considered a little fanciful by Ellie. But then, what of Seafields next door? Where were the fields? Come to that, where was the sea? The Firth of Forth was an estuary. But then that house had been divided into flats, its name didn't really matter.

Both houses were three storeys high, solidly built of local stone, with good large rooms and basements. Ardmore, however, looked rundown; it bore the signs of its Edinburgh landlord's neglect. Seafields, as a conversion, had fared better, with each tenant taking a share in the repairs, in painting and pointing and the upkeep of the roof.

When the Morrows first moved into their house in 1939, the Braids were already next door in their ground-floor flat. Arthur Braid worked at the town's distillery plant, the family wasn't too badly off. But after the war, with Arthur gone and money to find, Kitty had sacrificed her front room for a hairdressing salon where she permed and pincurled for reasonable prices, and somehow fitted her family of four into the rooms behind. It was Angus who did the repairs for her, when he had time at weekends, but John Morrow, who couldn't of course go up ladders, always turned down Angus's offers of help on principle. If it was that Edinburgh fellow's responsibility to look after the house, John argued, why should he no' do it?

'Och, Dad's great on matters of principle,' commented Josie. 'While he's talking, Ardmore goes down.'

'Write another letter to the landlord,' Angus advised.

But letters to the landlord brought only promises. One day, someone would come to mend the chimneys and the

10

doors that didn't fit, paint the window-frames, fix the bell-push. Until then, thought Josie, coming back with the shopping, she'd just have to do what she could herself. At least inside the house was as neat and clean as she and her mother could make it. Net curtains snowy, furniture polished, worn carpets brushed. Even the faulty bell-push gleamed with Brasso.

'It's no' too bad once folk are inside,' Josie said to herself, humping the shopping through the hall to the kitchen. 'We've just got to get them through the door.'

Just at that time, they were doing well. Because it was summer, people were booking up. All the rooms were taken, with the exception of the best room, the first-floor back, which had a beautiful view of the Forth. They'd had a cancellation for that only yesterday morning, which had resulted in bent brows and bad tempers all day, but looking at her mother's sunny face now, Josie guessed that something good had happened.

'Josie, Josie, where've you been?' cried Ellie Morrow, starting up at her entrance. 'I've just let the first-floor back. Oh, Josie, you should see the man who's taken it! He's like a film star. And a gentleman!'

'Oh, yes?' commented Josie, without interest. 'Shall I get on with the tatties?'

'No, no, Josie, listen!'

Mother and daughter faced each other in the long, narrow kitchen that was filled with light from its high windows overlooking the water. This was the room where the Morrows spent most of their time, their living room being given over to the 'guests'. There were chairs by the stove that was always on because it provided hot water, a second-hand fridge clanking in the corner, a great scrubbed table, and a gas cooker where that evening Ellie would fry her fish.

She was a slender woman in her late forties. Her eyes, a paler blue than Josie's, were large and beautiful, her brown hair thickly silvered. On her short imperious nose was a pair of shell-framed reading glasses which she now

11

removed and waved, to emphasise her point.

'Josie, I tell you, Mr Guthrie's really handsome. Black hair, very dark eyes, that pale skin some folk have with that kind of colouring. When he knocked on ma door and said he'd seen the Vacancies sign and was there a room, I didn't know where to look! I mean, I could tell at once he was a professional man. It was his accent, you see, and his manner – you'd never mistake them!'

Josie, shovelling the potatoes out of their brown paper bag, gave a wry smile. 'Don't wish to be rude, Mum, but why's a guy like that taking a room here?'

Her mother flushed. 'Well, you *are* rude, Josie, and very unfair. You know how hard I work to keep this house looking nice.'

'So do I work hard, but I know very well we're no' the Caledonian Hotel. Who is this man? What's he doing here?'

'He's a civil engineer,' her mother answered eagerly. 'He's doing a maintenance survey of the bridge with some other engineers. They're booked into the Bell but he couldn't get in, so he's having his meals there and just wants room and breakfast here.'

'That's a relief. I was thinking I'd have to go out and get some more fish.'

But Ellie was already planning the excellent breakfast she would give Mr Guthrie the following morning.

'As long as we have enough kippers,' she murmured. 'Though I say it maself, there's no one cooks a better kipper than me.' Suddenly her blue eyes were sharp. 'Josie, if you see Mr Guthrie now, be sure to be polite.'

'When have I no' been polite to our boarders? I mean, guests?'

'Well, I mean 'specially polite.' Her mother hesitated. 'He'd be – a good person to get to know.'

There was silence as Josie, turning round from the sink, easily read her mother's mind. Then she laughed.

'Angus is coming round tonight, Mum. With Lina. We'll probably go out.'

12

'Angus,' her mother repeated coldly. 'If you ask me, you see him too often, Josie.'

'We do have an understanding.'

'You're too young to be thinking of getting married. Your dad and me've said that all along.'

'And understanding just means you'll get married some time, Mum, Not tomorrow.'

'Aye, well, I hope that's true. I'm no' saying I've anything against Angus, he's a nice enough lad, but —'

But you think I could do better, thought Josie, and felt a sudden rush of loyalty to Angus. As for the unknown Mr Guthrie, she didn't feel like being polite to him at all, never mind 'specially so.

There was a step in the hall and John Morrow came in, carrying the evening paper. He took off his cap and hung it on a peg on the back of the door.

'Could do with a cup of tea,' he said, nodding to his wife. 'All right, Josie? Get the messages?'

'Fine, thanks, Dad. Yes, I got everything.'

John unfolded his paper and limped to his chair by the stove. At one time he had been a tall man, but since his accident he had lost his height, had become crooked and frail. His hair, once as richly brown as Josie's, had turned into a grey bush; his eyes, dark-blue like hers, were shadowed with pain. Yet there were still signs in him of the handsome young man Ellie McIver had married in the kirk that was central to his life. And his character was as the same as ever. Firm as a rock.

Ellie made the tea and Josie paused in her work to have another cup. Sitting at the table, her eyes looking nowhere in particular, she said idly, 'Know what Mrs Tassie said today? I'd make a good teacher.'

Her parents looked at each other.

'What's Beryl Tassie's opinion got to do with anything?' asked Ellie, after a pause.

'She was just saying.'

'Makes nice scones,' John remarked. 'No' much good for anything else.'

13

'Thing is, I agree,' said Josie desperately. 'I think I'd make a good teacher, too. I mean, I got ma certificates and Miss Riley was always telling me I should go to college.'

Her father finished his tea. 'Waste of time for a woman, having a career. Only have to give it up when she gets married. Who'd take care of the bairns, eh?'

'Aye, you have to think of that,' chimed Ellie. 'Bairns come first.'

'They grow up,' said Josie. 'Then you can go back.'

Her father fixed her with a darkened gaze.

'We let you stay on at school to do your exams, Josie, and then you did that typing course. Was that no' useful?'

'Oh, yes.' She shrugged. 'I type out the bills for Mum.'

'There you are, then. Let that do you.' John rose with painful slowness and laid his hand on his wife's shoulder. 'You know your mother couldn't have any more children after you were born. You're all we've got.'

'To help, you mean. Well, I think I do all I can!'

'Nobody could do more,' Ellie said warmly. She pressed Josie's hand. 'And we're very grateful, pet. I don't know what we'd do without you, and that's a fact.'

'Supposing I do get married one day?'

'To Angus Braid?' Her father was unworried. 'He's a good lad. Good kirk-goer. You'll be all right with Angus.'

'But we might move to Edinburgh, you know.'

'No, no, he'll find a place here. He's a Queensferry man, he'll no' want to move to Edinburgh.'

Josie stared from one parent to the other, from her father, complacently smiling, to her mother, frozen-faced. She leaped to her feet and ran out of the kitchen, banging the door behind her. Again, her parents exchanged glances, but in a few moments Josie was back and slicing the potatoes into chips without saying a word.

Chapter Three

While Josie and her mother served high tea to their guests –
the two ladies from Aberdeen, the hikers from the Borders,
the married couple from Glasgow – the Braids next door
were having sausages and mash with baked beans and fried
tomatoes.

'This is no' healthy food, Mum,' said Lina (christened
Paulina, a name she disliked and never used).

'I notice you're no' leaving it,' her mother retorted.

Kitty Braid was forty-six. She had green eyes and
copper-red hair she coloured herself in her front room
salon. None of her children was like her in looks. They all
had the fair hair and golden-brown eyes of her late
husband, which suited Kitty, for Arthur had been the love
of her life. Most like him in character was Angus, on whom
she leaned heavily, and though she was fond of Josie
Morrow and knew she would make a good wife, Kitty
always felt a little pain around her heart when she thought
of Angus marrying her. Or anyone.

'Should be having salad, though,' Lina went on. 'I mean,
in the summer.'

'Salad!' jeered George, who was twenty and working at
the local distillery. 'Catch me eating salad!'

'Catch me,' echoed Bernie. He was sixteen and also
working at the distillery. In two years' time, he would have
to leave to do his National Service. Kitty thanked God

every night that Angus and George had come back safely and that the terrible Korean War was over, but was already worrying about Bernie. Now if she'd had all girls, she wouldn't have had to worry. Or, would she? Eyeing Lina, who was looking as pretty as a picture in a new cream dress, Kitty wondered.

'There's trifle to follow,' she announced. 'Suppose you'll say that's unhealthy too?'

'Mum, stop teasing!' shrieked Lina. 'I never say no to trifle!'

'Have to let the belt of that dress out, then,' observed George. 'Why are you all toffed up, anyway? Thought Callum was away.'

'I said I'd go round to Josie's. We might go out somewhere.'

'You said what?' Angus, who had been grinning with his brothers, was frowning now. 'You know very well I'm going to see Josie tonight. I 'specially want to see her tonight.'

'I thought I could go with you.' Lina was looking to her mother for support. 'Why should I no' come too? Josie said it was OK. I mean, Callum's away, I've nowhere to go.'

'I told you, I 'specially want to talk to Josie tonight. On her own.'

'Why?' asked Kitty swiftly. 'What's so special about tonight, Angus?'

They all turned their eyes to him, watching his handsome face colour and his hand go up to push back his plume of fair hair. Kitty felt that anxious little squeeze of her heart again. What was this news he hadn't told her?

'Nothing much,' he muttered. 'Mr Johnson just said he was thinking of retiring early and his son would be taking over the business. He wants to expand, open another shop, take on a partner. Could be me.'

'A partner! With Niall Johnson!' Kitty's fear vanished. 'Angus, that's wonderful!'

'Nothing much?' repeated George. 'I'd say it was plenty. Will you no' need some cash?'

16

'Aye, I'll have to get a loan.' Angus's broad brow was clearing. 'Mr Johnson says he'll speak for me at the bank.'

'You should have told us all this before, when you first came in,' said his mother. 'We could have had a drink or something.'

'It's no' certain, Mum, it's no' time yet for celebrating.'

'You just wanted to tell Josie first?'

'No, no – well – like I said, it's no' definite.'

'We'll leave it, then.' Kitty stood up and began to clear away the dishes. 'But you let Lina go round to Josie's with you. After all, the news is no secret now. And no' definite, as you say.'

Angus glanced at his sister. 'As long as I get some time with Josie on ma own, OK?'

'OK,' she answered blithely.

Upstairs at Ardmore, Josie was getting ready to go out. Her room on the top floor was scarcely more than a cupboard, but at least she faced the back and had a view of the Forth. On her narrow bed were her old teddy, a china doll named Shirley, and a rag doll named Rita. Pinned to the wall were a number of pictures of film stars she had cut out from magazines when she was still at school; Stewart Granger, James Mason, Van Johnson, Gregory Peck. Along with these were a couple of framed certificates for Sunday School attendance, and a text worked in cross-stitch that her mother had once bought at a sale. Josie was rather fond of it.

'The Path of the Just is as the Shining Light', she would spell out as a little girl, and think of moonlight shining over the Forth. Once she had asked her mother, who were the Just?

'The righteous,' her mother replied, and at Josie's blank look, had expanded, 'the good. Folk who do what is right.'

'Oh.' Would the moonlight be hers? Josie wondered. She always tried to do what was right. Did trying count?

Of late she had scarcely looked at the text, but sometimes

17

she thought she should take down the film stars, get some proper pictures. After all, she was a bit old now for pin-ups.

That evening she was worried about her hair. Did it smell of fish? She brushed it hard and sprayed it with eau-de-Cologne because there wasn't time to wash it, then put on a cardigan over her pale green dress and decided she would do. Her father didn't approve of make-up and though sometimes she added lipstick when she left the house, she didn't really need it. Besides, she was only going for a walk with Angus and Lina, it wasn't as if they were going to a party or anything, or even into Edinburgh.

She ran lightly down the stairs from the top floor, heels tapping on the linoleum – carpet, such as it was, didn't start till the first-floor landing – and it was there that she saw a dark-haired man in casual tweeds closing his door. The famous Mr Guthrie.

Well, she'd promised to be polite. Josie smiled at him.

'Hello, I'm Mrs Morrow's daughter. Everything all right?'

He smiled back and she thought, yes, he's handsome. Or maybe striking was the word. Those very dark eyes, the pale skin – you'd have thought he'd be tanned, being out on bridges so much. But he was tall, a good deal taller than Angus, and her mother'd been right about his manner. Cost a lot of money, a manner like his.

'Everything's fine, thanks,' he told her, and his voice was like something on the wireless. 'The view's beautiful.'

He was looking at her with some interest and making no move to go. She felt a little self-conscious.

'I – I thought you'd gone out for your dinner,' she said at last, making towards the stairs.

He followed. 'Yes, I've eaten. Came back for some notes I needed. I'm working this evening.'

'Shame, it's so fine.'

All the way down to the ground floor, she was aware of his firm tread following her. Was he noticing the shabbiness of

18

the hall? she wondered. The faded distemper? The ancient hatstand that had to be propped at just the right angle, or it swayed like the Leaning Tower of Pisa? Worst of all, the smell of fish that lingered everywhere?

Oh, Lord, her mother had appeared, pale blue eyes lighting up at the sight of the new guest.

'Mr Guthrie, have you met ma daughter, then? This is Josie.'

'We've introduced ourselves, Mrs Morrow.' He gave a slight bow, but as Ellie was smiling delightedly and about to speak again, a knock sounded on the front door. Angus and Lina had arrived.

'My friends are here,' Josie called back hurriedly, as she let them in. 'We have to go.'

'Why, Josie!' cried her mother, vexed. 'There's no need to rush off. Mr Guthrie here might like to know about Queensferry—'

But Mr Guthrie was staring at Lina.

She's wearing her new dress, thought Josie. She looks as luscious as a peach. Oh, poor Mum!

Instantly, the air was electric. Angus's hand was pushing back his hair, Ellie was biting her lip, Lina's wide eyes were looking into the depths of Mr Guthrie's dark gaze. Only Josie felt herself an onlooker. She murmured some names, no one else spoke. She said they were just going out, maybe down to the harbour, such a nice evening.

'I wish I could join you,' Mr Guthrie said hoarsely.

'Why don't you?' asked Lina, and Angus stiffened, like an animal scenting danger.

'Mr Guthrie has to work this evening,' said Josie.

'I could be free tomorrow,' he said eagerly, his eyes still riveted on Lina. 'If you'd care to join me then? All of you?'

'I've to work late,' snapped Angus.

'Josie's not doing anything,' Ellie said quickly.

'And I'm not,' said Lina.

'Shall we meet here? At the same time?'

'We'll look forward to it, Mr Guthrie.'

'You must call me Duncan.'

As they walked away down the High Street, Josie looked back. Duncan Guthrie was still standing in the doorway of Ardmore, watching them. And behind him was her mother, watching, too.

Chapter Four

Only a few fishing boats used the harbour now, and there were no longer any ferries coming in to the old slipway. There was still plenty of activity, though, particularly on a fine summer's evening when the pleasure craft were out and about, and people sat with drinks from a nearby pub, watching the boats, looking out to Fife.

Josie, Lina and Angus sat with drinks, too. John Morrow disapproved of Josie's going into pubs, but she didn't see anything wrong in sitting outside and having a lemonade. That evening the frost between the Braids was so thick, she felt she could have done with something stronger. They'd walked the length of the High Street and Angus had said nothing, until he brought out the drinks. Then he let fly.

'What the hell did you think you were playing at back there?' he demanded of Lina. 'Inviting a fellow you'd never seen before to come out with us?'

'Keep your voice down! Everybody's looking!'

'I'm no' worried if they are.' Angus drank some beer, his eyes stormy. 'I tell you, when you said what you did, I couldn't believe my ears!'

'Och, it didn't mean a thing. I was just being friendly.'

'I'll say! And how d'you think Callum would feel about you being friendly with a stranger, an old guy like that?'

'Old? He's no' old!' Lina turned a flushed face on Josie. 'Josie, would you say Duncan was old?'

21

'Duncan, is it?' rapped Angus. 'He's thirty, if he's a day, and probably married. You don't know one damn thing about him.' He also turned to Josie. 'And neither do you, Josie, but you still agreed to see him tomorrow. That was another thing I couldn't believe.'

'I didn't actually say I'd go,' she said defensively. 'But if Lina's going, maybe I should. It's true, you know, Lina, we don't know anything about Mr Guthrie.'

'We're going for a walk round the town, we might have a drink. Does a fellow need references for that?'

'You know Callum wouldn't want you seeing another man,' Angus said doggedly. 'He thinks the world of you, Lina.'

'Well, we're no' engaged, I'm free to do as I like. So give it a rest, Angus!'

They sat in silence, bitterly aware that their pleasant evening was ruined. Angus, in particular, remained on edge, all his usual cheerfulness gone. As he darted glances from his sister to Josie, drawing deeply on his beer, he was an Angus they rarely saw.

'Och, I've had enough of this!' cried Lina, jumping to her feet. 'You can stay with Angus, Josie, and welcome to him. I'm off home.'

In fact, she didn't go home. They saw her being greeted by Patty MacAndrew and others Josie remembered from school. Soon she was sitting down with them and Josie and Angus heard her high laughter.

'Looks like you're stuck with me,' Angus muttered.

Josie took his hand. 'Come on, didn't you want to be alone with me?'

'I did,' he sighed. 'I've looked forward to it all day. In fact, I told Lina not to come with us, but you know what she's like, can't bear to stay in.'

'She didn't mean any harm, Angus, talking to Mr Guthrie like that.'

'I know, but I can't help thinking of Callum.'

They both thought of Callum. His long, solemn face, his

22

straight ginger hair, his sharp mind. Everyone at the local school had tipped him for university, but he had opted for a business course and a job in a travel firm instead. Well, he seemed to know what he was doing. Except when it came to falling in love with Lina.

'I'm sure Lina does care for Callum,' Josie said now. 'She's probably just too young to want to settle down.'

'She's your age,' Angus replied.

Josie looked away, said something he couldn't hear.

'What did you say?'

'I said, maybe I'm too young, too. To want to settle down.'

He caught his breath. 'Josie, what are you saying? You don't want to marry me?'

'I do, I do.' She raised a direct gaze to his. 'But no' for a while. I mean, until I've done something.'

'Done what, for God's sake?'

'I don't know.' She laughed weakly. 'Got some training – started a course – and I'm no' talking about typing. When I was at school, I always thought I'd have a career before I got married.'

'I thought your dad was no' in favour of careers for women?'

She shrugged, but Angus picked up her hand and held it.

'Listen, you'd have a better chance of a career if you married me, than staying put and cleaning your mum's house.'

'How d'you mean?'

'I mean you could go on courses in Edinburgh. I wouldn't mind, I'd be happy to let you do what you want. You could go to Moray House, train to be a teacher.'

'You think we would live in Edinburgh?' she asked thoughtfully. 'Dad was saying you'd want to set up here.'

At last Angus smiled and was himself again. 'There's something I want to tell you, Josie, something I've been dying to tell you ever since we came out. Then we got side-tracked, with Lina and that Guthrie fellow.'

'Well, tell me now!' she cried.

'Old Johnson's retiring. His son wants to expand the business and there's talk I could be a partner.'

'Angus!'

'Aye, it's a grand opportunity.' His eyes were alight with enthusiasm now. 'I know I'm a bit young, and I'm no' experienced, but Niall Johnson says he wants me and that means a lot, eh?'

'It's wonderful, Angus, it's really wonderful!'

'It's no' definite, but I think I can promise we're on our way, Josie. We could be married next year. What do you say?'

She didn't know what to say. Next year? So soon? Angus took her hands again.

'I've been saving up,' he said softly. 'Haven't bought it yet, though.'

'Haven't bought what?'

'The ring.'

'Angus ...'

He took a piece of string from his pocket and wound it round the third finger of her left hand.

'Just measuring.'

'Angus, we should talk about this. I mean, we've plenty of time and there's ma folks—'

'They know we have an understanding.' He sat back, twining the string round his own finger. 'Though I don't suppose I'm your mother's first choice, eh?'

'She likes you, Angus, she thinks you're a good lad, she said so. But she doesn't know what she'd do without me, that's the problem.'

He leaned forward. 'If some guy like Guthrie asked you to marry him, your mother'd be glad to do without you,' he said distinctly.

Josie flinched. 'Angus, that's a terrible thing to say.' She knew it was true.

They began to walk back towards Ardmore, the light of the

24

evening still as clear as ever. They were used to long light evenings at that time of year. Some people called them white nights. Angus said they were hopeless for lovers.

'How can we kiss in broad daylight like this?' he asked, outside the house. 'I'd no' mind, but I know you'll be worrying about the neighbours.'

They kissed anyway, long deep kisses that made them both feel good.

'Are you really going out with that Guthrie fellow tomorrow?' Angus asked, at last letting Josie go.

'Well, I think it'll be better if I'm with Lina.'

'I don't think either of you should be going out with him.'

'He's all right, Angus, I'm sure you don't need to worry.'

'You like him?'

'I'm no' interested in him at all. Anyway, he won't be staying long. He's just a ship passing in the night.'

'Wish he'd sail on, then,' Angus said glumly. Suddenly he brightened. He took the piece of string from his pocket and again tied it round Josie's finger.

'Don't forget,' he whispered. 'You're promised to me.'

Chapter Five

Everyone in Ardmore's dining room sat at one long table, which had been set for Mr Guthrie's first breakfast with Mrs Morrow's best white tablecloth. It'll be the devil to wash and iron when somebody spills the ketchup, thought Josie, who hadn't wanted to use it. But there'd been no arguing with her mother that morning as she tied a scarf around her hair and prepared to cook the kippers, conducting a monologue as she went.

'Now, don't you forget, Josie, Mr Guthrie asked you out as well as that cheeky little Lina. I never was so ashamed in ma life as when she invited him to join you last evening. I mean, what must he have thought! Kitty Braid's made a very bad job of bringing up that girl and I've a good mind to tell her so.'

'Mum,' groaned Josie, 'don't go on.'

She was already wrinkling her nose at the smell of the kippers, but they certainly looked delicious when they were cooked and were appreciated by the guests, smell or no smell. Mr Guthrie seemed quite happy at the top of the table, even though he did look as though he were conducting a board meeting, and after she'd seen the way he'd looked at Lina, Josie found she'd quite lost her shyness in his presence.

'An excellent breakfast,' he told Ellie as he was leaving the dining room, and she blushed and glanced at Josie, who

26

was clearing away. But it was John Morrow who wanted to speak to the new guest and buttonholed him as he was about to go up the stairs.

Oh, poor old Dad, thought Josie, running the hot tap over a pile of dishes. He wants to talk about the bridge.

No doubt her father would be telling Mr Guthrie all about his accident, and Mr Guthrie, with his perfect manners, would be listening gravely, and then would say he'd have to go but they'd have another chat anyway and her dad would feel better. Mum could never understand how much the bridge still meant to Dad. He'd had nothing to take its place for so long.

'See you this evening, Miss Morrow,' Mr Guthrie said to her as he passed her in the hall on his way out.

'Please call me Josie,' she answered, thinking again how striking his looks were, how different he was from anybody else she'd ever met. Could he really be thirty? It seemed pretty old. She couldn't imagine being attracted to him. Or even calling him Duncan.

Unlike Lina, who had lain awake for what seemed most of the night, thinking of 'Duncan'. It was true that she was very fond of Callum, who had always been special to her ever since they'd all played together as children: riding their bikes down the promenade, peeking at the Forth through wartime barbed wire. He was steady, Callum was, he would always be there, to be counted on, but compared with Duncan and his dark eyes and BBC voice, his tweeds and good shoes, his lovely manners ... och, you had to admit it, Callum was left at the post.

On the other hand – Lina punched her pillow – it was true what misery-guts Angus had said. She didn't know one thing about Duncan Guthrie. He might be married. Probably was, because he wasn't very young. Not thirty, maybe, but not twenty-one either. And while Callum came from Queensferry, knew everybody she knew, was a part of life hereabouts, Duncan came from she didn't know where and when he'd finished the bridge job would certainly be moving on. That was really the only thing she knew about him. He would not be staying.

At breakfast next morning, when they were all shaking out Cornflakes and hastily drinking tea, she was relieved that Angus said no more about her meeting with Duncan that evening. She'd already cleared the ground with her mother who'd said she was quite right to go for a walk or a drink with someone new. After all, she wasn't engaged to Callum Robb.

Exactly my point, thought Lina, to quell the small voice of protest at the back of her mind. She wondered if Angus had persuaded Josie not to come this evening. Didn't matter if he hadn't. Lina knew she faced no threat from Josie.

The day passed somehow, and then they were meeting at Ardmore, Lina and Duncan, and, yes, Josie too. How pretty she was looking, thought Lina, who could always afford to be generous in praise of other women. She was wearing a blue cotton dress; her beautiful hair burned darkly in the evening sun.

'Had to wash it,' she whispered to Lina as they waited for Duncan. 'Cooked kippers this morning – need I say more?'

Duncan, immaculate in a dark blazer, clapped his hands at the sight of them.

'Where to, then? Anywhere but the bridge!'

Mrs Morrow was hovering. Putting her eyes through me, thought Lina, who shrugged and suggested the harbour again. After all, they could sit outside the pub there, and that suited Josie whose father didn't like her to go into pubs.

'No need to worry about me,' Josie said quickly. 'Anyway, I thought we were supposed to be going for a walk, not a drink.'

'How would it be if I took you girls for a drive instead?' Duncan was swinging his car keys.

28

A drive? Their eyes lit up. They didn't know anyone who owned a car. Angus and Callum could drive, and drove for their work sometimes, but they couldn't as yet afford cars of their own.

'That all right, Mrs Morrow?' Duncan asked, and Ellie cried, 'Oh, yes, certainly!'

'We won't be late,' he promised. 'And I'll drive very carefully. This way, girls, the car's parked at the Bell.'

Seventh heaven was something the girls had heard about but never experienced. Now, even Josie, who knew she was playing gooseberry, felt they were in it, a seventh heaven of their own, bowling along down quiet country roads in Duncan's sports car, letting the wind blow through their hair, feeling they were young and beautiful and life could only get better.

I shall never forget this evening, thought Josie. This summer world. Only yesterday she had been standing in rain at the bridge, but now she couldn't imagine rain or dark clouds, or trouble of any sort. Things would work out for her, suddenly she felt sure of it, and Lina would be all right, too. Callum would come home, she would see that he was the one for her, and Duncan Guthrie would be just a memory. A very pleasant memory. Like his car.

They did stop for a drink, at a large country hotel where they could sit outside in the garden, but only after Duncan had scrupulously checked that it was all right with Josie.

'Of course it's all right, Duncan,' she told him, now using his first name with ease. 'I always feel a bit of a fool about not drinking. It's just a bee Dad's got in his bonnet.'

'I can understand. As a matter of fact, I drink very little myself. I've seen the effects of too much drink too often.'

'You mean accidents?' Josie nodded. 'Mum said some folk thought ma dad might have been drinking before he fell. They didn't know him. He was always stone-cold sober.'

'He told me this morning what had happened,' Duncan

said sympathetically. 'It's everybody's nightmare to think of falling like that. You can't help but be afraid sometimes.'

They were silent for a moment, sitting on the hotel terrace, surrounded by fragrant shrubs and trellises with climbing plants, drinks in long glasses on the wicker tables before them.

'Oh, don't,' Lina said softly, and Josie knew what she meant. Don't spoil this. Don't spoil our seventh heaven. They began to talk of other things.

Without being asked, Duncan told them that he wasn't married. He had once been engaged but it had fallen through by mutual consent. Lina opened her eyes wide at that, but said nothing. His parents lived in Edinburgh, where his father had been an advocate but was now retired.

'Wanted me to follow him into the law,' Duncan went on, 'but it wasn't for me. I'm an engineer. I work on bridges and that's what I want to do.'

'Your parents live in Edinburgh?' Josie repeated. 'Why don't you just drive home every night?'

He smiled. 'I don't live with my parents. I'm based in Edinburgh but I've my own flat. At the moment it's let. Anyhow, I like to be on the spot.' His gaze rested on Lina's face and his voice faltered. 'Very much so.'

They had another round of soft drinks and Duncan, lying back in his wicker chair, said it was the girls' turn to talk about themselves.

'You know all about us,' Lina said uneasily. 'Our lives are no' so interesting. Josie works for her folks, I work in a teashop. I've got three brothers, ma dad died in the war, ma mum does hairdressing for a living. That's it.'

'Not quite.' Duncan offered cigarettes and when they shook their heads, lit one himself. 'You haven't mentioned young men.'

'What young men?'

'Well, I met Angus last night. Isn't he your young man, Josie? Please forgive my asking.'

'That's OK.' She knew why he was asking her, he was working his way round to asking Lina. 'We have an understanding.'

The dark eyes moved to Lina.

'I will have a cigarette,' she said abruptly, and when he lit it for her, coughed and blushed and said she wasn't much of a smoker. Duncan waited. Josie stared fixedly at a tub of pink geraniums.

'I suppose I have an understanding, too,' Lina said bravely. 'I'm going out with a fellow from a travel agency. He's abroad at the moment.'

'Ah,' said Duncan. 'I was sure there'd be someone.'

The drive home was just as lovely as the drive out, but somehow the feeling of being in seventh heaven had evaporated. Well, you couldn't be up there all the time, the girls knew that, and no doubt Duncan knew it too. He didn't talk much on the way back and Lina, in the front seat, kept glancing at his sculpted profile and away. When he'd parked the car at the rear of the Bell, the three of them walked back to Seafields without speaking.

'Goodnight, then, and thanks ever so much,' said Lina. 'Wasn't it lovely, Josie?'

'Oh, it was,' she answered.

'Perhaps I'll see you again,' Duncan said to Lina, his gaze not leaving her. 'Come into your teashop for a buttered scone.'

'Why not?' She gave her high laugh. 'Well, goodnight again.'

She opened the door to her mother's flat and vanished inside. After a long moment, Duncan turned to Josie.

'Not too late, are we? I've got you home in good time?'

'Oh, yes, it's not late at all.'

Josie knew that whatever time it was, her mother would still be waiting up and her heart sank at the thought. In the hall, she thanked Duncan again for a wonderful drive.

'My pleasure,' he said courteously. 'Goodnight, Josie.'

31

When she had watched him climb the stair to his room, she did her duty and faced her mother in the kitchen. Ordeal by question. Get it over. But though she accepted a cup of tea and told her mother all that Mr Guthrie had told her, she did not say anything about being in seventh heaven. Anyway, she'd come down from that now.

'And did he ask you out again?' her mother asked eagerly. 'Did he ask Lina?'

'No, he didn't ask either of us out again. I told him about Angus and Lina told him about Callum.'

'Oh, Josie, why ever did you mention Angus?'

'You know why, Mum. It was the right thing to do. In fact, he'd already guessed about Angus himself.'

'And Lina told him about Callum?' her mother said thoughtfully. 'I must say, I'm surprised.'

Josie yawned. 'I don't suppose we'll be going out with Mr Guthrie again. Goodnight, Mum. I'm away to ma bed.'

For no particular reason, once in her bed she found herself reading that old text again as the moon went gliding by her window.

'The Path of the Just is as the Shining Light'.

She smiled as she closed her eyes. She felt quite pleased with herself and Lina. They had done what was right.

Chapter Six

The days went by. Callum was due home any time. Mr Guthrie moved out of Ardmore, telling Mrs Morrow he'd been very comfortable indeed, but a vacancy had cropped up at the Bell Inn. It made sense for him to be with his colleagues, he hoped she understood?

'Oh, yes,' she told him, with her frozen look. 'I'm glad you found us satisfactory.'

'Shan't forget your breakfasts in a hurry!' Duncan turned to John. 'And, Mr Morrow, I've really enjoyed meeting you and talking about the old days.'

'Aye, well, I was only involved in the painting but the bridge still means a lot to me,' said John. 'It's been grand hearing what the fellows are up to these days. Good luck, Mr Guthrie, and all the best.'

'Thank you, but you know, you'll soon have someone else to talk to,' Duncan said, with a smile. 'We've a marine team and a superstructure team starting work tomorrow. I believe a couple of chaps are coming here.'

'That's right,' Ellie said coldly. 'There are two bridge workers booked in for tonight. Goodbye, Mr Guthrie.'

Later that morning, to take her mind off her troubles, Ellie went round to Kitty Braid's for a shampoo and set. She was relieved to find herself the only client, for Kitty hadn't enough space to have cubicles and everybody had to sit together in her front room, listening to what everybody else said. The one bright spot in Ellie's darkness was that if Mr Guthrie had not taken up with her Josie, at least he hadn't fallen for Kitty's Lina, either. In spite of her pushing herself at him!

'Lovely to see you, Ellie,' cried Kitty brightly, as she ran the hot water. 'Just the usual, eh?'

'Aye, the usual. I'm no' due for another perm yet.'

'And what do you think of our Lina?' asked Kitty, rubbing away with the scented shampoo.

Ellie made strangled noises, her face being covered with a face cloth pressed against the wash-basin. Some hair-dressers had what they called the backwash, but Kitty hadn't got round to that yet.

'I mean Lina and your Mr Guthrie, Ellie. Or has he moved out yet? Och, I'm no' sure whether I'm on ma head or ma heels.' Above Ellie's head, Kitty gave a peal of laughter. 'Lina's the same.'

Ellie felt all the blood draining away from her face, then rushing back again. As Kitty brought her head up and wrapped her hair in a towel, she could not look at herself in the mirror, could not meet Kitty's reflected eyes either.

'How d'you mean?' she asked in a whisper. 'Lina and Mr Guthrie?'

'Well, it's a sworn secret so don't you go telling anybody – but they're engaged!'

'Engaged?' Ellie's mouth was dry. 'They can't be, they've only just met!'

'Aye, but he's been taking her out all over the place. The theatre in Edinburgh ... drives ... dinner-dances. You know Lina's always been a lovely dancer? Ballroom, jiving, jitterbugging – you name it, she can do it. Not that Duncan'd ever go in for jitterbugging!' Kitty laughed again. 'But Lina says he's very good at ballroom. Och, they've been out so much, I've had to lend her the money to buy two new dresses. I mean, she wants to look her best, eh, with a guy like him? Did you hear he went to Loretto?

34

That's a public school near Musselburgh.'

'I know where Loretto is,' Ellie answered shortly, wincing as Kitty stranded her hair into pin-curls and stabbed them into place with grips. Whatever happened, she told herself, she would not let Kitty see how she had been cut to the heart by her news.

'And what about Callum?' she asked. 'Is he no' due back any day? What's he going to say when he finds out about Mr Guthrie?'

'Callum?' Kitty's tone was vague. 'Well, that was only a boy and girl thing, you know, Ellie. Him and Lina were never officially engaged.'

'I'll bet Callum thinks it was more than a boy and girl thing!'

'Yes, well, that's why the engagement's a secret. Lina wants to tell him first, that's only fair. So she's no' wearing the ring.'

'She's already got the ring?'

'Aye. Oh, Ellie, you should see it! Two great diamonds – one for him, one for her, Duncan says – clasped together!' Kitty tied a large net over Ellie's hair and pulled back her chair. 'Now, I'll pop you under the dryer, eh? My eleven o'clock's due any minute.'

'Josie, Josie, are you there?' Ellie, newly curled and scarlet-faced, hurried into her kitchen where Josie was making pastry. 'Have you heard? Lina Braid's engaged to Mr Guthrie! I can't believe it, I can't take it in! Make me a cup of tea, pet, and I'll sit maself down. Ma heart's knocking like somebody at the door!'

Josie put down her rolling pin and washed the flour from her hands. She warmed the teapot and put in the tea leaves. Then she took the kettle from the stove and made the tea.

'Where did you hear this?' she asked evenly.

'From Kitty, of course! You know I've been to have ma hair done. She said Mr Guthrie's been taking Lina out all over the place, wining and dining and all that sort of thing, and now he's bought her a ring but she's no' wearing it yet. The engagement's a secret till Callum comes home.'

'I can't believe Lina wouldn't have told me.' Josie set a cup of tea before her mother. 'There must be some mistake.'

'When she's got the ring? How can there be a mistake?' Ellie gulped her tea and fanned her face with a drying cloth from the rail at the stove. 'Och, I feel so upset, Josie! That cheeky little thing taking Mr Guthrie from right under your nose ...'

'Mum, I wish you wouldn't talk like that. I was never interested in Mr Guthrie and he was never interested in me. Anyway, I've got Angus.'

'Angus!'

'He's got a good job, Mum, if that's what you want for me, a fellow with a career. A pharmacist is a professional, you know, he has to pass exams.'

'Aye, aye, you could do worse.' Ellie set down her cup. Her colour had faded, leaving her looking drained and weary. 'He's the brightest of that family, eh?'

Josie stood looking down at her half-finished pastry.

'And what about Callum?' she asked in a low voice.

'What about Callum, indeed? That boy's going to be heartbroken.'

'I'm going round to the Queen Margaret,' Josie said firmly. 'Soon as I've finished the pie.'

'No, better leave it till this afternoon. You could get me some more margarine on the way back. And a pound of collar bacon. Smoked. Here, I'll give you the money.'

Even though envy and chagrin lay upon her like a great suffocating weight, life had to go on for Ellie. She still had her guests to cook for, even though Mr Guthrie had deserted her. In more ways than one.

The afternoon was fine. Josie didn't need to have her coat dried in the Queen Margaret's back room on this visit. In fact, she went only so far as the doorway and kept her coat on.

36

'Hello, Josie!' cried Mrs Tassie again. 'Want to see Lina?' She gave a knowing smile. 'You're a change anyway from you know who!'

'Is she due for a teabreak?' Josie asked. 'I'd like a word with her outside, if possible.'

Beryl Tassie hesitated. 'Well, I could spare her for ten minutes or so, but we're awful busy – Lina ... Lina, Josie's here!'

'Josie?' Lina's eyes widened in apprehension. She tried to smile. 'Are you coming in for a coffee?'

'I want to speak to you. Mrs Tassie says you can have a few minutes off.'

'Oh.' Lina untied her apron. 'Nothing's happened, has it?'

'Depends what you mean by happened.'

They left the café and walked towards the pier. People were strolling up and down, looking across the water to see if the ferry was on its way; there was the usual queue of cars. Josie and Lina gazed up at the bridge towering on the right. They could see men working amongst the girders and supporting steel tubes, but could not make out their faces.

'Is he up there?' asked Josie.

'No.' Lina lowered her eyes. 'He's in Edinburgh today. Look, don't be mad at me. I was going to tell you about me and Duncan. Soon as Callum came home.'

'Callum.' Josie repeated the name heavily. 'Lina, how could you? How could you do this to him?'

'I couldn't help it, Josie. I fell in love.'

'Fell in love with Duncan? You mean with what he is?'

'No, that's no' true.' Lina looked up. 'Mebbe to begin with I was a bit carried away, you know, with his voice and his clothes and the car and that. I mean, he was no' like anybody I've ever been out with before. But now ... well, it's different.'

'Is it?' Josie was still looking up at the bridge. 'How different?'

'It's him I care about, Josie. Just him. If he didn't have a

37

bean, I'd still care. That's the truth.'

'You were supposed to care for Callum at one time.'

'You used to say I kept him on a string.' Lina put her hand on Josie's arm. 'The thing is, I never cared for Callum like I care for Duncan. I tell you, it's different.' She dropped her hand and stood back, breathing hard. 'You must know what I mean, Josie. You've got Angus. I mean, he's the one for you, isn't he? And Duncan's the one for me.'

'There's such a thing as loyalty, Lina,' Josie said, after a long silence.

'No. No, there isn't. Not when it comes to love. I couldn't give up Duncan to be loyal to Callum, I couldn't!' Lina's voice had risen, she was staring blindly about her, no longer afraid of Josie it seemed, only of what she was asking.

'I've got to go,' she said finally, catching her breath. 'Mrs Tassie'll be wanting me back. We're busy, we're always busy. I'll – I'll see you soon, Josie. We'll talk then, eh?'

She ran back across the road to the café, attracting attention as always with her dazzling hair, her obvious beauty. Josie watched but made no move to follow. There would be no point and anyway there were the messages to get. Margarine. Smoked collar. She checked her purse for the money her mother had given her and set off down the promenade towards the High Street.

There was no one around when she arrived back at Ardmore with the shopping. Her mother, it seemed, had worked herself up into a headache and was lying down until it was time to start the high tea. Her father was out, probably gone for his paper and to sit watching the Forth for a while. Josie hung up her coat and put away the messages. She was deliberately keeping her mind a blank. That way she would not have to worry about Callum.

Somebody was knocking on the front door. Josie could see

38

through the frosted glass the silhouettes of two tall figures.

Must get that bell fixed, she thought, opening the door. It's ridiculous that everybody has to knock the way they do.

'Yes?' she looked out at two young men on the doorstep, both carrying large holdalls.

'Ken Pearce and Matt MacLeod,' said one, who was lank and bony with dark slicked back hair. 'We've rooms booked.' He had a Glasgow accent.

'Is it OK?' asked the other, whose voice was softer and rather musical. 'May we come in?'

Oh, yes, the two bridge workers. Josie stood back to let them move past her into the hall. They were expected.

'We've a book for you to sign,' she said over her shoulder. 'Then I'll show you your rooms.' They were on the top floor, next to her.

'We both sign?' asked the Glasgow man.

'Please.'

He wrote his name and handed the book to the other. As he bent his head to sign, Josie saw that this man's hair was thick and straight and very light, almost yellow in colour. When he straightened up, he looked directly into her face and smiled. His eyes were dark grey, deeply lidded, his skin tanned. He had a beautiful smile.

'Your pen.'

She took it, flushing.

'I'm Mrs Morrow's daughter. I – would you like to come this way?'

They followed her up the carpeted stair and then the poorer little stair to the top floor. She opened the doors of their rooms which seemed small to her, yet were larger than her own. The two men put their bags down and said, 'Very nice.'

'You've a view of the Firth of Forth,' she said hesitantly.

The dark man twisted his head and looked out of the blond man's window.

'Here, you can see the bridge,' he said with a laugh.

'We'll see enough of that, eh?'

'There's a bathroom on the floor below,' Josie told them. 'And towels on the chairs. Will you be wanting a meal tonight?'

'We're just booked for breakfast,' said the blond man. 'We never know when we'll be finishing.'

'I see. Well, please let me know if there's anything you want.'

How stilted she sounded, as though she was acting some sort of part. Yet she had said these words so many times and had never thought such a thing before.

Again the blond man smiled at her, and the dark man said they'd everything they wanted, they were fine. Josie looked from one to the other and retreated down to the hall where she looked at the two signatures in the register. Which was which of those two men?

Ken Pearce was the dark one, he'd signed first, in a firm upright hand. Matt MacLeod was the blond one; his writing was round and careful, the signature of a man not used to writing. No reason why he should be, he spent his life repairing bridges. Both men had given Glasgow addresses, but the blond man didn't sound as though he came from Glasgow. Josie closed the book and looked up. Matt MacLeod was standing in front of her.

'Hallo.'

'Was there something?' Again, she felt a strange flush rise to her face.

'We've a free evening tonight. Start work tomorrow. Wondered if there was anything – you know – going on? Anything for us to do in Queensferry? We're strangers to it completely.'

'I – well – I don't know of anything special. There's plenty of places to have a drink, of course.'

'That's what I like to hear.' His heavy-lidded eyes gave his face a look of tranquillity. He would never be hurried, she thought, never be quick to show anger. 'We'll take ourselves out, then.'

For a moment she had the crazy idea that he was going to ask her to go with them. What a relief she was meeting Angus! But he didn't ask her. After he had turned and made his way back up the stairs, she went into the kitchen and sat down on a chair by the stove. It was too warm there for a July day. No wonder the flush wouldn't leave her face.

Chapter Seven

Callum was back. Angus told Josie when he came round that evening. She had been waiting for him in the hallway, near the precarious hatstand and the noticeboard where her mother pinned up snippets of information for her visitors. The two new fellows had asked if there was anything on, but they would have meant entertainment in the town. Josie doubted if they'd be interested in the opening hours for the local stately homes or boat trips round the islands. They wouldn't have time anyway, they were workers, not tourists. Still, they'd have days off. Maybe they'd be glad of the bus and train times to Edinburgh, maybe they'd like to see the Festival Tattoo. Why should she care what they'd like anyway?

'Josie, Callum's back!'

Angus, when she let him in, held her only briefly, brushing her cheek with his lips. His look, so sombre, chilled her.

'Today? I never thought he'd be back today.'

'Aye. Came straight round from his mother's to our place.' Angus sighed. 'He'd brought presents.'

'Oh, no!'

'Shawls. Spanish wine.'

Shawls. Spanish wine. She wanted to put her hands over her ears, as though blocking out the words would block out the thought of Callum, prepared for celebration, finding heartbreak.

'Angus,' she said breathlessly, 'let's go.'

They left the house and began to walk unseeingly down the High Street, past shops and buildings they had known all their lives. The evening was warm, there were plenty of people about, strolling as they were. Happier than they were. Some knew Josie and Angus and called to them and smiled and they smiled back. Two young lovers out for a walk without a care in the world. So they must seem. Oh, but wait till folk heard about Callum!

He had been so happy, Angus said, hadn't had an inkling – well, naturally. Lina had come in from the café just as Angus had come back from the station. He had seen her turn quite white when Callum had snatched her into his arms. Then they'd left the house together. Where had Lina taken him to break the news? The strip of shore, the Sealscraig Rocks? They'd watched for seals as children, rarely saw them now. Wherever it was, the two of them weren't out long. In no time Lina was back, crying her eyes out. And alone. She didn't know where Callum had gone.

Angus loosed his hand from Josie's and stood staring out at the Forth through a break in the buildings. This part of the town was full of little vistas of that sort; everywhere you went, you were conscious of the water out there.

'You know,' he said huskily, 'this has broken me up. I'm no' being selfish, I am thinking of Callum, but it's hit me hard as well as him.'

'Well, he's your friend, Angus, you'd be bound to feel it.'

'Aye, but Lina's ma sister. We've always been so close, I thought I knew her like maself. Wasn't true, was it?'

'You're being too hard on her. She never was engaged to Callum, remember?'

'He thought he was the one, I know he did. He was making plans, saving up. Then Lina throws him over for a guy with a public-school accent and hand-made shoes.'

'It's no' like that, Angus! Be fair ... you have to be fair.'

'She's no' interested in what he's got?'

'No! Well, mebbe at the start she was a wee bit dazzled. I mean, she'd never met anyone like Duncan before. But now she's genuinely in love with him. It's the real thing, Angus, for both of them.'

Angus was silent. For some time his tired eyes dwelt on Josie's face, as though there he could find what he was looking for, and she stayed quite still, letting him find it.

'I'd feel better,' he said at last, 'if I could believe that.'

'You can. You can believe it, Angus.'

They clasped hands again and walked on. Past the fine elevated houses of the Terraces, with their views of the Forth from their high windows. Past the little closes and glimpses of gardens, crazy little flights of steps and railings, old shops and picturesque pubs: the Tolbooth where the taxes had been collected long ago, the Rosebery Hall presented to the town by the Fifth Earl whose Dalmeny estate lay beside the Forth. All this, so familiar, so much a part of them, yet that evening, because of Callum, seeming strange.

Suddenly they saw him, Callum himself. Standing at the Binks, one of the rocky edges of the Forth where the ferries had landed in the old days; the true site, it was said, of that first crossing by Queen Margaret to the holy man in Fife.

'Callum!' cried Josie, and ran swiftly to the tall, motionless figure. Angus followed more slowly, his expression wary. Though he knew Callum so well, he wasn't sure what to expect of him now. Rejection could do strange things to a man, even one so hard-headed and well-balanced as his old school friend. Callum might keep all that balance for business. Where love was concerned, he might just go berserk.

But he seemed just the same as usual. Except, if anything, he looked rather better. Because of his time in Spain, of course. Not that he was tanned, because he didn't take a tan, but his face had been brushed by the Mediterranean sun, his ginger hair had lightened so that it

44

looked almost fair. Glowing skin, shining hair. Och, who am I fooling? thought Angus. Callum wasn't the same. Look at his eyes. They were colourless. They looked as if somebody had forgotten to paint them in.

'Hello, Josie,' he said. 'Hi, Angus.'

'Oh, Callum,' Josie said, her voice shaking, 'I don't know what to say.'

'That's fine by me. I don't want anybody to say anything.'

Still holding his arm, she drew him towards a bench facing the water.

'Why don't we sit down for a bit?' she asked quietly.

'I've got a better idea,' said Angus. 'Let's go for a drink.'

Angus had brought the drinks to a table inside the harbour pub, for instinctively Callum had avoided the crowd outside and made for the shadows. He had not asked Josie if she minded, though he knew her father's views, but she had signalled to Angus that she was not going to cause problems. Not tonight, when Callum was feeling so bad. After all, her father needn't know she'd entered a pub, need he? And she'd just drink lemonade.

It was only when her eyes had adjusted to the half-darkness that she saw across the floor two men looking at her. One dark, one fair. Ken Pearce and Matt MacLeod. Eating pie and peas, and smiling at her. After a moment's hesitation she smiled back then hastily turned away, feeling the warm colour rising again to her brow. Callum had noticed nothing, but Angus's tone was sharp as he asked who were those fellows who seemed to know her.

'Just two new boarders. Bridge workers.'

'Seem friendly.'

Josie split open a packet of nuts. 'Nice enough.'

Angus gave them a hard stare, then he and Callum drank their beer. The pall of gloom hanging over their table seemed like a fog, stifling their usual pleasure in being

45

together. And now Josie had begun to worry that the new boarders might just happen to see her father back at the house, might just happen to say, 'Saw your daughter down at the pub. Inside, not outside, definitely inside the pub.' They wouldn't do that, would they? Well, what if they did? It was about time she told her father she was old enough to do what she thought was right and not what he said was right. But her heart sank at the prospect. The truth of it was, she wasn't yet twenty-one. In her parents' eyes, she had no rights at all.

Suddenly, Callum spoke. 'Mebbe I should no' have left her, eh? Mebbe girls like Lina should never be left.'

'That's bloody rubbish,' snapped Angus.

'Aye, it is.' Callum lit a cigarette. 'But how was I to know some Edinburgh toff would take ma place before I'd even got it?'

Josie, gladly forgetting her imaginary arguments with her father, said earnestly, 'Callum, this has nothing to do with who Duncan is. I know everyone'll say that – I said it maself at first – but it's no' true, you must believe that.'

'I'm supposed to feel better because she loves him for himself alone?' Callum's Spanish ruddiness had deepened into scarlet, his colourless eyes were pebble-hard. 'Well, it doesn't make me feel better, Josie. It makes me want to wring her neck, OK?'

'Callum!'

'That's enough,' snapped Angus. 'That sort of talk does no good at all.'

'Think not?' Callum laughed, and watched the smoke rise from his cigarette. 'Does me a hell of a lot of good, as a matter of fact. But don't worry, I'm no' the type to lose ma head. Talk is all there'll be.'

'I'm glad to hear it. Look, I'll get you another beer.'

'No, thanks all the same. I'm off. I've got to pack.'

Pack? They stared. Hadn't he just come back from his travels?

'I've left the travel agency, I'm going to London. When I

was in Spain, I got in with a new firm. A consortium, looking to build hotels where there's sun. They've offered me a job and I'm taking it.' He made an attempt at a smile. 'I was going to take some leave first, now I'm no' bothering.'

London ... Josie's thoughts went to the cars rolling off the ferry. Going places. And here was Callum, going places.

'Did Lina know you were planning to go to London?' she asked.

'No, I only got the offer in Spain.' His eyes flickered. 'What difference would it have made?'

Josie was silent. No difference, of course.

'How about your mother?' asked Angus. 'She's going to miss you, Callum.'

'Aye, I know. I'm sorry about Mum, but what can I do? I'd ask her to come with me, but she'd never settle away from here. Could no' expect it, eh?'

'Think you'll settle?'

'You bet.' A sudden flash of feeling brightened Callum's eyes, then died. 'I'll make a new life for maself, I'll put everything behind me.'

'You will,' Josie told him. 'And one day you'll be happy again, you'll see.'

He stood up. 'That's what I'm aiming for, Josie. Don't worry about me, I'm going to be fine.' He put his hand in his pocket and took out a package. 'Nearly forgot. This is for you.'

'For me?' Her eyes widened. 'Why, Callum!'

'It's no' much. Only a doll. A tourist thing.'

'Oh, but it's sweet! I love it!' Josie gently touched the little doll's lace mantilla, then laid it down and saw its eyelids close. 'Callum, thank you.'

She kissed his cheek and he gave another of his attempts at a smile.

'It's me should thank you, Josie. And you, Angus. I'm grateful, you know, for – look, I'm no' one for making speeches. You've been good friends and I'll no' forget you.'

'You're no' going back without us?' asked Angus. 'We'll walk with you.'

'No, you two have a bit of time on your own. I'll go home and pack.'

'We'll see you before you go?'

'Sure. I'll say goodbye.'

They watched his tall, straight-backed figure leave the pub, red-blond head held high.

'He's right,' Angus said, after a moment. 'He'll be OK.'

'Eventually.'

'Aye. Like another lemonade?'

'No, thanks. I think we should go now.'

'Miss Morrow?'

She jumped. Ken Pearce and Matt MacLeod were standing at their table. Angus was frowning.

'Sorry to interrupt you,' Ken said politely.

'That's all right.' Making a great effort, Josie summoned her self-possession and introduced Angus to the two men. At their friendly smiles, he nodded briefly.

'We meant to ask your ma, Miss Morrow, will it be OK if we have our breakfast early? We have to be at the bridge by seven.'

'Oh, I see.' Breakfast at Ardmore was never a minute before eight. 'So, you'd be wanting it around six?'

'That would be fine,' said Matt. 'I'm sorry we're being such a nuisance to you.'

Josie again noticed his way of speaking, the soft sibilants, the lilt that was so musical. Was he a Highlander? A Highlander from Glasgow?

'Don't worry,' she said quickly. 'I can get the breakfast any time.'

They were effusive in their thanks and apologies, said they'd not intrude any further, be on their way.

'Well, talk about a damned nerve!' Angus exploded when they had left the pub. 'Coming up like that when

48

you're off duty, and then expecting you to get up at crack of dawn to get their breakfast! Josie, I don't like it. I don't want you to be at the beck and call of fellows like them!'

'Oh, come on, it's no trouble, I'm always up early anyway. And they have to have something to eat before they go out to work.'

'Josie ...' Angus reached for her hand. 'Why don't we get married soon as we can? I've had enough of you skivvying around for your mother. I want you living your own life, with me.'

She was silent, her dark-blue eyes troubled. He sat back.

'Too soon, is it?' he asked quietly. 'I mean, after Lina and Callum?'

'Yes, it's too soon. Let Lina get things sorted at first, that'd be best.'

'OK.' He heaved a long sigh. 'But I just wish to hell you didn't have to run round after guys like those two.'

'I told you, it's no trouble. It's ma job, I really don't mind getting their breakfast.'

All the way home, she wouldn't admit, even to herself, that she was looking forward to it.

Chapter Eight

By six o'clock next morning Josie had everything ready. Porridge made and simmering, bacon snipped and rinded, eggs cracked for frying, bread and tomatoes sliced. Her mother had already laid the dining-room table the night before, in between complaining about her new boarders and the trouble they were causing. If she'd known they were going to be so awkward about mealtimes, she'd have sent them on their way. It wasn't as if she couldn't get other visitors at this time of year. It was lucky for those fellows that Josie was willing to get up in the middle of the night to cook for them because if it had been left to her, she'd have put out the Cornflakes and a loaf of bread and let them get on with it.

Thank goodness she's letting me get on with it, thought Josie, humming to herself as she waited. It was a beautiful morning. Sunny and warm, the waters of the Forth beyond the kitchen window dancing under a clear blue sky. And Josie was in blue, too, a cotton blouse and skirt that matched her eyes; she knew she looked well. The kettle was joining in her singing. As soon as the men came down she could make the tea.

She heard their steps on the stair, their voices murmuring, as she had heard them last night when they came up to bed. They must have gone on somewhere after they'd left the pub by the harbour, for they'd come in after her and had had to get her father to unlock the door. She'd crept to the top of the stairs and listened to him warning them to be in by eleven in future, that was when he locked up, see? If they wanted to be in later than that, he'd have to have due warning. Presumably they'd agreed for there'd been no arguments; they'd come tramping up the stairs and she had fled back to her bed. It was the man with the yellow hair who was in the room next to hers and she'd wondered if she'd hear him moving around, but the walls of Ardmore were solid. She couldn't hear a thing. Yet had been conscious for a long time before she fell asleep that Matt MacLeod was just the other side of the wall.

Now she braced herself to go into the dining room and say good morning. But they took her by surprise, coming into the kitchen, carrying knives and forks they'd taken from the table.

'Och, we'll no' sit in state next door,' Ken Pearce said with a laugh. 'OK if we come in here, Miss Morrow?'

'Where's your manners, Ken?' asked Matt MacLeod. 'Say good morning.'

They all exchanged good mornings, and Josie, flustered, told them yes, they could sit at the kitchen table if they liked (though privately she didn't know what her mother would say). Would they be taking porridge or cereal? They took porridge. Just the thing, summer or not, for fellows working on high.

'Always cold up on a bridge, Miss Morrow,' said Matt, shaking salt over his porridge. 'Whatever the season.'

He too was wearing blue, a bright blue checked shirt and workman's trousers. His face was scrubbed and shining, his thick yellow hair brushed back from his brow. All this Josie saw only from the corner of her eye, as she did not at any time look him full in the face. Anyway, she had the bacon to cook. It was a relief to be able to turn away, busy herself with that, not to have to meet the eyes she knew were following her.

'Smashing breakfast,' commented Ken, as she set their

51

plates before them. 'Makes a difference with no rationing, eh?'

'Meat's just come off and that's the last.' Josie smiled. 'About time. I mean, the war's been over nine years!'

'Aye, I thought we'd niver see the end of thae damned coupons. Big relief to us, no' having to cart our books around.' Ken waved his fork. 'Want to say we're very grateful to you for obliging us like this, Miss Morrow.'

'I wish you'd call me Josie.'

'Well, I'm Ken. He's Fingal.'

'Fingal? Why, I thought—'

'His joke,' Matt told her. 'My first name's Fingal, but Matthew's my second. I'm always called Matt.'

'Isn't Fingal a Gaelic name?' Josie asked, at last finding the courage to look into his face.

'It is. It means fair-haired stranger.'

Ken gave a burst of laughter. 'And is that no' what he is, Josie? A fair-haired stranger from the Highlands.'

'You're a Highlander?' Josie poured second cups of tea. 'I thought you might be. From your voice, you know.'

'Ah, you've a good ear, Josie, and Glasgow's not taken away my birthright. Yes, my dad was a fisherman up near Skye. Lost his boat, and nearly lost himself and one of my brothers. "That's enough of risk," says Ma, and anyway, there was no more work. So down we came to Glasgow.'

'Aye, Glasgow's full of folk from elsewhere looking for work,' put in Ken. 'Just hope the work lasts oot, eh?' He glanced at Matt. 'Enough o' risk, though? That's a laugh, Matt, and you a bridge man!'

Matt gave his lazy smile. 'Felt like something different from the shipyards.'

'Like risk?' asked Josie.

'Like the open air. Like working in the sky. Up there, over the water, it's like nowhere else you can imagine.'

'He gets poetical,' said Ken, grinning. 'No' me. Up, doon, it's just a job.'

'Each to his own,' replied Matt. 'I am not saying other

52

men are like me. My brothers are in the yards, they wouldn't do what I do for any money.'

'How many brothers have you?' asked Josie with interest.

'Two. Fergus and Sandy. And I've two sisters, Iona and Marie. Only Marie and me aren't married.'

'And he'll niver get married!' cried Ken. 'Now me, I've a bonny wife and three wee girls. I keep telling this guy to get a move on, but he's having too good a time, see, foot-loose and fancy free!'

'Lies,' retorted Matt, 'all lies. Don't believe a word of it, Josie.'

She gave a faint smile and began to clear away.

'Here, let me.' He carried their plates to the sink and gave her a long look. 'Thanks again for looking after us so well.'

'Better get going,' called Ken from the door.

'Take care,' cried Josie with sudden urgency.

'We'll do that all right.' Ken picked up a canvas bag and slung it on his shoulder. 'It's three hundred and sixty-one feet to the top of the bridge. We'll take care.'

She bit her lip as she watched the two men go, Matt looking back once more. Then she stacked the dishes and began to run the water into the washing-up bowl. Her high spirits had faded. She could not stop thinking about her father and his fall, about the fifty-seven men who had been killed when the bridge was being built, about later accidents. Of course, things were much safer now. There was even a special rescue boat that kept watch for anybody working on the bridge. And the men knew what they were doing, didn't they? But even Duncan, she remembered, had been afraid.

It was much later, all the morning chores over, her mother away to the butcher's, her father closeted with the minister at the kirk, when Lina came round, so drenched and woebe-gone she looked like a doll that had been left out in the rain.

53

'Josie, is your mum in?' she asked fearfully.

'No, she's gone to the butcher's to get the stewing beef herself. Last time I got it, she said they'd given me too much fat.' Josie rolled her eyes in exasperation. 'But what are you doing, Lina? Why are you no' at the café?'

'Och, I couldn't go in, I told Mrs Tassie I felt too bad.' Lina blew her nose. 'Look at me, Josie! I've been crying all night over Callum. Honestly, I never thought in a million years he'd take it like he did. It was if I'd turned him to stone, I've never seen anybody look so cold!'

'I don't know what you expected, Lina. You must have guessed he'd take it hard.'

'Oh, but he was horrible, Josie! He looked at me as if he hated me, said he'd never been so wrong about anybody in his life as he'd been about me but I needn't worry, he wouldn't be staying around, he wouldn't be dancing at ma wedding. He was going to London where he was going to put me right out of his mind!'

'Well, that'll be just as well.' Josie filled the kettle and set out two cups. 'Do you want a coffee, Lina? I got some of that instant stuff from the stores, I like it better than the essence.'

'Anything,' moaned Lina, 'anything'll do.'

They drank the coffee and ate two chocolate biscuits each, after which Lina said she felt a wee bit better. But she had other things to worry about as well as Callum, because now Duncan would expect her to meet his family and she didn't know how she was going to face it.

'I mean, his dad was something grand in the law and they live in the New Town and go to garden parties at Holyrood and all that kind of thing. I ask you, are they going to want somebody like me for Duncan?'

'You're a lovely girl, Lina,' cried Josie. 'Why should they no' want you?'

'Och, you know what I mean, I don't have to spell it out. Families don't care about looks, they want somebody suitable, they want somebody who'll fit in.'

54

'You're marrying Duncan, Lina, not them, you needn't worry what they think. Anyway, they'll like you.'

'No.' Lina shook her head. 'No, they won't. And supposing they turn him against me?'

'He bought you that ring, he wants to make sure of you.' Josie gave Lina her most encouraging smile. 'Come on, fix up to see them, get it over with and then you can relax. What are you going to wear?'

'Duncan's given me twelve pounds to buy a new outfit. Will you come with me to choose something? I thought I'd go to Logie's.'

'Logie's? Wow! I'd love to help you spend twelve pounds in Logie's!' Josie laughed. 'Any time!'

'Duncan says his mother has an account with them, so I won't go far wrong if I get something there.' Lina stood up, looking a little less damp, though her eyes were still red and swollen. 'Och, why has everything to be so difficult, Josie? At least for me. With you and Angus it all seems so pleasant and easy.'

At the mention of Angus's name an arrow entered Josie's heart and she stood without speaking, bearing the pain, not asking why. Maybe she knew why, but she wasn't going to let herself face it, because to face it would make it seem true. And she wasn't prepared to admit that, either.

Lina was moving slowly towards the door, talking now about her wedding. Duncan wanted it as soon as possible, and so did she. Josie must be a bridesmaid. She'd like to be in blue, wouldn't she? They could have a look at material when they were in Logie's. Would Josie be willing to make her own dress? She was a good needlewoman. Lina's mother had already promised to make the wedding dress. They'd look out patterns at Logie's as well.

After a coffee and two chocolate biscuits, she's progressed from eternal misery over Callum to patterns for her wedding dress, thought Josie, as Lina said goodbye. Then thought perhaps she wasn't being fair. There were tears again in Lina's lovely eyes as she spoke of Callum.

Did Josie think he'd be happy in London?

'Yes. I do. Not at first, perhaps, but in time. He's a survivor.'

'I'd like to believe that, I do want him to be happy.'

'He'll be happy and so will you.'

'Maybe. When I've seen Duncan's folks. I think you're right, we should fix up to see them as soon as possible.' Lina wiped her eyes and pushed back her bright hair. 'I'll have to try not to cry any more, I suppose. I mean, I'll have to look ma best.'

Chapter Nine

Look her best Lina did, for her Ordeal by In-Laws, which was her way of describing her eventual meeting with Duncan's family. But in fact it wasn't as bad as she'd feared. His parents were very kind, very welcoming, even his mother, and Lina had been particularly apprehensive about meeting Duncan's mother. Everyone knew how mothers-in-law felt about daughters-in-law, especially daughters-in-law who came from different worlds, but Mrs Guthrie, in her fifties and fadedly pretty, seemed not the least bit possessive over Duncan. And his father, the retired advocate, dark-eyed and handsome still, had been as unfailingly courteous as his son, making Lina feel quite special.

'Och, what a relief!' she told her mother after the lunch in the New Town was safely over. 'Duncan's dad's so clever, I was really scared of meeting him. I mean, he might have expected me to be clever, too, and there's only Angus in our family who's got any brains.'

'Lina, what a thing to say!' cried Kitty, but Lina shook her head.

'Come on, you know it's true. Anyway, it didn't matter, Mr Guthrie just talked to me about the things I liked – he seemed to know what they'd be – and I talked back the way I never thought I would and did pretty well. At least, I think I did.'

'Of course you did!' her mother said fondly. 'But tell me

about the flat, tell me what you had to eat?'

'Nothing special to eat. I mean, it was nice, but just salad stuff to start with, then lamb cutlets with a sauce, and strawberry tart. No' bad pastry.'

'And Mrs Guthrie'd cooked it all herself?'

'Aye, they had a cook before the war but now they only have a cleaning lady.' Lina wrinkled her small nose. 'And no' much of a one at that. The whole flat could do with a good turn out, if you ask me, but folk like them'd never notice.'

'But it's a smart flat, isn't it?' asked Kitty, anxious that the Guthries' reputation for grandness should not be unfounded. 'I mean, in Heriot Row, it must have nice rooms and that?'

'Oh, lovely big rooms and plaster-work, but the curtains haven't been cleaned in a month of Sundays, and the leather chairs were all scratched. Still, the dining table was lovely. Real silver cutlery, Mum, and candlesticks and roses in a bowl. Antonia'd done all that.'

'Antonia? That'd be Duncan's sister?'

'Yes, she's supposed to be clever, too. Writes articles for the newspapers.' Lina's tone was cool. 'She's just getting divorced.'

'Did you no' like her, then?' asked Kitty, picking up on the tone.

'Och, she was OK.'

Lina rose, saying she would go and change out of the new silver-grey dress and jacket that had been such a success. In her tiny room, however, she didn't immediately change but sat on the bed and ran her fingers through her flaxen hair, going over and over the events of the day in Heriot Row, conducting her own post-mortem on her performance.

Only Antonia Fearn had been difficult, though obviously she had been primed by Duncan, as her parents it seemed had been primed, for she knew all about Lina and didn't ask any questions. But when she and Lina were alone

58

together, combing their hair in the spare bedroom after lunch, there had been some sticky moments. Very sticky moments, remembered Lina, sighing with relief that she had got through them.

First, Antonia had taken out her cigarettes and offered them to Lina, who had refused. She still hadn't mastered the art of smoking gracefully and was not going to be seen coughing in front of Duncan's sister. Antonia, lighting a cigarette for herself, had studied Lina through a haze of smoke.

'Did Duncan tell you he'd been engaged before?' she asked abruptly.

'Oh, yes.' Lina could see Antonia reflected in the dressing-table mirror and thought how like her mother she was, how thin and pretty, with the sort of delicate looks that did not wear well. 'He told me it hadn't worked out.'

'You can say that again! It was my friend Pamela who was his fiancée, and goodness, did he lead her a dance!'

Lina put her comb away in her new bag. 'Doesn't sound like Duncan,' she said quietly.

'No, well, I daresay you've only seen one side of him. And he's obviously very much in love with you.' Antonia gave a brief smile. 'He's fallen for you in a big way, Lina, and I must tell you, I think you'll be good for him. Calm and easy-going. That's the sort of woman he needs, because he's so up and down himself.'

'Up and down? I've never seen him like that!' Lina's cheeks were flushed, her eyes indignant. 'I don't even recognise this man you're talking about, if you don't mind me saying so.'

'Lina, he's moody. It's a family trait. I'm the same, I admit it, that's one reason why my own marriage is falling apart. We get it from Father.' Antonia drew on her cigarette, and shook her head as though marvelling at her family's faults. 'He can be very sweet and charming, just like Duncan, but on the day the black dog descends ... my God, you have to watch out then, I can tell you! Well, you've seen Mummy, how worn out she looks? Who wouldn't be, coping with us?'

'Just what are you trying to say to me?' Lina asked tremulously. 'I shouldn't marry Duncan because he'll make me unhappy? Is this your way of telling me I'm no' wanted in this family?'

'No! No, it's not!' Antonia stubbed out her cigarette and put her hand on Lina's arm. 'Honestly, I'm not trying to put you off – I *want* you to marry Duncan. I told you, didn't I, he needs someone like you? Mummy and Daddy have spotted that, too. They think you're the one to make him happy.'

'So, why are you talking like this?' cried Lina. 'Why tell me everything that's wrong with him?'

'I'm warning you, that's all. Preparing you, if you like to put it that way.' Antonia gave a brilliant smile. 'Forewarned is forearmed, you know!'

Lina, returning to the drawing room, had not smiled, and when Mrs Guthrie served the coffee, had looked at her with new eyes. It was true she was very thin and lined, but then she didn't seem particularly anxious or unhappy. Her clothes were lovely, she wore beautiful rings, she seemed only what she should be, a well-to-do, middle-aged lady with no particular worries. And Mr Guthrie, attentively handing sugar and cream – was he really the one everyone feared when the black dog descended? Lina's great brown eyes rested on him for a moment and moved away. She couldn't believe it. Furthermore, she wouldn't believe it. Antonia, whatever she said, was just stirring things up, trying to make trouble.

'Penny for them, darling,' Duncan whispered, bending over her. 'You look so sad, so far away. Not thinking of Callum, are you?'

'No.' She looked into his dark eyes and felt a great rush of love, mixed with regret that she had ever listened to a word against him. Forewarned is forearmed, Antonia had told her. Well, I don't need to be forearmed against

Duncan, thought Lina, wishing she could take him in her arms in front of everyone and kiss him on the lips. But of course she only drank her coffee then, at Duncan's signal, made her polite goodbyes as though to the manor born.

'Oh, well done, darling!' he had said to her as they drove back to Queensferry. 'I'm proud of you, I really am. They loved you, didn't they? I knew they would.'

'I don't know about Antonia,' Lina could not help herself saying.

'Antonia? Take no notice of her. She's just in a mood over her divorce.'

'She gets in moods?'

'Oh, yes, from time to time.' Duncan laughed. 'Who doesn't?'

'I didn't think you did.'

'Not with you, Lina. Never with you. You're good for me, you see.'

'Am I?'

'Yes, and I'm good for you. We're going to be very happy together, you know that, don't you?'

'Yes, I do,' she said sincerely.

Well, here she was, the big day over. Duncan had to work that evening, so it was a little bit of an anti-climax that she should be on her own. Never mind, she felt so wonderfully content, it really didn't matter that for once she was not with him, kissing and caressing and talking wedding plans. She looked down at her engagement ring and turned it so that its diamonds caught the light. How beautiful it was! How lucky she had been, in so many ways! Why couldn't everyone be as happy as she was at that moment? A shadow crossed her face as Duncan's words came back to her. Not thinking of Callum, are you? Now why had he reminded her?

She leaped to her feet, took off her dress and jacket and hung them on the back of her door, because she had no proper wardrobe. A cotton dress lay across her bed where

61

she had left it earlier and now she put it on again, fastening the belt at her waist that was not quite as slim as she would like. Callum had already gone to London, Angus had told her. Down there, he'd be so busy, he'd soon forget her. Soon meet someone else. Mebbe an English girl, a Londoner. In no time, he too could be talking wedding plans and she needn't worry about him any more. She brightened at the thought. Maybe she'd go round and see Josie that evening, tell her how things had gone, fix up to buy the material for the bridesmaids' dresses. Patty was to be a bridesmaid, too.

'Lina, do you want any tea?' Kitty's copper-coloured head came round the door. 'Mebbe after that big dinner you'll no' be hungry?'

'Oh, no, I couldn't eat a thing.' Lina hesitated. 'Well, it wasn't that big ... are you doing chips?'

'Aye, with a bit o' gammon. And fried eggs.' Kitty laughed. 'No' healthy food, Lina!'

'Oh, well, I've had some salad today.' Lina's face was wreathed in smiles. 'Had a lovely day all round, Mum. Now there's nothing to stop Duncan and me fixing our wedding date. Next thing'll be to get Josie to fix hers.'

'No hurry about that,' retorted her mother. 'No hurry at all.'

Chapter Ten

Every weekday Josie was still getting up early to make breakfast for the bridge workers. Every weekend, though, they went home to Glasgow with their washing. She was ashamed to feel so bereft.

Those early hours with Matt and Ken had come to mean so much. Somehow the kitchen always seemed sunny, the men always smiling, everything golden. All they did was talk, as easily as old friends, with Josie sharing their pot of tea, throwing back her beautiful hair, sending her blue gaze from one man to the other, relaxing as she had never relaxed in her parents' house before. Ken talked about his wife and little girls, showed photos that Josie fulsomely admired. Matt talked about his mother, who was the strong one of the family but sweet with it, and his dad, who worked at the ship-yard but was happiest playing his fiddle in the tenement, just as he'd played for the Highland *ceilidhs* in the old days. All his family was musical, Matt said, everybody played something except himself, and he could sing a bit.

'Aye, sings all the time up on the bridge,' said Ken. 'Lucky for us, eh, the wind blows his voice away?'

'I'm sure Matt sings well,' Josie said earnestly. She met his eyes, colouring up as she usually did. 'He has such a nice soft speaking voice.'

'Aye, that's how he charms the birds off the trees. Girls and all.'

Matt only smiled.

How could she not enjoy those mornings, Josie asked herself, when she felt such a different person, in a different, golden world? Instinctively, however, she knew that her parents would not approve, and because her father couldn't manage the stairs and they slept on the ground floor, they might hear all the talking and laughing that was going on in the kitchen. It was one of Josie's fears that they would come in one morning and break things up. It was another that her mother would suddenly offer to cook the men's breakfast herself. Once or twice she'd said she felt bad, letting Josie get up every time, and Josie hadn't dared to keep on saying she didn't mind in case her mother wondered why.

In fact it was her father who appeared one morning, just as she was serving up the finnan haddie, but he didn't seem to be annoyed. Only wanted a chat with the fellows. Never seemed to see them around. What did they do in the evenings, then?

'Want some of the fish, Dad?' asked Josie apprehensively.

'No, thanks, I'll just take a cup of tea.'

Fitting himself with some difficulty into a chair at the kitchen table, John stirred sugar into his tea and fixed the young men with a questioning eye.

'We generally work pretty late,' Ken told him. 'Make the most of the light, eh? Same as the painters.'

'Aye, I remember.' John gave a reminiscent sigh. 'Have to get through what you can when you can. You ken there's one hundred and forty-five acres to paint? And they might have to use five coats o' paint? Only the top one's red.'

'Tough job,' agreed Ken. 'But good lads, the painters. Sometimes come with us for a bit to eat at the Hawes, or mebbe drive into Edinburgh. One or two've got cars.'

'All right as long as you give the drinking a miss,' said John.

'Drinking?' Ken sounded as though he'd never heard the word. Matt was concentrating on his breakfast.

'Aye, it's the drink that does for men up aloft. There were fifty-seven briggers lost their lives here when the bridge was being built. And plenty more had accidents. Now, I'm no' saying that all of them were due to drink, but they used to say at the time, if the Hawes Inn had no' been so close, the figures'd have been different.'

'Believe you fell yourself some years ago, Mr Morrow?' Matt asked, looking up. 'But you're not a drinking man.'

'Aye, well, like I said, no' all accidents are due to drink.' John set down his cup. 'But you can't afford to take chances. Got to keep your head clear, working in the sky.'

Josie was making toast, trying to keep calm. The atmosphere in the kitchen had changed since her father's arrival. Sitting there between the two young men, his shock of grey hair on end, his dark-blue eyes very direct, very intense, he had somehow brought her new golden world crashing down from wherever it had been floating. He carried his own very different world with him, and Josie, who had always lived in that world, knew he would expect even these strangers to respect its rules. But Matt and Ken, they wouldn't know what he expected, they might say something or do something that wouldn't suit.

Please God, don't let them say anything, she prayed, as she cleared the plates and set the toast on the table. Don't let them argue or say what they think, just make them leave for work. Now.

She had the feeling her prayers were already too late.

'Must ha' been terrible for you, Mr Morrow,' Ken was saying sympathetically as he buttered a slice of toast. 'I mean, when you fell.'

'Aye, I fell through the girders, hit the walkway at the side of the railway lines.' John smiled grimly. 'Damaged ma spine. Was lucky to walk again, the doctors said.'

'He's in constant pain,' Josie said in a low voice. 'Never complains.'

65

'We're no' put here to complain, Josie. What the Lord sends, we accept.'

'You're saying God sends you the pain?' asked Matt. 'Did He cause the accident, then?'

John drew his thick brows together. 'You've a strange way of putting things, Mr MacLeod. But mebbe you'll know the words of the old hymn? *"God moves in a mysterious way, His wonders to perform"*? What you have to remember is that God's way is no' our way. We can't know why He sends us our trials, all we can do is accept His will.'

Matt tilted himself back in his kitchen chair, his grey eyes thoughtful.

'Must be a great comfort to you, Mr Morrow, to believe as you do.'

Oh, no, groaned Josie inwardly. Oh, Matt, why did you have to speak?

Her father was studying him, his gaze cool.

'Are you saying you're no' a believer, Mr MacLeod?'

'That's right, Mr Morrow.' Matt's tone was pleasant. 'I cannot believe that there's anyone up there taking an interest in anyone down here.'

'Me, I'm the same,' chimed in Ken. 'Aye, takes Glasgow to tell you the truth o' things, eh? I used to go to the kirk when I was a laddie and the minister, he'd say, "The good Lord loves you." But all I knew was I'd nae boots. Now why'd the good Lord no' give me any boots, Mr Morrow?'

'Boots?' cried John. 'You want the Lord to give you boots when He has given you life? When he has given you your immortal soul? Shame on you, to talk of Him in that way! And as for you ... ' He swung round on Matt. 'You say there is no one in heaven to care for you? Why, even a sparrow can no' fall to the ground without the Lord knowing! Aye, and the very hairs of your head are all numbered! Your own namesake tells us that, Saint Matthew himself in his Gospel. Go find a Bible, Mr MacLeod, and read what is written, read and understand!'

'Words, Mr Morrow.' Matt tilted himself forward to the table again. 'Anyone can write words. They mean nothing.'

John was silent. He had gone very white and against the pallor of his face, his blue eyes appeared black. He rose slowly to his feet and stood looking down at the men at the table. Though his disability had reduced his height, he seemed for one strange moment to have regained it, seemed to them in their surprise a tower of a man. Or else an angel, thought Josie, struck dumb by misery. An avenging angel. It did not seem fanciful to see him as that, for it was clearly how he saw himself. The Angel of the Lord, defending the Lord's name from the infidels. Men who could not see that there was purpose in suffering, that the Lord was a good Lord, that there was not one repentant sinner He would not take to Himself and Heaven. But for those who did not repent ...

'Mr MacLeod, Mr Pearce,' John said hoarsely, 'you will please leave this house. Go upstairs and pack your bags and leave. Now.'

No one moved.

Do they think he doesn't mean it? wondered Josie, trembling with apprehension.

Matt was smiling incredulously, Ken's mouth had fallen open. The air in the kitchen seemed to be thickening. Soon, thought Josie, they would surely not be able to breathe.

'You are asking us to leave because we do not believe what you believe?' asked Matt at last, his smile dying.

'In this house, we love and trust in the Lord,' John replied. 'Those who are no' willing to do that are no' welcome.' His face had turned yellowish, he was beginning to breathe fast. 'Will you go?' he cried, and sat down heavily, his new strength vanishing, his eyes beseeching Josie.

'You'd better do as he says,' she murmured. 'He's no well, you can see that. Please – just go.'

'It's no right,' cried Ken. 'We're due at work, we're

already late. How can we pack our bags and go just like that, eh? Where'll we stay?'

'Anywhere, anywhere,' gasped John. 'Anywhere out of here!'

'What's going on?' cried a voice from the door, and Josie stiffened as her mother, her hair straight out of curlers, her reading glasses trembling on a chain around her heaving chest, came hurrying into the kitchen.

'It's all right, Mum, it's all right,' Josie said desperately, but John raised his head.

'These two fellas are leaving, Ellie. I've given them their notice.'

'You've no' given us any notice!' shouted Ken. 'And we're entitled to notice. I've no taking this lying doon, I promise you, I'm taking it up with the authorities!'

'Josie, have they ...' Ellie's pale-blue eyes flew to her daughter, but Josie shook her head.

'They haven't done anything, Mum. Dad's throwing them out because they aren't church-goers.'

'Atheists!' cried John weakly. 'Unbelievers! I'll no' have them in the house. Out they go, Ellie, out they go!'

'Och, you've knocked yourself up, John! What were you thinking of? Why did you no' fetch me? I'd have told 'em what to do!' Ellie turned with satisfaction on the two young men who had now moved to the door. 'You heard what Mr Morrow said. Please pack your things and leave. I've had people on the phone just now asking for rooms, so I could do with yours and that's a fact. Josie, make out their bills!'

There was an ashen taste in Josie's mouth as she left the kitchen. Her head was throbbing, she felt ill. Ahead of her, standing in the hall, were the two men. They looked back at her then Ken ran up the stairs, slapping down his feet as though he wanted to relieve his feelings with the noise. But Matt's eyes were on Josie's. She supposed she should be typing out the bills but she made no move. Nor did he. Only their eyes exchanged messages. Then Matt turned and went up the stairs and Josie followed.

68

She knew he would be waiting, and he was. As she rounded the first turn of the staircase, he held out his arms to her. Though she was taking a terrible risk, for at any moment someone could come down the stairs or her mother could come up, she went to him. As his arms enfolded her and she rested against him, her head on his shoulder, she felt wonderfully, strangely, at peace.

It didn't last, of course. She knew it couldn't, she wasn't entitled to peace with Matt MacLeod. With a long sigh, she pulled herself away.

'Don't think too badly of ma dad,' she said quietly. 'It's just that the kirk's his life, he can't imagine anyone not believing – you know – the way he does.'

'He's stopped me seeing you.'

She looked into Matt's face, read what was there, and lowered her eyes.

'Shall I see you again, Josie?'

'I don't know.'

'Are you thinking of Angus?' he asked urgently, but there was a door closing on the landing above them, someone coming down. As Mr Benson, a Yorkshireman from one of the first-floor rooms, came stolidly advancing towards them, they sprang apart.

'Morning,' he called cheerfully, and they stood aside to let him pass.

'Morning,' they replied.

'I must go,' Josie said distractedly. 'There's the breakfasts – and I haven't done your bills.'

Matt put his hand on her arm, but she shook it free and ran blindly down the stairs.

'Have you done those bills yet?' cried her mother, from the kitchen door. 'Be quick, be quick, we want those fellows out as soon as possible. I've the breakfasts to get and your dad's no' well, he's away to his bed, fretting and worrying. Och, he's no business to go working himself up like that.'

'He shouldn't have told them to leave,' Josie said

69

brusquely. 'He'd no right to do that.'

'No right? In his own house!'

'He didn't give them any notice. They were entitled to notice.'

'I never liked them anyway, they were a nuisance. Hurry up and do the bills, then you can give me a hand.'

Josie had been thinking that she would see Matt once more, but when she had typed out the bills and put them into envelopes, her mother took them from her.

'You cook the fish,' she ordered. 'I'll see to these.'

There was nothing Josie could do.

'Could I say goodbye to Miss Morrow?' Matt asked as Ken stood by, counting his change and simmering with rage. 'You will not refuse me, Mrs Morrow, your daughter has been so kind?'

Ellie hesitated, affected against her will by Matt's appealing grey eyes beneath their heavy lids.

'She's busy, she's cooking the haddie,' she said hastily. 'Anyway, she's no' wanting to say goodbye to you, Mr MacLeod.'

'Come on, Matt!' roared Ken, stamping to the door, and Matt turned away.

In the kitchen, Josie, listening for it, heard the front door bang. She took down the warm plates and began to serve out the haddock.

'Good riddance to bad rubbish!' cried Ellie, bustling back into the kitchen. 'At least, there's one good thing come out of all this, Josie – you won't have to get up so early in the mornings now, will you?'

'No, I won't.'

Her mother gave her a quick glance. 'You're very pale. You've no' let this upset you, have you? Tell you what, why don't you and Angus go out tonight? Take yourselves to the pictures in Edinburgh? There might be a Grace Kelly film on, she's so lovely and ladylike – have a look at the paper.'

'You want me to go out with Angus?' Josie's voice grated. 'Oh, well, Dad'll approve, won't he? 'Specially if we go to see Grace Kelly who's so *ladylike*. Excuse me, I'd better take this fish in now, folk are waiting.'

'Aye, mustn't let it get cold,' agreed her mother, narrowing her eyes as Josie disappeared into the dining room with her tray.

Chapter Eleven

It was August. Ferry Fair time.

'Can't believe that's come round again,' said Ellie, who'd been a great one for the Ferry Fair ever since Josie as a schoolgirl had been crowned Ferry Fair Queen. Aye, that had been a grand day, even though John had gone around muttering, 'Vanity of vanities, all is vanity,' even though Lina Braid had had her turn the following year. Nothing could take away Ellie's proud memories of her daughter's crowning and triumphant procession through the town with her little retinue. It had seemed a forecast of Josie's future success, a promise that her life would be better than her mother's. And that was all that Ellie wanted for her daughter. Surely it was what every mother wanted? But things had gone sour, the promise had not been kept. It was Lina who was making the good marriage while Josie was drooping around, getting nowhere.

'You take the afternoon off,' Ellie told her. 'Go and see what's doing at the fair, cheer yourself up. I don't know what's got into you lately.'

'Nothing's got into me,' Josie retorted.

'Why are you so snappy, then?' Ellie sniffed. 'Mebbe you're just sick of all the wedding talk from next door. The Lord knows, I am!'

'I'd no' mind going down to the fair,' Josie said, after a moment. 'It'll make a change from sewing in ma time off.'

'Och, you're too soft, you are, Josie. Making Patty MacAndrew's bridesmaid's dress as well as your own. If she can't put a needle through a bit of material, she should have paid a dressmaker!'

'It's no trouble.' Josie, brightening, was already on her way upstairs to get ready to go out. 'See you later!'

The town was full of people, come from all over the area to laugh at men climbing a greasy pole; to watch the races and the fancy dress competitions; to see the Ferry Fair Queen bowing to her admirers. Most fascinating of all to some would be the Burry Man, a fellow dressed from head to foot in burdock burrs, who would make his awkward progress through the streets, assisted by his helpers, two strong young men who had helped to cover him earlier in the day. What a strange throwback from some earlier time was this figure walking the town to bring good luck! Everyone looked out for the Burry Man.

Amongst the crowd somewhere would be the two young women from Newcastle who had taken the rooms vacated by Matt and Ken. Nice girls, with cameras and touring maps, who'd had no idea, as they'd asked Josie about the Ferry Fair and the Burry Man and all the customs of the day, that they were twisting her heart because they were there and Matt was not.

She had never seen him since he left. Not once. Wouldn't even know what had happened to him, except that Angus had told her the two bridge men had found lodgings with Mrs Robb. Yes, Callum's mother, who had put another bed in his old room and was said to be glad of the extra money the laddies were paying her. So much for Matt's asking if he might see Josie again. She must have dreamed his arms had ever been around her, must have dreamed the look in his eyes. But if her heart was sore, her head told her things were better this way. Much, much better.

'The fair used to be a sort of hiring fair, where people

73

came to find work,' she explained to Sally Smith and Norma Fenwick. 'Now it's just for fun. And the Burry Man – he's part of the ritual. He always walks the town on the first Friday in August, to bring good luck, so you'd better watch out for him. First time I saw him, though, when I was little, I howled ma head off!' She laughed at the memory. 'I thought he was a bogeyman!'

'Aye, well, you would, wouldn't you?' Sally had commented. 'Covered in all them sticky things!'

'Is it true he wears long johns underneath?' Norma asked, giggling. 'Suppose he'd have to or he'd die scratching!'

'It must take hours for the poor guy to be covered,' cried Sally. 'How do they ever get anybody to volunteer?'

'Always do,' Josie replied. 'Suppose it's fame for a day.'

She didn't tell the two girls that she too had had her fame for a day, but it still made her happy to remember her mother's pleasure when she'd been crowned Ferry Fair Queen. It was a happiness mixed with bitterness now. Seemed a long time since she had been able to please her mother in that way.

She walked slowly down the crowded esplanade towards the bridge, remembering how much the fair had meant to her and her friends as children, how they'd missed it during the war, been thrilled when it returned. Probably it didn't mean as much to today's children, who had so many other diversions. Even television, though Ardmore had yet to obtain its first set. Still, there were plenty of families about now, all appearing to enjoy themselves. Josie wished she were not on her own but Angus was working, and even her mother, who loved the fair, wasn't able to leave the house. Dad couldn't look after things, he wasn't well, his blood pressure was up. He'd been on tablets from the doctor ever since his row with Matt and Ken. Though she made an effort to understand her father's views, Josie couldn't help but believe he'd brought his troubles on himself. Och, here she was, thinking of Matt again.

Stop it, she told herself. Stop thinking of him. And don't go to the bridge.

Already, and she was ashamed to admit it, she'd been several times to study the distant figures working on the bridge, but so far had never seen Matt. Her father owned a pair of field glasses but she'd drawn the line at using those. No, she wouldn't be seen scanning the bridge for Matt MacLeod. She would put him right out of her mind.

'Josie!'

He was in front of her, conjured up by her thoughts, it seemed. But no, physically, wonderfully present. People were walking round him but he wasn't moving. He wore a dark blue shirt and trousers that weren't his work trousers, and carried a jacket slung over one shoulder. The sun was on his hair and some of the people walking past were looking back, caught by its colour. Some of them looked at Josie's hair, too, for its mahogany brown was aflame. Burning in the light. She too felt herself aflame.

Time passed, they had no knowledge of it. They knew they were walking together, and stopped once to buy ice-cream, but they couldn't have said, if anyone had asked, what they saw. Everything had taken on the golden haze that Josie remembered from those mornings in the kitchen when she had cooked the early breakfasts. It must be generated by Matt, she thought, half laughing at herself. Where he was, was summer.

'Why didn't you try to see me?' she asked, turning to look into his eyes, knowing she hadn't imagined what she'd read there on the stairs at Ardmore. No, she hadn't imagined anything.

'I didn't know if you'd want me to,' he said quietly. 'And I didn't want to upset your folks.'

'You were never going to find me?'

'Ah, now, I didn't say that. I don't know how long I'd have lasted out.'

'You're here today anyway. Why are you no' working?'

'Had a few hours owing. Thought I'd see this wonderful fair people keep telling me about.'

'And now you've seen it, what do you think of it?'

'Why, I haven't seen it at all!' he cried. 'I have only seen you!'

'You've no' even seen the Burry Man?' she asked, laughing.

'Oh, God, yes, I did see him. Before I met you.' Matt rolled his eyes. 'Frightened the hell out of me.'

'He's meant to bring good luck.'

'He's done that, then.' Matt took her hand. 'Josie, where can we go? To be alone?'

She stopped laughing. 'I don't think we should be alone.'

'Why?'

'You know why.'

'Because of Angus? Are you engaged to him?'

'In a way.'

Matt touched her left hand.

'No ring, Josie.'

She remembered the piece of string Angus had tied around her finger and another arrow pierced her.

'We're to be married next year,' she cried, snatching her hand away. 'You don't need a ring to be engaged.'

'You will not be married to him next year,' Matt said slowly. 'You do not love him, Josie.'

'I do! I do love him!'

Matt shook his head. 'You know you do not. Maybe you guessed before? But you know now.'

Her eyes on him were anguished. 'Matt, don't talk to me like that. I could never let Angus down, I could never do to him what Lina did to Callum Robb.'

She had to explain. Callum was his landlady's son, now in London, he knew that. Well, Callum had had an understanding with Lina, who was Angus's sister. She had given up Callum for Mr Guthrie.

'Mr Guthrie?' Matt gave a faint smile. 'Now he'd be considered a catch?'

'Lina is in love with him. And he's very much in love with her.' Josie hesitated. 'She's very pretty.'

'Yes, I've seen her. Passing the house, you know.'

'You think she's pretty?'

'Yes, and her brother is handsome, they must be a handsome family. But she is not beautiful like you, Josie.' The yearning in Matt's eyes was in his voice, in all of him, as he caught her hand again. 'For God's sake, let's go somewhere we can get away from people. We don't know when we'll have another chance.'

They went to the woods on the way out of town on the Hopetoun road. It was a long walk they didn't notice, through crowds they didn't see. Once in the trees, there was no one about anyway. They fell into each other's arms.

'Remember that time I held you on the stairs?' Matt asked softly.

'I'll never forget it.'

'But you knew before that how I felt about you? Women always know.'

'I didn't know,' she said faintly.

'You did. From the moment you took the pen from my hand in your hallway. You looked into my eyes and you knew.' Matt laughed, gently caressing her. 'And I knew, too. Oh, Josie, you were always blushing! Don't you remember? That lovely rose colour, coming up to your brow?' He smoothed back her hair. 'Listen, I want to thank you for giving me this time. If you say it's all I can have.'

She shook her head against his shoulder. 'Matt, I should no' be here with you like this. It only makes it harder.'

'A few kisses, that's all I ask.'

'Kisses,' she echoed.

Their mouths met.

Kisses were all he asked and all she gave, but for each they were a revelation. Josie, who had only known Angus's quiet embraces, was dazed by them. Dazed and even frightened, not of Matt but of what she found in herself. She felt different. Older. A woman who had glimpsed passion, and

77

wanted it. But even on Matt, who had kissed many other women, the kisses had a profound effect.

'Oh, Josie, I love you,' he stammered, finally releasing her. 'You're so strong, so beautiful, I've never known anyone like you.'

She smoothed the damp hair back from his brow.

'Have you known many, Matt?'

'Well, I'm twenty-six years old.' His smile was disarming. 'You'd expect me to have had a few girlfriends. Hadn't met you, remember.'

'There goes the charm,' she said with an attempt at lightness. 'Ken was right, Matt. You could charm the birds off the trees. Or someone like me.'

'Listen, I've never felt about anyone as I feel about you, Josie. So, in that way, you're the first. Am I the first for you? Or do we talk about Angus again?'

She turned her head away and said nothing.

'You still say you're going to marry him?' Matt pressed.

'I have to. If I said I wouldn't, I'd break his heart. I couldn't do it.'

'Ah, Josie.' Matt held her close. 'Haven't you done it already?'

'Not when he doesn't know. What you don't know, can't hurt you.'

'It's better to face things.'

'I don't want him to face things.'

'He's lost you, Josie. He lost you when we first met. Come on, admit it.'

She pulled herself away from him, took her comb from her bag, pathetically tried to make herself look as usual when her whole world had burst into flames.

'I think I could be happy with Angus,' she said at last. 'I've known him all ma life. I don't really know you at all, Matt.'

'Don't know me? Josie, we're made for each other! Didn't we both know that from the beginning?' He held her

78

arms and looked into her face. 'Didn't we? Didn't we know that from the beginning?'

She shrugged, looking unseeingly about her.

'We'd better be getting back.'

He let her go, giving a long sigh of defeat. 'If that's what you want.'

'What time is it?' she asked, as they came out on to the road. Beside them lapped the Forth. In the distance was the bridge. Matt's bridge, as it seemed to Josie now.

'I don't wear a watch in my job.' He looked up at the sky. 'But I'm good at guessing. I'd say it was five o'clock.'

'Help! Ma mother'll kill me!' Josie gave a strangely uncaring laugh.

'No point in hurrying, then,' said Matt, who never hurried.

As they reached the High Street, Josie began to walk a little apart from him. This was where everyone knew her and she was vulnerable. Already she could feel the eyes at the windows, hear the whispers. 'Isn't that Josie Morrow? Who's the young man? No' Angus Braid, anyway.'

'Is this where we say goodbye?' asked Matt.

Josie went pale. She put her hand to her mouth that had known his kisses.

'I suppose it is.'

'I won't be here for much longer, anyway.'

'Why? What do you mean?'

'My job finishes in September. The undersea work's already done.'

'I didn't know that,' she said blankly. 'I didn't know you finished in September.'

'Can't last forever.'

'No.' She could not take her eyes from his face. 'Matt, I don't want to say goodbye to you here. Everyone can see us, it's like being in a goldfish bowl.'

'Wouldn't do to meet again, though.' He looked away from her, down the High Street. 'You're right, I think. You could be happy with Angus. Your parents'll accept him, and they'd never accept me. Be easier for you this way.'

'Easier? You think I care about that?'

'No.' He pressed her hand. 'But I know you care what they think.'

'The funny thing is, I never gave them a thought this afternoon.'

'That's because you chose Angus, not me.'

He's changed, she thought desolately. He's saying I've done the right thing. If it's easier for me, it's easier for him. Could she blame him for not wanting another battle with her father?

'Josie,' he said gently. 'I'll say goodbye now.'

'Matt!'

He lifted his hand in a melancholy wave. 'Goodbye, Josie.'

She did not watch him walking away from her, that would have been asking too much of herself. It was almost a relief that when she raised her head, he had gone.

'Josie, where have you been?' cried her mother frantically. 'I've had everything to do, and your dad's lying down again. Is that ice-cream you've spilt on your good blouse?'

'I'll go and change, won't be a minute.'

In her room, Josie stood swaying with the pain. She had never imagined it would be like this. Physical. A physical pain behind her breastbone. She felt like running to the window and screaming: 'Matt, come back!' But he would be too far away by now. And she'd never have done it, anyway.

She changed her blouse and went downstairs.

Chapter Twelve

The night before Lina's wedding, Josie and Patty MacAndrew went round to her home for a last try-on of their bridesmaids' dresses. They found Lina in a bad state of nerves, fiddling with a cigarette and bewailing the fact that Duncan had to spend the evening at his stag party in Edinburgh. What a silly idea it was, that bride and groom had to be separated, just when they needed each other most! And it wasn't as if Duncan wanted a stag night out anyway, him no' caring about drink and having no young friends.

'Come on now, pull yourself together,' her mother told her briskly. 'And put that cigarette out before you get ash all over the girls' dresses. Och, you both look beautiful, so you do! I'll away to make some tea. No room for me in here anyhow.'

'Think I'll try ma dress on again,' Lina murmured as she ground out her cigarette. 'Makes me feel better somehow.'

'Just try to relax,' said Josie, as she and Patty, resplendent in their dark blue taffeta, slid the cloud of white silk over Lina's flaxen head. 'Everything's organised, there's no' a thing to worry about.'

'Aye, and nobody's going to look better than you,' Patty added fervently. 'Och, you're a dream, Lina! Your mum's made a marvellous job of that dress!'

'I helped, you know.' She turned herself around for their inspection. 'I'm no' as good as Mum or Josie, but I'm no'

81

so bad either.' She took a deep breath in and held her hands to her waist. 'You don't think I look too fat? I mean, here?'

'Fat? What are you talking about?' cried Patty. 'You look like a model!'

Lina shook her head. 'It's no' fair, eh? Here's me, slimming like crazy and getting nowhere, and there's Josie, losing weight without even trying!'

'I've no' lost weight!' cried Josie. 'Why d'you say that?'

'You have, Josie,' Patty said solemnly. 'That dress is hanging on you like it wasn't yours. No' fretting, are you?'

'Why would I be fretting?'

Josie's cheeks burned scarlet as the two young women considered her figure.

'No' had a row with Angus?' asked Lina.

'No, I have not had a row with Angus! Look, will you two stop staring at me as though I'm a freak or something?'

'It's supposed to be brides who lose weight, no' the bridesmaids,' sniffed Lina. 'Where's Mum with that tea?'

'*What will the wedding breakfast be?*' sang George, coming in with a tray and grinning. '*Two green beans and a black-eyed pea!* Hey, Lina, get out of thae glad rags before you get chocolate cake on them!'

'Chocolate cake?' her eyes lit up. 'Och, too late to worry about ma waist-line now, eh? George, you push off, then we can change.'

'You girls look pretty good, but wait till you see me in ma hired kilt! Och, I'm never going to live it down at work, me in bloody Highland dress, eh? I mean, we're Lowlanders. What was wrong with ma good dark suit?'

'Out, and watch your language!' ordered Lina, and when the door had shut on him, she and her bridesmaids rapidly changed back into their ordinary clothes and started on the cake.

'Och, you'd never believe the fuss George and Bernie have been making about wearing the kilt!' Lina exclaimed. 'But they are ushers and I said all along that they'd to be the same as Duncan and the best man, and *they're* wearing the

Black Watch tartan, like they did in the war. Angus said he'd wear the Henderson, because that's Mum's, but the boys have done nothing but moan and I can see I'm never going to hear the end of it. As though I care what the guys at work think! This is my wedding and I want things done my way!'

Her bridesmaids knew, but of course made no comment on the fact, that Lina was only able to have things done her way because of Duncan's money in the background. It was he who was paying for the reception at Brackens Park, the country hotel where he'd taken Lina and Josie on that first drive when they'd all just met. Though Kitty said she felt embarrassed and would have been glad to have booked the local hall, Lina had set her heart on Brackens, and what Lina set her heart on, Duncan provided.

'Do you remember driving to Brackens?' Lina asked Josie softly. They were standing together at Kitty's front door. Patty had already gone home.

'I remember,' Josie replied.

She had been happy that evening, happy and hopeful. Everything was going to work out, everyone was going to get what they wanted, it was always going to be summer. How quickly she'd had to learn the lesson, never to think like that again.

'I think I knew then that I was falling in love with Duncan,' Lina murmured. 'Oh, Josie, everything's been so wonderful for me, but I want to tell you, I've no' forgotten Callum.'

'You've been in touch?'

'Och, no, he'd never want that! He said, if you remember, he'd never dance at ma wedding.' Lina shivered, for the September evening was chill, the sky already dark. 'But I do think about him sometimes, hope he's OK. Did you hear he'd given his mum a television set? Had it sent over from Edinburgh.'

'Mrs Robb's got a telly?' Josie's heart leaped, because now she could legitimately speak of Matt. 'I suppose Matt MacLeod and Ken Pearce'll like that.'

'Aye, only the best for them, Mum says Mrs Robb spoils 'em like she was their mother.' Lina drew her cardigan around her shoulders. She grasped Josie's hand. 'Oh, Josie, it keeps coming over me and I can't believe it. Tomorrow is ma wedding day!'

The two girls hugged each other, half-laughing, half-crying.

'It's all going to be perfect,' Josie said at last, pushing Lina towards the door. 'Even the weather forecast's good. You're lucky, Lina, and that's the thing to be.'

'I know. I know.' She rested her glowing eyes on Josie's face. 'Wish you'd get yourself some luck and marry Angus, Josie. What's the point in waiting?'

'I am going to marry him. We'll be getting engaged very soon.'

'Josie! Oh, I'm so happy for you, and for Angus. Can I be your matron of honour?' Lina gave her high little laugh. 'Hope I'm no' in the family way by then!'

Josie, looking out at the night from her bedroom window, was reflecting on the decision she had just taken. What's the point in waiting? Lina had asked, and she was right, there was no point. At least, marrying Angus, Josie could make somebody happy. Might even be happy herself. In time. As soon as the wedding was over, she would write for a prospectus from the teacher-training college. Make a new life. She turned back to her bed, thought of Lina sleeping alone for the last time, and of Matt MacLeod who had once slept in the room next door. Was he watching Mrs Robb's telly now? A great sob racked her, but she stifled it. Matt had called her strong, and strong she would be. She still could not sleep, was glad when her alarm went and she could get up to face the day. Lina's wedding day.

Chapter Thirteen

The ceremony had been arranged for three o'clock at the kirk. By half-past two, a small crowd had gathered and guests were beginning to arrive. One of the first to be greeted by her own sons acting as ushers was Kitty Braid, wearing a restrained dark suit that was not her choice. Emerald green would have gone with her hair, she had argued, but Lina was adamant. No green, it was unlucky. Then didn't Kitty see Duncan's mother come wafting up in a forest green two-piece, complete with matching gloves, hat and bag! No worries about bad luck for her, it seemed! You only had to look at her and Duncan's father, so distinguished in his morning dress, to see that they'd never had to worry about the luck that came their way. Still, they were very nice to Kitty, as they'd been when Duncan had taken them all out for a meal in Edinburgh, never put on a bit of style, and even Duncan's nervy sister seemed in a good mood today and was managing to do without her cigarettes.

Outside, the crowd was admiring the smart folk still arriving from Edinburgh. So many pricey outfits and big hats, morning-suits and Highland rigs! Had they mistaken the kirk for a Holyrood garden party? 'Hey, where's the Queen?' shouted a cheeky errand-boy, pausing with his bike, and John Morrow, limping along with Ellie, told him sharply to be off.

'Young folk, these days, I don't know what they're

coming to,' he muttered, 'the world's gone mad.'

'Now, don't get started,' warned Ellie, though she was privately relieved that he'd been sidetracked from estimating how much money was on the backs of all these guests. She didn't want him coming out with his Old Testament 'vanity of vanities, all is vanity' speech. As a matter of fact she'd spent some money on a new outfit for herself, but she'd already told John he'd better not say anything about that. She owed it to Josie to look her best at this wedding, even if she and John couldn't go on to the reception because of having to do the high teas at Ardmore. Amazingly enough, he had only said she looked very nice and the navy suit was worth every penny, at which she'd blushed like a girl and given him a kiss.

Mrs Tassie, by dint of getting her cousins over from Fife to look after the café for a couple of hours, had also managed to make it to the kirk. After all, as she whispered to Ellie, squeezing in beside her, she couldn't possibly miss Lina's big day, eh? And seeing Patty and Josie as bridesmaids as well!

A ripple went round the guests in the kirk as the tall, straight-backed bridegroom entered with Roderick MacKean, his best man, both in Black Watch Highland dress. The girls who had been at school with Lina giggled and sighed and thought how well she had done for herself and whispered to one another, were there any more at home like them? Was the best man married, did anybody know? Suddenly, the organ struck up, the guests sprang to their feet, and Angus, solemn in his Henderson tartan, walked slowly up the aisle, with Lina in her white silk dress and floating veil clasping his arm.

Well, it had to be admitted, Ellie grudgingly agreed, she did look a perfect picture. All blondness, creamy skin and, big brown eyes, a little smile playing at her delicate mouth, pale pink roses and carnations in the bouquet she handed to Josie when she tremulously reached Duncan Guthrie. Oh, heavens, see the look he gave her! Now shouldn't all that adoration have gone to her Josie, thought Ellie, for didn't her daughter in her dark blue taffeta look as beautiful as the bride, even if she had lost weight recently? Why has she lost weight? wondered Ellie, but having to join in 'Love divine, all loves excelling', in her reedy soprano, quite put the question out of her mind.

Josie too had seen the look Duncan had given his bride and had been consumed with memory that was bitter-sweet. Another man had looked at her in just that way, but she must no longer think of him. She had put that man out of her life and he had agreed to go. Now she looked down at Lina's exquisite flowers trembling in her hands, studied their petals, smelled their scent, as Lina and Duncan, 'In the presence of God and before this congregation', made their vows. Oh, how solemn the words, how awesome the promises! They seemed to be burning into Josie's soul. She raised her eyes and met those of Angus, standing close. Our turn next, he seemed to be saying. Their turn. Her turn. To move from the sidelines to the starring role. Would she soon be promising her love and her trust as long as she and Angus both should live?

I won't, thought Josie, I can't. Even if she never saw Matt MacLeod again, she couldn't marry Angus. She loved him as a friend, as a brother, she would always love him in that way. But never in the way you had to love to say the words of the marriage service. She felt quite sick and wondered how she would get through the day.

Somehow the hours passed, the rituals were observed. Photographs taken, champagne corks drawn, food handed, wedding cake cut. The groom made a speech, the best man toasted the bridesmaids, the band arrived, the dancing began.

'You're looking pale,' Angus told Josie as they danced together.

'Got a bit of a headache.'

'You'll no' be coming back to Mum's afterwards?'

'Oh, I don't think so, Angus, I'll be away home.'

She couldn't look him in the eye but at least the headache was real enough. It was a relief when she and Patty had to slip away with Lina to the room the hotel had provided and help her change into her going away clothes.

'I can't bear to take it off,' Lina sighed as she emerged from the swishing silk of her wedding dress. 'Oh, it's so lovely, eh?'

'You can always wear it for dancing,' Patty said cheerfully. 'Mebbe dye it a nice pink?'

'Never!' cried Lina. 'I'm going to keep it just the way it is, always.'

To Josie, it seemed an age before they could get Lina into her turquoise suit, watch her re-do her makeup, find her bag and gloves, set her little hat on her flaxen hair, but she was ready at last and out on the hotel steps with Duncan at her side.

'Here!' she cried, looking straight at Josie. 'Catch!'

And threw her bouquet.

Oh, no, I can't take it, thought Josie, she means it for Angus, I told her I was going to marry Angus.

But she could only hold on to the flowers and fling her confetti with the rest of the guests as the bride and groom made a dash for the car that was to take them to the airport at Turnhouse.

'They're away to Paris, you know,' Kitty told Josie as the car disappeared, trailing cans and ribbons and 'Just Married' signs. People were turning back into the hotel, the confetti drifting forlornly at their feet. There was the usual feeling of anticlimax in the air, now that the newly-weds had gone, but Kitty was taking comfort. Lina was on her way to Paris and the start of a wonderful life.

'They're no' going away for long,' she told Josie. 'Duncan has to be back for the end of the bridge job.'

'I knew it was nearly finished,' said Josie.

'Aye, and then, who knows, eh?'

And Josie echoed, 'Who knows?'

Chapter Fourteen

It was a wonderful relief to arrive home, put the flowers in water, change into a jumper and skirt, pull on her raincoat.

'I'm going out for a breath of air,' Josie called to her mother. 'I've a terrible headache.'

'Going out? In the dark?' Ellie's face was a study in disappointment. 'Your dad and me were looking forward to hearing all about the reception.'

'You were looking forward,' said John, turning a page of one of the kirk's account books.

'Well, it would be nice to know what everybody had to eat. Are we going to get any cake?'

'Mrs Braid's cutting it up tonight.' Josie took a torch from a shelf. 'Won't be long, must clear ma head.'

'Did you drink any of that champagne?' John asked sternly. 'No wonder you feel ill.'

'Dad, I had to drink the toasts. I just had a sip.'

'See where it's got you, then.'

'Keep to the road,' Ellie cried as Josie left them. 'I'm no' keen on you wandering on that shore by yourself.'

'It's safe enough, Mum. Stop worrying.'

She was leaning against the esplanade rail, looking at the bridge, marvelling at its amazing silhouette, dark against the paler evening sky. The waters of the Forth were black, covering the strip of shore where the Braid boys had once dug for crabs and Josie and Lina had played their own games. That had been after the war. A long time ago. Josie felt older, but no wiser. It was clear enough she had no idea how to manage her life. Didn't really know what she wanted. Oh, but that wasn't true! She *did* know what she wanted. She had just thrown it away.

There were people about, mostly making for the Hawes Inn. They all seemed to be couples. She didn't look at them, didn't want to see couples happy together. Anyway, the wind was turning colder, she might as well go back. A man's melodious voice said, 'Josie?'

She turned, her heart rising, and as she had so gladly done before, went straight into Matt MacLeod's arms. It was enough for a while just to stand there with him, resting against him, switching off from her troubles, but finally she drew a little away.

'Thought you'd be at Mrs Robb's,' she said lightly. 'Watching telly.'

He laughed. 'I like to walk, I like a bit of air.' He touched her face gently. 'Why aren't you dancing at the wedding?'

'The dancing's over.'

'Suppose it would be by now.'

'Did you no' want to go to Glasgow today? It's Saturday.'

'I stayed to see the wedding.'

'You were at the wedding? Where? I didn't see you!'

'I was in the crowd, saw you in your blue dress. You looked beautiful.'

'I wish I'd seen you.'

'You've lost weight, though, haven't you?'

'Everyone says that.'

'Why? Why've you lost weight?'

'Because I'm unhappy.'

Matt laughed shortly. 'I should be a skeleton then, the way I feel. And I've given up the drinking. Ken thinks I've lost my senses.'

90

'I never knew you'd taken to walking here,' Josie murmured. 'Seems like fate I came tonight.'

'I don't believe in fate,' Matt said firmly.

'Somehow, I didn't think you would. You're no' like me, you can do without believing.'

'I believe in you and me, Josie.'

The lights of a train shone at the far end of the bridge and they watched it come closer, rattling across the rails until it reached the viaduct approach and was gone.

'Like to go to the Hawes? asked Matt.

She shook her head. 'I'm already in disgrace for drinking champagne.

He hugged her but did not smile.

'Josie, are you still going to marry Angus?'

'No. Not now.'

He gave a long sigh. 'What made you change your mind?'

'It was the service today, it was hearing the words. They're beautiful words, Matt, but they have to be for the right people. I knew they weren't for Angus and me.'

'For you and me, then?'

'You don't believe in church services.' She searched his face. 'I don't even know if you want to be married.'

'To you, I do.'

'Ken said you'd never want to settle down.'

'We'd never settle down, Josie.' He waved his hand. 'We'd be up there with the clouds.'

'We're a long way from the clouds, Matt. And I've still got to tell Angus.'

They were at Ardmore, looking up at the lights in its windows. Josie's room, of course, was at the back and could not be seen.

'Who's in my old room?' asked Matt. 'Who's next to you?'

'A cyclist from London. He brought his bike up by train, he's planning to ride round Fife.'

'Hope he doesn't want his breakfast early?'

'No, he's no trouble.' Josie felt the tears prick her eyes. 'Oh, Matt!'

'Used to lie awake, you know, thinking of you next door. Did you ever think of me?'

'All the time.'

'We won't be separated for much longer. When will you see Angus?'

Josie bent her head. 'He's away next week. Mr Johnson's sent him to London on a business course.'

'A breathing space for you.'

'I don't want it, I'd rather get it over with. By the time he comes home, Lina will be back, too.'

'And Mr Guthrie will be finishing the contract.' Matt was determinedly cheerful. 'Then it'll be back to Glasgow for me.'

'Glasgow? Matt, what'll I do?'

'Don't worry.' He shook her gently. 'It won't matter where I am, we'll keep in touch. And you'll be planning our wedding.'

'Yes.'

She did not mention her parents, and neither did he. But when they kissed goodbye, both were conscious of the house before them and its windows. Josie did not linger and Matt did not try to keep her. Anyway, they could afford to be apart for a little while, now that they had found each other again.

Chapter Fifteen

The week that followed was the longest of Josie's life. For Lina, it was the shortest. Oh, how she wished her honeymoon need never end! It was not only the passion of the nights that thrilled her, but the pleasure of the days: the promenading round Paris in her trousseau clothes, eyeing the fashionably dressed citizens, listening to their rapid speech, watching their gestures, eating in smart restaurants with Duncan to translate the menu and gaze soulfully into her eyes. These were experiences she soaked up greedily, treasuring them for memory, though Duncan told her as they were returning home that it was all just the beginning, they had a whole lifetime of happiness ahead of them. Looking out at Turnhouse as their plane landed, Lina took his hand.

'Do you ever feel you're too happy?' she asked.

'No, I feel just right.' He squeezed her hand in his. 'We're perfect for each other and always will be.'

Probably all newly-weds felt that way, thought Lina, but sometimes things went wrong. Look at Antonia's marriage, for instance. But we'll be different, she promised herself, and could not imagine a time when she would not be ecstatically happy with Duncan. She shifted her thoughts to her mother, the boys and Josie; to the fun she would have giving them the presents she had bought, showing them the New Town flat Duncan had rented until he could get the tenants out of his own. She had invited them all over for a cup of tea on Sunday. Though she would scarcely have had time to unpack, she felt she couldn't wait to see them and knew they couldn't wait to come.

They all went over to Edinburgh on the train – Kitty, George, Bernie, Josie and Angus, who had arrived back from London the night before. Josie had been dreading seeing him but he was so full of the course he'd been attending, he failed to notice her uneasiness when they met.

'I think it was very good of old Johnson to get me some business training,' he told his audience in the dusty carriage rattling towards the capital. 'I mean, it's one thing to have professional knowledge, but it's quite another to run a business. If I'm going to go into this thing on an equal footing with Niall, I've got to know what's what.'

'That's right,' agreed Kitty. 'But if you ask me, you'll end up running the show for that Niall Johnson before you know where you are. You just be sure you get equal shares and equal treatment, because he's the boss's son and he'll no' let you forget it.'

'Och, he's no' like that, he's a good chap.' Angus's golden-brown eyes moved to Josie, who shifted in her seat. 'Saw Callum when I was down in London.'

'How is he?' asked Kitty, before Josie needed to say anything. 'No' still fretting?'

'It's no' been all that long, Mum, since Lina gave him the push.'

'Gave him the push? What a way to talk!'

Josie looked out of the window. 'We're nearly there,' she said quickly, thanking God that the train journey to Edinburgh was so short.

'Callum's OK,' Angus said shortly. 'Managing.'

'And making money, I expect?' Kitty was powdering her nose as the train ran into the station. 'Have you seen that telly he's bought his mother?'

'He's doing well. Some compensation, I suppose.' Angus

94

rattled down the window and opened the compartment door. 'Now, where's Duncan? He said he'd meet us.'

'Och, I'm so excited,' Kitty whispered to Josie. 'To think of our Lina living in the New Town! Can you believe it?'

'New Town?' Bernie repeated, leaping out on to the platform. 'Old as the hills, seems to me.'

'Aye, but no' Old Town all the same,' said George. 'Damn' funny place, Edinburgh, eh?'

'There's Duncan!' cried Kitty. 'Now, have you ever seen anyone look happier?'

The rented flat was what was known as a double-upper, the top two floors of a terraced house in one of the New Town's Georgian crescents. There was a central garden, shared by all the tenants, but as Lina said, she was not going to have time to sit around in a garden, with all the sorting out she had to do! It was true, the fine drawing room was still crammed with unpacked wedding presents, boxes and cases, pictures and pieces of furniture sent over by Duncan's parents to complement the rented furnishings. Lina told her family she was longing to get into Duncan's own flat, but they would just have to be patient and wait for the end of the tenants' lease. In the meantime, this was nice, eh?

'Nice? It's grand!' cried Kitty. 'Och, you're a lucky girl, Lina. Look at the ceiling ... look at the mantelpiece!'

'Where's the tea?' asked George.

'Now, you'll no' have to expect marvels,' said Lina. 'I had to rush out soon as I got back and buy what I could, so it's no' home-made. No need to worry, though, there's plenty!'

That was true enough, thought Josie, who was finding it hard to eat anything and was relieved when tea was over. But then the presents from Paris were distributed. A pretty necklace for Kitty, cuff-links for the brothers, a silver brooch for Josie. Her heart sank.

'Oh, no,' she protested, 'you shouldn't have bought me

anything else. I've already got the lovely locket Duncan gave me at the wedding.'

'You're special, Josie,' Lina told her. 'You're family. Well, nearly.'

As Josie lowered her eyes, Kitty said crisply, 'Lina, are you no' going to show us upstairs?'

'It's so nice having two floors,' chattered Lina, leading the way up a spiral staircase to the upper rooms. 'This is our bedroom – sorry it's such a mess, I've no' even unpacked the cases. But is this no' a sweet room? They told us it was the nursery in the old days. See the little cupboards? That's where they must have kept all the clothes and nappies and stuff.'

'Lina, you sound broody already,' Kitty teased, but Lina tossed her head and said she certainly was not!

'Are you all right?' Angus asked Josie, keeping his voice down. 'You're pale again. I'm worried about you.'

'Angus, can I talk to you?' she asked urgently. 'Could we slip away somewhere now?'

'Now? How can we?'

'There's the garden, we could go there, Lina said she had the key. Please, Angus?'

Kitty and Lina exchanged significant glances when Angus said he and Josie would like to go down to the garden, but Duncan, finding the key, said, 'It's just grass and trees, really. We don't seem to run to flowers.'

'They're no' worried what's in the garden, Duncan,' Lina laughed. 'Angus has been away for a week, right?'

'Ah, I see.' Duncan joined in the laughter, but Kitty said sharply, 'Don't be too long, you two, we've our train to catch, remember, and there's no' much of a service on a Sunday.'

'I won't be late.' Josie, paper-white, was not looking at anyone. 'It's just cold supper on Sundays, but Mum'll want me back.'

'Better get going, then,' said Angus. He was already looking a little strange.

96

Chapter Sixteen

From the viewpoint of the garden, the houses of the cres-
cent seemed towering. Solid walls, long windows looking
down, closing in. Josie stood for some time gazing up at
them before she spoke.

'Can anybody see us?'

'There's nobody here. Well, one old lady with a dog.'
Angus peered through the dusty trees that edged the
garden's central plot of grass. 'And one guy on a bench
reading a newspaper.'

'I meant, from the windows.'

He knew she meant only one window.

'We could go to the far end, if you like. The trees'd
shield us there.'

They walked towards the boundary of the garden where
they found another bench and sat down.

'Everybody's crazy about the New Town,' Josie said
after a pause, 'but if I lived here, I'd feel so shut in.'

'You're too used to sky.'

'Yes.' Josie's laugh came out a sob. 'Angus, I don't
know how I'm going to tell you this—'

He waited while she cleared her throat, folded her hands.

'Come on, then,' he said at last.

She had meant to be so gentle, so considerate, but the
words came out in a torrent, as though a dam had collapsed
and all that she'd had in her mind for years could come

tumbling out, pouring over Angus as he sat on the bench and listened to her and made no move.

'I can't marry you. I'm sorry – I'm really sorry. I should have told you years ago, but I never sorted things out, I never tried to understand what was wrong. I knew I loved you, and I do love you, Angus, I'll always love you as a friend, but I never saw that that was no' enough, you see, and now I have seen, and I know it would be wrong if you and me were wed. It's no' anything new, it's just that I've understood. There's nothing we can do. It's just the way it is.' Josie snatched a glance at his face but it was expressionless, told her nothing. 'Angus!' she cried. 'Say something!'

'What do you want me to say?' he asked evenly. 'You've been talking rubbish. What can I say to that?'

'You call it rubbish? All I've been trying to tell you?'

'Aye, it makes no sense at all. You say you love me like a friend. Well, of course you do, we've been friends all our lives. That's what makes it right for us to marry. We're in love and we're friends as well. Our marriage'll be solid, Josie, it's built on rock.' Angus took a breath. 'Now tell me you're no' talking rubbish!'

'The thing is,' she said painfully, 'we're no' in love.'

'We are, Josie, we are!' He took her hand. 'You've just got romantic ideas of what being in love is like, and you compare what we have and think it's no right. But it is right. It's real. Can you no' see that? We're no' in some film, Josie, we're just ordinary folk who love each other.' He dropped her hand and sat back on the bench. 'Oh, God, why can I no' get through to you?'

'Angus, don't say any more, it won't do any good.' Josie turned her eyes to his face. 'I've met someone else.'

Minutes ticked by. The old lady with the dog walked past, smiling and nodding. Maybe she said something. They didn't hear.

'I'm sorry,' Josie said again. 'Angus, I'm sorry.'

'Who is he? Tell me his name.'

She was silent. She couldn't seem to say Matt's name.

'Tell me,' Angus repeated, his voice shaking. 'Tell me who he is. Or do I know? It's that bridge guy, isn't it? The one your father threw out of the house? It's Matt MacLeod!'

'Yes, it's Matt.' Josie's eyes were full of tears. 'We love each other, Angus, and it is the real thing. Please try to understand.'

'Understand? I think I understand, all right.' Angus's voice was strangled with misery. 'You know, when I was in London and I met Callum, he said to me, "You're lucky, Angus, you don't know how lucky you are, you've got a girl who will never let you down." That's what Callum said.'

Josie sat with bowed head. 'You're right to make me feel bad, Angus,' she said, her voice a thread. 'I feel bad, anyway. I know what I've done to you.'

'No, you don't know what you've done. You've given me up for a waster, Josie. A waster and a womaniser.'

She raised her head. 'You don't know him!'

'I know him.'

'You thought you knew Duncan, but you were wrong about him.'

'At least Duncan will take care of Lina, and that's what she needs. But Matt MacLeod will never take care of you. I saw what he was the first time I met him, when he came up to our table in the pub. I thought then: I wouldn't trust that guy, I wouldn't want Josie being mixed up with him. I didn't even want you to cook his breakfast for him, if you remember. I knew here –' Angus struck his chest ' – that he was no good and that he could be dangerous.'

'Dangerous? He's no' dangerous, Angus. He's honest, he's gentle!'

'I meant dangerous to us. And you see, I was right. He's destroyed us.' Angus groaned. 'And you've let him do it.'

For some time they sat on, and the autumn dusk came up around them and they grew cold but did not feel it.

'How you must hate me,' Josie said quietly. 'I know I hate maself.'

'I don't know what I feel.' Angus had been staring at his hands on his knees; he looked up. 'Have you told your folks yet?'

'No,' she answered reluctantly.

'You'll have to be prepared for trouble.'

'Yes.'

Angus searched her face. He took her hands in a fierce grasp.

'Josie, why do you have to do this? Ruin both our lives? Look, will you just listen a minute? You don't have to marry me. If I'm no' what you want, OK, I'm no' what you want. But for God's sake, don't marry MacLeod. That's what I'm asking now, Josie, that's all I'm asking. Because I can't bear to see you doing this to yourself, I can't stand by and let you do it.'

Why can't I love Angus the way he loves me? she wondered dully. It would be right, he would be happy, I could make him happy. For a moment she wavered. Everything would be so easy. No need to face her family, or Angus's family, or the people they knew. No risk, no going into the unknown. Just love and security with Angus. She closed her eyes, she almost spoke.

'Josie?' Angus said softly, and the spell was broken. It should be Matt who was saying her name, she only wanted Matt. Angus loved her, but she loved Matt. There was nothing she could do.

'We must go back,' she stammered, pulling her hands from his. 'Angus, let's go back.'

Without a word he stood up and walked with her from the garden.

'Don't say anything, will you?' she asked as they came to Lina's house. 'I mean, when we go in.'

'They'll have to know some time.'

'But not yet. Not now.'

He shrugged. 'I'm no' going in anyway.'

'What do you mean? Where are you going, then?'

'Hey, you love-birds, where've you been?' called Bernie. He was running down the stairs to meet them. 'You're late, Mum's creating.'

'There's plenty of time for the train if that's what she's worried about,' said Angus curtly. 'Tell her to go on without me, I'm no' going back just yet.'

'What's up?' asked his brother, staring from one desolate face to the other. 'Have you two had a row?'

Neither Angus nor Josie made any reply. Angus began to walk away, slowly at first, then faster, and as he passed under the street lamp, Josie saw the light shine on the plume of his bright hair.

Chapter Seventeen

Monday morning. It seemed strange to Josie that everything appeared so normal. Sheets out, blowing on the line. Handkerchiefs, boiling. Her mother shaking Rinso into a tub, ready for the coloureds.

'No' a bad day for drying,' said Ellie with satisfaction. 'Sets you back when Monday's wet, eh?'

Josie, stirring the hankies with a wooden stick, knew that her mother had been brought up to do the washing on a Monday, 'hail, rain, snow, or blow', as she put it. Well, today was 'blow', so that was all right. As though Josie cared. As though she cared about anything. She had not been able to sleep for thinking about Angus. She felt as though she might never sleep again.

'One of these days, I'm going to get rid of this old tub,' Ellie was murmuring. 'Get maself one of thae new washing machines. Folk say they tangle everything, but think of all the effort saved, eh? And it's time we got a telly as well. Of course, your dad's no' in favour. Folk come to see scenery on their holidays, he says, no' a black and white box. But I say we could put it in our adverts. "Television Lounge". That'd be an attraction. What do you think, Josie?'

'Where'll you get the money?'

'Och, I'm only talking, you know that. I'll have to save up.' Ellie frowned as she looked at her daughter. 'You've awful black bags under your eyes, Josie. I think you should go to the doctor's. Ask for a tonic. I mean, it's all on the National Health now. Might as well get what you're entitled to.'

'That's true,' said Josie, who had no intention of going to the doctor's, but was not prepared to argue about anything that morning.

Her mother was right, all the laundry dried well and they were able to bring it in and fold it ready for ironing before they had their dinner. Cold meat and pickles – didn't take long to eat or wash up. As her father went along to his room for his nap, Josie said she'd be away for the messages.

'I don't think we need anything,' said Ellie. 'I've got what I need for tonight, and we're no' a full house now.' She bit her lip. 'Summer seems to be over already.'

'We always get people in the autumn, Mum, don't worry.'

'We get some people, no' many. Och, it's the same every year, eh?' Ellie hooked on her reading glasses and opened the newspaper. 'But you go on out, get some colour in your face. You could bring me a loaf if you pass the baker's.'

As Josie put on a warm plaid jacket, her mother suddenly took off her glasses again.

'You've no' had much to say about Lina's place, Josie. I thought you'd be full of it.'

'Well, it's only rented. Very nice, but no' theirs.'

'In the New Town, though. I bet Kitty was impressed, eh?'

Josie shrugged. 'I'll away, Mum.'

When she heard the front door bang behind Josie, Ellie put down her paper. The same old record was playing through her mind. Should have been Josie in the New Town, should have been herself and John being entertained to tea by their married daughter and elegant son-in-law. Strange, the way luck went. Fate, some called it. John didn't believe in fate. Sometimes Ellie wasn't sure what she believed.

Josie was on her way to the bridge. It drew her because of

103

Matt. If she could just see him, remind herself of his love, of what had made her love him, she felt her bruised spirit might be comforted. Self-hatred was not something she'd ever had to confront before; now she knew she must learn to live with it. Undoing what she had done was not possible, because she didn't want to undo it. As Lina had said, loyalty had to give way to love. The only person who might help her to live with her herself, who would be sure to think she'd done the right thing, was Matt.

The breeze that had dried the washing was stronger now, more like a real wind. As it blew Josie along the esplanade, along with grit, leaves and flying papers, she thought of Matt and the rest of the bridge workers and was glad their work was finished. All of them hated high winds, for the wind was strong up aloft even on the calmest days, and gales caused accidents. Even Matt, who so loved to be above the world, had once admitted to Ken in her hearing that if he was afraid of anything it was a gale. And Ken had agreed. Aye, when the wind got above a certain strength, it was solid earth for him. Even when the bridge was being built, when the engineers had not wanted to lose a day, they'd never tried to carry on in a gale. Och, no, they'd send the laddies home, Ken had said, laughing, back to their lodgings wherever they were, but no' to the Hawes Inn, eh? That'd have been a big mistake!

Would Matt and Ken be in the Hawes Inn now? wondered Josie. Having a few drinks to celebrate the end of their contract? Maybe that wasn't cause for a celebration, for where would they go next? Matt had said once he would go wherever he was needed, and if no bridge work was immediately available, he'd work in Glasgow until something turned up. Same for Mr Guthrie, he had added. His little Lina would never be sure where her husband would be working next.

Josie missed Lina's not being at the Queen Margaret any more, but she wouldn't have wanted to go there now. It had been bad enough avoiding Lina's puzzled eyes last night;

she was glad she didn't have to face them today. Or Mrs Tassie commenting on how thin she was, or Patty asking if everything was all right between her and Angus? All she wanted to do was find Matt.

The wind was so strong now, she was almost catapulted into a crowd of people standing around the pier. The usual queue for the ferry, she thought, until she saw the ambulance. Ambulance? Instantly, her heart was on the alert, beating so hard she felt it would leap from her breast. She put her hand to her side and stood quite still, looking from face to face, looking for Matt.

'It's coming,' she heard someone say. 'The boat's coming in now.'

'What boat?' she asked urgently. 'What's happened?'

A man with a pair of binoculars hung around his neck turned excited eyes on her.

'The rescue boat's picked up a guy. He fell off the bridge. I saw him go. It was the wind took him, it was the wind, gusting.'

'You saw him?' Josie could scarcely get the words out. 'Who was it? One of the workmen?'

'I couldna tell you. Had a hard hat, saw it fall.'

'He fell to the water?' she whispered.

'No, he saved himself, caught at one o' the girders.' He pointed a thin finger. 'You see the girders?'

Oh, yes, she saw the girders, she'd been seeing them all her life. Like the great steel tubes, they were an integral part of the cantilever sections. Below the water, as her father had explained to her, the cantilevers rested on platforms supported from the seabed by massive cylinders called caissons. John Morrow had been full of stories about the construction of the caissons, how hazardous it had been for the men, working down there under the water. Yet most of the early casualties occurred when men were working above, not below, the Forth. It seemed it was the same today. Working among those girders, those tubes, men were vulnerable. The image of the hard hat falling turned

105

Josie sick, but she grasped the arm of the man with the binoculars.

'What did he do? Did he jump to the boat? How did he get down?'

'Och, he couldna jump! The rescuers were lowered, then they lowered him. Aye, it was tricky – I saw it all – they did a grand job.' He shook her hand free. 'But look there, it's in, the boat's at the pier!'

She stood in silence with the rest of the crowd as the man who had fallen was brought off the rescue boat by stretcher and carried to the waiting ambulance. It was not possible to see his face through the press of people and she hadn't the courage to push herself forward. The longest moments of her life ticked by. And suddenly were over. One of the men who had been helping to carry the stretcher stood back as the doors of the ambulance were closed. The man was Matt.

'Oh, Matt, I thought it was you!' she cried, sobbing with relief as she fell into his arms. 'Oh, God, I thought it was you!'

'Josie,' he said gently, 'it was Mr Guthrie.'

Matt had made her go into the Queen Margaret café, had made her sit down and drink tea brought by Patty while Mrs Tassie clucked in sympathy, saying she'd never seen Josie look so white. But then it was worry, eh? Worry for poor Lina. And her such a new bride. Och, didn't bear thinking of, that she must be on her way to the hospital now. Where'd they taken poor Mr Guthrie, then?

'The Royal in Edinburgh,' Matt told her, keeping his eyes on Josie. He put another spoonful of sugar in her tea. 'Drink up,' he whispered. 'It's good for shock.'

'Aren't you the fellow who used to lodge with Mrs Morrow?' Mrs Tassie asked, suddenly taking an interest in Josie's companion, suddenly remembering what had happened.

'I am,' he replied, with his clear, open look. 'That's how I got to know Josie here.'

'He got Duncan into the boat,' Josie said faintly, as Mrs Tassie gazed with fascination at Matt. 'He rescued him.'

'Helped,' Matt corrected. 'I helped to rescue him.'

'And is he going to be all right?' Patty asked eagerly. 'He's no' badly hurt?'

'Too early to say. There's a broken arm and a dislocated shoulder, maybe internal injuries, the ambulance men said.'

'But he will be all right?'

'They seemed to think so.'

'Thank God, thank God,' cried Mrs Tassie. 'Patty, go and get some teacakes for poor Josie and Mr—'

'MacLeod. Matt MacLeod. But do not trouble with anything to eat for me.'

'Nor me,' sighed Josie. 'Oh, I feel so awful!'

'Why, Josie, there's no need for you to cry!' Mrs Tassie put her arm around her. 'It's nothing to do with you, what happened!'

But tears still welled from Josie's eyes and she couldn't explain her shame at praying for Matt and not thinking of Duncan. Oh, poor Lina! When could she go and see her? Not now, that wouldn't be right, maybe tomorrow? But what if Lina didn't want to see her, after what she'd done to Angus? Oh, God, Angus ... Josie thought her world had never seemed so dark. Only Matt brought her comfort, as she had known he would, and looking at him with her tear-drenched eyes, she longed with all her soul for them to be alone.

It was better outside the café, when he quite naturally put his arms around her, holding her close, as though protecting her from her own thoughts.

'It's terrible, what happened,' he said softly, 'but it could have been a hell of a lot worse. Mr Guthrie's going to be OK, we're all OK. And I love you. Remember that.'

She was leaning against him, luxuriating in the way she had of being close to him, of shutting out the world, when she felt his arms slacken, saw his eyes darken. Turning her

107

head, she saw two women looking at her, looking at Matt. One was Kitty Braid, one was her mother.

There was no scene. Nothing was said. Kitty, her lipstick a scarlet slash against her pallid face, stalked into the café, her coppery head held high, and after a long terrible moment, Ellie followed. She had given just one last look at Josie and one at Matt and her fine eyes had flashed blue fire, but her lips had remained closed. It was a measure of the seriousness of her situation, Josie thought dazedly, that her mother would not even speak to her.

'Oh, Josie,' Matt was saying ruefully, 'I'm sorry, I'm sorry. Oh, hell, hell ... what'll we do?'

'It's all right,' she answered, and heard her voice as a stranger's. 'Mum had to know some time. She knows now. What difference does it make?'

'Poor, brave, Josie!' He tried to gather her into his arms again, but she pulled away.

'I'd better go home, Matt. Wait for her.'

'Tell your dad?'

'No, no, I'll tell them both together, it'd be better.' Josie began to walk on and Matt caught up with her to take her arm. The still powerful wind dragged at them, buffeting their two forlorn figures as they fought their way along the esplanade.

'Oh, I never thought to see Mum here!' Josie groaned. 'She must have heard about Duncan, must have seen Mrs Braid running out of her house and come with her.'

'Aye, someone'll have told Mrs Braid, all right, seeing as Mr Guthrie's her son-in-law.'

'She's probably going on to the hospital after she's seen Mrs Tassie, she'll want to be with Lina.' Josie stopped and suddenly flung her arms around Matt. 'Oh, think of Lina, Matt! What does it matter what ma parents say about us? As long as you're all right and we're together?'

'That's the way to look at it,' he told her, but his eyes were uneasy. 'Only I want you to let me come in with you

108

to see your dad. That's the right thing to do, and I want to do it.'

Josie shook her head. 'No, Matt, better not. You saw ma mother's face. She won't think it's right, whatever you do. Neither will Dad.'

'I know, I'm prepared. But I don't want you talking to them on your own. I don't want them thinking I'm skulking outside, leaving you to speak for me.'

'Matt, honestly, it'd be better if you didn't come in. They're ma parents, I know them. I know I've a better chance of making them understand things if you're no' there.'

As they stopped at the door of Ardmore, he stood hunched against the wind, his yellow hair blowing across his brow, his gaze troubled.

'I'm afraid for you,' he said at last. 'That's the truth of it.'

'Afraid?' Josie tried to smile. 'They're not going to hurt me, Matt. They've never laid a finger on me in all ma life!'

'Maybe I should've said "afraid for us". They'll persuade you to give me up. They'll tell you all the things against me and there'll be plenty, according to them.' He took her hands. 'And you're so used to doing what they say, how will you stand out against them this time?' He shook his head. 'I don't see it.'

Josie, ignoring the fact that there were people passing, kissed him full on the mouth. 'That's how I'll stand out this time,' she said breathlessly. 'I love you and I want you, Matt. And what nearly happened to Duncan today has made me see what's important. It's us, our life together. Nobody is going to make me give you up, I promise you! Now, you go back to Mrs Robb's and wait for me there.'

'Mrs Robb's? No, I want to be here, Josie, I can't just go back to Mrs Robb's!'

'You mustn't be here when ma mother comes back. Please, Matt, you go home and I'll come to you, I'll tell you what they said.'

He slowly let go of her hands. 'I always said you were strong, Josie. Strong and beautiful. OK, I'll go to Mrs Robb's and wait for you there.' He flung back his head against the wind. 'Remember what you promised!'

She smiled and took out her key. But when she had opened the front door to her parents' house, she didn't feel beautiful and she didn't feel strong.

Chapter Eighteen

'Is that you, Josie?' called her father.

'Yes, Dad.'

Josie went into the kitchen where there was the savoury smell of a beef stew cooking. John Morrow was sitting in his chair by the stove, more kirk papers on his knee. He seemed tense, excited. It was clear he'd heard the news about Duncan and had been reliving his own experience.

'Seen your mother? She's gone to the bridge with Kitty Braid. There's been an accident, Mr Guthrie's fallen.' John's lip trembled. 'Aye, taken by the wind seemingly. Should never have gone up, eh? That's one lesson we all learned. Never underestimate the wind.'

'He's OK, Dad.' Josie, taking care to disregard the question about her mother, pushed back her wind-tossed hair. 'He fell, but he saved himself. He hung on till they got to him and lowered him to the boat.'

'He's no' hurt? Thank God for that!'

'Well, he's hurt, but maybe no' seriously. They've taken him to the Royal Infirmary.' Josie tied on her apron. 'Smells as though Mum's got the stew in, I'd better do the vegetables.'

'I've done the tatties and the carrots.'

'You have, Dad? What's come over you?'

'Felt so worked up, had to do something. Brings it all back, eh?' John was shuffling his papers with trembling hands when the front door banged. 'That'll be your mother.'

As Ellie walked in, without taking off her coat or hat, Josie felt a strong sense of relief. All her play-acting at being just as usual with her father was over. Here was the real challenge. She wanted to meet it.

'So, you're back.' Ellie was strung up, stretched tight as a drum, her eyes on her daughter glittering. 'I wonder you've the nerve to show your face back here!'

'What's up?' asked John, creaking to his feet.

'Did she no' tell you? Did Josie no' say I found her kissing Matt MacLeod in the street in broad daylight, for all the town to see! I was never so ashamed, never!' Tears were spilling down Ellie's cheeks, but she dashed them angrily away. 'Och, I'll never be able to hold up ma head in this place again. And Kitty Braid there and all, to see it and tell everybody!'

'We were not kissing,' Josie said swiftly. 'And Mrs Braid'll have other things to think about than me.'

'Aye, her Angus, that you've given up for an atheist and good-for-nothing!' Ellie threw her hat and coat over a chair. 'Josie, how could you? How could you?'

John had been staring at Josie with eyes that had been growing harder and colder as his wife's words sank in.

'Hold on, Ellie,' he said hoarsely, 'let me get this straight. You say you saw Josie with that fellow I threw out of the house?'

'Is that no' what I'm telling you? They were together outside Beryl Tassie's café, kissing and cuddling—'

'He was comforting me,' Josie said desperately. 'I was upset about Duncan Guthrie.'

'And why should a man like that be comforting you?' Her father's blue eyes seemed to boring into her soul. 'What's this MacLeod to you? Have you been seeing him behind our backs?'

'We love each other,' she said bravely. 'We want to be married.'

There, it was said, and she felt the better for having said it; lighter, easier, as though something festering had been removed from her heart. She wasn't used to keeping secrets. But the relief was short-lived. The effect of her words on her parents was worse even than she'd anticipated.

'Married?' breathed Ellie, and sank into a chair. All the colour left her face, leaving her looking old and ill, her hold on beauty quite gone. 'Married?' she said again. 'John, do you hear?'

'I hear.' He too had sat down, he too was ashen pale. 'But I'm no' taking it in.' His blue gaze beat fiercely on Josie's face. 'Josie, are you trying to tell your mother and me you want to marry a man without God?'

'And a womaniser and a waster!' cried Ellie. 'Kitty told me that's what poor Angus said about him, but I knew it anyway, I saw it for myself, it's written all over his face, what he is. Oh, Josie, Josie, this is just madness, can you no' see that?'

'Madness,' John slowly repeated. 'Aye, it's what they call infatuation. No' real love, Josie, just an illness, a fever. Goes as quickly as it comes. You give it time and you'll see. You give it time and you'll no' ruin your life and ours. You're no' wanting to do that, eh?'

'No, I don't want to hurt you or Mum, Dad. You know I've always done ma best for you.'

'That's true, you've been a good daughter.'

'And we've appreciated it,' said Ellie. 'But we've always done our best for you, too, and wanted what's right for you. We can't stand by and let you throw yourself away on somebody like Matt MacLeod. Look how he's changed you already! You've never kept secrets from us before, and here you've been, meeting him on the sly without a word to us!'

'I'm sorry about that, Mum, honestly I am, but it was only because I didn't want to upset you,' Josie said earnestly. 'I knew Dad had taken against Matt over the religion, but he's

113

no' what you say, he's no' a waster or a womaniser. Angus said that, but he doesn't know him. None of you knows him but me, and I know he is a good man.'

'A good man?' Her father laughed harshly. 'A man who cannot believe in God? A man who admits it, who's proud of it! You call him a good man?'

'Watch yourself, John,' said Ellie. 'Don't let yourself get upset.'

'Don't let maself get upset? Our daughter wants to marry a man we can no' accept in our own house and you tell me no' to get upset? What's it take to get you upset, Ellie?'

'I'm heartbroken,' she said quietly. 'All I'm telling you is to think of your blood pressure. I'm no' wanting to lose you as well.'

'Mum, don't talk like that!' cried Josie. 'Oh, I never wanted to make you feel so bad!'

'Well, you know what to do, then. Say you'll give that fellow up and we'll just forget that this ever happened. We'll get back to normal and be happy again.'

For a long moment, Josie let her eyes rest on her mother. As when Angus had pleaded with her in the garden, she could see how easy it would be just to let go. Just do what they said. Give up Matt. Give up the fight. Get back to normal.

'Angus still loves you, he'd take you back tomorrow,' Ellie pressed, taking a step forward, ready to fold Josie in her arms. 'And he's right for you, Josie, you know that in your heart, he's the one for you.'

'Aye, and he's the one who's good,' put in her father. 'A fine, clean-living lad. You'd be safe with him.'

A great shudder went through Josie's frame. She closed her eyes and saw Matt's face, handsome, resigned, beneath his blowing yellow hair. She heard his voice. 'They'll persuade you to give me up, Josie ... how will you stand out against them this time?' She opened her eyes to meet her mother's intensely pleading gaze.

'I'm sorry,' she said in a low voice. 'I've always tried to

114

do what you want, but this time – it's no good – I can't. Matt's the one for me, no' Angus. I'll always feel bad about what I did to Angus, but it's Matt I love. I'm going to marry him.'

She waited for one of her parents to speak. When neither of them said a word, she gave a nervous little laugh.

'I think – I think the stew must be ready. I'll take it out, shall I?'

'Leave the stew,' said her father, clearing his throat. 'Go upstairs and pack.'

'John!' shrieked Ellie. 'No!'

'It has to be, Ellie. Go up and pack, Josie, and leave the house.'

She was bewildered. 'What – what are you saying? You're telling me to go? Where? Where will I go? You can't throw me out, I'm your daughter!'

'No,' he said simply. 'Not now.'

'John, what are you thinking of?' moaned Ellie. 'Where is she to go? Oh, I never thought you'd no' let Josie stay, no matter what she'd done!'

'I'm no' having her marry MacLeod from this house, Ellie. Best for her to go now and think on what she's doing.'

'But where can she go? If she stays here, we can talk to her, we can make her see what's right ...'

'She knows what's right and she's chosen to follow her own will, not God's. There's no place for her here.' John slowly rose from his chair and limped to the door, from where he looked back at his wife. 'Better get the tatties on, Ellie.' His voice faltered. 'Time's going by.'

Chapter Nineteen

Strangely enough, it was Ellie who shed the tears as Josie packed the cheap little case she so rarely used and tore down the posters from her bedroom walls. Josie's own eyes were dry.

'I never thought, never, that he'd no' let you stay,' sobbed her mother. 'But you have to look at it from his point of view, you see, he think he's right.'

'I know what he thinks.' Josie took down the text worked in cross-stitch and threw it on the bed. 'He thinks that's for him, he thinks he's the just, he thinks he walks the path of the shining light. So why don't you put it up over *his* bed? It's no' suitable for me.'

'Oh, Josie!'

As she looked around the room she had known all her life, Josie's gaze rested on her teddy and her dolls. For a moment she hesitated over the little Spanish doll Callum had given her. She picked it up but put it down again.

'You're leaving your dolls?' asked Ellie tremulously.

'No space. They're no' exactly a priority.'

'That's all you have of your life, Josie, in that one little case?'

'Looks like it. You can pack ma stuff up when I'm gone, if you want to let ma room.'

'I'll no' be letting your room, Josie. It'll always be here for you.'

116

'Please yourself.' She closed the suitcase and picked up the carrier bag that contained her shoes, hairbrush and spongebag.

'That's it, then. I'm off.'

'Josie – where will you go?' whispered her mother. 'You wouldn't – you wouldn't go to him?'

'Not the way you mean,' Josie said curtly. 'But I am going to see him, tell him what's happened. He's waiting for me at Mrs Robb's.'

'And then what? Oh, if only we had someone we could turn to, some family. I've only ma cousins in Aberdeen—'

'I'm no' going to Aberdeen,' said Josie. She walked to her window and looked for the last time at the view of the Forth she had loved so much. 'I thought of going to Mrs Tassie's. She's got a spare room, she'd take me in.'

'Beryl Tassie?' screamed Ellie. 'Oh, no, Josie, no! Och, I'll no' have Beryl Tassie knowing all our troubles!'

'You mean, knowing ma own dad has thrown me out?' Josie shrugged. 'Why not? He's only done it because he thinks it's right.'

Ellie bit her lip then suddenly threw her arms around Josie, and Josie, after a moment's astonishment, dissolved into tears.

'Oh, Mum, I wish it didn't have to be like this! I wish you could have just tried to get to know Matt, liked him a little bit—'

'I wanted the best for you, Josie, that's all I ever wanted. And you wanted something different yourself, didn't you? Different from what I had. But what sort of a life are you going to have with Matt MacLeod? It'll be hard. Hard as mine. Mebbe even worse. I can't try to like him, Josie. I can't accept him.'

'You'll no' come to ma wedding then? It might be in the kirk. Matt's agreed.'

Ellie let Josie go and stood aside, her face working. She shook her head.

'It'd be too much for me. Too different from all I'd hoped.'

Josie gave a long, resigned sigh. 'All right, I won't ask you again. Look, I think I'd better go. I don't want to be too late, finding a place.'

How quickly you appeared to get used to things, she thought drearily. Already on the surface she was accepting that her parents' home was no longer hers, that she must find another place to lay her head. At the same time, it all seemed so incredible, must surely be some sort of nightmare. She would surely soon wake up?

Her mother was scrabbling in the pocket of her apron. She took out an envelope.

'Here, I want you to have this.' She put the envelope into Josie's hand.

'What is it?'

'It's a few pounds from ma savings. Whatever you've done, I'm no' letting you go out of here without something to tide you over.'

'Mum, I can't take it,' Josie said softly. 'You'll need it, to pay somebody to take ma place.'

'Josie – I never thought! Oh, what'll I do?' Josie, what'll I do without you?'

'Get somebody in. You'll have to. And I've got some money anyway. Ma own savings from ma tips.' She put the envelope back into her mother's pocket. 'But thanks, Mum, I'll no' forget this.'

She picked up her case and the carrier, slung her handbag over her shoulder, took a last look round her room and walked slowly down the stairs.

'You'll no' say goodbye to your dad?' her mother asked in the hall. 'He'll be suffering, you know. You're the apple of his eye, he'll be lost without you. It shows how much his religion means to him that he could send you away.'

'His God's no' mine,' Josie answered bitterly. 'My God's kind and forgiving, He'd no' let a father throw his

118

daughter out of the house. And no, I won't say goodbye to
Dad. I don't want to see him again.'

'Oh, Josie!'

'Will you keep in touch?' Josie asked fiercely. 'If I
write, will you reply?'

'I'll see. I'll try.'

Mother and daughter stared hard into each other's face,
then clung together, holding back tears.

'Shall I no' phone for a taxi?' asked Ellie. 'You've that
case to carry.'

'It's no' heavy. I've no' taken much.'

Ellie opened the front door. 'The wind's dropped, that's
something.' She brushed her eyes with her hand. 'Oh, I
can't believe this is happening, it's a nightmare!'

'We're no' going to wake up from it.' Josie, ready to go,
gave her mother a quick, awkward kiss, and walked away.
A few paces on, she turned to look at Ardmore and Ellie
standing in the doorway, but she could not wave, her hands
were full. Anyway, she didn't feel like waving.

Plum Tree Cottage, Mrs Robb's house, had no view of the
Forth. It stood by itself in a little street at the back of the
town, not pretty but in good repair, thanks to Callum's
efforts before he departed. It had a large patch of ground at
the back where Mrs Robb was often to be seen in her
wellingtons, digging and planting, for she was a great
gardener, growing all her own herbs and vegetables, and in
the autumn gathering apples and plums from her withered
old trees that still produced crop after crop.

Josie had always got on well with Mrs Robb, who was lean
and ginger-haired like her son, and was said to be brainy,
too, though she'd never found any work but cleaning. It was
many years since her husband had died at sea and her life had
been a struggle, but she never complained, which was what
Josie liked about her. All the same, Josie was nervous when
she knocked on the cottage door. What must she look like,
with her tear-stained face, and her suitcase and her carrier-

bag? Really, she only wanted to see Matt.

'Hallo, Josie!' cried Mrs Robb, answering the knock. 'Why, it's an age since I've seen you. Come in, come in!'

'I was wondering if – if I could speak to Matt, Mr MacLeod?' stammered Josie.

'I'm here, Josie,' said Matt, and took the suitcase from her hand.

They had been having their tea, he and Ken, and Mrs Robb insisted on setting another place for Josie, who said she wasn't hungry, then found she was starving. It was another dream world, here in Callum's home, but no longer a nightmare. No, all was golden again, as it was when Matt was with her, and it wasn't too hard to recount what had happened, accept Ken's sympathy and Mrs Robb's amazement. Though he hid it well, Matt was shaken. Josie knew he'd never imagined John Morrow could treat his daughter as he had treated strangers. Not surprising, Josie thought wryly, when she had never imagined it herself.

'So, you and Matt are engaged,' Mrs Robb murmured, pouring Josie another cup of tea. She made no mention of Angus, but Josie knew he was in her mind. Thinks me faithless like Lina, thought Josie, and was saddened because it was true. Or partly true. But when she looked at Matt, she could not believe she had ever made promises to any other man. No one but Matt existed for her now, and even the memory of Angus's pain was dimmed.

'So, Josie, what are you going to do?' asked Ken. 'I mean, now?'

'I'm no' sure. Book in somewhere for the night, I suppose.'

'Why, Josie, you silly girl, you can stay here!' exclaimed Mrs Robb. 'I've a couch, I've blankets! You've no need to be going around the town looking for a room!'

'That's very kind of you, Mrs Robb,' said Matt. 'But I've already decided what Josie's going to do.' He stretched out his hand and took hers. 'She's coming to Glasgow with me.'

120

'Glasgow?' Josie's eyes grew wide. 'Glasgow, Matt?'

'Aye. We've finished here, the job's done. Ken and me were leaving tomorrow anyway. But if we hurry, we can get a train tonight. What do you say?'

Josie looked at Ken. 'We'd all go to Glasgow tonight?'

'No' me,' he said, grinning. 'I'm no' playing gooseberry. The two of you can go, I'll wait till tomorrow.'

'But, Matt, where would we go in Glasgow?' cried Josie. 'Do you mean to your mother's? We couldn't do that, she wouldn't be expecting me.'

'She's not the sort to worry if folk turn up out of the blue. Did I not say we lived in Liberty Hall?' Matt was laughing, his worries for Josie melting away. 'Will it not be the answer to everything now?'

She was stunned, could say nothing, and it was left to Mrs Robb to speak.

'Matt, can you no' see it's all been too much for the girl? She doesna ken whether she's coming or going. But you go and pack your bag and Ken can phone from the callbox for a taxi to Dalmeny station. Then you'll be on your way.'

On their way. The dream was continuing, first in the little train to Waverley, then in the station buffet, having a coffee and waiting for the Glasgow train. Josie knew, even in her golden haze, that the pain of her father's action was not gone, only anaesthetised, it would come back when she was on her own. But when she was with Matt, nothing could hurt her, nothing could touch her. She was free to be happy.

'How could your dad have done that to you?' Matt was asking wonderingly. 'His own daughter! You told me not to think too badly of him, but that was when he'd only thrown me out. What am I supposed to think now?'

'Don't let's talk about him,' Josie answered, looking into her coffee cup. 'I don't want to talk about him, or think about him. I'm just grateful that ma mother's no' the same as him. She was so mad with me when she first came home,

121

but when Dad told me to go, she changed. Even tried to give me some of her savings.'

'That's good. You'll not feel so bad, then.'

'But she won't come to our wedding. Whenever it is.'

'You still want it to be in the kirk?'

'I don't think it matters now.'

'Just as long as it happens.' He grasped her hand and pulled her to her feet. 'Let's see if the train's in yet.'

But on the way out of the buffet bar, Josie saw a callbox telephone and stopped.

'Matt, there's still some time, isn't there? I'd like to ring Lina.'

'She might still be at the hospital.'

'I could try her home number, I've got it written down. I want to ask about Duncan, anyway, but I really want to tell her about you and me. Tell her maself. All she'll know is what her mother will have told her.'

'Mothers,' muttered Matt. 'Thank God, mine's not one for making trouble.'

'Could you let me have some change?' asked Josie, hauling open the door of the callbox. 'I'll probably need more than tuppence.'

Lina answered on the first ring. Maybe she thinks it's the hospital, thought Josie, and felt ashamed to be worrying her. When she gave her name there was silence until Lina spoke, her voice strained with tears and weariness.

'Josie?'

'Lina, I wanted to ask about Duncan. I've been so worried since I heard – what happened.'

'Yes. Well, I've just come from the hospital. He's sleeping comfortably. They've set his arm and shoulder, taken X-rays.' Lina drew a long shuddering breath. 'They think he'll be OK.'

'Oh, Lina, that's wonderful! Oh, I'm so relieved!'

There was another silence, then Josie, feeling the receiver damp under her hand, said, 'There's something else I wanted to tell you about—'

122

'Angus? I know. My mum's here. She told me.'

'I suppose she told you about seeing me with Matt MacLeod as well? She hates me, doesn't she? Och, I don't blame her.'

'You know how she feels about Angus, Josie.'

'Yes, and I feel terrible about what I've done to him. It's the worst thing I've ever done in ma life.' Josie took a deep breath. 'But I couldn't help it. I'm going to marry Matt. I'm going to Glasgow with him now, to his mother's. We'll be married there.'

'You're what?' Lina's voice had taken on a sudden animation. 'Josie, I don't believe it! Married in Glasgow? It can't be true!'

'It is. Ma dad's thrown me out because he doesn't approve of Matt – oh, Lina, the pips are going! I'll have to put some more pennies in—'

'Josie, Josie . . . reverse the charges!'

'It's OK, I've put the money in. Listen, I had to speak to you, just to try to make you understand about Angus – about Matt—'

'For goodness' sake, Josie, who'll understand better than me? I'm heartbroken for Angus, but I was beginning to wonder if you felt the same for him as he felt for you.'

'How is he?' Josie asked fearfully.

'Mum says very quiet. I suppose what you'd expect. Look, I know how you feel, Josie, but these things happen. Try not to blame yourself too much.'

'I suppose so,' said Josie, knowing she would always blame herself.

'Will you come over and see me from Glasgow?'

'If you want me to. Oh, it's such a relief to know you're not mad at me. So many people seem to be!' Josie gave a slightly hysterical laugh. 'Lina, I've got to go. Matt's tapping on the window, the train must be in.'

'Keep in touch!' cried Lina. 'And ask me to your wedding!'

'You'd really come?'

123

'I'll come, Josie, I'm your friend.'

'Come on, come on!' cried Matt, picking up the cases, and Josie, bitter-sweet tears streaming down her face, ran with him through the barrier towards the Glasgow train.

Part Two

Chapter Twenty

Marie MacLeod and Josie were window-shopping in Buchanan Street, staring glassily at the lovely clothes, handbags and shoes, whistling at the prices.

'Och, is it no' a shame you couldna buy your wedding dress here?' asked Marie, clutching Josie's arm and going off into gales of laughter at the idea. She was Josie's age, slim and lively, not at all like Matt. Her hair was dark, very short, with a strong wave, her eyes bright hazel. This was her half-day off from the optician's where she worked as a receptionist. Now that the torrential rain of the last few days had stopped, she was taking Josie sightseeing again, for she had already shown her the Barras, the famous hand-barrow market, Paddy's Market, where they'd picked over second-hand clothes but hadn't bought any, and the People's Palace, a museum of social history that had been a bit of an eye-opener for Josie. Today they were doing the 'posh' bits, as Marie called them: the City Chambers in George Square, the Merchants' House, the Cathedral, the fine shops and restaurants of the city centre.

Josie laughed with her. In the three weeks she'd been in Dow Street with the MacLeods, she'd found herself laughing a lot. Though she'd shed tears, too. On her first night, she'd wept long into the night on the little bed they'd made up for her in Marie's room. Not because she felt unwelcome – Matt's mother and father had been very kind – but because she'd just been so exhausted, so suddenly bewildered, by events. In the end, Marie had got up and made her a cup of tea, and Matt had got up too, because he slept in the kitchen alcove anyway, and they'd sat together, the three of them, till the small hours, by which time Josie had begun to feel better.

It was only natural she should feel strange and homesick, declared Marie. Look how she'd been thrown in at the deep end! One minute in peaceful Queensferry, the next in noisy Glasgow! And her folks had shown her the door, too, so she'd be missing them and feeling mad at them at the same time, was that no' true?

'Oh, yes,' Josie had sighed, 'it's true.'

She was missing her parents – even her dad, though she couldn't forgive him for what he had done. She was also missing her familiar surroundings and apprehensive that she might never get used to Glasgow, a city without sky from what she'd seen so far – which admittedly wasn't much. And though it seemed ridiculous, she was even missing the bridge. Felt disorientated without it, felt she would never find her way about the network of streets in this city of tenements.

At least the MacLeods' flat in Turngate, a district in the heart of shipbuilding Glasgow, was not as bad as she had feared. Not as bad, they told her, as their first Glasgow home off the High Street, since demolished. Two rooms with shared toilet and no hot water, rising damp and rubbish in the close. That had been in 1948 when post-war housing conditions were appalling; they'd had to take what they could get. The main thing was there were still jobs. The unemployment of the thirties had vanished with the war, the shipyards and allied industries were still busy. That was why, apart from fearing the sea, Agnes MacLeod had dragged all her family down from the Highlands, and she'd been right to do it, because they'd all found work. And she'd never given up until she'd found them a better place to live, and by that time Fergus, Sandy and Iona had married and were living with their in-laws. Only Matt and Marie were still at home, to make the move to Dow Street with their parents.

Josie wasn't quite sure what she'd been expecting, that first evening she'd arrived with Matt. Something on the lines, perhaps, of the place the MacLeods had left: the cold-water tap, the shared WC, the rubbish in the close. But Fifty-five Dow Street wasn't too bad at all. A four-storeyed Victorian tenement in a street of similar tenements, its sandstone darkened with time and pollution but solid enough and by no means a slum. The ground-floor flat had two bedrooms, a living room, a kitchen with sleeping-alcove, a toilet and even a bath (with a lid) in a space that was no more than a cupboard off the living room.

'No' what you're used to, eh?' Marie had asked at one point, and Josie noticed a quick glance from Matt's mother as she poured tea from a large brown pot. Matt's heavy blond father was looking at her, too, wondering what this stranger made of them, wondering what they should make of her.

'I think it's very nice,' Josie said honestly, and indeed the living room was good-sized and comfortable. There was a large bay window and a fireplace with a mantel, several heavy chairs, a sofa, a piano, and a square table covered with a plush cloth. Everything, Matt told her, had been his grandmother's and had come down with them from the Highlands, but if it was old-fashioned and shabby, it was well looked after. In fact, the whole flat was clean and neat, for Agnes could not endure clutter. Though she worked full-time in the office of a laundry, she was famous for going through her house like a whirlwind, tidying, dusting, shaking mats, as soon as she came home. Washing she did down the stair in the washhouse provided, and hung it out in the court leading off the close; she did not care to go to any local 'steamie', that was not her style. After her chores, she liked to play the piano a bit, sometimes with her husband when he got out his fiddle, or sew or read or dash off letters to old friends in the Highlands. One thing she never did was sit still.

'Your mother is a remarkable woman,' Josie was later to tell Matt, to which he fervently agreed.

'Aye, Ma's a character, and that's a fact. Pity there's only Marie like her for that.'

It was true that Marie, the only one to look like Agnes, was also the only one to inherit her nervous energy. As Josie was to discover, everyone else in the family was like Brandon, Matt's father. 'Yellow yins', as Matt said in the Glasgow voice he could use at will, for like his brothers and sisters, he could switch from Lowland Scots to a Highland accent depending on circumstances. Marie, the youngest, was the only one to sound a true Glaswegian always.

'And we're all of us slow,' Matt added, grinning, but Josie said that that wasn't true. Unhurried, gentle, serene, were the words she would use to describe his family. Apart from his mother and Marie, of course.

As the days went by, Josie's spirits had rallied, in spite of the bad weather. Matt's golden aura, faint for a time, came back stronger than ever, and there was so much for her to do, she couldn't think of home too much. Apart from helping to cook, shop and look after the flat, there was her wedding to arrange and the rest of Matt's family to meet.

It was difficult at first to sort them out, remembering which was Fergus and which was Sandy, or that Fergus was married to Gillie, Sandy to Heather, and Iona to Lew. And then there were the children! Fergus had two, Sandy and Iona one each, but they were all girls, all fair and small, all constantly wailing and being picked up. Josie did her share of picking up and soothing, but was never sure whether she was kissing Polly or Ailie, Shona or Midge. Never mind, they all seemed to like her anyway.

Every day, someone in the family would turn up at Number Fifty-five for this or that reason, and at the week-ends there was always a crowd for Sunday dinner or tea,

130

and then there might be a singsong round the piano, or a bit of a concert, with Dad on his fiddle and Sandy on his accordion. So far, no one had acquired a television, and Ma said she hoped they never did, for the men would be sure to do nothing except watch football or whatever sport was on. Och, it would be the end of everything. Families'd never be the same with the box in the corner.

When the married ones had gone home, there'd be another pot of tea brewed and Ma would shake out some of her oatmeal biscuits from their tin and they'd all feel pleasantly relaxed. Then Ma would give Dad a look and off they'd go to bed, followed tactfully by Marie, so that Josie and Matt could have a little time to themselves, to kiss and caress, before tearing themselves away, Josie to Marie's room, Matt to his bed in the alcove. They felt as tragic as Romeo and Juliet, saying goodnight like that, but at least it wouldn't be long to their wedding, and it was very pleasant, anyway, being engaged. Josie did wish, though, that her mother would answer her letters. Every day she looked for a reply, and every day found nothing. 'Never mind, pet,' said Agnes. But it was hard, not to mind.

'I don't need a wedding dress,' she told Marie as they strolled down Buchanan Street. 'I've got ma suit. Or will have, when I've finished it.'

After she was married, Josie intended to find a job. Matt was temporarily working at Turngate Yard, but they'd need more than his money to afford somewhere to live. For the present, Josie was busy making her wedding outfit on Mrs MacLeod's sewing machine. She'd bought the material out of her slender savings, not from Buchanan Street – to think of shopping there was a laugh, all right – but from the local Co-op store. It was dark blue tweed, which would be smart for the big day and serviceable for the future. A good suit was always useful, particularly if it was in your mind to try for interviews, as it was in Josie's. In spite of everything, she still hadn't given up her teaching plans.

131

'Your suit'll do fine,' sighed Marie, 'but you'd have made such a lovely bride in white with all the trimmings!'

'I really don't care about that sort of fuss.'

'I do! When I meet Mr Right, it'll be the works for me.'

'And then *you'll* make a lovely bride with all the trimmings!'

'Och, I know I'm no beauty.' Marie shrugged. 'I leave that to Iona – and you, of course.'

'Why, you're very attractive, Marie,' Josie said sincerely, and couldn't help adding, 'and so is Matt.'

'Aye, he is.'

Marie was leading Josie to her favourite little tea shop, tucked away in a side street. Here they ordered the set tea of sandwiches and cakes and pot of tea for one shilling and sixpence, and set back with easy sighs, to take the weight off their feet.

'I think you and Matt are going to be very happy together,' Marie remarked. 'He's really crazy about you, and if you take him as you find him, you'll be OK.'

'What do you mean?' asked Josie, but the waitress had appeared and was setting out the contents of her tray.

'All right, hen?' she asked, pushing the metal teapot towards Marie.

'Fine, thanks,' said Marie. 'I'll be mother, eh?'

'What did you mean, take him as you find him?' pressed Josie, her dark-blue gaze very direct on Marie's face.

'Och, you know—'

Josie did know. When people said to take folk as you found them, they usually didn't expect you to find anything good.

'Well, he's just an ordinary fellow,' Marie answered. 'No' perfect.'

'I don't expect him to be perfect. I'm no' perfect maself.'

'There you are, then.' Marie passed Josie her tea. 'Folk getting married should no' expect miracles.'

Josie sat back, laughing uneasily. 'You're quite the expert, Marie.'

'Onlooker sees most of the game, they say. Listen, when we've had this tea, let's go to Glasgow Green. It's a grand park – should have dried out by now – and I bet you'd like to see some open spaces, eh?'

'Oh, I would!' cried Josie, and was embarrassed to find her eyes stinging with tears again. She kept her head down over her tomato sandwich, but Marie, who missed very little, leaned forward and pressed her hand.

'Sorry, Josie. I know how you feel. When Ma made us all come down here, I was still a kid but I cried like you, for what we'd left. Och, I think we all did.'

'Was it very beautiful, where you used to live?'

'Aye.' Marie stirred her tea. 'Right opposite Skye. You should go there some day.'

'I'd like to.'

They were silent for a while, finishing their tea in companionable silence. Josie was thinking how much she liked Marie, whose shell might seem brittle at times but whose centre was soft. All the same, Josie wished she hadn't made that remark about Matt.

Chapter Twenty-One

The quiet wedding was arranged for Saturday, 27 November, in the register office. Though she still had her beliefs, Josie felt it would not be right, after what had happened, to force Matt to be married in the kirk. No one in his family was religious, and obviously her own parents would not be attending the ceremony, so she and Matt could do just as they liked. It was strange for Josie to realise that she had, in effect, achieved freedom. She couldn't take much pleasure in it, the price had been so high. Yet she knew she would have paid that price again, to spend her life with Matt.

No new bridge contract had appeared for him, which suited Josie, who knew he would have to leave Glasgow when one came through. Though he had to work long hours, at least he was home every evening, and at the weekends they could spend time together. Once, Josie felt sure, he would have gone drinking with his friends on Saturday nights, but now they went to the pictures, taking it in turns to choose the film, with Matt sitting through Doris Day musicals and Josie sweating it out with his choice of giant creature fantasies or Marlon Brando being violent. Either way they were able to cling together in the back seats, the nearest they could get to love-making apart from the snatched kisses in the kitchen at Dow Street.

'Oh, God,' Matt would murmur, 'why do we have to

wait till November? What difference do a few words in a register office make?'

But he didn't press Josie not to wait. Sometimes she wondered what she would have said if he had. She wanted him so much she might have said yes, but then where would they have gone to make love? He didn't ask her, anyway.

At some time during the weekend – usually fitted in round Rangers' football matches – he would show Josie his Glasgow. Not the 'posh' bits or the people's bits, he didn't bother about grand Victorian architecture or galleries or markets. What Matt liked to show Josie was the Clyde.

'My forebears were all fishermen,' he told her. 'We like to be near the sea, and the best we've got here is this river.'

Josie, walking with him through the mass of quays and docks that lined the banks of the great river could see nothing but evidence of intense industrialisation. She found it difficult to think of the Clyde as a waterway, it seemed to have become so much a part of shipbuilding. Yet, of course, it was full of steamers and riverbuses, passenger ships and ferryboats. 'Going doon the watter' meant a lot to the people of Glasgow, she knew that. Perhaps she just compared it unfavourably with the Forth at home. Perhaps she was just being unfair, because this wasn't home to her. Yet she was gradually getting used to Glasgow.

'I like to think of the Clyde going westward,' Matt once remarked, when they were on the docks again. 'Westward to the open sea. You'll never have seen a liner being launched, have you, Josie? Och, it's a grand sight. I wish I'd seen the Queens launched before the war. The *Queen Mary* and the *Queen Elizabeth*. Beautiful ships.' He shook his head. 'I'll always be a bridge man, but there's something draws me here as well. Don't know what it is, can't put it into words, but it's there.'

'You do put it into words,' Josie said warmly. 'Why, you're quite poetical, Matt! Isn't that what Ken said about you?'

'Ken.' Matt stared up at an enormous crane towering

135

over the dock where they stood. 'Got some gloomy ideas, has Ken.'

'Has he?' Josie's eyes widened. She had seen Ken and his pretty wife, Millie, only a few days before when she and Matt had been invited round for a fish supper. 'I've never noticed. What's he gloomy about?'

'Jobs. Glasgow.'

'They're no' laying off, are they? I thought there was plenty of work.'

'He's looking into the future.' Matt waved his hand to their surroundings. 'Thinks all this'll go.'

'The shipyards?' Josie was astonished. 'Oh, Matt, that's crazy! Ships'll always be needed!'

'Maybe, but Ken's been reading the figures. Road transport's up, coast transport's down. Firms are finding it cheaper to move their stuff by road.' Matt put back his yellow head and stared into the sky. 'And folk are starting to think about travelling by air.' He drew back his gaze and met Josie's. 'Ken says when air travel gets cheap, no one'll go on liners.'

Josie remembered Callum and his talk of package holidays with people flying to the sun. If they could get to where they wanted in hours, why should they choose to spend days or weeks at sea? She searched for a bright spot.

'What about the goods, though, Matt? The cargoes? You couldn't send them by air.'

'That's true.'

'So they'll still need ships and ports, won't they?' Josie took Matt's arm. 'Och, Ken's worrying over nothing. They'll never lose the shipping from Glasgow. Why, it wouldn't be Glasgow without the ships on the Clyde, even I know that!'

'Aye, you're right.'

But as they walked home to get ready for their cinema outing, Matt's face was strangely bleak. He had not liked his look into Ken's crystal ball, thought Josie. But who could tell what lay ahead? Things could turn out better than you feared. That thought must have occurred to Matt, too, for by the time they'd reached home, he was his usual serene self.

At one of the gatherings for Sunday tea, the women's talk was of the wedding. While the men kept to football and ate their way solidly through Ma's sandwiches, drop scones, fruit loaf and coconut buns, the women discussed numbers for the 'do' back at the house, continually picking up and putting down wriggling children, getting up to make more tea, cutting more sandwiches and the bought Battenberg cake that was Iona's contribution. ('Iona never was a baker,' muttered Ma, in an undertone. 'Now Josie, she's a natural, have you tried her pastry?')

'Can we work out exactly how many folk are coming back here?' asked Marie, who had a notebook by her cup and saucer. 'Trouble is, Ma, you keep changing your mind about asking the neighbours.'

'Aye, well, it's difficult,' sighed Agnes. 'I mean, they know we're having a wedding, and you have to keep in with folk you see every day.'

'But we're limited for numbers, when we have to fit everybody into this room.'

'And there's enough of us anyway,' Iona said lazily.

The older of Matt's sisters was more like him than either of his brothers. They had his colouring, but not his well-cut features or his beautiful smile. Iona could have been his twin, yet they were not particularly close; perhaps because she could never stir herself sufficiently to be close to anyone. Lew Jameson, her husband, ran a small dry-cleaning business. Everyone knew he worshipped Iona as though she were a goddess in a temple, and she just let him do that. And even though she dearly loved her little daughter, Ailie was almost always on someone else's knee. Now Iona turned her large grey eyes on Josie.

'How many are you inviting, Josie?' she asked casually. 'Not your parents, eh?'

'Iona!' snapped her mother. 'Show a bit o' tact!'

'Well, just want to be sure, Ma. I mean, if we're catering—'

Gillie, Fergus's tiny, red-haired wife, gave a snort of laughter. 'Since when have you done any catering, Iona?' she asked tartly. 'Josie, it's just the one guest for you, is it then?'

'My friend Lina,' she answered, keeping her eyes on her plate. 'And mebbe her husband.'

'No' that grand feller frae the New Town?' cried Heather, tall, statuesque, dark-haired, and married to Sandy. 'I'll no' dare open ma mouth if I have to talk to him!'

'He's nice, you'll like him,' said Josie. 'But he might no' be well enough to come.'

'He's the one had the accident?' whispered Gillie, with a sidelong glance at Ma, who did not like to hear about accidents on bridges.

'He's fine,' called Matt from across the table. 'What's a broken arm? Have you put Ken down, Marie? And Millie?'

'They'll make fifteen,' said Marie, writing in her notebook. 'Ma, you can't have the neighbours. No room.'

'They could sit on the stair,' suggested her mother. 'We do that at Hogmanay.'

'But this do's meant to be just for family and special friends. The neighbours don't even know Josie.' Marie turned to her. 'What do you think, Josie? It's your wedding.'

She reluctantly looked up. 'Whatever Mrs MacLeod wants suits me. Everybody's being so kind and I feel so awful – her voice faltered – 'that I'm no' paying ma share.'

'Ah, now, don't talk like that!' Agnes cried. 'We know what's happened, and we're glad to be able to help out. Matt's paying something anyway.'

'But it should be the bride who pays, and I've got a bit saved up—'

'You keep that, you'll need it.' Agnes stood up. 'Och,

let's do the washing up and be done with all this!'

'Well, I want you to know I'm grateful,' Josie went on stubbornly. 'You'll have to let me say that.'

'You say whatever you want,' said Matt, coming round the table to take her hand and draw her to the window, away from the activity of clearing the table.

'I should be helping,' she murmured.

'There's plenty to help, let them get on with it.' Matt stood looking out at the dull autumn evening. The windows of the tenement houses opposite were yellow squares in the gloom, the street lamps already lit. 'I wish I could've given you an engagement ring,' he said, keeping his voice low. 'You'd have liked a ring, eh?'

'No, I wouldn't! Not when we've so many things to buy.' Josie glanced back at the women rushing backwards and forwards with plates and dishes, while the men sat about, picking up the Sunday papers, and the children wailed as someone stopped to wipe their jammy faces. If only we could have been on our own, she thought. She already loved Matt's family, was deeply grateful for the home they had given her, but oh, how wonderful it would be when she and Matt had their own place! Tomorrow she would start looking.

But the next day brought something she'd never expected to see, though she'd been looking for it every day.

'Josie, Josie, there's a letter for you!' cried Marie, bringing in the post before she ran out to the station for the subway train to town. Matt and his father had already left for work, Agnes was buttoning on her coat, Josie was at the sink, washing up the breakfast things.

'A letter?' She thought it must be from Lina. But it wasn't from Lina.

'Everything all right?' asked Agnes, putting the bills that were her post behind the clock over the kitchen range, as the street door banged behind Marie.

'Oh, yes!' Josie was radiantly studying the looped and

139

flamboyant handwriting she knew so well. 'It's from my mother.'

'Ah, that's nice. You've been waiting for that for a long time, eh? Now you sit down and read it in peace.' Agnes adjusted her hat in the mirror by the window. 'I'm away.'

'No, wait!' Josie had opened the letter. 'She's sent me a postal order, Mrs MacLeod. A postal order for ten pounds! It's towards the expenses.'

'Josie, that's grand, but you know I told you not to worry about money.'

'Oh, but I want to pay something, Mrs MacLeod, and now I can.' She swallowed hard. 'It means a lot to me.'

'I'll see you tonight, pet,' Matt's mother said softly, and closed the door as Josie's eyes went down to her letter.

It was written on the pale-blue lined paper Ellie bought at the post office, and instantly conjured up for Josie a picture of her mother sitting at the kitchen table under a dim electric light, ink bottle to hand, thin-nibbed pen sputtering as the elaborate writing flowed. Since Josie had learned to type and taken over the business correspondence, Ellie had not had occasion to write many letters, but she was proud of her handwriting and style. Perhaps she was pleased, thought Josie, at having to write letters again, now that there was no one to type them.

This letter was quite short. Ellie said she hoped Josie was managing all right. Her father was not too bad, but low in spirits. The minister had talked to him. Mrs Robb was now helping out at Ardmore. Not as good as Josie, but another pair of hands. Several guests from England at present, which was a nice surprise for the time of year. The letter closed with Ellie's love and the hope that the enclosed would be a help with expenses. No need to worry, she could afford it. There was a postscript.

'Sorry not to see you, Josie. Cannot see myself getting through to Glasgow. But glad to hear from you. Your affectionate Mother, E. Morrow.'

Josie read the letter through twice, her eyes filling with

140

tears. It meant so much, that letter. More than her mother could possibly know. Her father would probably never accept her again, which hurt, hurt a lot, but at least she was no longer forsaken. She had family again, her past still meant something, her roots were still hers. Drying her eyes, Josie put her letter carefully into the zip-pocket of her bag and stood up. She had not forgotten her promise to herself to start looking for somewhere to live. Also, she wanted to telephone Lina, who had not been in touch. At the back of Josie's mind was always the guilt she felt over Angus. Maybe Lina would have news of him, would say he was OK, coping well without her. Though Josie felt she had no right to expect news of that sort. Why should Angus give her peace of mind, when she had taken away his own?

Chapter Twenty-Two

Lina was waiting to be collected. Duncan's parents were coming to take her to Lawn House, a private hospital on the south side of Edinburgh where Duncan had been transferred from the Royal Infirmary some two weeks before. If the doctor gave the OK, it was possible he might be allowed home that afternoon, but Lina was not allowing herself to look forward to it in case it didn't happen. The weeks without him had been so long, she didn't know if she could face more. Had only managed so far by living from one hospital visit to the next. And smoking.

Since Duncan's accident, she'd become quite proficient in the art of smoking gracefully. There were no more coughing fits, no more tears in the eyes. Cigarettes, in fact, were so much a part of her life, Lina felt she could outsmoke Antonia, and was ashamed to need such a prop. There had never been any real worry about Duncan, he was clearly going to make an excellent recovery. It was true he had been moved to Lawn House when Lina had expected him home, but as Dr MacIver had explained, he had been deeply shocked by his accident and still needed a little extra rest under supervision. And could afford to pay for it, too, of course. So Lina smoked on, drawing in comfort with every inhalation, swearing to throw her cigarettes away the instant Duncan was returned to her. She wouldn't need comfort then.

Everything in the flat was in apple-pie order, ready for the homecoming. Mr Guthrie had been surprisingly handy, putting up pictures and unpacking boxes, doing all the jobs Duncan would have done. Antonia had buzzed around, arranging books and china, while her mother had sent her cleaning lady to give Lina 'a few hours', an offer she had tactfully declined, preferring to do her own housework. Now there wasn't a thing left for Duncan to do. He could just come home and get himself completely well. And make love? Lina, grinding out her cigarette in one of the many ashtrays she'd placed around the flat, could only live in hope. The accident had followed so quickly on her honeymoon, she'd had no time to dwell on its pleasure, but she knew she wanted to experience it again.

She glanced at the clock on the fine plasterwork mantelpiece. Still a little time before Duncan's parents arrived. In spite of Mr Guthrie's having been so helpful, Lina had grown somewhat afraid of him in these last weeks. She could believe now, as she had not done before, that the black dog could land on his shoulders. Had seen signs of it herself and was terrified of seeing it again, so trod carefully, never disagreeing, always playing the part of the dutiful daughter-in-law. Today she had even dressed the way she knew he liked, which was the style of the debs photographed for *Scottish Field*, in a plain jumper and tweed skirt and the seed pearls Duncan's mother had given her on her wedding day.

She was smoothing her hair at her mirror when the telephone rang. As usual her heart leaped in fear. The hospital? It was Josie, her voice sounding strong and confident from a callbox, as they discussed Duncan.

'He might be coming home today? Lina, that's wonderful! But why have you no' written? No' kept in touch?'

'Och, Josie, I'm sorry, but you know how it is. How are things with you?'

Josie told her about hearing from her mother, about looking for a flat, no luck that day, but of course she'd just

143

started. About wedding plans – Lina was still coming, wasn't she?

'Of course I'm still coming! I'm looking forward to it.'

'And Duncan?'

'We'll have to see how he is. He'll come if he can. Has a soft spot for you, Josie.'

Josie laughed and paused. Lina had the feeling she was just approaching the purpose of her call and Lina knew what it was.

'If you're wondering about Angus, he's all right,' she said quietly. 'Mum says he's no' pining.'

'I see,' Josie said blankly. 'Oh, well, that's good. How is your mum, then?'

'Fine, when she isn't blaming Duncan's mother for the accident. For wearing green at the wedding, you remember? When I told Mum it was bad luck.'

'Folk feel better if they've somebody to blame. Listen, Lina, you will keep in touch now?'

'Josie, there's the doorbell, it'll be Duncan's dad, he's taking me to the hospital. I'll write, I promise.'

Lina replaced the receiver and ran downstairs to open the door to Mr Guthrie. But it was Angus waiting there.

'No' pining' their mother had said. So why did his collar look too big for him? Why had his eyes, so much like Lina's own, taken on that look she had last seen in Callum's?

'Angus!' Lina exclaimed, trying to sound pleased to see him. 'What a shame, I'm just off to the hospital. We have to see Duncan's doctor, see if they'll let him come home.'

'That'd be grand, eh?' Angus stepped inside. 'I only want a word, won't keep you.'

'But why aren't you at work?' she called over her shoulder as she led the way into the flat.

He stood in the drawing room, warming his hands at the electric fire and looking about him in a lost, vague fashion that had never been his. Already Lina was beginning to feel apprehensive.

'I've left work,' he said abruptly, and sat down on Lina's carefully plumped up Chesterfield. 'That's what I came to tell you. I finished yesterday.'

'Left work? Left Mr Johnson's?' Lina's eyes were enormous. 'Angus, what are you talking about? You can't have left work!'

'I have. I've got a job in London. One of the big pharmaceutical firms has given me a temporary contract. I start next week.'

'Pharmaceutical?' she repeated uncertainly. 'Can you do that sort of work?'

'It's an admin post, it's something different, but I want to do it.'

'I can't take this in.' Lina sat down heavily. 'What does Mr Johnson say?'

'He's been very helpful, very understanding. So has Niall. They realise I can't stay here.'

Lina gave a long sigh, opened the lid of her cigarette box, then shut it. 'I'm lost, I'm all at sea. I mean, how did you get this job?'

'It was Callum's idea. He suggested I should go south and try my luck. I got an interview with a firm a couple of weeks ago – told Mum I was away on business. They offered me six months, to see how I made out. I accepted. Came back and put ma notice in. End of story.'

'Callum.' Lina's mouth was dry. 'So he's made you do what he did?'

'It's exactly what I want, Lina. Hell, I might have wanted it anyway. I can do something better than run a chemist's shop.'

'It was your dream once, I thought.'

'Aye, well, I had a lot of dreams once.'

As Angus stared at her woodenly, Lina caught her breath.

'What about Mum? What does she think about this crazy plan?'

'It's no' a crazy plan. Can you no' see it's right for me? After what's happened?'

'OK, it's right for you. What does Mum think?'

He lowered his eyes. 'I haven't told her yet. Thought I'd tell you first.'

'And get me to tell her?' Lina laughed shortly. 'Think again, Angus. I'm no' going to break that sort of news.'

'I just thought, if you were there—'

'I won't be. Duncan's coming home. I can't go rushing off with you to Mum's.' Lina put her hand to her eyes. 'Angus, it'll break her heart if you go away. You're her favourite. The most like Dad.'

'I know,' he said huskily. 'But there's nothing I can do. That was said to me, you know. Maybe you said it, too. Now I have to say it.'

A deep flush rose to Lina's face. Her gaze locked with her brother's, then fell. As the doorbell pealed again they both stood up.

'It'll be the Guthries,' Lina murmured. 'They're taking me to the hospital.'

'I'll go, then. Look, I'm sorry I've only been talking about maself. I hope Duncan gets on all right.'

She pressed his hand. 'Write to me, Angus, eh? Tell me how things go?'

'I will.' But at the top of the stairs, he stopped.

'Have you seen her?' he asked roughly.

'No, but she's been in touch.'

'When's the wedding?'

'The end of the month.'

He ran on down the stairs. 'I'll be away by then, thank God.'

The Guthries, immaculately dressed, their faces a little more lined, a little more strained than Angus remembered from Lina's wedding day, greeted him with kindly politeness as Lina buttoned up her outdoor coat and closed the door of the flat. Angus said how glad he was to hear of Duncan's recovery, they agreed it was wonderful that he

146

might soon be home, then Andrew Guthrie opened the door of his Armstrong-Siddeley, his wife and Lina took their seats, and Angus, with one last dark searching look at his sister, waved them away.

Chapter Twenty-Three

Everything about Lawn House was green. Smooth grassy slopes outside, bounded with evergreen shrubs and trees. Soothing green carpets inside, plus matching curtains, chairs, upholstery. Only the blonde receptionist in a beautifully tailored grey suit provided contrast, but she was very soothing anyway.

When Duncan's parents and Lina presented themselves at her desk, she greeted them in hushed tones and escorted them personally to a nearby lounge, so quiet the air appeared not to have moved in weeks and the large arrangements of chrysanthemums looked as though they were nodding off to sleep.

'If you wouldn't mind waiting here for a moment? Dr MacIver will be with you shortly.' She gave them a practised, professional smile. 'May I get you something? Tea? Coffee?'

They shook their heads with thanks and, as she withdrew, Erica Guthrie sank into a chair and loosened her coat.

'How hot they keep these places, don't they?' she murmured. 'I'm sure I don't know how anyone gets better in such heat.'

'Well, Duncan *is* better,' her husband said shortly. 'That's all we need to worry about.'

I could do with a cigarette, thought Lina, pacing the thick carpet. I wish I'd said I'd have a cup of tea. Where is the doctor? I want to see Duncan.

Dr MacIver did not keep them waiting long. A quiet, steady Scotsman in his forties, he cast a glance around the room, said, yes, it was empty but might not remain so – better come to his office, if they wouldn't mind? Just down the corridor.

More green carpet, more nodding chrysanthemums, but in the doctor's office a sudden change to stark white and fawns and browns. Not so soothing, really, thought Lina, who was beginning to feel alarmed. She glanced at Duncan's parents and read her own anxiety in their expressions. Dr MacIver was being very easy and relaxed, motioning them to chairs, taking his own seat at his desk, but there was something not quite right about him. Yes, they could all feel it. He had bad news.

'What is it?' asked Erica quickly. 'What's wrong? Has Duncan had some sort of relapse?'

'No, no.' Dr MacIver did not flinch from her frightened gaze. 'Mr Guthrie has made an excellent recovery from his physical injuries.'

No one missed the slight stress on the word 'physical'.

'And the shock?' Andrew asked sharply. 'Has he recovered from the shock of the accident? We were led to believe he only needed more rest.'

'That's true. We did hope rest was all that was needed.'

'Did'. Another significant word. Andrew and Erica exchanged looks. Lina's large eyes were on the doctor, who cleared his throat.

'It seems, I'm sorry to say, that Mr Guthrie – Duncan – has been more deeply affected by his experience than we thought. He is going to need time – a good deal, perhaps – to make a full recovery. Time, rest, and medication.'

'What sort of medication?' asked Andrew. 'He's scarcely taken as much as an aspirin up till now.'

'Sleeping pills … something to relieve his anxiety. There are one or two things out now that are better than barbiturates—'

'Are you saying Duncan's depressed?' cried Andrew. 'Got melancholia or something? That's absurd!'

'There are signs we can recognise, Mr Guthrie. I'm only trying to prepare you as a family for what might be necessary.'

'Our son is a very brave man, Dr MacIver,' Erica said earnestly. 'He was with the Black Watch in the war, you know, he fought in Germany and Sicily. I'm sure he must have seen terrible things—'

'But never suffered from shell-shock, battle fatigue, anything like that!' snapped Andrew. 'He's a moody devil, I'd be the first to agree, but he's never been depressed.' He glanced at Lina trembling in her chair. 'Good God, he's just back from honeymoon, Dr MacIver! Don't tell me that a fall from a bridge can affect a fellow who's got everything he wants to make him happy!'

'I do appreciate the situation,' Dr MacIver said quietly, resting his eyes compassionately on Lina. 'But the brain is a strange master. We're a long way from fully understanding it, as you'll be aware. All I can tell you is that your son says he can never climb a bridge again. He feels his working life is over.'

There was a silence during which Erica put her handkerchief to her eyes and Andrew, his jaw muscles working, stared at the doctor's cord carpet. It was Lina who suddenly leaped to her feet.

'Can he still come home?' she cried. 'Does he want to come home?'

'Oh, yes, Mrs Guthrie, he wants that desperately.' Dr MacIver left his desk to open his door. 'Which is why I've taken the decision to let him try it, on the strict understanding that if it's necessary he returns here, or to some other hospital. There will also have to be regular outpatient visits and he must follow instructions for his medication to the letter. That's absolutely essential.'

As Lina said faintly that she understood, the doctor gave her an encouraging smile.

'I do sympathise. Just back from honeymoon and now this, eh? But remember you'll have all the support you need. From myself and the hospital and your family.' He glanced at Erica who caught Lina's hand.

'Oh, my dear, you can count on us!' she cried. 'We'll do anything we can to help you and poor Duncan!'

'Let's go and see him, then,' said Dr MacIver. 'He's waiting for you in his room.'

On the way home in the rear seat of his father's car, Duncan sat without speaking, one hand clasped in Lina's, but his gaze fixed on the passing views of the city. If he was aware of Lina's desperate regard, or his mother's trying to catch his eye as she turned constantly from her front seat, he gave no sign. It was only when his father drew up outside the rented New Town flat and said, 'Glad to be home, Duncan?' that he roused himself.

'Very glad,' he said quietly.

'You'll soon be your old self now,' his mother told him bravely. 'Everyone feels better at home.'

Lina said nothing. She felt divorced from reality as she switched on the electric fire again and watched Duncan follow his parents into the drawing room, his father carrying his case, his mother fluttering round like some fine moth that had found its flame. To outward appearances Duncan appeared his old self already. He looked just as handsome, just as elegant, even though one sleeve of his jacket swung free over his left arm, from which the plaster had only recently been removed. But he was not his old self. He was not the Duncan Lina had married. That was where the unreality came in. All the time she had been longing for him to come home, she had been picturing the old Duncan. When she'd visited him in hospital it was true he'd seemed subdued and different, but he was a patient, you could expect patients to be like that. Now he was home and she had to face it. He was a stranger and her life had become something that didn't belong to her. She couldn't think what she was going to do.

151

'Well, there we are!' cried Erica. 'Everything's unpacked and sorted out. Lina, shall we make a cup of tea?'

'Good idea,' said Andrew heartily. 'Duncan, sit down and relax. Got to rest, you know, the doctor said to get plenty of rest.'

'The doctor's wrong, I don't need any rest at all.'

'Come on, old chap.'

'I need something else to do.' Duncan lit a cigarette with shaking fingers. 'Only I don't want to do something else. I want my old life back.'

'Well, why shouldn't you have it? You'll get well again, there's no question of that. It's only been a few weeks since the accident, you've made excellent progress—'

'I've made no progress. Unless you're talking about my shoulder. That's better. So's my arm.' His cigarette hanging from his lip, Duncan took off his jacket and swung his left arm to and fro. 'See – there's my excellent progress. Make the most of it, that's all there is.'

'Lina, have you got Duncan's tablets?' Andrew asked in a low voice as she came in with the tea tray.'

'You think all I need is a few bloody tablets?' asked Duncan. 'The next thing you'll be telling me is to pull myself together. As though you've never had the black dog on your own back!'

'Let's all have tea,' said Erica, sending warning glances to her husband, whose eyes were smouldering and who had turned rather white. 'Lina dear, you're looking so tired, would you like me to stay on and help you with dinner this evening?'

'I'm sure the young people would like to be on their own, Erica,' Andrew said swiftly. 'We'll go home and give Antonia a ring, she'll be wanting to know what's happened.'

'Could you no' ring her from here?' asked Lina. 'We'd really like you to stay.' She turned a nervous gaze on Duncan. 'Isn't that right, Duncan?'

He gave a sardonic smile, as though he knew she was

152

putting off as long as possible being alone with him.

'Oh, yes, do stay. Both of you.'

But his parents had to go home some time. By the time they left, everyone was waxen, reeling with fatigue and stress, but at least Duncan and his father parted on good terms.

'I'm sorry I spoke to you as I did,' Duncan muttered, his dark eyes starting from his head. 'You'll have to excuse me.'

'Nothing to excuse,' Andrew replied hastily. He clapped his son on his 'good' shoulder. 'I understand, you know, how things are.'

'I know you do.'

'We'll be in touch,' Erica said, kissing first Lina, then Duncan. 'Oh, do take care, dear, take care!'

'Lina will take care of me.' He drew her to his side and put his arm around her. 'Goodnight, then.'

'I'll have to show them out,' gasped Lina, ducking away from him and running down the stairs to lock up after his parents had left. When she returned, Duncan was already in the bathroom, and from behind the closed door, she could hear the water running.

'Do you want any help?' she shouted, rapping on the door.

His head came round it. 'No, thanks. Amazingly enough, I can still manage to bath myself.'

Oh, God, thought Lina, undressing in the bedroom. What's going to happen? Will it always be like this? How can I manage? I can't, I don't know what to do.

She put on a plain cotton nightdress, but her dressing-gown had been bought for her trousseau and was pink and fussy and not at all warm. There was no heating in the bedroom and she sat shivering, wrapped in her honeymoon frills, until Duncan came out of the bathroom, in his own plaid dressing-gown.

'It's all yours,' he told her, combing his damp black hair. But as she quickly got up to go, he caught her arm.

153

'I'm not going to go berserk,' he said quietly. 'Not going to chase you with a carving knife or anything like that.'

She gave her little laugh. 'Duncan, what are you talking about?'

'Lina, your lovely face – it's like a piece of glass. I can see right through to here.' He put his hand quietly to her brow. 'I can see everything you're thinking. What did that doctor tell you about me, to make you so afraid?'

'I'm no' afraid, Duncan! It's just all so strange, and I'm so tired ...'

'Yes. Well, go and have your bath. Hope I haven't taken all the hot water.'

'It'll be OK – the immersion's very good.'

She backed away from him, then skimmed along to the bathroom and shut the door. How warm and safe it was in there! She would have liked to stay forever, but when she had soaked herself as long as she dared, she had to return to the bedroom where Duncan was waiting. He was lying in bed, wearing pyjamas, which he'd never worn on honeymoon. His eyes were closed, his hands were folded on the coverlet, and he was so pale in the subdued bedroom lighting, Lina gave a little gasp of fear. At once, his eyelids flew open and his sombre gazed was fixed on her.

'How pretty you are,' he murmured. 'I used to try to think of you in hospital, you know. If I could see your face, that was a triumph. That meant I might not have the dream.'

'What dream?'

'The dream I had most nights.'

'About – the bridge?'

'Always the bridge.'

Lina turned desperate eyes to the bedside table where she had put his medication.

'Have you had your sleeping pill?' she whispered.

'No, I don't want it. I don't want to sleep.'

'Duncan, you have to sleep! You must take the pill. And that other one the doctor left you. It's important.'

154

'To hell with the pills. I'll start tomorrow.' He held out his right arm. 'Come to bed, Lina.'

She crept in beside him and he held her close. He did not have to tell her that there would be no love-making. Already the passion of their honeymoon seemed something that had happened in another age. Now they lay fearfully together until sleep, against their will, claimed them.

A sound woke Lina. A terrible sound. Someone calling, sobbing. An arm was round her, holding her in a vice, hurting her, so that she too was calling, trying to get free. It came to her that a man had broken in, this was an intruder holding her, and she began to scream. But as she came fully awake, she saw that the man holding her was her husband.

'Duncan!' she shrieked. 'Wake up! Wake up, you're dreaming!'

His hold on her slackened, his head fell back against his pillow, his eyes opened, and she snapped on the bedside light.

'Lina?' he whispered.

'You're safe,' she whispered, wiping the sweat from his face. 'You're at home, you're in bed. Duncan, you're safe.'

'Oh, God.'

He sank against her, breathing hard, and she cradled him, soothing him as though he were a child. But Lina had no experience of children and didn't even like them very much, had never been one for looking in prams or holding other people's babies. Maybe if she'd been like that she would have held Duncan now and not minded, but she wasn't like that and she did mind, for a desolate knowledge was beginning to consume her. Duncan, who had been the man to take care of her, as all her life she had been taken care of by somebody, had changed roles. It was he who now needed her. It was she who would have to take care of him.

It's no' fair, she wailed inwardly. I'm no up to it. What can I do?

Great tears filled her beautiful eyes and rolled down her cheeks as Duncan began to talk – to her or himself, she didn't know.

'I'm with all these men,' he whispered, 'all the briggers who fell, they're running and leaping – they used to leap across the girders, you know, they'd take any risks, the crazy devils – their hats would go down, then they would go down, and I know in my dream that I'm next, I'm going down too, and there's no boat, there's no one to save me – no one to save me!'

He was growing wilder, thrashing in the bed, leaving her arms. She drew him back, still shedding tears over him.

'There's always a boat, Duncan,' she murmured. 'There's always someone to save you. And you were saved, you were saved. Remember that.'

He seemed comforted, but would not close his eyes, would not sleep again, he said, not that night. That was the way it went. And so the two of them sat up, staring into the shadows cast by the light, Lina with Duncan, her husband, her child.

Chapter Twenty-Four

It was a mark of Lina's distress that she wrote so quickly to Josie, to tell her the bad news about Duncan. Come over and see me, she begged, come as soon as you can. Meet me in town, we can't talk at home. Deeply shocked, Josie sent a postcard, arranging to meet her at Logie's for coffee. Not her sort of place, but maybe such easy, pleasant surroundings would make them both feel better, for Josie had her own troubles too.

As soon as she saw Lina, however, she knew neither of them was likely to feel better, however swish the restaurant, however good the coffee. For Lina, smartly dressed and carefully made up, still had the look of one whose life has fallen apart with the suddenness of a bomb-blast. Why me, why me? Josie could see her thinking, and remembered her as a plump little girl, crying in the school playground because her skipping rope had broken. Josie had lent her her own rope and the next day Mrs Braid had bought her a new one. No more tears then, only radiant smiles and the confidence that there would always be someone around to fix things for Lina. Who would fix them now?

'Oh, Lina, I'm so sorry,' Josie murmured, as they sat in their comfortable chairs, looking out at the shoppers in Princes Street. 'I thought Duncan was nearly better, I thought you'd nothing to worry about.'

'So did I,' said Lina thickly. Her eyes were red-rimmed,

the colour she had brushed on her cheeks standing out against her pallor. 'It'd no' be so bad if it was something physical, I mean, like his broken arm or mebbe a broken leg, but this is in his head, Josie, and there's no getting it out. No' as far as I can see.'

'Lina, you mustn't talk like that. Duncan'll get better from this, just as if it was a broken leg, you'll see. He's got a very good doctor, he'll get Duncan well.'

'Dr MacIver said it would take time. A very long time.' Lina shook her head. 'The way Duncan is, I think it'll take forever.'

Silver pots of coffee arrived, with large soft scones, butter, jam, a plate of pastries, and though the two young women felt guilty, they couldn't help but take comfort in the delicious things to eat.

'The days are awful,' Lina said mournfully, 'and the nights are worse. Every morning, if it's fine, Duncan takes the paper into the gardens, but he never reads it. He just sits and smokes and stares into space. Then we have lunch and sometimes Antonia or Mr and Mrs Guthrie come over for that. Sometimes they take Duncan for a drive, or Mr Guthrie takes him to the New Club, but I'm sure he never says much, wherever they take him. He won't go out in the evening, just doesn't want to do anything, he says. Mrs Guthrie said we should get a television set, but Duncan says he's no' interested. I make the meal and wash up, I mebbe do a bit of sewing, listen to the wireless, then we go to bed.' Lina pushed her plate away and took out her cigarettes. 'But no' to sleep. Duncan's afraid of sleeping. That's when he relives it all, one way or another, falling from the bridge. Sometimes he's on his own, sometimes he's with the briggers from the old days. Whatever happens, he always falls.' She lit a cigarette and watched its smoke. 'Sometimes I think I'll go mad, Josie.'

Josie, horrified, said throatily she'd have a cigarette, too. She rarely smoked, but at that moment felt as Lina felt, the need of support.

158

'Surely you can't go on like this?' she asked, as Lina lit her cigarette for her. 'I mean, I know Duncan's no' long out of hospital, but should he no' go back?'

'Aye, he might have to do that. But he just wants to be at home, Josie, he just wants to be with me. He leans on me full weight, he takes all ma strength, and the thing is, I'm no' up to it, I'm no up to it at all!' Lina looked wildly round at the well-dressed Edinburgh ladies, their lipsticked mouths hard at work, talking, eating, sipping coffee, but their eyes, thank God, on one another, not on her. She kept her voice down all the same. 'I'm no' strong like you, Josie. You could cope, you could manage.'

'Manage?' Josie repeated, drawing awkwardly on her cigarette. 'I don't know about managing. What have I done so far? Broken Angus's heart. Probably broken your mum's heart as well, now he's gone to London. And then there's ma folks—'

'I broke somebody's heart, too,' Lina whispered. 'Oh, Josie, do you think it's judgement on me, what's happened?'

'No, I do not!' she cried. 'Don't talk that way! Would Duncan have to suffer because of something you did?'

But Lina's eyes stayed large and wondering, until the waitress brought them their bill, when she said she would pay, no argument.

'The one thing I've got is money,' she said, bitterly, putting coins for the tip under her plate. 'I daresay some folk would say that that was all I was after, anyway, but it was no' true, it was never true.'

'Of course it wasn't,' agreed Josie warmly. 'I know how much you love Duncan.'

They walked out into the chill of the November day which was grey and dripping, even without the haar. Josie said she'd better go for her train, Lina said she must get back to Duncan even though Antonia was with him at the flat. He didn't like to be left alone.

'Josie, I feel so bad,' Lina went on. 'I've never asked

159

how you were getting on. Och, am I no' selfish? Always was.'

'I'm OK,' Josie answered quietly. 'Just a bit down at the moment because I can't find us anywhere to live. Lina, you would never believe how bad the housing is in Glasgow. I mean, there's nothing! Council waiting lists a mile long, no hope there. Flats – och, you should see them! It'd break your heart to see how some folks have to live.'

'Aye, everybody knows what Glasgow's like.'

'But this is no' Victorian times, Lina! It's no' even the twenties. I never thought things could still be so bad.'

'Are they no' making any improvements?' Lina asked listlessly.

Josie shrugged. 'There's plans to pull half the city down – the Gorbals and such – and mebbe put up big new blocks of flats. I don't know how it'll all work out. Meantime, Matt and me are getting married in three weeks and we've nowhere to live.'

Lina shivered. Her face was pinched and not so pretty. In spite of her smart warm coat, she looked chilled to the bone as she put her gloved hand on Josie's arm.

'I wish there was something I could do.'

'I'll say the same, Lina. Listen, if you ever need me, get in touch, eh?'

Lina nodded. 'I'll be over for your wedding, anyway. I've got your present already. Well, two presents, as a matter of fact.'

'Two? Oh, Lina!'

'One's cutlery – you said you wanted that, didn't you? And the other's just for you.' Lina smiled. 'It's a nightie.'

'A nightie?'

'For your honeymoon. I wanted to give you something you hadn't had to make yourself.'

'Oh, Lina!' Josie said again, and they clung together, both laughing bravely. But when they drew away and Josie sent her best wishes to Duncan, Lina's little laugh died and her face took on its now familiar chill. They waved as they

160

separated to go their different ways, each soon lost to the other in the Edinburgh crowds.

Poor Josie, thought Lina, walking home. Nowhere to live. Still better off than me.

Poor Lina, thought Josie, in the Glasgow train. Who'd have thought things'd turn out like this for her? Fancy her worrying about judgement ... I don't believe that, I don't believe anybody's punishing me now for what I did to Angus. Anyway, even if I can't find anywhere for Matt and me to live, I'm happy. Oh, poor Lina, that's the difference.

Chapter Twenty-Five

It was Matt's birthday the following Saturday and instead of going to the pictures, he and Josie went dancing. Glasgow people liked dancing, there were dance-halls in all the main areas of the city. During the war, folk said they'd been packed out and there'd been jitterbugging and jive and all the sort of thing you saw in American films. These days, it was modern ballroom that was popular – the foxtrot, quick-step, slow waltz – with a few old-time dances thrown in for variation. Like Lina, Matt could do them all. It was Josie who said she had two left feet.

'Not you,' said Matt, skilfully leading her in the foxtrot. 'Just remember, all you've got to do is follow me.'

'Aye, I know, but I just seem to get in your way.'

The problem was Angus hadn't cared for dancing and Josie's parents hadn't really approved of it anyway, apart from the Scottish and country sort, so she'd had very little practice. She felt self-conscious about it, wanted to be as good as Matt so that he would take pleasure in dancing with her. He said, couldn't she see that holding her was pleasure enough for him, he didn't give a damn about the steps?

'If you could just relax, Josie, let yourself go, you'd be fine.' He leaned his cheek against hers. 'Come on, give yourself to me, that's the way.'

'Give maself to you? No wonder Dad used to say modern dancing was sinful!'

Josie was laughing and excited, but later, when the band had gone for their beer and she and Matt were sitting with their own drinks, she seemed so subdued he asked her what was wrong.

'It's my birthday, you're not allowed to look blue. What's up, Josie?'

'I was just thinking about Lina. She loves dancing and going out, and she used to have such a good time with Duncan.' Josie heaved a sigh. 'Now she just sits and listens to the wireless, or does a bit of sewing. I mean, it's all so sad.'

'He'll get better, Josie. Folk do.'

'Aye, but when?' She raised her eyes to Matt's. 'Then there's us.'

'Us? What's wrong with us?'

'We've nowhere to live, Matt. What are we going to do? I've tried everywhere. There's nothing we can afford.'

'You mean nothing you like. What about the ones you don't like?'

She shuddered. 'I couldn't, Matt. Some of those places, I can't tell you ...'

'You don't need to tell me. I've been down that road, I've lived in one of those places.'

She caught at his hand. 'I know, I know. But your ma got you out, she'd no' want you to go back.'

'Josie, sweetheart, you're worrying about nothing.' Matt gave her one of his beautiful smiles. 'We just stay where we are. Problem solved.'

'Stay where we are? With your folks?' Josie was beginning to breathe hard. 'You can't mean that, Matt. It'd never work out!'

'I thought you liked my folks?'

'I love them!' Her lips were trembling, she couldn't get her words out fast enough. 'But we'd no' be on our own, Matt, and newly-weds have to be on their own, isn't that true? And where would we sleep anyway? There's no room for us in Dow Street!'

'There's Marie's room,' he answered mildly. 'She could have the kitchen bed, where I sleep now.'

'The kitchen bed? You mean, you'd ask her to give up her own room? I could never do that, Matt, it wouldn't be fair!'

'She's willing to do it. I've already asked her.'

Josie coloured furiously, her eyes flashing. 'You've already talked to Marie, without talking to me first? Matt, I never thought you'd do that!'

'I knew you were worried,' he answered calmly. 'Had to come up with something, and this seemed the best plan. Look, there's no need to get all steamed up. Marie'll probably move out soon anyway. She's got this new fellow she's meeting, Ma says she's keen, could get married herself before long.'

It was true that Marie was now going out with Colin Howat from the optician's where she worked, but to say that she was 'likely' to get married soon, that she would 'probably' move out, was wishful thinking on Matt's part in Josie's view and didn't make her feel any better about depriving Marie of her room. As she sat staring at him, her eyes still stormy, he reached across and fondled her unresponsive hand.

'Josie, you don't understand about Glasgow,' he said softly. 'Nobody here expects to walk into a home of their own when they get married – I mean, people like us. For a start, they haven't the money for high rents. For another there's a shortage of places to live anyway.' He stroked her fingers. 'As you've already found out, eh?'

'So what do people do?' she cried, snatching her hand away. 'You're telling me they all live with their in-laws?'

'Most of 'em, yes.' He sat back, still being infuriatingly calm. 'Take Fergus and Sandy, they're still with their wives' folks, and Iona's only just managed to get into a couple of rooms over Lewis's shop.' Matt lit a cigarette. 'Because somebody died.'

'I'll have a cigarette,' snapped Josie, shifting restlessly

164

as the band began to drift back and people left their seats to stand around the dance floor. 'If you don't mind.'

'Hey, since when did you start smoking?' he asked in surprise, and Josie, pleased to have shaken him for once, tossed back her beautiful hair and cried, 'Since I've had things to worry about!'

'Ah, Josie, you're not angry, are you? I was only trying to help when I talked to Marie.'

She took the cigarette he gave her, but did not light it. Tears she did not want to shed were gathering in her eyes.

'I know, but I can't help feeling upset, Matt, that you don't mind us having to live with your parents. They're lovely people, but what will it be like? We won't have any privacy, we'll never be alone.'

'We'll have our own room, with our own double bed,' he said gently. 'We'll be alone, all right.'

She bowed her head, could not bring herself to speak, but was aware of Matt's trying to take her hand again, then rising to his feet and murmuring something she couldn't hear. She looked up and saw him standing with two people she didn't know. One was a short, rough-haired young man in a tight navy-blue suit, the other a girl with dark permed hair and a narrow freckled face. She had high cheekbones and cool blue eyes. Josie thought her very attractive. And would not have trusted her an inch.

'Oh, Josie, this is Rena Cameron.' Matt said easily. 'Used to live near us when we first came to Glasgow. Rena, meet Josie Morrow. We're engaged to be married.'

'Engaged?' The girl raised her plucked eyebrows. 'Dinna say somebody's caught you at last, Matt MacLeod! Niver thought I'd see the day. Pleased to meet you, Josie. This is ma friend, Jimmy Fraser.'

There was an awkward pause. The band was tuning up, any moment now the music would start, and Josie turned her eyes on Matt, willing him to ask her to dance. Too late. As the band moved into a quickstep, Rena Cameron had already taken his hand and was leading him on to the floor.

'You'll no' mind?' she called over her shoulder to Josie. 'This is just for old times' sake.'

Jimmy Fraser pulled up a chair near Josie.

'Want to dance?' he asked hoarsely, clearly expecting her to say no.

She didn't surprise him. 'No, thanks.'

They both watched, fascinated, as Rena and Matt stood for a moment eyeing each other, waiting for the beat, then glided off across the floor, perfectly matched, perfectly attuned, a couple moving as one. So that's what it should be like, thought Josie, sitting very straight as though feeling no pain. That's what dancing should be. Oh, God.

It was easy to follow the progress of the yellow head leading the dark one, for other dancers seemed to be making way for them, glancing at them sideways with admiration as they so smoothly covered the floor, doing all kinds of elaborate things with their feet, running and tapping, then turning their heads this way and that, Rena imperiously ignoring everyone around her except Matt, his body close to hers, his hand on her back, his deep-lidded eyes on her little freckled face.

'They've danced together a lot,' Josie stated harshly. 'You can tell.'

'Aye.' There was a bitter expression in Jimmy Fraser's small eyes. 'He used to take her dancin' in the old days.'

'They're very good.'

'Should be on the telly,' he said contemptuously.

How long can I stand this? thought Josie. When can I go?

Somehow, she didn't picture herself leaving with Matt. In the acuteness of her misery, it seemed to her that he would stay, permanently dancing with Rena Cameron, round and round, away from her, who was to marry him in two weeks' time.

'Like a smoke?' Jimmy Fraser asked, taking out cigarettes.

'Thanks, I've got one.'

166

He gave a loud bray of laughter. 'Hen, you'll no' do much good with that!'

When she looked down, Josie saw that the cigarette between her fingers was in shreds.

In the end, she didn't go home alone. Of course not. That had just been a silly fantasy. Matt had brought Rena back at the end of the quickstep, she had given no more than a shuttered smile at Josie and immediately gone off with Jimmy.

'Had enough?' Matt had asked. 'Oh, yes!' Josie had cried.

They had walked home arm in arm but hadn't said much. Perhaps Matt had realised how Josie was feeling. She herself was too numb to speak, until they reached Dow Street, when she knew she must say what was in her mind while they were still alone.

'I don't think I'll dance with you again, Matt, now I've seen you with Rena Cameron.'

'You don't mean that, Josie? I've told you what dancing with you means to me.'

'But she's so wonderful.'

'Aye.' By the light of the street lamp, she saw him smile. 'She certainly makes a grand partner. Took her Silver, you know.'

'Silver?'

'Silver Medal. For Ballroom Dancing. Spent all her money on lessons when I knew her. And she didn't do too badly, with tips and that.'

'She's a waitress?'

'Chambermaid. In one of the big hotels.'

'I can just see her,' said Josie. 'I bet she wears high heels and a little frilly apron.'

Matt took her by the arms and turned her towards the light. 'Josie, that girl means nothing to me. Do not be steaming yourself up again for no reason.'

'Did you take your Silver Medal when she took hers?'

'What Silver Medal? I never took any medals for dancing.'

167

'How do you dance so well, then?'

'Natural genius.' He laughed. 'Och, she used to get me to practise with her. I picked up what I know from her.'

Josie gazed earnestly into his face. 'Was she no' one of your girl friends? Those girls you said I should expect you to have had because you were twenty-six years old?'

'And now I'm twenty-seven,' he said banteringly. 'And I only have you.'

'Was she? Was she one of your girls, Matt? Tell me.'

'All right, she was. For a wee while only. She was always more interested in the dancing.'

Josie leaned against him. She felt sick. Knowing about Matt's anonymous girls in the past was one thing; knowing one of those girls by name was another. Seeing Rena's cool blue eyes, her high cheekbones, seeing her hand in Matt's, her body against his, brought such a fine, exquisite pain, Josie had to bite her lip to stop herself from crying out. Jealousy. She was eaten up with jealousy. One of the Seven Deadly Sins. Shouldn't she be ashamed?

'Can I ask you something?' she asked, as Matt's arms came round her. 'Will you please no' dance with Rena again?'

'I'll never dance with her again,' he said solemnly. 'That's a promise. After all, I'm nearly a married man.' His arms tightened. 'And, oh, God, Josie, I wish I was a married man now!'

Chapter Twenty-Six

The night before the wedding, Matt went round to sleep at Sandy's.

'Aye,' said his mother, 'have to follow custom, eh? The groom must never see the bride before the wedding.'

'Damn' silly custom,' murmured Matt, kissing Josie who was giving the skirt of her blue suit a final press. 'I'd rather be with Josie here than round the pub, I can tell you.'

'Round the pub?' She set down her iron. 'You're going drinking, Matt?'

'Just with a few of the lads from the yard.'

'And Fergus and Sandy and Dad,' put in Marie. 'In other words, all the men you know.'

'Stag night,' said Josie, frowning, 'I see.' She picked up the iron and thumped it over the pressing cloth. 'Why do men have to have stag nights?'

'One o' these days, women'll go out, too,' said Marie. 'Why not? 'Course there is the worry of looking sloshed on your wedding day.'

'I shall not be looking sloshed on the wedding day,' Matt announced with dignity. 'Come on, Josie, no need to look like thunder, it's only a few drinks.'

'A ritual,' said Marie. 'Fellow has to say goodbye to the friends he thinks he'll never see again, once he's wed. Och, it's the way things are, Josie. Women plan weddings, men plan pub nights.'

Josie shrugged, hung her skirt on its hanger and unplugged the iron. 'I'll see you tomorrow, then,' she said coolly, not looking at Matt, who burst into laughter.

'Och, Josie!' He swung her round and hugged her. 'Crack that face, eh? Have you forgotten what tomorrow is?'

As Agnes and Marie laughed with him, Josie gave a reluctant smile. 'I've no' forgotten what tomorrow is,' she said softly. 'Think I must be a bit worked up, that's all.'

''Course you are,' said Agnes, as Matt finally departed with a case that contained his new grey wedding suit, paid for with the cash he'd made on overtime. 'Night before the wedding every girl's in a state. Or should be! Marie, put the kettle on, eh? We'll have a nice little break without the men.'

'Can I make a sandwich, Mrs MacLeod?' Josie asked. 'I don't know why, but I'm starving.'

'Mrs MacLeod?' repeated Agnes. She put her arm around Josie's slender shoulders. 'It's time you called me Ma. Aye, see if you can find something to eat now. The place is that full o' food for tomorrow, we've forgotten about today!'

Later, after they'd had their tea and worked through a plateful of potted meat sandwiches, Agnes took off her shoes and stretched her feet out on the couch.

'That's grand, that is,' she sighed gratefully. 'Just look at these ankles! Like balloons.'

'You should rest more, Ma,' Marie told her. 'Though it's a waste of time saying it.'

'I feel bad you've done so much for me,' said Josie. 'All this food for the wedding breakfast—'

'Och, it's all cold stuff, I've done no baking, 'cept the cake, and Betty MacRae's iced that.'

Betty MacRae was a thin little widow who lived on the top floor of Number Fifty-five and worked for one of the big bakery firms as a confectioner. 'An artist with the

170

piping' was how Agnes described her. She was bringing the cake down first thing in the morning, and they should see it! All the little whirls and scrolls and shells, and Josie's and Matt's initials intertwined in silver. A poem, no less!

'I'm so happy, I feel worried,' Josie said in a low voice. 'When you want something so much, it seems funny to get it.'

'Only you would talk like that, Josie!' Marie exclaimed. 'There's no need to feel guilty because you're getting what you want. And, like I keep saying, you're going to be very happy with Matt, he really loves you and you're good for him. Is that no' right, Ma?'

'That's right,' Agnes agreed comfortably. 'He's got his faults, I'd be the first one to say so, but he's a good lad at heart. A wee bit wild, like his dad – but see how his dad's settled, eh?'

'Wild?' Josie repeated, her eyes very bright. 'But Mr MacLeod's so calm! And so is Matt!'

'Well, you know what I mean, pet. Just the way men are, when they're young and bonny.' Agnes swung her legs down and squeezed her feet into her shoes. 'Now, I'll go and see if there's another drop o' tea left and then I'll clear up next door. No, you two stay where you are, I like to crack on in my own way.'

When Agnes, her energy restored, went off to do battle in the kitchen, Marie leaned forward to look into Josie's face.

'No' worrying about what Ma said, Josie? Look, Matt's no' wild. I don't know why she said that.'

'You said yourself I'd to take him as I found him. Why did you say that, then?'

'I can't remember! But it's true that he's a good fellow, he has a good heart.'

'I believe that,' Josie said slowly. 'I've always said that.'

'There you are, then. All you have to do is manage him the way Ma's managed Dad.' Marie sat back. 'The way I'll manage ma Colin if we ever get wed, eh?'

'You think you might?' asked Josie, trying to focus on something, anything, but what was filling her mind.

Marie's eyes danced. 'Who knows? He's coming here tomorrow so he'll see us in all our glory, find out just what he's taking on. If I tell you his folks live in Kelvinside, you can see he might have a problem.'

'Kelvinside's a good area?'

Marie laughed. 'Well, it's no' the Gorbals! Och, it'll be a test, eh? If he passes, watch out. I might be getting you to make ma wedding dress!'

It was late when Matt's father returned from the pub. Josie, lying awake in her collapsible bed in Marie's room, heard his ponderous step moving through the flat, accompanied by a baritone rendering of 'Ma luv is like a red, red rose', until Agnes called, 'Quiet!' in a whisper guaranteed to wake anyone but Marie, who slept like the dead.

'Aggie, where's the bed?'

'Where it always is, you great loonie! Here, over here! Come on, now, stop falling about before you wake poor Josie, and her getting married tomorrow!'

There were more mutterings, whisperings and a few mild curses before the creak of the bed springs in the room next to Marie's signalled that Brandon MacLeod, the managed man, was settling himself down for what remained of the night.

'All you have to do is manage him the way Ma's managed Dad,' Marie had said. Josie, staring into the darkness, listening to Marie's regular breathing and the snores and sighs coming from next door, wondered what was meant by 'manage'? Supposing she didn't want to 'manage' Matt, anyway?

As she tossed around in her narrow bed, it came to her that this was the last time she would be sleeping in it and sleeping alone. When she and Matt came back from North Berwick, where they were to spend their short honeymoon, a second-hand double bed, newly bought, would be installed in this

172

room and poor Marie would be outed to the kitchen alcove. She had insisted she didn't mind, and perhaps she didn't if she was really planning to marry Colin Howat. But Josie minded. Still minded that she had lost the battle to find somewhere for herself and Matt to live. Maybe she would try again, when she came back from honeymoon.

Honeymoon? A tremor went through her body. How casually that word had drifted through her mind, as though it meant nothing special! Fears she had not let herself examine suddenly came rushing out of the night to confront her. Supposing she wasn't very good at sex? All her passionate exchanges with Matt had made her feel she would be. But supposing she wasn't? Supposing the honeymoon was a fiasco? She'd heard of that happening. Lina had said she'd had a marvellous time, but had given no details. Well, of course, you couldn't expect details. But Josie wished now that she knew a little more. A lot more, in fact. She could have talked to Matt. But all she'd talked to him about was not having a baby. They'd agreed she should go to a clinic and get herself 'fitted up'. Her cheeks flushing at the memory of that, Josie crossed her fingers. Just hoped she'd be OK.

The old clock in the living room gave a single chime. Half-past two, was it, or three? Josie wished it was dawn. She longed for the day so that she could get up and get on with the wedding. Be married. Be on that honeymoon. She closed her eyes and Matt's face swam before her. Matt! In all her ponderings, she had been missing the point. Tomorrow she and Matt would be made one. That was what marriage meant. She would be his, he would be hers. The golden haze he brought with him would surround them. It would be November and it would be summer. Sleep was claiming her at last and as she sank into rest, her lips curved in a smile. Who cared about managing? She and Matt were in love, and always would be.

The next thing she knew was Marie shaking her awake in a room filled with light.

173

'Josie, wake up, wake up! Betty MacRae's brought the cake, it's gorgeous! Come on, come on, it's your wedding day!'

Chapter Twenty-Seven

The register office service seemed so short. That was what struck Josie, when it was over. The most important thing that had ever happened to her and it was over before she'd had time to take it in. The words had been said, the signatures written, then Matt was kissing her, his parents hugging her, and Marie, Lina and Fergus, who had been Matt's best man, were waiting their turn. Josie and Matt were married.

They came out into the cool November day and posed for people's cameras, Josie in her dark blue suit with a brimmed hat that Marie said made her look like Ingrid Bergman, Matt in his grey. After more kisses and hugs and a shower of confetti from Marie, the wedding party, all sporting white carnations, piled into taxis for Dow Street. Josie gave a last look round for her mother. She wasn't surprised when she didn't see her, hadn't really expected her to come. Too late now, anyway.

It was clear that Agnes had decided after all to invite the neighbours, and a good many other people too, for when Matt and Josie arrived back at the flat they could hardly get into the living room.

'Standing room only!' cried Sandy, looking out of the door. He was scarlet in the face and holding a beer glass. 'Och, it's the bride and groom! Folks, get ready, get singing! Here comes the bride, here comes the bride!'

As the people behind him began to chant with him, Agnes said in another of her stage whispers, 'Fergus, go out and put Sandy's head under the tap, he's been at the bottle already.'

'Hasn't stopped since last night,' muttered Fergus, leading the still singing Sandy away as Josie and Matt were dragged into the throng of guests and kissed and embraced, and Agnes bustled around, giving orders right and left. 'Iona fetch the boiled ham, Gillie, the pork pies, Marie, the plates ... now be quick!'

'So you did ask the neighbours, Ma?' Marie whispered, hurrying to put the plates on the table, all that was left of the furniture apart from the piano, for everything else had been shunted into the bedrooms by the MacLeod brothers, hangovers or no hangovers. 'Thought we'd said no.'

'It was you said no. Anyway, there's plenty to eat, I made sure of that.'

'Just hope we all fit in.'

'Aye, well, I'm not the only one asking extra folk. Your dad's brought in Georgie Adair and Freddie King, and Matt's asked two or three more mates, and Josie said could she have another girl from Queensferry, and some lady who runs a teashop ...'

'Oh, Patty!' Josie was crying, as Patty MacAndrew flung her arms around her. 'And Mrs Tassie! Oh, Lina, is it no' lovely to have these two here? Oh, I'm so glad to see you!'

To be with familiar faces from home made a lump rise in Josie's throat. It was some time before she could collect herself enough to introduce the friends from Queensferry around, though she was aware of the looks of interest at Lina, so grand in her suit with a fur collar and the great stones of her engagement ring blazing on her finger. To Josie, though, she didn't look well. Pale and anxious, which was not after all surprising. Duncan was in hospital again, they were trying out some new treatment.

'Poor wee girl!' exclaimed Mrs Tassie. 'Och, is it no' a

176

shame? And Josie, when I think of the way your dad – well, better no' say any more, eh? But it's grand to see you looking so happy, pet, on your wedding day.' Her eyes strayed to Matt in the distance, being kissed by some elderly neighbour. 'Grand,' Beryl Tassie said again absently.

'Josie, Josie, Colin's here!' cried Marie. 'Come and meet him!'

A tall young man in a dark suit shook Josie's hand. He had large horn-rimmed glasses and pale brown hair, well-Brylcreemed, and was unmistakably nervous. Who wouldn't be? thought Josie, who knew what it was like to meet a loved one's family on uncertain terms. But it had worked out for her and would work out for this fellow if the looks he was casting at Marie were anything to go by.

'Congratulations,' Colin murmured, as somebody pushed a plate into his hand. 'I do hope you'll both be very happy, you and—'

'Matt,' prompted Marie. 'You remember, my third brother? Josie, have you shown your friends the cake?'

'It's beautiful, Mrs MacRae,' Josie said fervently, as they joined little Betty MacRae in admiring her handiwork. 'I've never seen such pretty icing.'

'Aye, it's no' so bad,' Betty agreed. 'Thank God there's no more rationing, eh? When I think what weddings was like in the war ... you couldna get sae much as a currant or a sultana, and we'd to make the cakes oot o' dried egg and God knows what, then put a bit o' decoration on top. Pretend icin', you ken? Aye, but the lassies was happy and that's what matters, eh?'

'Josie, can I have a word before you go away?' Lina whispered.

'Of course, but you're no' rushing away yourself, are you? There'll be plenty going on here, even when we've gone. If I know the MacLeods, they'll be here till all hours!'

'I think I'd better get back, thanks.' Lina huddled herself

177

into her fur collar as though she were cold, though the room, filled with so many people, was hot and Josie had already taken off the jacket of her tweed suit. 'Patty and Mrs Tassie are staying the night with somebody Mrs Tassie knows, but I've booked a taxi for the station.'

'Why, we're going to the station! We could have given you a lift!'

'Och, Josie, don't be so daft! As though I'd go with you on your going away!' Lina allowed herself a smile. 'Where are you going anyway, if it's no secret?'

'Don't laugh – North Berwick.'

'Why should I laugh? We used to think North Berwick was lovely, didn't we?'

'Well, it's no' Paris,' Josie said cheerfully, then seeing Lina's face crumple, was overcome with contrition. 'Oh, Lina. I'm sorry. I know it must hurt—'

'Aye, it hurts.' She dabbed at her eyes. 'Thinking of the happy times.'

'Josie, have you had anything to eat yet?' asked Matt as Lina moved away. 'Better grab something quick – it's going fast.'

'I'm sure I did eat something. Or maybe I didn't? Oh, Matt, what does it matter? I'm too happy to eat!'

'We'll be leaving soon, remember. Can't stay for the knees up.'

'Matt, I thought you'd be singing!'

'I can sing any time.' He put his face close to hers. 'Tonight, I want to make sure we catch that train.'

'Break it up, you two,' ordered Fergus, putting a large hand on Matt's shoulder. 'Ma says it's time to cut the cake.'

After Matt had said a few words about how lucky he was to have found Josie, and Fergus had made the toast to the bride and groom (which people drank in whatever they had in their glasses, champagne not being expected), Matt gently pushed Josie towards Marie's room, which would soon be theirs.

'Go on now, get ready.'

'Your dad's getting his fiddle out, could we no' just stay a while?'

'Don't you want to be alone with me?'

'You know I do.'

He gave her the smile that had first drawn her to him.

'Get ready, then.'

She had closed up her case and was putting on lipstick at Marie's mirror when Lina came quietly in and closed the door on Brandon's fiddle playing a Scottish air.

'Anything I can do, Josie?'

'No, thanks, I'm just wearing ma same suit, I'm pretty well ready.' Josie gave Lina a radiant smile. 'I've packed your present, Lina. Oh, it's so lovely! Silk! I've never had anything silk before. You're too good, though, to give me something like that.'

'Somebody should be good to you, Josie. It's what you deserve.'

'In spite of what I did to Angus?'

'There's no point in thinking about that now. You've made your choice and life goes on, eh?'

'Yes,' Josie sighed, then straightened her shoulders, buttoned up her jacket and put on her Ingrid Bergman hat. 'How do I look?'

'Beautiful.' Lina's golden-brown eyes filled with tears. 'Oh, Josie, remember when I was going away? You and Patty helping me? It seems like a million years ago now.'

Josie put her hands on Lina's shoulder and looked into her face. 'Listen, Lina, Duncan's going to get better. You have to believe that. Things are going to be all right, just the way they used to be.'

Lina pulled herself away. 'Things are not going to be all right,' she said in a low voice. 'They're going to be quite different.'

'How d'you mean?'

Lina looked up. 'I feel such a fool, I don't know how to

179

tell you. I'm – well, you know what.'

Josie's lovely face flushed beneath the brim of her hat.

'Lina, you're not!'

'I am, then. Can you believe it? A honeymoon baby?' Her full scarlet mouth twisted bitterly. 'Just what I need, eh?'

'But you can't be sure yet. I mean, how many weeks is it?'

'Never mind about the weeks, I'm sure.' Lina gave a great sigh. 'And what I'm going to do, I don't know. I just can't face it, Josie, I've enough to do, looking after Duncan. How can I cope with a baby as well?'

'Oh, you will cope, Lina, people always do,' Josie said comfortingly. 'And when the baby arrives, it'll be wonderful!'

'If it's so wonderful, I suppose you'll be wanting to have one yourself as soon as possible?' Lina asked acidly.

Josie hesitated. 'I do want a family, but I'd like to qualify as a teacher first. And to begin with, I'll have to work. Matt doesn't earn all that much, and you know what rents are like.'

'Better watch your step, then. Get yourself sorted out, Josie, don't leave it to him. That's my advice.'

'I have got maself sorted out,' she answered, with an embarrassed smile. 'But nothing's a hundred per cent, is it?'

'You can say that again!' Lina laughed, then burst into tears and flung her arms round Josie's neck, knocking her carefully tilted hat awry. 'Och, I'm sorry, Josie, coming in here and depressing you, when you're just going away! Take no notice of me, I'm just a sour little cat. Have a wonderful time, and get in touch when you come back. Don't forget now!'

'Are you ready, Josie?' came Matt's voice at the door. 'Ken's got the car round, it's time to go!'

Chapter Twenty-Eight

They had to go into a station waiting room to shake the confetti from their clothes. Even so, there was plenty of it still sticking to their hair and Josie's hat, and how Ken was going to get it out of the Morris he'd borrowed, nobody knew.

'Och, nae bother,' he laughed, as he left them at the platform. 'What's wrong with a wee bit o' confetti, then?'

'Thanks, Ken,' said Matt, shaking his hand. 'We appreciate the lift.'

'It was very good of you, Ken,' Josie added, kissing his cheek. 'Much better than a taxi, to drive with you.'

He stood back, smiling in the harsh station light.

'Canna get over it somehow, you two married ... When you cooked us that first smashing breakfast, Josie, who'd have thought that you and Matt'd soon be wed?'

'I would,' said Matt simply.

There were other people in their carriage, reading their evening papers, trying not to smile at the confetti trailed in by Josie and Matt.

'Feel such a fool,' Josie whispered, taking off her hat and shaking it.

'I don't mind,' Matt whispered back. 'I like folk to see I'm married.'

Josie turned her wedding ring. 'Should have got you one of these, should I?'

181

'No, thanks! Men don't wear wedding rings.'

'Some do, I've heard. Why not, anyway?'

Matt shook his head, smiling, and lay back in his seat, closing his eyes, but Josie still turned the ring on her finger. She'd never thought about it before, but now she saw it was really a sign of possession. Hands off, said engagement rings and wedding rings, this one's mine! And straightaway men knew a woman's situation. But that wasn't true the other way round. Some men might wear rings, most of the men Josie knew did not. She looked at Matt's ringless hands lying on his lap. No one would know he was married.

The train gave a shriek and rattled on through the November night. The lights were on in the carriage, she could see nothing out of the window except her own ghostly reflection. The other passengers were nodding over their papers, Matt too seemed to be dozing. Then suddenly his grey eyes were open and fixed on her with one of those yearning, melting looks that gave her a such a feeling of power, at the same time turning her weak with longing. What did it matter that he didn't want to wear a ring? He was hers anyway, ring or no ring, and had her trust. As Matt's eyelids closed again, Josie tried closing her own eyes, tried thinking of all the dear faces of her friends and Matt's family as they stood on the stair and waved goodbye, so that her mind would be occupied with what had already happened and not with what was to come.

Don't you want to be alone with me? Matt had asked. She did, she did, he knew she did. It was just that she was nervous. All brides were nervous. Or should be, as Ma had said, with a grim smile. Would there ever be a time when women were as experienced as men before marriage? Josie couldn't imagine it. There'd always be the worry about pregnancy, women were saddled with that. Take poor Lina. She'd manage, though, people did, and money would make it easier. Money. There was another worry. As soon as Josie returned home, she would be starting in her new job, doing shop accounts for Iona's husband, Lew, Iona having given up her so-called assistance, saying she'd enough to do. If only the extra money would help Josie to find a decent place to live! She stirred in her seat and felt Matt's hands grasping hers.

'Coming into Edinburgh,' he told her. 'One more train trip and we'll be there.'

North Berwick, a popular east coast resort in the summer, was dark and quiet in November. People played golf, of course, and walked on the beach, looked out to the famous Bass Rock with its sea-bird colonies, but did not take boats out. Not a place for holidays, then, so late in the year, but honeymoons were different. You took your own sun on honeymoon, thought Josie, especially if your bridegroom was someone like Matt.

They'd booked a room in a boarding house with sea views. Not that they could see any views at all when they arrived from the station at Pebbledene, but even what she could see of the house made Josie's heart ache.

'Oh, Matt, it's so like Ardmore!'

'Ardmore? Come on, it's nothing like Ardmore!'

'No, no, it's just done up, that's all, painted and that.' Josie looked round the entrance hall, with its notice-board of local events, its desk and plants, and smell of polish and cooked food. I should be wearing my apron, she thought, running along with a tray, asking folk to sign the book.

'Mr and Mrs MacLeod?' asked a middle-aged woman in a cardigan suit, with glasses on a chain round her neck. Oh, Mum! thought Josie, and left the talking to Matt. It was he who signed the register, said they didn't want a meal, thank you, but yes, they'd like a cup of tea.

'You can have it in your room, if you like.' The woman with the glasses had friendly brown eyes and a pretty mouth that only twitched a little over the confetti that was now leaking out of Josie's suitcase. 'I'm Mrs Barclay, by the way, owner of Pebbledene. Would you like to come this way?'

They followed her up a carpeted stair to the first floor, where she showed them into a spacious room with a walnut double bed and matching wardrobe and dressing-table. On the walls were several framed photographs of North Berwick, showing the beach, the Bass Rock and the other famous landmark, the volcanic mound known as Berwick Law. One of the best rooms, thought Josie, usually booked up first in the season, but of course at this time of year, business would be slack.

'There's a lovely view of the sea,' Mrs Barclay announced, waving her hand to the curtained windows. 'You'll have to take my word for that, though, till tomorrow. I've put the electric fire on to warm the room up a bit – don't forget to switch it off, will you? There's a wash-basin there and the bathroom's just next door. Now, I'll get you your tea, shall I?'

When the door had closed on her, Josie and Matt turned to look at each other.

'This is just like our first-floor back,' said Josie. 'One of our best rooms. Mum let it to Duncan Guthrie.'

'Josie, sweetheart, let's not think about all that now, eh?'

Matt took a step towards her, but she was busying herself opening her suitcase.

'Who put all this confetti in ma case?' she murmured. 'Honestly, it's everywhere! I hope they haven't messed up ma new nightie.'

'Josie!'

'No, wait, Matt, wait till she brings the tea.'

'I'll find the bathroom,' he said with a sigh.

When he came back in new blue pyjamas and a dressing gown he'd borrowed from Lew, he found Josie sitting at a little table, a tray with tea-things and a plate of mixed biscuits in front of her. She was wearing a clinging ivory silk nightdress, so delicate, so light, it seemed to cover her

184

body and yet reveal it at the same time, causing Matt to stop in his tracks and gaze at her without a word.

'I found another bathroom,' she told him. 'Thought I might as well get maself ready.'

'Good idea.' He cleared his throat.

'Do you want any tea, then?' Her hands rattled the cups in their saucers.

'Tea?' Matt flung his clothes over a chair and sprang to pull Josie into his arms. 'Oh, God, Josie, just come to bed!'

'I thought you said you wanted tea – they've brought it.'

He was peeling away the new nightie, tearing off his own pyjamas. 'Don't be afraid, Josie, don't be nervous, it's going to be all right!'

'I'll just put the light off, Matt, and the fire, I know how much these things cost.'

'For God's sake, Josie ...'

'Won't take a second.' She snapped off the light and the electric fire, and as its rosy glow faded, came back to Matt and slid into his arms. 'I'm not nervous, Matt. I know it'll be all right.'

It was true. Maybe it had been the voluptuous feel of the silk nightdress on her skin, maybe its obvious effect on Matt, but all Josie's anxieties had fallen away and she was feverishly, passionately confident. She remembered how she'd felt when he had first kissed her, how she'd known then what she wanted, even though she'd known so little of love. Now love was here and even before their bodies met and Matt guided her into real ecstasy, she was filled with joy. In a way it was like the dancing, she thought afterwards, lying spent beside him in the hard old bed, he was so expert, he knew just what to do. Only it was not like the dancing, because this time somehow she knew too, just what to do.

'Watch your step, Rena Cameron,' she murmured sleepily. 'I'm better than you at this.'

'What are you talking about?' asked Matt, kissing her gently.

185

'Nothing, nothing at all,' she answered, kissing him back.

'Josie, you're so beautiful. I knew you were, but when I saw you – oh, God – listen, it was all right, wasn't it? Not too bad?'

'All right? Not too bad?' She laughed. 'Matt, you've no idea how I feel.'

'I know how I feel,' he said softly. For some time they lay together in the darkness, Matt's arm around Josie, her head on his chest. Then he said, 'You know what? I'm hungry.'

'Me, too.' Josie sat up. 'Go and get those biscuits, eh?'

He crept, naked, into the cold air of the room, found the plate of biscuits and took them back to bed.

'I feel better now,' he said, when they'd eaten all the custard creams and digestives. 'Don't feel like sleep, though, do you?'

'Oh, what's sleep?' she asked.

Next morning, looking at their tumbled sheets, she felt embarrassed. What on earth would the girl who made the beds think? She remembered what she'd thought herself sometimes, when she'd been making beds.

'Funny honeymoon couple,' giggled one of Mrs Barclay's helpers to another as they made the double bed, while Josie and Matt ate their full Scottish breakfast downstairs. 'Biscuit crumbs everywhere – had they no' got anything better to do?'

Chapter Twenty-Nine

They spent the days visiting places, because they had to fill in the days somehow until it was night and they could go to bed. Most of the other people at Pebbledene were residents. They didn't visit places, they went into the town to do a little shopping, have their hair done (or cut, in the case of the only two men) and buy their papers, then they spent the rest of the day in their particular chairs in the lounge, looking out at the view or at any new guests, and waiting for high tea.

It was clear that Josie and Matt, and the business rep who was the only other non-resident, provided great interest, even though Matt got off to a bad start by accidentally taking one old lady's chair. But as soon as she had quavered glacially that he was sitting in *her* seat, he had leaped to his feet with apologies and his beautiful smile, and she was as captivated as the rest of the onlookers.

'Poor old things,' Mrs Barclay had murmured confidentially to Josie and Matt. 'They get special rates for the winter. Helps them, helps me, but they're mostly on their way to residential care. Don't mind if they take an interest in you, will you? Apart from Francie, they don't see many young people.'

Who's Francie? they had wondered. Next morning they met her.

*

They had been to Musselburgh and Dunbar, had walked on the sand dunes behind Dirleton and imagined Robert Louis Stevenson's characters coming ashore in *Catriona*, a book they'd both read at school, along with *Treasure Island* and *Kidnapped*. This was all Stevenson country and exciting enough, but today they were bound for Tantallon Castle, a huge ruined fortress rising ominously from the Firth of Forth. It was only a couple of miles from North Berwick. They stopped at the reception desk to ask the way.

'Good morning!' said a young woman they hadn't seen before. She was dark-haired and slightly built, wearing a fawn suit and crisp dark blouse. Her eyes were brown, less warm than Mrs Barclay's but sufficiently like to make it no surprise when she said, 'I'm Francie Barclay, Mrs Barclay's daughter. Can I help you?'

Another pull at Josie's heart. Mrs Barclay's daughter ... How often had she introduced herself in similar terms. 'Mrs Morrow's daughter, can I help you?' Oh, it brought it back, staying here, in a smarter, brighter version of Ardmore. Brought all that old world back, made her realise afresh that it had gone. Why should she mind so much? Sometimes she didn't; other times the memories pierced her with a dagger's pain. She lowered her eyes as Matt gave their names and asked for directions to Tantallon. When she looked up, it was to find Francie Barclay's eyes fastened on him.

'Why, it's just down the road,' she said, her mouth with its glossy lipstick trembling slightly. 'I – I could draw you a little plan.'

'That's very kind,' said Matt, resting his heavy-lidded gaze on her, giving her his famous smile. 'Don't want to put you to any trouble.'

'It's no trouble.'

'Matt!' called Josie from the door. 'Come on, we'll find it!'

He turned in surprise. Francie Barclay, her pencil poised, stood rigidly to attention behind her desk.

188

'Come on,' said Josie again. Her eyes were stormy, her cheeks a glaring red, she felt strange, as though she were not in command of her own speech, her own thoughts.

'OK,' said Matt. He gave a quick, rueful glance at Francie, whose mouth relaxed, whose eyes softened. Go on, I understand, she seemed to be saying, mustn't upset her, must we? After only the slightest hesitation, he turned and joined Josie outside.

'What's up?' he asked quietly, as she began to stride ahead down the street lined with boarding houses, all more or less like Pebbledene. Opposite was the sea, dark grey and churning white under a dark grey sky.

'What's up? I should think you'd know what's up! When a girl like that makes sheep's eyes at you, and you go smiling at her as though she's somebody special!'

The way you first smiled at me, Josie added to herself, tasting iron in her mouth. The way you smile at everybody.

'Ah, come on now, you're not being fair!' Matt caught up with her and took her arm, but she shook away his hand. 'Josie, I don't understand, what's got into you? That girl was just being friendly ...'

'Friendly!'

Josie hurried on, walking blindly, her hands in the pockets of her raincoat. She felt as churned as the sea over there, blown by the wind.

'If you'd just tell me what I'm supposed to have done?' called Matt.

'Let's find Tantallon,' she hurled over her shoulder. 'Let's not talk.'

The land around the castle was empty. So was the sky. It reminded Josie, in turmoil as she was, of home. So much space, so much freedom from tall grey buildings, closing in. Then there was the sea, crashing around the rocks at the base of the promontory on which the castle stood. Fierce, hungry, answering some need in herself as she felt that day. Beyond was the Bass Rock, with its crying sea-birds. Then

189

more space, more light, more emptiness. As she and Matt climbed further into the framework of the ruined castle, Josie's bitterness began gradually to slip away.

'That's better,' whispered Matt, who had been closely watching her face. 'There's my Josie back again.'

They were the only visitors to Tantallon that morning. There was no one to see as he turned Josie towards him and sank his mouth on hers in a long sweet kiss.

'Oh, Matt.' She leaned against him as though she had been a long time away. She felt that she had, that she had moved so far, she had almost lost him.

'I feel so bad,' she whispered, as they stood together in an arch of stone that might have once been a window. Below, if they had dared to look down, was the sea battering the cruel rocks, but Josie's eyes were for Matt alone. She wanted nothing then but to be a part of him again, to make herself and him forget those black moments when she had deserted them both.

'Don't think about it,' he answered, covering her face with small kisses. 'It's over.'

'I don't know what got into me. I suppose, it's just loving you so much, I couldn't bear to share.'

'Share? One smile?' He laughed, smoothing back her splendid hair. 'Josie, you can afford that!'

'I know, I know, but women always seem so attracted to you—'

'What women? The old ladies in the lounge?'

'Rena Cameron.'

'Rena? She was my dancing partner, you know that.'

'She was one of your girls, you said so. You said you'd had a lot of girls.'

'In the past, Josie, in the past. I told you, you're different, I've never felt the same for anyone else as I feel for you.'

She gave a little sigh of satisfaction. They left each other's arms and continued their explorations. If she had not had so much on her mind, Josie thought, she would have been

190

terrified by her surroundings. Not so much because she was afraid of losing her foothold on battlements or spiral stairs, but because around this huge ruin of a fortress, unoccupied now for three centuries and scene of frightful siege bombardment from Cromwell and others, there still hung an atmosphere of violence that chilled her spirit. Even for the family who had built the castle in the fourteenth century, this could never have been a place of refuge or comfort. As for the poor wretches who had been imprisoned here, in various cells and pits still existing, Josie could only shudder to think of their fate and move hastily on.

It was a relief to her to make a perilous descent from the upper ramparts down to the Close, or central courtyard, and from there return through outer fortifications to the road and civilisation.

'Glad we live nowadays?' asked Matt cheerfully. 'And not here?'

She laughed, crushing his hand in hers.

'I'm glad about a lot of things. Oh, I wish I hadn't gone on like that, Matt! Spoiling everything. It was just, I started remembering, you know, what people had said ...' She stopped, drawing in her breath as Matt looked down at her.

'What people had said?' he repeated. 'What did they say?'

'Nothing, Matt.'

'Come on, no secrets. What did people say about me?'

'I don't want to say any more. I've done enough damage today.'

'Aye, and you'll do more if you leave me wondering what people have been saying about me behind my back.'

'It was just what Angus said, and ma folks. You can't go by them.'

'You can tell me what they said.'

'They said – they said – ' Josie twisted wretchedly as he held her hand fast. 'They said you were a womaniser.'

He dropped her hand. 'Is that all? I thought you were going to say a murderer at least.'

He showed no anger, as she had known he wouldn't. What he was feeling, she couldn't tell.

'I told them I didn't believe it,' she said quickly.

'Until now.'

'No, no, I don't believe it at all, Matt! Look, I've said I'm sorry for this morning, I won't be like that again, I promise.'

'It's not fair to call me a womaniser,' he said quietly. 'I've always liked girls, I admit it, but there's nothing wrong in taking girls out, is there? Why shouldn't a guy like me be attracted to women? I mean, before he's married?'

'Women are attracted to you, Matt.'

'Fergus and me, we're the same as Dad,' he went on, not listening. 'Sandy was more for the drink, till he met Heather. "One for the girls," they used to say about Dad up home, so Ma told us. "Watch out, he's a one" – things like that. But then he married Ma and you see how he is now. Just wanted the right woman.'

'And she managed him,' said Josie.

'Managed him? Who told you that? Marie?' Matt laughed, pushing back his yellow hair that the wind was catching. 'Well, it's true, she sorted him out, same as Gillie's sorted out Fergus. Same as you'll sort out me, Josie.'

'I don't want to, Matt, I don't want to sort you out or manage you. I just want us to trust each other and be happy.'

'I want that, too.'

They clung together, on the windswept road, where there seemed to be no traffic or people, only the glowering castle on its mound behind them, and beyond that, the sea.

They felt weary as they arrived back in North Berwick, not only with walking and battling with the wind, climbing and scrabbling round Tantallon, but with the mental exhaustion of their first quarrel. But of course they couldn't return to

Pebbledene until evening, couldn't run the gauntlet of those eyes in the lounge if they appeared for lunch or went up to their room. Josie, in particular, didn't want to go back until she had to, for fear or seeing Francie Barclay again.

'Let's have fish and chips and go to the pictures,' she suggested. 'It'd be lovely just to sit down out of the wind.'

And lovely it was to sit holding hands in a cinema again, losing themselves in Hitchcock's *Rear Window*, coming out and finding it was time to go back to Pebbledene, meeting only Mrs Barclay in the hall, not Francie.

'You met my daughter this morning?' she asked pleasantly. 'Oh, it's such a help having her here this year before she goes to university. She's going to Aberdeen, you know, to study languages.'

'She's not in this evening?' asked Josie casually.

'No, had to go into Edinburgh, but she's very good, does as much as she can. I'm a widow, you see, there's just the two of us.'

When they had made sympathetic noises, Mrs Barclay smiled and said she'd a nice piece of beef for the meal that night, with plum tart to follow. Always bottled her own plums. So different from tinned, eh?

Two days later, Josie and Matt left North Berwick, having kept as much as possible out of Francie Barclay's way.

I'll never see her again, thought Josie, but I'll never forget her.

She knew that she had learned something from that tiny brush with Francie. Something about keeping a marriage together, something about herself. She would never again give way to that self-inflicted pain that could so easily destroy her. If she'd believed in punishment, she might have thought it had come for her when they arrived home, for Matt found a letter waiting. There was work to be done on a Highland bridge, he had been offered a short contract and would be away until after Christmas. At least.

193

Part Three

Chapter Thirty

'Churchill Resigns!' roared the newspaper headlines. 'Eden New Premier!' 'Farewell Dinner For Queen At Number Ten!'

It was April, 1955. The start of a new era, as some liked to see it. Farewell to old-style Toryism, hello to a younger, more dynamic government, for Eden was strongly tipped to win the next election and would serve a more prosperous nation and a Queen still under thirty. World War II had been over ten years. Everyone was looking for better times.

All Lina cared about was that on the day Churchill finally gave in to pressure and resigned, she had only two months to go until her baby was born. Two more months of heartburn and discomfort, of iron pills and Welfare orange juice, of taking her little specimen bottle along to the doctor's, of being prodded and weighed. 'Oh, dear, up again, Mrs Guthrie! And not still smoking, are we?'

Well, she had tried to cut down on her cigarettes, but there were times when she just had to light up, and having lunch with Duncan's parents was one of them. They were so generous and thoughtful, had given her so much, especially since the start of her pregnancy, but watching them watching Duncan was enough to wind her up to screaming pitch. She didn't know which was worse, feeling like that, or having to hide it. And she was supposed to be the calm one, she was supposed to be so good for Duncan!

Today's lunch had been rather worse than usual, because he was supposed to be feeling better and had even had an interview with his firm that morning about getting back to work, which meant his parents were painfully cheerful, but still watching his every move. Watching, questioning, although trying not to, with Duncan so obviously not co-operating.

'Well, nothing's decided yet.' And there went his melancholy gaze roving the room. 'Yes, plenty of options ... we'll have to see how it goes.'

Lina had to have another cigarette with her coffee, avoiding Erica's reproachful glance over the tiny white jacket she was knitting with much clicking of needles. While Andrew made small talk, discussing Churchill's going, saying he supposed it had to happen, the old boy was desperately unfit, but he wasn't sure he trusted Eden, Lina's thoughts went skidding away to Duncan. The awful thing was, the awful thing she couldn't tell anyone was, she didn't believe he was better. It was true that the terrible nightmares had ceased and he was now so ashamed he had ever clung to her in the night, he scarcely touched her at all. But there was a darkness that still surrounded him, an emptiness in his eyes, that made her feel he was still away somewhere, far, far away, from his real self and from her. In any case, the doctors were being very cautious. They weren't claiming any miracles, were still keeping him on medication, giving him regular checks. All they would concede was that he was improving and if he felt like work, he should certainly try it, perhaps in some limited form. Erica, however, was sure it was the coming baby that had made the difference.

'Oh, yes,' she declared, 'there's no doubt about it. As soon as he took it in that he was to be a father, he really made the effort to get well. You could see it happening.'

'Mummy, that's just not true,' Antonia told her. 'And it's not the way depression works. Anyway, the baby's not even here yet. Men don't relate to what's on the way.'

'I don't either,' said Lina, suddenly feeling the need to be frank. 'It's all happened too quickly. I can see maself getting bigger and bigger, but it doesn't mean a thing.'

'Lots of women feel like that dear,' Erica said comfortingly. 'I remember crying my eyes out because I'd no waist and just not associating it with the baby. Then, when Duncan was born, it all made sense!'

'I'm sure I'm going to have a boy, it kicks so hard.'

'Poor Lina. Just make everything white or lemon, dear, then you can't go wrong.'

But Lina wasn't making anything. With her mother and Duncan's mother knitting and stitching, Antonia ordering pram sets from Logie's, and Josie sending over lovely little matinée jackets and bootees, there didn't seem much point. However did Josie find the time to do all she did? Lina wondered. Working full time for Matt's brother-in-law, doing her share of the housework at Mrs MacLeod's, and now preparing for that teacher-training course she was so set on. She'd been offered a place in October, and was certain to do well, bright Josie. Lina had already asked her to be Master Guthrie's godmother.

Duncan was up and catching her eye.

'Thanks for the lunch,' he told his parents. 'We'd better be on our way.'

'Yes, Lina should have her rest,' Erica agreed. 'Get those ankles up, my dear, and don't try to do too much.'

When Lina had lumbered to her feet, Duncan took her arm and they progressed slowly into Heriot Row, waving to his parents at their window before driving away.

'Oh, I could do with a rest,' Lina sighed. 'It's terrible, being two everywhere I go.'

'I'll drop you off at home,' Duncan said, driving very slowly; he had only recently found the confidence to take the car out again.

She sat upright with a jerk. 'What do you mean? Where are you going?'

'Queensferry.'

'Queensferry?' She caught her breath. He had not been there since the accident. 'What for? Why do you want to go to Queensferry? I don't think you should.'

'I need to go. Please don't argue with me, Lina.'

'You're not – you're not going to try to – climb the bridge?'

'No, I am not going to try to climb the bridge. Look, will you stop worrying?' Duncan's expression was set and hard, but when he turned his eyes briefly from the Edinburgh traffic, Lina saw that they were anxious. 'You go home and rest,' he finished curtly. 'Leave things to me.'

'I will not go home and rest, Duncan! I'm coming with you. Why should I no' go to Queensferry, anyway? I could look in on Mum.'

'She'll be working.'

'She'll still want to see me.'

'She's always seeing you, you're always over there. Talking about me, no doubt.'

'Talking about the baby!' cried Lina. 'You know that's all she thinks about!'

Duncan shrugged. 'All right, we'll both go to Queensferry. But I draw the line at calling in at the Queen Margaret café. I can't face your Mrs Tassie today.'

'No, we won't go to the café,' Lina agreed, who didn't herself want to see Mrs Tassie, or Patty. Not when Duncan was with her. Not with that look of anxiety in his eye.

After a silent drive down the roads they knew so well, they parked in Queensferry away from the café but in sight of the bridge. Lina could feel the tension mounting in Duncan as he switched off the engine and sat looking out at the great red structure straddling the Forth. There were the usual tourists taking photographs and the usual queue of cars waiting for the ferry.

'Look at them,' Duncan said in a low voice. 'They'll be lucky if they get on the next ferry but one.'

'It's always like that,' Lina answered without interest.

'There'll have to be a road bridge, that's the only solution. The government's been told. Why are they not coming up with the funds?'

'Oh, God, we don't want any more bridges, Duncan!'

He gave a wry smile. 'A strange thing for the wife of a bridge engineer to say.'

Does he still call himself a bridge engineer? she wondered. Perhaps it was true, he was really getting better? But she couldn't imagine him on a bridge again. As she was sure, he couldn't imagine himself.

'You stay here,' he told her, opening the car door. 'I won't be long.'

She was instantly apprehensive. 'What are you going to do?'

'Nothing, nothing. Just look at the bridge.'

'Why? What's the point?'

'Wait for me,' was all he replied.

At first, she tried to follow his tall elegant figure threading through the people on the pier, but when a ferry came in and cars and passengers began leaving, he was lost to her. She sat back, feeling exhausted, longing for a cup of tea and wishing she could pop over to the Queen Margaret and use the cloakroom. Maybe, as Duncan was not with her, she could do that? No, better not. He would soon be back and wonder where she'd gone. She closed her eyes and opened them to see him returning, but he stopped and turned away from the car to lean over the esplanade rail.

'Duncan?' She opened her door to call to him. He made no reply, and now she could see his shoulders drooping and his head bent low.

'Duncan!' She left the car and hurried to him as fast as her heaviness would allow her. 'Oh, what is it? You should never have gone to the bridge, it's only upset you, I knew it would!'

But already he had straightened up, composed himself.

'I'm all right, don't keep on.'

201

'Keep on? I've no' said a word! Look, come back to the car. Please, just come back to the car!'

He did as she asked, politely seeing her into her seat as he always did, taking his own behind the wheel. But then he sat, staring sightlessly ahead, and she felt his despair like a cold wave of the sea wash over her.

'I feel so ashamed,' he said, after a long silence. 'When I think of the war – what we went through – all of us together. And we were so young, you know, just boys, really. But there was no refusing, then, no saying you couldn't do whatever you had to do.' As though Lina had made some point, he nodded. 'OK, a few guys cracked, yes, that's true.' He gave her his dark gaze that was tragic now, rather than fearful, for his fears had been realised. 'But I didn't, that's my point. I did everything that was expected of me.'

'And more,' Lina whispered. 'You were very brave, Duncan, everyone says so.'

'Brave?' He laughed. 'Well, look at me now. What do you think the fellows I knew would think of me now?'

'Duncan, it's different, you can't blame yourself for what's happened!'

'Not for what happened. But for not being able to take it. I can blame myself for that, all right.' He took her plump hand and stroked her fingers. 'And look what I've done to you, Lina. All I ever wanted was to make you happy, and all I've done is make you wretched. You'd a right to expect something better than that, poor girl.' He kissed her hand gently. 'The thing is, you see, I can't promise that things are going to get any better.'

'They will, they will, they're better now!' she cried. 'You're better yourself, Duncan, you don't have the nightmares so much, you're not so depressed—'

'You know,' he said thoughtfully, 'there was a time when I thought I might be involved in building the new road bridge, if my firm could get a part of the contract. I used to picture myself up there, over the Forth again,

202

creating a new wonder of the world! Does that seem crazy?'

She stared at him, her eyes glistening with tears. 'Don't talk like that, Duncan, don't make yourself so unhappy.'

'No, mustn't do that. Because I know I won't be involved with the new road bridge, or any bridge come to that. Remember what I said when I first came round after the accident? I'd never work on bridges again? It was true. It's still true. I settled that today when I went to look at the bridge. I looked up at the girders where I fell, and I knew I'd never be up there again, or anywhere else like it.'

'Did they say you couldn't work?' Lina asked fearfully. 'When you saw the directors this morning, is that what they told you?'

'No, they're leaving it to the company doctor to decide. If he gives me the OK, I can work in Head Office doing some damn' job or other. What the hell's it matter what? But I thought I'd give myself one more try. I'd go to the bridge, I'd look at it. I knew if I looked at it, I'd know. So, I do know. That's it. I won't try again.'

'Duncan, I'm very sorry, I'm really sorry, but at least you've still got a job, eh? I mean, it might no' be just what you want—'

'Not' just what I want? Oh, God, Lina ...' Duncan suddenly switched on the engine and roared away down the esplanade. 'Forget it, forget it! Don't think about it! Let's just go and see your mother. Let's just go and have a bloody cup of tea!'

Chapter Thirty-One

Kitty was thrilled to see Lina. Less so to see Duncan. She knew that what had happened to him wasn't his fault but still couldn't forgive him for changing so dramatically. One minute the ideal husband, everything she'd ever wanted for Lina; the next, someone she didn't even want to talk about. And it had been nice talking about him, she'd enjoyed it, enjoyed the showing off. Not much to show off about now, was there?

'Is it no' lucky, I'd just finished Mrs Winn's perm!' she cried, taking Lina and Duncan into the living room at the back of the house. 'Now I've nobody till ma half-past four colour, so we can have a nice cup of tea and a chat. Now you come and sit down here, Lina pet, and put your feet up. You're no' looking well.'

'I'm fine, Mum.' Lina lay back in her chair. 'And Duncan's much better, too. He's even thinking of getting back to work.'

'Is that right?' Kitty made an effort to smile. 'I'm very glad to hear it. Been a long time, has it no'?'

'Long enough,' Duncan replied shortly.

'So, what happens now? You move on to another bridge?'

'Maybe he'll just be in the office for a while,' Lina said hastily. 'That'd be best.'

'Aye, no point in taking risks.'

Kitty poured the tea and passed round sandwich cake of her own making which Lina ate hungrily and Duncan refused. Lina asked after George and Bernie, though she'd only seen them the week before. George had a new girl-friend, Kitty told her. Came from Bo'ness, worked in the Post Office, he'd met her at a dance. Lina expressed inter-est, though keeping an anxious eye on Duncan, who was shifting in his chair.

'And how are the Morrows?' she asked, giving herself more tea.

'The Morrows?' Kitty tossed her bright head. 'Don't ask me! Ellie Morrow knows what I think of that girl of hers, she doesn't try to come round here these days. Gets her hair done elsewhere.'

'Mum, you shouldn't think so badly of Josie!' cried Lina. 'She didn't want to hurt Angus, it was just one of those things. You know it was the same with me—' Lina glanced again at Duncan. 'And Callum.'

'We won't discuss that,' Kitty said sharply. 'But if you're interested, Callum's doing well down south, and so is Angus. He's on the permanent staff now, they said they were very keen to have him. Both thae lads are doing very well indeed!' Her green eyes went to Duncan, but his own gaze was cast down. She wasn't sure he was even listening.

'I do think Mrs Morrow's behaved badly to Josie,' Lina murmured, after a pause. 'You know, Josie asked if she could meet her at Christmas, but Mrs Morrow just sent a card and said they'd better leave it for the time being. Josie was so upset!'

'Should have thought of her mother before she went off with that bridge fellow, then,' retorted Kitty. 'I've no sympathy for John Morrow - even the minister's told him he should make his peace with his daughter and he'll no' do it. But Ellie has suffered over Josie, and I can understand the way she feels. Aye, it's the mothers who suffer in this world, Lina, and you might as well face it.'

'Thanks, Mum!' She smiled wearily. 'That's nice to

know!' While Duncan stayed silent, lost to their world, she and her mother chatted on until Lina rose heavily to her feet and said they must be going.

'Just dropped in to see how you were, Mum, as we were passing.'

Passing? thought Kitty. Through Queensferry? I bet Duncan's been back to that bridge and it'll have done him no good. If he's better, I'm Elizabeth Taylor ...

'I'm always glad to see you, pet,' she said aloud, 'you know how I worry about you.'

'There's no need to worry about Lina, Mrs Braid,' said Duncan, finally rousing himself to speak. 'I can take care of her.'

'I hope so,' Kitty replied.

She saw them to their car and stood back to wave as Duncan drove slowly down the High Street, her heart as heavy as stone. It was the contrast that hurt. She'd been so proud once of that same car, of Duncan driving, so handsome, so assured. You could tell just by looking at him he'd never had to struggle, never had to make his own way. Could she be blamed for believing that Lina would be safe with a man like him? Would be loved and cherished, as Callum Robb could never have loved and cherished her?

We live and learn, thought Kitty, tears filling her eyes as she took out her shade cards ready for her half-past four client. But what wouldn't she give now for Lina to have been Mrs Callum Robb, especially as Callum was doing so well! The one bright spot on the horizon was the baby, and she just hoped everything was going to go all right with that.

'Pretty clear what your mother thinks of me, isn't it?' asked Duncan, speaking for the first time as they approached the suburbs of Edinburgh. 'Thinks I've let you down. Haven't turned out the way she thought I'd turn out. Can't blame her for that. When she's right.'

What does he expect me to say? thought Lina. Everything he says is true.

She put her hands over her bump and closed her eyes. All she wanted to do was get home and rest. Would Duncan wash the salad stuff she'd got to go with the cold chicken? It wasn't beyond him to do that, and she felt so drained. Like a doll without stuffing.

'Seems you agree with her,' came Duncan's voice, through the mists of her weariness. 'You think what she thinks.'

'I don't know what Mum thinks,' Lina sighed. 'Duncan, I feel ever so tired, would you make the salad tonight? We've got some cold chicken for supper.'

'For God's sake, who cares about supper?' he cried.

But when he saw her face in the hall of the flat, the old courteous Duncan fleetingly returned. He held her gently, smoothing back her hair, made soothing murmurs and helped her, half-carrying her, into the bedroom, where she lay down immediately, just as she was, and fell asleep. For some moments he looked at her with a tenderness she would have liked to see, then darkness touched his brow and he turned away.

The room was still light when Lina awoke; she felt she couldn't have slept long. As she struggled to sit up, feeling hot and sticky and regretting having lain down in her clothes, she wondered what had disturbed her, what had brought her up from such deep exhausted sleep? There were no sounds around her, only the usual hum of traffic outside that she never noticed. No murmur from Duncan's wireless, no clattering of dishes from the kitchen. But noise did not carry in these solid rooms. You could never tell where people were. Suddenly, she felt very much alone and wanted Duncan, needed him. But as she opened her mouth to call him, was seized by pain.

No, not pain, she told herself swiftly. You couldn't call it pain, more like a squeeze, that was all. A strong sharp squeeze somewhere inside her, a squeeze that didn't last more than a second or two. It had woken her up, all the same. After how long? As another strong pain – no, squeeze – caught her, she gathered her strength. 'Duncan!' she cried. 'Can you come? Duncan!'

He stood in the doorway of the bedroom, a glass of red wine in his hand.

'Are you wanting to eat? I haven't done the salad yet.'

'I don't want to eat.' She sat upright against her pillows, her eyes large and terrified. 'Duncan, I think the baby's starting!'

He set down his glass and came to her, sitting on the edge of the bed and holding her hand that was hot and slippery with sweat.

'The baby's not due for two months, Lina, it can't be coming. Lie back and rest.'

'Babies often come early, Duncan, they can come at seven months – this could be a seven months child!' Lina ground his hand in hers. 'I think I should go to the hospital.'

'Darling, you've been asleep, you've got yourself into a state—'

'I'm having pains, the baby's coming, I tell you!'

Duncan turned white. 'Severe pains?'

'No, but it's starting, I know it is, it's different from anything I've ever known before. I want to go to the hospital, I want to be safe.'

'It could just be a false alarm, Lina. Often happens, doesn't it? It would be silly to go all the way to hospital without being sure.'

She lay back, sighing. 'Mebbe you're right.'

'You just stay there,' he said with relief. 'I'll go and get the supper, shall I?'

'I'd just like a cup of tea.'

But when Duncan returned with the tea, he found Lina up and changed into a fresh maternity dress, her face scrubbed, her hair brushed.

208

'I'm no' staying, Duncan,' she told him. 'I can't. Oh, I can't! Will you get me that case down from the wardrobe? I packed it last week. Must've had a premonition, eh?'

He could see there was no point in further argument and when he had lifted down her suitcase, rang the private maternity hospital where she was to have the baby.

'What did they say?' asked Lina, gulping her tea. 'Did they say I should come in? I'm going, anyway, whatever they say.'

'Thought it might be as well to let them see you, though the nurse said it was early days.'

'Early days!' she repeated. 'Och, it feels like years already!' She set down her cup and reached out her hand to Duncan. 'Hold me, will you? Just hold me for a minute. I'm so afraid.'

'Oh, God, Lina, don't say that!' he groaned, as he took her ungainly body into his arms. 'I can't bear to think of your feeling like me!'

In the event, there was no need for Lina to be afraid. Her labour was quick and easy, and though the baby was taken to a special unit after the birth, the doctors were confident that she would pull through. It would be some time before she would be able to leave hospital, but she was a strong little bundle, was Miss Guthrie.

'A girl?' Lina had whispered. 'I don't believe it! I was so sure I was going to have a boy!'

'She's a girl, all right,' said the nurse cheerfully. 'And as pretty as a picture, even if she is a wee scrap. Have you got a name for her, dear?'

Poor child, she had no name, she had not been expected for weeks or even planned in the first place. And there wasn't a single pink thing in her entire layette. As Lina looked through glass at her tiny flailing daughter in the premature babies unit, her conscience burned. I'll make it up to her, she promised, I'll make her the most wanted baby anyone could have, and the most wanted daughter.

And as soon as I get out of here, I'll buy her something pink and pretty, she needn't wear just yellow and white. In fact, the more Lina thought about it, the more she realised that having a daughter all of her own was just what she wanted.

'You don't mind, do you?' she asked Duncan, when he visited, bearing sheaves of flowers. 'I mean, having a daughter instead of a son. They say fathers always want sons.'

'I don't, I've always wanted a daughter, and she's lovely, just like you.'

Lina lay back smiling. All her beauty that had been in abeyance during her pregnancy had returned, and in her joy over the birth of her baby, her anxiety for Duncan had for the moment been smoothed away, as the little lines had been smoothed from her creamy brow. In fact, she was so relaxed and happy, she felt she really might be able to give up smoking.

'I've decided to call the baby April,' she said dreamily. 'Because she was born in April and that's going to be special for her. What do you think?'

'April Guthrie,' Duncan murmured. 'Yes, it goes well.'

'You don't think your mother will want her called after her? I don't want her called after anyone, I want her to be just herself.'

'Quite right,' said Duncan. 'Let's cut out the family baggage.'

Whatever she thought of the baby's name, Erica, like Kitty, was ecstatic about having a granddaughter. And as poor Lina had done all the work, her choice of name should be accepted.

'Between you and me, I think Andrew would have liked a grandson,' she told Kitty as they left the hospital together after a joint visit. 'But I say girls are much less of a worry, and every mother wants a daughter, doesn't she?'

'Aye, that's true,' agreed Kitty. 'Sons'll no' go shopping

210

with you, for a start, Och, I'm just so happy it's all over, and the baby's all right. Ma Lina looks a different person!'

'And Duncan looks different too, wouldn't you say? So much better? So much more relaxed?'

Kitty, seeing the anxious question in Erica's eyes, agreed again. No doubt about it, Duncan looked better.

'Yes, he's on the mend,' said Erica happily. 'I always said the baby'd make all the difference.'

How people see what they want to see, thought Kitty. There was no difference in Duncan. He might go through the motions of being the happy young dad, might bring in the flowers, smile over the baby in the nursery, but you only had to look into his eyes to see that he was no better at all.

Chapter Thirty-Two

Like everyone else, Josie had been taken aback by the early arrival of Lina's baby. In fact, it took her some time to get used to the idea, for a baby expected is not the same as a baby arrived. Now Josie had to think of Lina as a mother. A parent. With all that that implied. It seemed to her that time had taken wings, pushing Lina and herself into another generation.

They'd always been the young ones, she and Lina, first as children together, then as girls. The world had been out there, waiting, and who knew what they might find in it? Josie remembered how she had watched the traffic leaving the ferry and yearned to be going places herself. Well, maybe she hadn't actually gone very far, but her whole life was different now, and so was Lina's. They'd grown up and no mistake, yet here was Lina taking another step, moving even further into maturity. As well as poor Duncan, she had a child to care for, she had the sort of responsibility Josie, who wanted to do some living of her own first, was not yet seeking. The wonderful thing for Lina, however, was that the coming of the child she'd so much dreaded had brought back her happiness. She was lovely, contented Lina again, and Josie gave thanks for that.

Her own life was not exactly ideal, because Matt was so often away and they still had no place of their own. She had schooled herself not to feel jealous of unknown women while he was away, concentrating only on her happiness when he came back. But she couldn't help being conscious, when they made love, of his parents next door and Marie in her bed in the kitchen alcove. Nothing was ever said, of course, no looks were exchanged, but just the fact that other people knew of their rapture tarnished it somehow for Josie. She dearly loved Matt's family, but couldn't wait to get away.

Then there was her continuing disappointment over her mother's failure to agree to a meeting. She could scarcely believe it when Ellie made an excuse not to see her at Christmas, had even thought wildly of going over to Ardmore with presents and cards and confronting her father as well as her mother. Of course, she'd thought better of it. To be turned out again would have been unbearable, she couldn't risk it. For some time she had made no contact with her mother, but after Ellie had sent good wishes on an Easter card, she'd written back. There'd been no further letters, but she still hoped for reconciliation. One day.

There were, however, bright spots in her life, for which she was grateful. One was getting her place at the teacher-training college. That had made up for so many frustrations in the past, and made her feel she had a chance to show what she could do. The other was her small success in her work for Lew Jameson. He was tall and spare, with a thatch of prematurely grey hair and an easy manner. Though he would not for the world have criticised Iona, he had to admit to Josie that the clerical side of his dry-cleaning business was much better run since she had taken over.

'Och, you're just so efficient,' he told her. 'You could be manageress of some big outfit, I'm telling you, you're wasted wi' me, hen, but I'm no' complaining!'

'I just want to do ma teaching course,' Josie replied, turning away in embarrassment. 'But it's really nice of you to say I'm doing well.'

'You'll make a good teacher,' Lew commented. 'I bet

you'll pass that course wi' flying colours! Marie ought to try for something like that, eh? Seeing as she doesny seem to be gettin' herself wed at the moment.'

The family was worried about Marie. Ever since Christmas when she had been invited home to meet Colin Howat's parents, she had lost her bubbliness, had become so cast down she was almost morose. It was only to Josie, some time later, that she had confided that things had not gone well. Mr and Mrs Howat had been cool, had made it plain that Marie was not going to be the daughter-in-law of their choice. Colin had felt wretched, had manufactured excuses for them, said they would 'come round'.

'Come round!' Marie exclaimed to Josie. 'I told him, they could twirl themselves to the moon as far as I was concerned, if they were going to look down on me because ma dad's a shipyard worker!'

'Why, Marie, that's awful!' Josie had cried. 'Why should they take that attitude? Duncan's parents have been really nice to Lina, they've never said a word about her different background!'

'Aye, but they've no need to worry, have they? They've got their place, nothing's going to change it. But the Howats were poor, they both came from a terrible tenement in Hutchesontown. Colin's dad was bright and got himself into an office, studied at night-school, finished up running one o' the big building societies. Now him and his wife don't want their dear little boy rocking the boat and bringing a tenement girl home to tea!'

Tears had thickened Marie's voice, but she would not cry.

'To hell with 'em, I say, Josie, and to hell with Colin, too!'

'But you're still seeing him, aren't you?'

Marie shrugged. 'Now and then. But things are no' the same. How could they be? Och, let's talk of something else, eh? But Josie-' Marie caught at her arm. 'Don't tell Ma, or Dad. I don't want them upset.'

'As though I would!' she cried. 'I'd never want to upset your folks, Marie. And things might still work out, you know.'

To that, Marie had made no reply. Throughout the winter she remained subdued, prompting her mother in despair to ask Josie if she knew what was wrong. Things were not going well with Colin, she had answered diplomatically, and Agnes had sighed and said she'd guessed as much, but why would children never tell you anything? Probably she'd also guessed where the trouble lay, but probed no further. Josie wasn't the only one who could be diplomatic.

Over in Edinburgh, Baby April was home from hospital and thriving. Her christening had been arranged for June, in the Edinburgh church attended by Duncan's parents, Lina's tactful choice to spare Josie the possible pain of meeting her father again at the Queensferry kirk. Antonia was to be second godmother; Roderick MacKean, who had been Duncan's best man, the godfather. Josie could not help wondering about Angus.

One Sunday afternoon, when she and Lina were gazing fondly down at April sleeping in her Moses basket, she ventured to ask if Angus would be coming up for the christening.

Lina said she wasn't sure. He hadn't said yet.

'Surely he'll want to see the baby?'

'Oh, he has seen her. He came up to see her in the hospital. Didn't I tell you?'

'You know you didn't.' Josie looked down at April, who was already showing signs of becoming a second Lina. Her eyes were closed but Josie knew that they had darkened and would be golden-brown, and the few wisps of damp hair on her brow were flaxen. 'She's so gorgeous,' Josie murmured, sidetracked for a moment. 'You must be so proud, Lina.'

'Och, I'm a real mother hen. And to think I didn't want

215

her! It's like Duncan's mother said, you don't think of the bump as being a person till it arrives.' Lina leaned over the cot, smiling. 'Oh, but you are a person, aren't you, darling? Yes, you are, a real little person—'

'Does Angus know I'm to be godmother?' asked Josie, interrupting the cooing.

'Yes, he does, I thought I'd better tell him.' Lina straightened up. 'Look, you can't avoid him all your life, Josie. What's past is past, and he knows that as well as you.'

'I suppose so.'

'Even if he does come, he'll probably keep out of your way. After all, you'll have Matt with you, won't you?'

'Yes, he wants to come. He's no church-goer, but he said he was looking forward to it.'

'So am I!' cried Lina. 'I can't wait to dress April in Duncan's old christening robe. Oh, you should see it, Josie! It's beautiful!'

'I'm sure,' said Josie, looking round the nursery Lina had created from her spare room. Everything was beautiful, including the baby, including Lina. In a way it was almost suffocating, to be surrounded by so much of the best, like living on chocolate or strawberries. But then Duncan came in, and Josie felt ashamed of her thoughts. As he brushed her cheek with his lips, she looked into his face and saw that beneath the rosiness of Lina's life, lay darkness still.

It seemed to cheer Marie up to go shopping with Josie. She knew just the shop off Argyle Street, she said, where Josie could pick up a marked-down christening present. Nothing grand, but that little Guthrie baby was going to be swamped with gifts, anyway, and who was going to expect Josie to be able to afford hall-marked silver? Not on her wages.

'Och, the Tories can say what they like about this being the age of affluence,' Marie added tartly, 'but it's no very obvious to me. Cars, tellies, washing-machines, we're all supposed to be buying like there's no tomorrow, but when

216

it comes down to it, folk like us still haven't got the money.'

'Things are better than in the thirties,' Josie replied. 'I think you'd have to say that. I mean, there's full employment.'

'Aye, but for how long in the shipyards?' asked Marie. 'There's trouble ahead there. It's all this air-travel and folk sending stuff by containers.' Seeing the downcast look on Josie's face, she put on a smile. 'But let's cross that bridge when we come to it, eh? Away and I'll show you what they've got in this shop, I saw the nicest little jewel case, if you could run to it. And Lina's baby'll have plenty to put in something like that, if I'm no' mistaken.'

Josie did manage to run to the pretty velvet jewel box, and felt a great relief that she had found something within her budget. Next, she had to find a hat to go with the pale blue dress and jacket she'd made for the christening. Matt was going to wear his wedding suit, but Josie had decided hers would be too heavy for a summer occasion. Besides, it was nice to have something new, wasn't it?

'Very nice,' Marie agreed, with a look in her eyes Josie did not understand. 'I'm thinking of buying something new maself. Tell me what you think of this two-piece I've seen.'

She hurried Josie along to one of the less expensive department stores, where she tried on a biscuit-coloured jacket with nipped-in waist and a long pencil-slim skirt.

'Why, it's lovely!' cried Josie. 'And so smart! But when would you wear it?'

'Och, I go out now and then. I might get a hat, as well.'

'Yes, I need a hat,' said Josie, who could not keep her eyes off Marie, trying so hard to tell her nothing when there was so obviously something to tell. They both found hats to suit, Josie's a light straw with a brim and a flower, Marie's a 'half-hat' that was no more than a handful of veiling and a band.

'Marie ...' Josie began, as they left the store carrying their large paper shopping bags.

'Yes?' asked Marie.

'Nothing,' said Josie.

'Och, I'll have to tell you, I'm just burstin' to tell somebody!' Marie cried, her face breaking into radiance. 'Thing is, I'm getting married next Saturday!'

'Married?' Josie came to a stop on the pavement, staring at Marie with astonished eyes. 'Why, I don't believe it! Married? And you've never said a word!'

'Too scared. I'm still no' keen to talk about it, really. In case it never happens, in case I'm imagining it, or something.' Marie gave a nervous laugh. 'Oh, Josie, come on, let's go back and have a coffee and I'll tell you what's going on!'

Over coffee and buns in the department store café, Marie explained that Colin had asked her to marry him anyway, regardless of what his parents felt about it. They'd decided to arrange a register office wedding without telling anyone. There would be no family present, not even Ma and Dad, just two officials to act as witnesses. Then his folks could make of it what they liked.

'You're not even going to tell Ma?' Josie asked breathlessly, 'Oh, that's not fair, Marie, that'd really upset her. Why treat poor Ma the same as Colin's parents?'

'I'm no' doing that, I'm going to tell her and Dad the night before. I'll just say that we want the wedding to be for ourselves.' Marie took another sugared bun. 'She'll understand, Josie, she knows I'm no' like other people, I like to do things ma own way.'

'I seem to remember you saying when you got married you'd want the full works,' Josie reminded her. 'White dress, veil, flowers, the lot.'

'Did I say that?' Marie was unconcerned. 'Well, that was then. Now, all I want is Colin, and I don't give a damn about the packaging.'

'Oh, Marie.' Josie leaned across the table to press her hand. 'I'm so happy for you, I'm so glad it's worked out – did I no' say it would?'

'We'll still have Colin's folks to face, but if they want to cast him off, they can cast him off. He's no' worried.' Marie put down her half-eaten bun. 'At least, that's what he says. Oh, God, Josie, I just hope he means it.'

'He does, he does!'

But Josie's eyes were shadowed, as she thought of Colin being 'cast off' by his parents. Cast off, thrown out. Only words you could say quickly. She knew what they meant.

'So what are you going to do after the wedding?' she asked, closing her mind to memories. 'Are you having a honeymoon?'

'Aye,' Marie looked a little shame-faced. 'We're going to be two of those people I've been complaining about. We're flying to Spain.'

'Flying?' Josie repeated. 'To Spain? Oh, Marie, what wouldn't I give ... Oh, you lucky so and so! You know, I can't take all this in – you getting married and flying to Spain – it's wonderful, Marie, isn't it? Just wonderful?'

'If it happens,' Marie said, stirring the last of her coffee. 'How'm I going to get through till Saturday, Josie?'

'I daren't ask you, have you found anywhere to live?'

'That's another thing I'm no' thinking about till everything's legal. Colin's found a couple of rooms in North Kelvin that he says we can afford. They're no' too bad – here, Josie, don't look like that!'

'A couple of rooms of your own?' she said slowly. 'That's wonderful, Marie, like I said – really wonderful.'

Marie was looking embarrassed. 'Josie, you'll find somewhere, eh? Things are getting a bit easier, they say. Mebbe a council house ...'

They both knew that Josie had as much chance of a council house as a flat on the moon, and were silent for a while.

'I understand why you want everything quiet,' Josie said at last, 'but I wish I could've seen you married, Marie.'

'You'll be there in spirit.' She stood up, gathering her shopping together. 'Better get back, eh?'

*

219

In the subway, rattling home, they studied each other's faces. Marie had lost some of her euphoria, was thinking, Josie guessed, of her coming talk with Ma. Josie knew she herself was looking dejected. She was genuinely happy for Marie, but couldn't help contrasting Marie's ease in gaining a home with her own struggle. If only Matt cared a little more about finding a place of their own, but he seemed happy enough to stay on in Dow Street. That was men for you. A home was not important to them, not in the way it was for women. Maybe in the future women would feel that way too, if they all got good jobs and could lead their own lives. But Josie's thoughts couldn't stay with the future. What she wanted was her own home now. Now was always the only thing that counted.

'I'm going to miss you,' she leaned over to say to Marie. 'I can't believe that after Saturday you'll be gone!'

'Fingers crossed!' Marie said sharply.

'Why do you talk like that? You know Colin loves you. I'm sure he's proved that already.'

Marie's face softened. 'Yes, that's true.'

'So, why not just trust him?'

'I do. Well, I want to. But I'm a pessimist, I suppose. I'm no' sure you can ever be sure.'

'What's love, if you can't be sure?' Josie asked quickly. 'I'm sure of Matt.'

'Of course you are,' Marie agreed, touching her hand. 'Aye, you're right. I'll stop worrying. It's bad to be thinking all the time of being let down.'

Chapter Thirty-Three

'Why, I never heard of anything so daft!' cried Agnes, when Marie told her of her plans for the wedding. 'Going off on your own to be married, with just a couple o' witnesses you've never met? That's a piece of nonsense, Marie, and you know it! What's got into you?'

'Ma, we just want it to be as quiet as possible,' Marie protested, her face already taking on a hunted expression. 'Lots of people get married that way.'

'Not in this family, they don't!' Agnes retorted. 'Brandon, you tell your daughter you're not having it. Go on, tell her. Why, we've Matt up from England for the weekend, we're all here, we can all come. It's too late to fix a proper do, but we can come back to the flat, just like we did for Josie's.'

'Ma, we're going to London straight after the wedding,' Marie said miserably. 'We're catching the train, staying in a hotel, then flying to Spain on Sunday. It's all arranged.'

Agnes bit her lip, sent her bright gaze around those members of the family who were present – Brandon, staring at Marie as though pole-axed; Matt, lolling next to Josie on the sofa; Josie, keeping her eyes down, to avoid any storm.

'How long have you got before the train?' Agnes finally demanded.

Marie hesitated. 'A couple of hours, I think. Ma, I'm

sorry, I wish now I'd done things differently, but it's just too late.'

'It's never too late,' Agnes said firmly. 'We'll sort it out somehow. Why, if we only have a cup of tea in the station café, it'll be something, eh? I mean, send you on your way? We can buy buttonholes tomorrow and take the camera, mebbe even get a cake from where Betty MacRae works – what do you think, Matt? You've got the day off, you could see what you could do. Brandon, you'll have to get the day off and all ... I don't know if Sandy and Fergus can manage it. Matt, go round to them now – go on, it's no distance. You and Josie go together, it's a nice summer evening ...'

'Oh, Ma,' cried Marie, half-laughing, half-crying, 'why did I ever think I could have a wedding without you?' She flung her arms around her mother and kissed her cheek. 'Och, I'm a fool, eh? I was just too scared of everything going wrong.'

'You've not the sense you were born with,' her mother said fondly. 'You know you'd have been miserable, getting yourself wed and none of us there! If Colin's folks want to play high and mighty, that's up to them, but we're your family and we stick by you. Come on, now, let's have a look at this dress you've bought, while your dad puts the kettle on. No going to the pub tonight, Brandon! We've things to do!'

'Who's going to the pub?' he asked dazedly. 'Our Marie's getting married tomorrow? I think I'm dreaming!'

It was his turn to be hugged and kissed, and as he smoothed back Marie's hair and looked into her rueful face, Josie said she'd put the kettle on, before she and Matt went out to spread the news of Marie's wedding.

That night Josie left the sleeping Matt to sit near Marie's bed in the kitchen, for Marie she knew would be awake. 'You know it's really what you want,' she whispered. 'I mean, you'd never have been happy getting married with no family there, now would you?'

Marie shook her head. 'I must have been a bit mad,' she confessed. 'Colin and me, we just got the idea of strolling out and coming back married. No fuss, no trouble. Let his folks like it or lump it. But I reckoned without Ma.'

'And just as well. Ah, it'll be lovely tomorrow, Marie, you'll see. Colin'll be glad for you, too, to have your own people around.'

Marie laughed. 'I can just see his face, Josie! When he comes to collect me and all the MacLeods descend on him!'

'Shall I make tea?' asked Josie, laughing too. 'We could see what's in Ma's tins, have a midnight feast!'

'Poor old Josie, you seem to spend your life with a kettle in your hand. Yes, let's live it up!'

'Know who I've been thinking about, lying here?' Marie asked, when they were drinking tea and nibbling Ma's Melting Moment biscuits. 'That poor woman.'

'What poor woman?'

'You know – Ruth Ellis.'

'Oh.' Josie's face grew bleak. She had been trying not to think of Ruth Ellis, a young woman who had that week been sentenced to death for the shooting of her ex-lover in a London street. 'I shouldn't have thought you'd want to remember her, the night before your wedding, Marie.'

'I know, but the thing is I'm so happy, I just can't imagine what it would be like to be her.' Marie shuddered. 'She's going to hang, Josie. And no' so long ago she might have been like you and me.'

'She did kill a man,' Josie said quietly.

'Aye, but maybe she didn't know what she was doing. They say she'd no' long got over a miscarriage.' Marie set down her cup. 'And who's to say they might not get carried away like that, do something terrible, and then be sorry?'

'I don't want to think about it,' Josie said, rising. Ever since she had looked into the abyss that time on her honeymoon, when she had become like another person because Matt had smiled at someone else, she had known the power

223

of emotion. It had been a lesson well learned. She couldn't bear to contemplate what was going to happen to Ruth Ellis. Lessons were too late for her.

'Come on, let's think of something cheerful,' she said briskly. 'Like tomorrow. Like your wedding.'

Marie gave a beatific smile. 'Thanks, Josie, thanks for everything.'

'I haven't done anything!'

'Yes, you have. Away now to your bed. I'll wash these cups up. On second thoughts, I won't wash the cups up, I'll away to ma bed too. Need ma beauty sleep, eh?'

Josie crept back to her room where she stood looking down at Matt, who had not stirred since she left him. They had made wonderful love together, as they always did his first night home. Now he lay in the darkness, but she knew his body so well, his handsome face, his thick, tangled hair, she didn't need light to see him, to love him, and slipped in beside him with joy and fear in her heart. Supposing he were ever to meet someone else to love, as she herself had come to love him in spite of her understanding with Angus? How would she feel?

'I couldn't kill you, ma darling,' she whispered against Matt's back. 'Suppose I might kill maself.'

But she knew she wouldn't do that. All her upbringing, all her instincts, would be against that. No, she'd just go on living in despair.

Why am I thinking like this? she cried in her mind. I trust Matt, he loves me. It's all Marie's talk of poor Ruth Ellis ... She's just nervous about tomorrow, and she's got me nervous too.

'Josie?' murmured Matt. 'What's the matter?'

'Nothing, darling, go back to sleep.'

As he turned his head to his pillow, Josie slipped her arm around his naked waist and lay in contentment that soon became oblivion. Until Ma bustled around the following morning, waking everybody up, while Brandon put the kettle on, singing 'Off to Marie's wedding' in as much of the Gaelic he could remember.

The little wedding went off without a hitch. If Colin Howat was taken aback to be greeted by a crowd of MacLeods all wearing buttonholes when he arrived to take Marie to the register office, he didn't show it. In fact, it relieved Josie's mind to see his good-natured smile as Fergus and Sandy clapped him on the back, the children clung to his knees, Rena gave his coat a brush and Iona planted a sisterly kiss on his cheek. Colin was going to be all right, Marie had known what she was doing when she fell in love with him. Different though he was from her family, and maybe not the obvious choice for her, they matched and that was what mattered. No one had been able to see that Josie and Matt had matched, too. They had just known it themselves. That was why they were so happy.

After the short register office ceremony, everyone adjourned to a café in the town centre, where Brandon had been able to book a room for a couple of hours. Tea, sandwiches and sausage rolls were served, plus the large layer cake that Betty MacRae's shop had been able to provide, and though the café wasn't licensed, a blind eye was turned when Colin ran out and brought back champagne. Champagne! Looks were exchanged and the message signalled – this fella might be an asset after all! Marie, who had that extra dimension of beauty brides seem to acquire, said she felt so bubbly already, she hardly dared take a drink. But she joined in the special toast made by Colin: 'To the MacLeods!'

'To the MacLeods,' cried Josie, keeping her eyes on Matt. This day was beginning to feel like a repeat performance of their own wedding, and that was all right by her. She could happily have relived it any time.

But time was running away. They had to take the newlyweds to the train, where Marie couldn't decide whether to look radiant with happiness at going on her honeymoon, or burst into tears at the thought of leaving her family.

225

Somehow, she managed both, as she and Colin leaned out of the carriage window, dodging the confetti Heather and Rena insisted on throwing in defiance of the scowls of the porters walking along slamming doors.

'Send us a postcard'! cried Agnes, dabbing her eyes.

'Aye, from SPAIN!' shouted Brandon. He blew his nose. 'Who'd have thought our Marie'd be travelling abroad, then?'

'Mebbe we'll go abroad one day,' Matt whispered to Josie. 'If we come up on the pools?'

'Far away places,' she sighed. 'I used to know a song called that.'

'I'll sing it for you, sweetheart.'

'Och, it's a shame we couldn't have had any music for Marie's wedding, I know she'd have loved what we had.'

'Looks happy enough anyway,' commented Matt, as the train began to glide away.

Everyone waved. The little girls tried to run along the platform, picking up the coins Colin had thrown to them, Agnes couldn't keep back a few more tears. Still, there were plenty of MacLeods left to go back to Dow Street and have a bit of a sing-song, even if the guests of honour were on their way to London.

'It's nice you've got your day out tomorrow,' Agnes said to Josie, as Brandon tuned his fiddle. 'Your little god-daughter's christening. Be sure to take plenty of snaps, eh?'

'Oh, I will, Ma,' Josie answered. 'I've got the Brownie all ready.'

Chapter Thirty-Four

At three o'clock the following day, Josie and Matt made their way to the church in Edinburgh's West End where April Guthrie was to be christened. Matt was wearing his grey suit with his yellow hair well brushed, while Josie was in the blue dress and jacket she had made for the christening but had already worn for Marie's wedding, plus a pair of short white Grace Kelly gloves. Her face was pale beneath her summer straw hat. She had told Matt she was worrying about her duties as godmother, how she would acquit herself in front of the Guthries' smart friends, at which of course he had only laughed. But her real worry was the prospect of meeting Angus again. She hadn't seen him since that terrible day in the city garden when she had told him she couldn't marry him. Even with Matt by her side, her heart failed her at the thought of looking into Angus's eyes again. But perhaps he would not be there?

He was. As soon as she and Matt approached the knot of well-dressed people standing outside the church, she saw him.

'Steady on!' Matt whispered, as she dug her fingers into his arm. Then he too saw Angus and glanced at Josie, whose lovely eyes were lowered. 'Come on, darling, look up, you're the godmother, you've got to meet people.'

'Josie!' Lina, plump and beautiful, in floating silk with a wide-brimmed hat, was swift to come to her side. 'Oh, I'm so glad to see you! Now, don't you mind, Angus is here.'

'I know.' Josie was forcing herself to smile and look about her. At Duncan, very pale, in a dark suit. But then he was always pale. At his so-elegant parents and their friends, at his sister in lilac, at Roderick MacKean, his former best man who was to be April's godfather. At Kitty Braid, in the bright green she had been denied for Lina's wedding, so perhaps Lina had said it wasn't bad luck for a christening. At Baby April, resplendent in the Guthries' christening robe, wriggling in her carry-cot. At Mrs Tassie and Patty MacAndrew, talking to George and Bernie, in best suits. At Angus.

He was wearing a good dark suit with a grey silk tie, and looking well. Not haggard or anything. In fact, Josie rather thought he'd filled out a bit. So that was a relief. Oh, no, he had seen her and was coming over! She looked round for Matt, but he was in polite conversation with Mrs Guthrie and Antonia. Lina, too, had moved away. Josie felt as exposed and vulnerable as if she were alone on a rock.

'Hello, Josie,' said Angus quietly. 'You're godmother, I hear.'

'Yes.' Deep colour rose to her face beneath the shade of her hat. 'How are you, Angus?'

'Fine. And you?'

'Oh, very well.'

'You're certainly looking well.' Angus hesitated. 'Marriage suits you,' he added curtly.

She raised her eyes and looked into his, but they were blank. In the old days, she had always been able to tell what Angus was thinking, but not today. After a moment, he turned his head and looked at Matt, who, feeling his gaze, turned and looked at him. Across the pavement outside the church, across the chattering christening guests, the eyes of the two men locked. Then Angus broke the spell.

'Will you excuse me?' he said politely and walked away to speak to his brothers. Josie, hurrying to Matt's side, felt unreasonably snubbed. But why should Angus be friendly?

228

He obviously no longer cared for her, and that was good. The last thing she wanted was to know that he was still pining for her. Well, he wasn't, and she was glad, very glad indeed.

'Josie!' called Lina, coming to her with April in her arms. 'Will you take the baby? We're ready to go into church now.'

It had to be admitted that April did not behave well during her christening. Perhaps she didn't like the minister or maybe it was the baptismal water. Whatever the reason, her face turned scarlet, her tiny hands went shadow-boxing, her mouth let out roar after roar, while Lina cringed and the guests suffered. When at last April was returned to Josie's arms, however, she quietened, fixing her godmother with a dark stare until her eyelids trembled and closed and she fell asleep.

Peace, wonderful peace! As the guests began to leave the church, Lina, walking on eggshells, transferred April to her carry-cot.

'I don't understand it,' she murmured to people standing around, taking out their cameras. 'I fed her before we came, she can't be hungry, and she's usually so good – och, it's so embarrassing!'

'Might be she's uncomfy in the christening robe?' suggested Mrs Tassie, dabbing at her moist plump face with her handkerchief. 'Babies hate being constricted.'

'And then it was very stuffy in the church,' Josie murmured, as she photographed the still-sleeping April. 'I felt faint maself.'

'Aye, you're a wee bit pale,' said Patty. 'Bet you were nervous, eh? But you were the one to get her to sleep, Josie, you must have the touch!'

'Unlike me,' said Antonia, winding on her camera. 'I was so dreading I'd have to hold her. Thank God for you, Josie. Let me take your picture now, you and your husband together. And one with Lina and Duncan. Duncan ... over here a minute!'

229

'Who'd like a lift back to the flat?' asked Roderick MacKean, and Josie with Matt was glad to accept. She really wasn't feeling too well.

'Must have been that champagne yesterday,' she whispered to Matt. 'Doesn't suit me.'

'Don't say that! If I'm not mistaken, it'll be flowing here today.'

'All I want is a cup of tea,' said Josie.

Lina's flat, so packed with people, was stuffier than the church. As hired waitresses served tiny sandwiches and pastries and poured the welcome tea, Duncan flung open the long windows, and everyone said, 'Ah!' Josie, giving Angus a wide berth, drank tea thirstily, but didn't feel like anything to eat. When the champagne corks were popped and Roderick proposed the baby's health, she did allow herself a sip, but just the sight of the rich dark christening cake made her stomach lurch and she shook her head at the smiling waitress.

'Hey, it's no' like you to turn down cake!' cried Mrs Tassie. 'Now I didn't make this maself, but I can tell you it's delicious!'

'Will you excuse me?' Josie asked faintly, and made for the bathroom, where she felt like death until she brought up the champagne and the tea, when the world cleared and she felt better.

'Are you all right?' asked Duncan, passing her as she came out of the bathroom. His sad eyes travelled over her face. 'Oh, you're not, are you? Would you like to lie down for a minute?'

He showed her to the main bedroom and when she sank on to the double bed, stood looking down at her with compassion.

'Shall I fetch Matt for you? Or Lina?'

'No, no, I'll be fine, I think it's just something that's disagreed with me.'

'Nasty ... well, you just stay there until you feel better.'

230

It was pleasant, lying away from everyone, just listening to the hum of traffic, the babble of voices from the next room. Or would have been pleasant, if a thought had not been nagging at her mind like a dog at a bone. She was late, that was the thing, and she was never late. And now she'd been sick. She'd missed a period, she'd been sick ... Did two and two make four? No, could be just a coincidence. Could mean nothing. Nothing at all. They'd been so careful. But whatever you did, you could never be sure. Never one hundred per cent sure. Drops of sweat shone on Josie's brow and she clenched her sticky hands. She would not give up her teaching, she would not! Because she was not going to have a baby, she was not!

The door softly opened and Matt came in, looking anxious. He dropped to his knees by the side of the bed and took her hand.

'Josie, you're not ill, are you?'

'No, I'm OK, I'm feeling better now.' She sat up, smoothing back her hair, and smiling. 'It was just something I ate.'

He let out a sigh. 'Had me worried. I mean, you're never ill.'

They clung together for a moment, then Josie said she'd get up, go back to the party.

'Well, folk are leaving now. Duncan said he'd give us a lift home, but I said the station would do.'

'Och, yes, he doesn't need to take us all the way to Glasgow!'

'Are you sure you're all right?' Lina asked worriedly when Josie reappeared. The room was emptier now but Josie, from the corner of her eye, could see Angus by the window looking at her.

'I'm better,' Josie said at once. 'I'm quite all right.'

'Were you sick?' asked Lina, with the look in her eye people always gave young married women who were sick.

'It was the champagne,' Josie said firmly. 'You know, at Marie's wedding.'

'Fancy Marie getting married like that, just out of the blue!' cried Lina, happily sidetracked.

Duncan came up with his car keys, accompanied by Antonia, who said he could give her a lift home on his way back from the station. When Josie and Matt had made their farewells to Duncan's parents, to Mrs Tassie and Patty and others still around, Lina, holding the newly awakened April, came down the stairs with them.

'Take care,' she said to Josie, kissing her cheek. 'And thank you again for April's lovely jewel case. 'Bye, Matt, be good!'

'I'm always good,' he retorted.

There were kisses for the baby, more farewells, and Josie was beginning to feel quite weary again when there was a sudden rush of footsteps down the stairs and Angus joined them.

'Goodbye, Josie,' he said quietly. 'Hope you'll feel better soon.'

He nodded to Matt, who gave him his beautiful smile, and before Josie could speak, had run back up the stairs.

'Still carrying the torch?' asked Antonia, who had evidently been told by Lina of her brother's one-time love.

'I don't think so,' Josie answered, no longer caring, as she was put into the front seat of Duncan's car. Nothing mattered to her now except being free again. Out of the trap. She could hear Antonia telling Matt in the back about some newspaper she was going to work for, and Matt was making polite noises, but Josie was envying Antonia from the bottom of her heart. She could get on with her life and her work. While I, thought Josie ... but she wouldn't even allow herself to consider her future. Not yet. Not till she was sure.

The first thing Matt did when they got home was to tell his mother that Josie had been ill. Oh, God, why didn't I tell him no' to say anything? thought Josie, who then had to go through her ritual of saying she was quite all right, it was just something she'd eaten.

232

'Been sick?' asked Agnes brightly.

'It was the champagne,' cried Josie, and vanished into her room.

'What are you thinking, Ma?' asked Matt, raising his eyebrows.

She shrugged, glancing at Brandon. 'Thinking we might be grandparents again. Why not?'

'We don't want a baby yet. Josie's got her teaching course.'

'Maybe nobody's told the baby!' laughed Brandon.

'Look, she's been sick once. Don't start counting grandchildren before they arrive!'

'Ah, well, if Josie wants to do her teaching course, I hope she can,' declared Agnes. 'She's got plenty of time for bairns. Want a cup of tea, Matt?'

'Aye, and then I'll get ma bag packed, I'm away at first light tomorrow.'

'Everybody's away,' his father muttered. 'We're left.'

'We've got Josie,' said Agnes stoutly.

'And she's looking to flit.'

'Aye, well, if there is a bairn on the way, she might want to stay with us. We'd be a help, eh?'

Josie, listening from the bedroom, felt like crying out. 'Oh, God, there is no bairn on the way!'

But she didn't know for sure. She no longer knew anything for sure.

Chapter Thirty-Five

Dr Norah Keir, a partner in Dr Ashton's practice where Josie was registered, seemed very sure. 'January the eighteenth, that's your date,' she said crisply.

But Josie still asked, 'Are you sure?'

'Sure of the date, or sure you're pregnant?' Dr Keir, a handsome woman in her forties, gave a thin smile. 'Well, with first babies it could be a week or two either side of the date. But there's no doubt about the baby, Mrs MacLeod. That's there, all right.'

Josie nodded dumbly. She couldn't think why she'd asked the question, when she knew the answer already. All the same, to have the doctor confirm what she dreaded seemed to slam home the door of the cell. She had been taken prisoner by what her mother would have called Nature. 'Nature knows best,' she was fond of saying. 'That's Nature's way.' 'Can't go against Nature.' Anything you didn't want, Nature seemed to fix it so you got it. But what would her mother say to her news now? Josie decided she wouldn't tell her just yet. After all, they didn't exchange letters very often.

'You're not looking happy,' Dr Keir was saying. 'Is there a problem?'

'I was due to start a teaching course in October.'

'October? I'm afraid you're going to have to postpone that. Well, I suppose you could ask—'

'Och, no, I'd no' try to do it with a baby on the way.'

'There's no one who could help you after the baby's born?'

Josie shook her head. Ma would have done it like a shot, but she had her own job to do. Anyway, in Josie's eyes it wouldn't be right to expect someone else to look after the child. It would be hers and she'd be stuck with it.

'You can always do the course later on,' Dr Keir said kindly. 'You're very young, you've time on your side. Try not to feel depressed, Mrs MacLeod. Remember, someone else's health is dependent on yours now.'

'Oh, I know.'

While the doctor outlined what lay ahead – booking in at the hospital, attending ante-natal classes, applying for all the things she was entitled to, working out a healthy diet, drinking milk, drinking orange juice, taking iron – Josie tried to look cheerful and interested, but could only feel herself sinking lower and lower under her new yoke. Only a few weeks ago she had been feeling sorry for Lina, lumbered forever with responsibility for another human being. Now that same responsibility was hers. When do I get to belong to maself again? she wanted to cry, but knew the doctor could only answer: When junior gets the key of the door. And maybe not even then.

It was true that Lina couldn't be happier, now that her baby had been born, but Josie couldn't take comfort from that. Things were different for Lina. She hadn't been looking forward to a career that had been snatched away from her, she didn't need the extra money a good job would bring, she had a place of her own to live.

'Thank you,' she heard herself saying to Dr Keir, and then was walking out through the airless little waiting room where people sat turning over old magazines with unseeing eyes. Walking out into summer sunshine, with the words 'January the eighteenth' hammering into her brain.

One good thing was that Matt's job in England was finished

235

and he was home again. She would be able to give him the news as soon as she got back. In fact he had been keen to come with her to the doctor's but she had said she wanted time to herself. Time to come to terms with the end of a dream.

Oh, don't be so soft, she told herself, as she paced slowly through the streets of Turngate that looked no less grey in the sunshine than in rain and cried out for a tree or two. You're just giving in to yourself, Josie MacLeod. You've no' lost a dream. Matt's your dream and you've still got him. The teaching course can wait, the doctor's right, you can do it later. She had the feeling she would not.

Glasgow was good for parks, but there was no park in Turngate, sandwiched as it was between Kinning Park and Govan. All you were conscious of were long streets of tenements, where washing blew like bunting and children played football, where women chatted at the entrances to closes and men were not seen until the hooter blew in the yards. Then the great wave of caps would come tumbling out until the streets emptied and were quiet, as the whole of Turngate sat down to its tea.

How she missed the Forth on days like this! The open sky, the sunlight on the water, white sails of yachts, pennants flying ... she felt she could have taken the houses lining the streets and pushed them apart, so that she might have space. Space to breathe! Oh, God, she felt queasy again! Might as well go back and tell Matt, he was going to be a father.

He was alone in the flat, lying on the couch, reading the paper. Nothing in it, thought Josie, taking it from his hands and tossing it aside. No horrors, now that Ruth Ellis had paid her terrible forfeit. No news to compare with her own.

'Oh, Josie!' He had leaped to his feet and put his arms around her. She hadn't needed to tell him her news. He had read it in her face. 'I'm sorry, sweetheart, I know you were set on that course. Mebbe you could still ...'

'No.' As she had told the doctor, she told him. It was out of the question. Even if had been possible, she wouldn't have wanted it. Couldn't have put her mind on it. Then, what would she do when the baby came?'

'When's it due?' Matt asked hoarsely.

'January. January the eighteenth.'

'My God. It's pretty wonderful, eh, when you think about it? Bringing another person into the world?'

'A lot of people manage it,' she said drily, and moved from his embrace. 'I could do with a cup of tea, Matt.'

'I'll make it!' He set off for the kitchen, then turned back. 'You lie down, Josie. Put your feet up. Got to rest, you know.'

'Put ma feet up? I'll be back at work tomorrow. Lew gave me the afternoon off, but we can't let Iona take over for too long.'

Matt put on the kettle and came back to sit beside her on the couch. 'I think you should give up working for Lew,' he said seriously. 'It's not good for you, working near those fumes.'

She ran her hand down his face. 'Matt, I'm going to work as long as I can, we need the money. You've no' even signed on yet, and even if you get a job at the yard, we could still do with something extra. I'm determined to find a flat. If I'm staying at home, I want it to be my home. You do understand?'

'Sure I understand. I'm as keen as you to get our own place.'

'Since when?' she asked, smiling faintly.

'Don't look like that, I mean it. In fact, I might already have found us something.'

'Matt!' Josie sat up straight, her eyes shining. 'Where?'

'Met an old friend this afternoon. She said there was a flat going at her place. The usual thing, a couple of rooms, but reasonable rent. And ground floor.'

'Old friend? What old friend?'

'Rena Cameron.' Matt's dark-grey eyes seemed translucent. 'She's got the day off from the hotel today. I said we'd go round when we'd had our tea.'

Chapter Thirty-Six

Josie agreed that they should look at the flat in the house where Rena Cameron lived. She did not let Matt see how she felt about it, and that was not for his sake but for hers. He had obviously forgotten the jealousy she'd displayed after he'd danced with Rena, but Josie had not. She was determined never to give way to that kind of emotion again. They would go and look at the flat and they would turn it down; at least, that was what she hoped.

First, of course, they had to have their tea and tell Matt's parents about the baby. It wasn't too bad. Brandon seemed pleased; didn't say much, but then, he never did. Agnes was delighted, said everyone would be – just wait till Marie heard! But she was sympathetic, too. What a shame about the teaching, eh? Maybe Josie could do it later on, she was a bright girl, she shouldn't waste her talents.

'Thanks, Ma,' Josie said, quietly. 'It's nice that you understand. See ma point of view.'

'Always try to see your point of view, pet. Even when you want to be away.'

'Just to a place of our own, you know how it is.'

'Aye, I've said I understand.'

'Young folk like to be on their own,' remarked Brandon. 'If they can afford it.'

'Think we can afford this flat,' said Matt. 'Needs doing up.'

His mother shrugged. 'All right, if you don't mind being mixed up wi' the Camerons again.'

'Mixed up? Who's getting mixed up?' Matt raised his fair brows. 'There's just Rena and her sister got this top flat in Piper Street. Their dad's married again and moved to Paisley. You remember Mrs Cameron died?'

'Jeannie, yes, she was no' so bad. Spoiled those girls, though. I used to say to her, "You're doing yourself no good, Jeannie, sitting up till all hours, stitching sequins on Rena's dresses, and doing without yourself so's Fay can go to college." I mean, you like to do what you can for your family, but there is a limit, and Jeannie never had a life of her own. And, you see, she never made old bones, did she?'

'Ma, we're only going to look at a flat,' Matt said patiently. 'Not move in with the Cameron girls.'

'Aye, well, Rena's awful bossy. Josie, just see she doesn't talk you into anything!'

'I'm no' likely to do that,' Josie said with feeling.

Piper Street was like the long streets Josie had passed through earlier that day, the houses four-storeyed as in Dow Street, built of the same darkened sandstone, but less well maintained. Children were out playing again, enjoying the summer evening, but there were few women about, probably most being busy with their chores while the men read the evening paper before departing for the pub. One or two roofs had television aerials, prompting Matt to say with uncharacteristic force, 'Somebody's doing bloody well, eh?'

Josie glanced at him in surprise. 'You want a telly, Matt? I'm no' keen. Seems to be all panel games and news.'

'I'd like to be able to afford one, that's all.'

'If we can get ourselves a flat, that's all I need.'

'Here we are, then. Number Seventy-two.'

The house was no better or worse than its neighbours, with a door hanging open to reveal a close that led to a back

240

court, window-frames that needed painting and net curtains that needed washing. There was no television aerial on its roof, but there was a tiny strip of garden between its front step and the street, where a few sooty marigolds clung to an uncertain life.

'Think that goes with the flat we're after,' said Matt. 'I bet you could make it nice, Josie.'

'It'd no' take me long!' she answered, with a laugh that soon died. Rena Cameron was on the step, smiling radiantly at Matt. No, that wasn't fair, Josie corrected herself, she's smiling at me, too. Must want us to come, she's really on her best behaviour.

'Been looking out for you!' cried Rena. 'The landlord's given me the key to show you round. Come on, Fay,' she called over her shoulder. 'Matt's here! And Josie.'

A second dark-haired girl appeared on the step. She had a strong likeness to Rena, with high cheekbones and freckles, but her eyes were different, a soft melting brown rather than piercing blue. They made her seem less formidable than Rena, even sympathetic.

'Ma sister Fay,' Rena said carelessly. 'You remember Matt MacLeod, Fay? This is his wife Josie, frae Queensferry.'

'Hi,' said Fay. 'Welcome to Number Seventy-two!'

'Haveny taken the flat yet,' snapped Rena. 'Away in, I'll show it you. Now, dinna be expecting too much, eh? It's got – what's the word, Fay?'

'Possibilities,' said Fay smoothly.

'Needs doing up,' Matt had said. You can say that again, thought Josie, after they had inspected the two rooms and tiny kitchenette that were on offer. There was furniture, of a sort. A horsehair sofa, two sagging armchairs and a deal table in the living room; a double bed, dressing-table and single wardrobe in the bedroom. Everything was as the previous owner had left it, with antimacassars, little lace cloths, curtains and bedclothes, all in need of washing or

241

throwing away. There were small ornaments, views of Edinburgh framed in passe-partout, crusted pans in the kitchenette, a lavatory that made Josie turn white. As for the cupboards, no one dared to look in them.

'Landlord hasny cleared it yet,' Rena told them, rather obviously. 'Old Mrs MacEwan only died in June.'

'Did she die here?' cried Josie.

'No, in hospital,' Fay said softly. 'She'd no relatives, might have had to go into a home, so it was a happy release, really.'

'Mr Moffat was just going to advertise when I told him I knew a really good tenant for the flat,' Rena said, fingering a dirty curtain and glancing at Matt. 'Of course, he's going to clear it out, except for the furniture – that's his. But he says he'll take out anything you're no' wanting.'

'Is he going to decorate?' asked Josie, staring at the old range in the living room. How long since anyone had black-leaded that?

Rena shrugged. 'Depends. If you do it yoursel', you can have the flat for nine shillin' a week. If he does it, he'll charge more.'

'I could do it,' said Matt. 'I like painting.'

'Once it's been cleaned,' Josie told him, with a slight shudder. 'I'd need a ton of soap and disinfectant.'

'Could be really nice,' said Fay. 'Do you no' think?'

'As we said, it's got possibilities,' put in Rena. Her sharp gaze went between Matt and Josie. 'Shall we leave you to have a think about it?'

'If you wouldn't mind?' said Matt.

'Nae bother. Come on up to our place when you've decided, eh? We're on the top, name's on the door.'

'Well, what do you think?' asked Matt, when the sisters had gone.

'I don't know,' Josie answered.

This was true. She had come with the intention of turning the flat down, whatever it was like, because it was in the same building as Rena Cameron's home. But now that she

242

had met Rena again, Josie felt she was not quite the threat she'd imagined. And then her sister was very nice. And the flat itself had – yes – possibilities. On the other hand . . .

'There's only a shared bathroom, Matt.'

'Lucky there's one to share.'

'I suppose so.' Josie tried and failed to pull up one of the sash windows. 'Och, I'd like to get rid of this stale smell!'

Matt came to her and put his arm around her shoulders. 'You wouldn't have to do the cleaning, Josie. I'd get the family in, they like giving a hand.'

'I don't mind cleaning. I mean, really getting a place to look good again.'

'Don't want you knocking yourself up now, sweetheart.'

'I'm OK, Matt, I can do it.'

'You want to? Want to take this flat? I don't think we'd get anything better.'

'No, I suppose we wouldn't.'

Matt was silent for a moment. His chest heaved in a long rueful sigh. 'Just wish I could – I mean, get you something better. I sometimes think you should have married some other guy.'

'Matt!' Josie took his hands. 'What are you talking about? I wanted you, you know that!'

'Aye, but think of Lina and her life. Thank what you might have had, if you'd married somebody like Duncan Guthrie.'

'You think I envy Lina? Are you crazy? With all poor Duncan's problems to worry about?'

'Angus has no problems,' Matt said quietly.

Josie's eyes searched his. 'Matt, I don't love Angus.'

He bent his head and kissed her and they clung together for a long moment.

'We'll take the flat, then?' asked Matt.

She nodded.

'We'd better go up and tell Rena.'

'Yes. All right.'

*

243

The Cameron sisters' living room in their top flat was small but filled with light. There was no black range here or clippy mats or old, deal furniture, no books or photographs or china ornaments. The walls were distempered in pale green, the curtains were fawn and matched the cord floor-covering, the chairs and table, thin and angular, could have come straight out of a contemporary magazine. In fact, the whole living room could have come out of a magazine, thought Josie, as she and Matt gazed around with astonished eyes.

'Different from our old place, eh?' asked Rena, watching their expressions while Fay stood modestly by.

'I'll say,' Matt retorted. 'How'd you do it, Rena?'

'Dinna look at me! It was Fay, here. Just threw everything out when we moved in, painted the walls, made the curtains, bought the furniture on the never-never. What do you think?'

'It's wonderful!' cried Josie. 'I could never do anything like it!'

'Just ma job,' said Fay. 'I work for a firm of interior decorators.'

'In Buchanan Street, no less!' cried Rena. 'Och, she should make a fortune, but she only gets buttons, is it no' always the same?'

'I remember now, you went to art school, didn't you?' asked Matt. 'We were all so impressed!'

'Och, Mum thought I was going to be another Constable!' Fay said, blushing. 'She had this picture she cut out from a paper – The Hay Wain – said, 'One day you'll be able to paint like that, Fay.' But I couldny even draw! I went to college to study textiles and design.'

'We've still got that picture,' said Rena. 'It's in the bedroom. Want to see the bedroom? It's just like everybody else's. I told Fay, I'm no' having all that modern stuff where I sleep! Fay, put the kettle on, eh?'

Josie couldn't help feeling a little relieved when she looked around at the normal clutter of the room shared by

244

the sisters. There were magazines piled in the corner, and beside the cut-out of The Hay Wain, posters of film stars (like I used to have, thought Josie, with a twinge), make-up on the dressing-table, clothes on chairs.

'Keep all ma dance-dresses in here,' said Rena, opening a long old-fashioned wardrobe. As she ran a hand down one of the frothy net dresses, she gave Josie a speculative glance. 'You and Matt still go dancing?'

'No' very often. I'm no' much good. Do you and Jimmy?'

'Jimmy? Jimmy who?' Rena laughed and closed the door of her wardrobe. 'Och, I've no' seen Jimmy Fraser for months. I'm no' one for keeping up with folks. Still go dancing, though.'

'They say there's some new dances coming over from America.'

'What new dances?'

'I don't know. Somebody said something at the dry cleaner's where I work.'

'There's always new stuff coming in, never stops people doing ballroom. Ballroom's the only proper dancing, that's why.' Rena gave Josie another of her sharp blue glances. 'You ought to take some lessons, then you could go dancing with Matt. He'd like that.'

'Bit late at the moment,' Josie said in a low voice. 'You might as well know, I'm expecting a baby next January.'

'Good God!' Rena's lips trembled into a smile. 'Matt's going to be a father! I canna believe it!'

'I think he'll make a very good father,' said Josie quickly.

'Sure he will!' Rena slid smoothly out of her bedroom and, catching Matt by the arm, turned him round and kissed his cheek. 'Congratulations, Matt! You never told me you were going to be a dad!'

He laughed and with an embarrassed look towards Josie, put his hand to his face where Rena had kissed it. 'Early days, yet, Rena. But that's why we want a place of our own.'

245

'Josie, you're going to have a baby?' asked Fay, appearing with a tray of mugs of coffee. 'Why, that's lovely! Rena, is that no' nice? We'll have a baby in the flats!'

'No novelty,' she answered drily, 'there's half a dozen here already. But it's lovely, so it is. When do you want to move in here, then? Shall I fix it up with Mr Moffat?'

As Matt enthusiastically agreed, Josie thought caustically, Yes, fix it up with Mr Moffat, Rena, you're the type to fix everything. Then she felt conscience-stricken, for Rena was pleasant enough, really, and would probably be quite a help once she and Matt moved in. Her sister, too. It wouldn't be too bad, living at Seventy-two Piper Street.

'Are you happy?' asked Matt, as they walked slowly back to Dow Street. 'I don't want you to do anything you're not happy about.'

'I am happy,' she told him. 'I'm sure it'll work out. But I'm no' Fay, remember. Our flat'll no' look like hers.'

'Thank God for that!' said Matt. 'I want a place that looks like home.'

'I liked it, I think it shows what can be done with tenements.'

'Aye, maybe. Listen, we're going to need money. There'll be the deposit, then there's the furniture—'

'We can make do with the furniture there, if we get it cleaned up. I don't want us to go in for hire purchase, Matt.'

'I'll check what we've got in the Post Office tomorrow, and get maself signed on again. Josie, I've decided. I'll not try for work away until after the baby's born. That suit?'

'Matt, that'd be wonderful! Oh, it'd make all the difference, no' to have you away!'

'Aye, and if I stay put, I might get the chance to do some evening classes at the Technical College. Learn a bit more about bridges.'

'I should think you'd know plenty about bridges already,' Josie commented in surprise.

246

'Some bridges. But I'd need training for anything new.'

'You're thinking of the road bridge? If it comes?'

He nodded. 'I'd like to be involved.'

'Lina says Duncan wants to be involved, too. She doesn't think he'll ever be well enough.'

'Poor devil,' said Matt. 'I think I'd die if I never got up aloft again.'

Josie paled. 'Matt, you don't mean it?'

'No.' He laughed and hugged her to him. 'Just mean I know how Mr Guthrie feels.'

She relaxed, smiling. 'Talking of Lina, I'll have to tell her about the baby. She'll be thrilled.'

'What about your folks? You going to tell them?'

Josie hesitated. 'Haven't heard from Mum for a while. I'll leave it for now.' She brightened. 'But I'll tell Lina tomorrow.'

Chapter Thirty-Seven

Lina was indeed thrilled by Josie's news, but she had news of her own. Duncan had been asked to move temporarily to the London office of his firm. He had said he was happy about it, provided he could eventually be involved in preparing tenders for the new Forth bridge superstructure. That had been agreed.

'Duncan's happy, how about you?' asked Josie.

'What do you think? I don't want to leave Scotland. All ma friends are here, and ma family. Mum's already in a state.' Lina's voice wobbled. 'There's April, you see. Duncan's parents are upset, too, but they just want him to do what he wants to do. So, we're going to London.'

'You couldn't stay on here? Say, if Duncan came up at weekends?'

Lina shook her head. 'I'd never do that to him, Josie. He needs me. We're a family.'

'Yes.' Josie thought of her own misery when Matt was absent from her. 'You'll have to go then. When?'

'Middle of August. We're going to try to get out of the lease here and rent a flat in London.' Lina sighed. 'I suppose, on the bright side, I'll be able to see Angus.'

She did not mention Callum Robb, Josie noticed. But then London was not exactly Queensferry. You could probably go forever without seeing somebody you knew in London.

*

The weeks went swiftly by. Josie and the MacLeods spring-cleaned the Piper Street flat from top to bottom, tearing off old wallpaper, sugar-soaping paintwork, throwing out old rugs and curtains, blackleading the range, blasting the gas cooker with oven cleaner, splashing so much disinfectant down the lavatory, Marie said the place smelled like a hospital.

'Better than what it smelled like before!' said Agnes.

By the time Josie and Matt moved in, however, the hospital smell had gone, to be replaced by the scent of furniture polish and the flowers they'd been given. At their little house-warming party, everyone agreed it was wonderful, eh, what a difference paint and soap and elbow grease could make! The only new piece of furniture was the bed Josie and Matt had brought over from Dow Street, but Brandon had given them a little money from a savings account so that Josie was able to buy floor coverings and make new curtains. While deeply admiring Fay's taste, she had followed her own, which had resulted in a plain easy style that Matt said proudly was just what he wanted.

'I can't believe it,' cried Lina. 'I mean, you'd never think this was ...'

'A tenement?' asked Josie. 'Och, you should see the Camerons' place upstairs! The thing is, folk forget that these houses are good and solid, they've got big windows and space, and all they need is a bit o' money spent to make them look grand. It's no' right just to pull them down and put something up that's no' as good!'

'Some of the slums have to go, Josie,' said Marie. 'I mean, they're just too bad, they can't be repaired. But I agree with you, the planners should be careful.'

'They say they'll be going for these tower blocks,' Agnes remarked. 'Now who wi' bairns wants to live up in the sky?'

'And who wants tae live out o' Glasgow, then, in these new towns they're planning?' asked Gillie. 'They shouldny

249

tinker about wi' folks' lives, eh?'

'We'll just have to hope for the best,' said Josie, moving away with Lina, who was looking lovely but despondent.

'It's next week we go, Josie. I don't know how I'm going to say goodbye to Mum and everybody. I've told Duncan I'm going to have to make a lot of trips home, he's just got to be prepared.'

'A long way for you to bring April,' sighed Josie.

'Oh, I needn't bring her every time. Did I no' tell you? Mrs Guthrie's insisting on getting me a nanny.'

'A nanny?' cried Josie.

'Well, there is a lot to do with a baby, Josie. You'll find that out.'

'I won't be getting a nanny, that's for sure.'

'I suppose you think I'm spoiled?' asked Lina, lowering her eyes. 'It's what the Guthries are used to, you see. I go along with it.'

'I don't blame you. If I was in your shoes, I'd probably do the same.' Josie undid a buckle on her skirt. 'Oh, that's better ... Lina, I'm really starting to show.'

'You are not! Well, if you are, you look fine, Josie. No, I mean it.'

'Don't always feel so good, though. Can't wait for January.'

'It'll all be worth it, Josie, believe me.' Lina set down her glass. 'I can see Duncan coming over, we have to go. Look, you will come and say goodbye to me next week, won't you?'

'I can't, Lina, I'm working.'

Josie was watching Duncan, thinking how well he looked and how for the first time in months, his dark eyes were not those of a dead man, but bright and filled with feeling. Others were admiring his looks, too. Rena and Fay, Heather, and even Marie, devoted as she was to Colin, were all covertly studying him, probably wondering where Lina had found him. Duncan had become a 'catch' again, and for Lina's sake, Josie's heart was glad.

'There go the toffs,' commented Fergus, when Duncan and Lina had made their farewells and driven away. 'Now we can relax and get down to business. Where's your accordion, Sandy? Let's have a tune!'

'Duncan isn't a toff,' protested Josie. 'I mean, he's no' standoffish, he likes to join in.'

'Och, he's OK,' Fergus conceded. 'But folks like him who live on Easy Street have no' got much in common with the rest of us. I mean, never had to suffer, has he?'

'You don't know the half of it,' said Josie.

'What a fine girl, Josie is!' Duncan remarked, driving home. 'I think she could make a success of anything.'

'Yes, that's Josie.' A tear crawled down Lina's cheek. 'I'm going to miss her, Duncan.'

'I know. I'm sorry. Feel bad, you know, taking you away.'

'You have to do what's best.'

'If you really can't face London, you can always come back north.'

'I'm staying with you,' she said firmly. 'It won't be forever anyway.'

Duncan smiled broadly. 'Know something, Lina? You're a pretty fine girl, too. I want to tell you that. I want to thank you for standing by me, in the dark days.'

'Are they over?' she asked quietly.

'They're over. I'm really better. This job, with the chance to do something for the new bridge, it's made all the difference. Cheered me up. Maybe I'd have cheered up anyhow, but I feel it's done the trick. I'm myself again.'

'And that's what matters to me,' said Lina.

She knew going to London was a small price to pay for Duncan's health and was very willing to pay it. All the same, when the time came to say goodbye to Scotland, she could not put a good face on it and collapsed, sobbing, in her mother's arms.

'Come on, pet,' Kitty said, crying herself. 'You're only going to London, you'll be coming back on visits, and I'll be coming down.'

'Yes, but it'll no' be the same as just popping down the road to Queensferry, will it?'

'Well, try not to cry any more.' Kitty lowered her voice. 'Think of Duncan, Lina, don't upset him.'

Lina blew her nose and managed a smile for Duncan, waiting with his parents and April in her carry-cot.

'Sorry, darling, I'll be OK once we're on our way.'

'Wish you weren't going all the way by car,' murmured Erica. 'It's just too much for April, in this summer heat.'

'We'll be taking our time, staying overnight at a couple of places,' Duncan told her. 'We'll give you a ring as soon as we arrive, try not to worry.'

There were kisses and hugs. April was stowed away on the back seat of the car. Lina, with her handkerchief still to her eyes, took her place in the front.

'Get in touch with Angus soon as you can!' Kitty cried to Lina as Duncan turned the key in the ignition. 'He'll see you're all right down there, pet!'

'*I'll* see Lina's all right!' retorted Duncan. 'No need to worry about that. Goodbye, everybody, keep in touch!'

'Oh, dear,' sighed Erica, as the car was lost in traffic, making for the Mound and the road out of Edinburgh. 'I feel so lost. Would you like to come back for a cup of tea, Mrs Braid?'

'It's very kind of you but I'd better get back,' Kitty answered. 'I've the lads' tea to get.'

'We'll give you a lift to the station, then,' Andrew said, with his easy politeness. 'Sad, this leavetaking, eh? But we really do feel that Duncan's going to London will be for the best.'

'I hope so,' Kitty said, with a sniff, letting the Guthries see that it was her daughter's happiness at stake as well as their son's welfare. Then, looking at their downcast

252

faces, she relented. They would be missing little April just as much as she would. They would be missing their son.

'Thanks very much, I'd be glad of a lift,' she told Andrew. 'Och, they'll be fine down there, don't worry.'

Chapter Thirty-Eight

Property in London was scarce and rents very steep. Without the private income left him by his grandfather, Duncan probably wouldn't have been able to afford anything to suit Lina whose sights these days were high. Anyway, they had April to think of, and her nanny, they needed space and a garden, access to shops, easy commuting to the West End for Duncan. All of these they found in an Edwardian terraced house in Barnes, and within a surprisingly short space of time, had settled in. Lina was still homesick, was often unable to keep back tears as she wrote to her mother and Josie, but as exile went, she had to admit, hers was not too bad.

If only she'd had someone to go to the shops with! The shops were so wonderful in London, you could get absolutely anything, you could spend your life just looking, though Lina was keener on buying and as soon as she had unpacked was out, adding to her wardrobe and April's. Nothing gave her greater pleasure than to find pretty clothes for her baby daughter who gave every sign of becoming a beauty, although Lina's purchase for herself of a pair of the blue jeans that were all the rage was certainly exciting too. Imagine wearing these in Princes Street, she thought, struggling to get into them, for since having the baby and giving up smoking, she had put on several pounds. But she was pleased with her new image and when

Duncan came back from work, asked what he thought.

'You look gorgeous, you always do,' he told her fondly.

'But in these jeans, Duncan? You don't think they make me look too fat?'

'Let's see.' He turned her round. 'No, you look just right.'

She moved to loosen her hand from his, but he did not let go.

'Just right,' he repeated, catching his breath. 'Lina, where's April?'

'Valerie's taken her to the common.'

Valerie was the nanny, a cheerful young woman from Surrey, highly recommended and very experienced, Lina had made certain of that.

'How soon will they be back?'

'Fairly soon, I should think.'

'We might just have time, though?'

'Time?' A tremor ran through Lina as she looked into Duncan's dark eyes. It was so long since they'd had sex, so long since he'd looked at her in that hungry way, she'd almost forgotten the pleasure she'd had on her honeymoon in Paris. But the memory was coming back to her now.

'Time for what, Duncan?' she asked teasingly, and began to wriggle out of the new jeans.

'Please, let me help you,' he said, laughing at his own exquisite manners, and carried her to bed.

It was the final touch, Lina decided, all that she needed to make her as happy as she'd thought she be, that day she'd floated down the aisle to marry her catch.

Angus came frequently to visit. He was doing well in his pharmaceutical firm, and had acquired a small flat in Fulham. He also had a girl-friend, a graduate chemist named Tammy Harley. He asked if he might bring her for a meal one evening.

'I didn't know you had a girl-friend,' Lina said, narrowing her eyes.

'So? What do you want me to do? Live like a monk just because Josie turned me down?'

'No, of course not. It's just that I'm surprised, that's all.'

'I still don't know why. Josie's married, for God's sake!'

'And expecting,' said Lina.

Angus looked away. 'I didn't know that,' he said carefully. 'When's it due?'

'January. She's had to give up her teaching course.'

'Had to give up a lot, I expect, being married to Matt MacLeod.'

'Don't talk like that, Angus. Matt's turned out much better than everybody thought.'

Angus shrugged. 'Tell me when I can bring Tammy.'

Surprise, surprise, she's Josie's double, thought Lina, shaking Tammy Harley's hand. Only not quite so good-looking. Very pleasant, though, and very keen on Angus. Is he keen on her?

Lina hoped so. She was so happy herself, she wanted everyone else to be happy, too, especially Angus, her favourite brother. Why, even George was going steady with that girl from Bo'ness, her mother had written, it really was time Angus settled down. Almost purring with contentment, Lina served supper and decided to do all she could to further Tammy's cause.

They had reached the coffee stage, with Tammy appearing to hang on every word of Duncan's monologue on bridge engineering and Lina preparing the tray, when Angus strolled into the kitchen and sprang his surprise.

'Got a message for you,' he said quietly. 'Callum would like to see you again.'

Lina, spooning brown sugar into a bowl, stayed her hand and stood quite still. Her large eyes went to her brother's face.

'Angus, what are you talking about?'

'I'm not doing the talking, I'm just a messenger.'

256

'Well, I'm surprised that you should give me a message like that! You know I can't see Callum. Why should I want to? And why should he want to see me?'

'Well, you're in London now, he thought it was only friendly to get in touch. Why shouldn't you be friends, anyway? He's just being civilised.'

'Civilised? Lina filled the sugar bowl, set cups on a tray and filled a jug with cream while the coffee in the Cona bubbled away, filling the kitchen with a delicious smell. 'I don't know what's civilised about stirring up old feelings! You tell Callum I think it would be better if we didn't meet.' She hesitated. 'I'm sure he'll understand.'

'Thanks very much,' Angus said bitterly. 'That's a nice answer for me to give him, I must say. All he wants to do is to see you and make sure you're happy. You could at least give him that.'

'I'm no' giving him anything, Angus. Duncan's just recovered from a very serious illness, he's happy, I'm happy and I'm taking no risks. Do I have to spell it out for you?'

'No.' Angus hesitated. 'I'm sorry, Lina, I didn't think. Didn't think about Duncan. You're absolutely right, you can't see Callum. Just forget I said anything.'

'Hasn't he got a girl-friend yet?' Lina asked, slightly mollified. 'I mean, you've got Tammy. I should have thought Callum would've found someone by now.'

'Probably has. All he wanted was to be friendly, Lina. He got over all the old feeling long ago.'

'Thank God.' Lina switched off the coffee. 'If I bring this, will you take the cups?'

'Just one more thing.' Angus looked down into Lina's flushed face. 'How do you like Tammy, then?'

'Why, I think she's sweet!' Lina cried enthusiastically. 'A really nice girl. You like her, don't you?'

'Oh, yes, we get on fine.'

Is that the same thing? wondered Lina.

*

Valerie's days off were Sundays and Wednesday afternoons. Sundays were Duncan's special time for April, the day he played with her, wheeled her out in her pram while Lina prepared the lunch, even bathed her and helped put her to bed. Lina thought she had never seen anything so sweet as Duncan's tall figure stooped over the cot containing the small bundle that was April, as he sang to her and played her little music box until she fell asleep.

On Wednesday afternoons it was Lina's turn to take April out, sometimes to local shops, usually to the common, where she would find a bench and push the pram to and fro with one hand while she looked at the daily paper. Nothing much in it, apart from rumours about Princess Margaret wanting to marry some divorced Group Captain, and news of the forthcoming independent television channel. Duncan often worked late into the evening, he had no time for television, but he had rented a set for Lina who loved it. She knew the stars of all the panel games and all the announcers, admired their clothes, their cut-glass accents, the women's chandelier ear-rings, and was only too ready to take to advertising jingles and a whole new range of programmes on a commercial channel.

On the first Wednesday after Angus and Tammy had come for supper, she was on her favourite bench, rocking April in her pram as usual and reading yet another report about Princess Margaret, when a voice said, 'Hello, Lina.'

The breeze turned chill, her heart bounded in her breast, as she looked up into Callum Robb's narrow hazel eyes.

'Callum!' She threw her paper to one side. 'What are you doing here?'

'Came to talk to you.'

'You can't talk to me!' She looked around distractedly, as though she expected Duncan to appear from nowhere. 'Not here, with all these people—'

'Somewhere else, then?' He sat down on the bench next to her and bent his head to smile at dark-eyed April, steadfastly fighting sleep.

'No! Oh, look, Callum, can you no' see that this is awkward for me? How did you find me, anyway?'

'The baby's beautiful, Lina. The image of you.'

'How did you find me?' she asked again. 'Have you been watching ma house? Why aren't you at work?'

'Questions, questions ...' He sat back, with his arm along the back of the bench, and gave her an easy smile. She thought he was thinner, had not filled out as Angus had done, and was rather more handsome than she remembered. His leanness suited him, and he had lost the slightly foxy look that had always made him seem like a man on the make. Perhaps he had already made what he had set out to make, he looked prosperous enough.

'I'm on leave at present,' he went on, 'making arrangements to go to America to do a recce on motels. So you see, you needn't worry about seeing me, I won't be around.'

Lina, relaxing a little but still keeping a wary eye on him, began to jog April's pram again.

'You're like Angus, losing your Scottish accent,' she remarked. 'You'll soon sound like a Londoner.'

'Och, you're joking, I'll no' do that!' he cried, exaggerating his Scottishness. 'It's an asset, ma Scottish accent, makes folk think I'm a hard-working Presbyterian Scot!'

'Which you are. But tell me the truth, how did you know where to look for me?'

'Angus told me you had a nanny. I guessed she'd take the baby out in the afternoons. I also guessed she'd have an afternoon off and that would probably be mid-week. Got lucky today. Satisfied?'

'Why all the bother?' Lina cried desperately. 'I mean, why try to see me? There's no point!'

'We were close once. I still care about you. Maybe not the way I did—'

'Oh, I hope not!' Lina groaned. 'Have you no' found yourself a new girl, Callum?'

'I've been seeing one or two people. No one special.' He

259

looked down again at April and put his finger to his lips. 'You can stop rocking her, Lina, she's asleep.' He bent to put on the pram's brake. 'Can't get over you as a mother,' he said with a grin as she straightened up. 'Taken to it like a duck to the water, haven't you?'

'Callum, it's nice talking to you but I think I'll have to go now. Duncan's been ill, I don't want him upset.'

'Nobody wants to upset him.' Callum suddenly grasped her hand. 'All I want is to see you and part on better terms than the last time we met. It's been bad for me, Lina, remembering that meeting, the things I said.'

'You talked as though you hated me,' she said quietly. 'Later on – I mean, when I thought about it – I didn't blame you.'

'You hurt me so much, I just said what I could to make you feel as bad as I did.' Callum let go of her hand and sat staring into the dust around the bench. 'Since then, it's all sort of – festered. When I heard you were in London, I thought it was my chance to see you again and part friends. You want that, don't you?'

'Oh, yes! Yes, I do! Because it's been bad for me, too, Callum. I've never liked to think of that last time I saw you, I've always tried to push it to the back of ma mind.'

'OK, so I take back the things I said.' He raised his eyes from the ground to Lina's face. 'And you agree it was hard for me, what you did to me.' He put out his hand again. 'We're both forgiven?'

'Forgiven,' she answered solemnly, shaking his hand. 'Oh, Callum, I feel better about you, I really do!'

'That's good, that's what I wanted.' He stood up, glancing at his wrist watch. 'Shall we go back now?'

'Not to the house!' she said quickly.

'Don't worry, not to the house. Just to the end of your street. If that's all right?'

They walked slowly from the common, leaving behind other young mothers pushing prams, dogs straining on leashes, children throwing balls, old folk strolling. Though

260

there was nothing particular to mark out the people on the common as different from Scots, the landscape with figures seemed very English to Lina. Perhaps it was being with Callum again that made her think of home, and to remember that home was a long way away. Perhaps it was being with her made him feel the same, for he said softly,

'Thinking of the 'Ferry?'

Ah, that hurt! Only Queensferry people talked of the 'Ferry. Who in London would even know where it was?'

'I do get a bit homesick sometimes,' she answered, pausing with the pram as they reached the busy main street.

'We've come a long way, eh? Not just miles?'

'But I'll go back.'

'We'll never be able to go back, Lina. Not to the old days.' Callum's fierce gaze held her. 'But they'll always be there.' He tapped his red-gold head. 'In there. Safe.'

'Yes,' she whispered, mesmerised. 'Safe.'

'Now.' He relaxed a little. 'You'll be wanting to go home. Before you do, I want you to listen to me.'

'I've no' done much else today, Callum.'

He smiled faintly. 'I just want to say, if you ever need me, for any reason at all, I'll be there for you. Got that?'

'Thank you, Callum, it's very kind of you, but I'll be all right. Duncan's better now, you see, he's really better.'

Callum shook his head. 'Lina, he'll never be better.'

'Why do you say that? You don't even know him!'

'I've known people like him, judging by what Angus has told me. He may be all right now, but he'll be lucky if he stays that way.'

Lina stared down at her sleeping daughter, her eyes glazed with unshed tears. 'I don't know why you want to talk like that to me, Callum. Duncan is well and he's going to stay well. His firm is hoping to get part of the contract for the new Forth bridge, and he's working hard. He's happy.'

'OK, that's fine.' Callum put his hand on Lina's shoulder. 'I'm sorry if I've upset you. All I'm saying is, if

261

there's a time when you could do with a friend, I'll be that friend. Will you remember that?'

'I'll remember.'

He stopped to kiss her cheek. 'Good luck, then.'

'And to you, Callum.'

'Thanks.' He smiled faintly. 'Take care. And of that baby!'

'Have a good time in America!'

People were swirling around them, the traffic noise beating against them. There seemed nothing else to do but go their separate ways and not look back.

Chapter Thirty-Nine

Josie was annoyed with herself. She had always been so strong, so oblivious of 'women's' problems of any sort, the idea that she would not take pregnancy in her stride had never occurred to her. Yet, from the time she'd become aware that there was a baby on the way, she had never felt well, battling against sickness, weariness and, lately, high blood pressure. Her job at Lew's was due to finish at the end of October. She thought she might just make the deadline, but had no heart to do much else. Even to make love. Though she had not told Matt that yet.

'Aye, that bairn's taking it out of you,' Agnes remarked when Josie and Matt were round at Dow Street one Sunday afternoon. Matt had found work locally again and was also doing an engineering course at night-school to help him, he hoped, in the future. They had established a weekend routine like all the other MacLeods, of seeing the family at Ma's place. Exhausted as she was, Josie always enjoyed that.

'Taking it out of me? Sometimes I feel there's nothing left of me,' she answered. 'I don't know whether it's a boy or girl. All I know is, it's strong.'

'It's a boy,' said Heather. 'Och, anybody can see that.'

'How can you possibly tell?' asked Marie, with interest.

'Well, Josie's so neat and tidy, that's a sign.' Heather nodded sagely. 'You'll see. Me, I was all over the place,

big as a house-end and lumpy with it. What did we get, eh?
A girl!'

'I was the same,' said Gillie. 'No shape at all, and
Fergus all for wantin' a boy. I says to him, "Want away,
I'm no' carrying high, it's a girl." Aye, and it was, both
times!'

'And bonny girls they are too,' Agnes declared. 'What's
it matter what you get, as long as the bairn's all right?
Now, have some more lardy cake, Josie, get back that
strength the baby's taking away. Or another soda scone?
Put plenty of butter on, that's the ticket!'

'How are you, then?' Marie asked Josie, later, when they
could snatch a few moments together. 'You've got those
violet shadows under your eyes again.'

'Just feel so weary, Marie. Och, I'm a drag on everybody these days.'

'Come on, you're nothing of the sort! But when are you
coming over to us again? You've only been once and I
wanted to show you ma paintwork. I've painted everything
in sight!'

'I want to come, but you know how it is, with ma job and
all.'

Josie had enjoyed inspecting Marie's new home in one of
the 'good' districts of the city, knew how much it meant to
her, whose in-laws had finally done what Colin said they
would, and 'come round'. No doubt the painting had been
done in their honour. Certainly Marie had had to take time
off work to clean the place from top to bottom, the day they
first came for a meal.

'As soon as I've finished work, I'll be in touch,' Josie
promised.

'I'll hold you to that. You take care of yourself, OK?'

'Leave that to me,' said Matt, coming up to put his arm
around Josie's shoulders, and she leaned against him with a
little sigh of content.

But it was that same night in bed, when he tried to turn her

264

towards him, that she found she could no longer keep up her charade.

'I don't want to, Matt,' she whispered, lying rigid under his touch. 'I'm sorry.'

'Don't want to?' She could hear the smile in his voice. 'Come on, you always want to!'

'It's just the way I am at the moment, I can't help it.'

'But, Josie, it's only September, you've months to go. We can still make love!'

'No. I just – don't feel like it.' Into his silence, she said again, 'I'm sorry.'

After a few moments, he got out of bed and she heard him scrabbling on the dressing-table for his cigarettes. Then a match flared and she saw his handsome face illuminated, until he lit his cigarette and blew out the match.

'Is it just tonight?' he asked, sitting on the edge of the bed. 'You don't feel well tonight, is that it?'

'I never feel well!'

He put out a hand and gently caressed the shoulder she had turned from him. 'I'm sorry it's so bad, Josie. I'd go through it for you, if I could.'

She laughed. 'And I'd take you up on that, if I could.'

'But—' he hesitated '– I thought you liked making love with me.'

'I do! Och, you know I do, Matt! When have I ever said no before? It's only while I'm like this that I don't want it.'

'So, when will you want it? Like I say, there's months to go before the baby comes.'

She pressed her head against the pillow. 'I think – we'll just have to be patient.'

'Patient?' He drew on his cigarette. 'It's a bit hard on a chap, Josie. Asking that.'

'And what do you think it's like for me?' she flared.

There was a silence between them.

'I'll put the kettle on,' said Matt. 'Get you some tea, eh?'

'That'd be nice. Thank you.'

*

265

In the morning they faced each other over a snatched breakfast, neither wanting to look the other in the eye after their sleepless night. Josie cleared her throat.

'Matt, you do understand? I mean, about last night?'

'Yes,' he answered tonelessly. 'Don't worry about it.'

'Well, I do worry. I don't want to let you down.' Josie's dark-blue eyes were filled with misery. 'Look, tonight it might be better—'

'No.' Matt stood up, gulping hot tea. 'I've said I understand. Let's leave it, eh?' He kissed her cheek. 'Got to go.'

Long after he'd gone, she sat on, knowing she was already late for work, feeling too leaden, too sick at heart, to move. Finally, she stood up, cleared away, made their tumbled bed, and left the house. She felt she might have been one of those creations from the films Matt loved, one of those things that went through the motions of living but was not living at all. Except that inside she was suffering.

Somehow they got through the days that followed. September crawled by. Nothing in the outside world deflected Josie from her own troubles. She had been mildly upset when the BBC killed off Grace Archer from their wireless soap-opera on the opening night of commercial television, but not enough to grieve, as apparently half the nation did. As for the independent television channel itself, that held no interest for her as she and Matt were a long way away from affording television rental. Lina, however, wrote to say she was thrilled, it was so lovely having two channels to choose from!

If only I were Lina, thought Josie, for it seemed to her that Lina had come through her storms to summer again, while Josie was battling once more in the cold and the rain. It was not that Matt was showing anger or even coldness towards her, rather that she was so desolately aware that something had changed between them. Their love-making had been so freely joyous, so much wanted by both of them, it had made them seem as one. Suddenly, its support

266

had left them and they had fallen apart.

Josie knew that Matt blamed her, though he had never said so, but she blamed him too, for not understanding how she felt. He claimed to understand, he clearly didn't. Why couldn't he see that this was just a temporary difficulty that would soon be over? Instead, he was being so patient and long-suffering about her shortcomings, she felt like throwing something at him. And the worst of it was she had to bottle all her feelings up inside, for she could never, ever discuss a problem like this with anyone.

Och, we'll get through it, she told herself. We'll have to.

Matt was working hard at his evening classes, held in a local technical college. Most evenings, while Josie doggedly knitted matinée jackets and leggings, he would spread out books and diagrams, studying modern designs and the most recent techniques of bridge-building. Josie would glance at him covertly, feeling surprise at this new, studious side of him, taking the old pleasure in his handsomeness, then lowering her eyes to her work, because it pained her to look at him too long when they were at odds with each other.

Once he felt her gaze and raised his eyes before she had time to look away. She hastily rose and came over to him, asking him if she could see what he was studying.

'Sure.' He pushed the plans towards her. 'You can see that all the new designs are different from the rail bridge. Lighter, more stream-lined, sort of smoother.'

'Did you ever think you might like to be an engineer yourself, Matt?'

'Like Duncan Guthrie, you mean? Och, no. I don't pretend to have the brains.'

'You're clever enough, Matt!'

'With my hands. I'm not ashamed of that.'

'You're studying now, though.'

'Just for interest, see what might be needed when they get going with this new bridge. Mind – nobody's even

267

promised any cash to build it with yet.'

'It'll come, though?'

'Aye, it'll come. And then I'll want to be there.'

'Back in Queensferry?' Josie didn't know whether to let her heart rise or fall. To be back home would be one thing. To face her parents would be another. 'I'd come too?' she asked.

'It's years away, Josie. No point in thinking of it now.'

That had been a pleasant little exchange, Josie reflected, as she heated her usual night-time milk, but it hadn't meant much. When they were lying side by side in bed that night, they were still strangers. She longed to turn and take Matt in her arms, knew it was all he wanted, yet somehow couldn't do it. Oh, God. Her eyes, staring into the darkness, seemed filled with grit, and now she longed to cry yet couldn't. Again, Matt got up and smoked a cigarette, and she waited for him. When he came back, she held her breath, but he made no move.

''night, Josie,' he said calmly.

'Goodnight, Matt.'

It was amazing that they did both sleep, in the end.

Chapter Forty

It was growing colder. Josie had taken to lighting the range in the living room, which meant more work – fuelling, riddling, cleaning out – but kept at least one room warm and gave hot water. In the evenings she liked to sit beside it with her knitting or her library book, just as she'd done back at Ardmore, sometimes opening out the damper to get a good blaze up, feeling as warm as a cat by a hearth, if not as contented.

It seemed to her that she was too often alone on these evenings. Matt was no longer spending time on his books and diagrams, he was always out. If not at his class – and he was always late back from that – he was attending union or Labour Party meetings, activities he'd always ignored before, or going for a drink with his mates, or watching football. Anything rather than be at home it appeared. Could that be true? Was he actually trying to avoid her? Even when he was at home, his eyes never seemed to meet hers. When she talked, he answered, but he rarely began a conversation. Most of the time, all she saw of him was his yellow head bent over a book or newspaper.

A great fear began to possess her. What was happening? Had he fallen out of love because she hadn't felt up to having sex? What sort of love was that? Her fear turned to anger. What right had he to treat her this way, when he knew the situation, knew how deeply she loved him? Her fear returned. If he no longer loved her, he wouldn't care how much she loved him.

Why don't you tackle him? she asked herself. Have it out with him, once and for all?

She hadn't the courage. Not just now. It was better to say nothing and not be sure, than to speak and be told the truth. The old text came back to her. 'The Path of the Just is as the Shining Light'. Hadn't she always tried to be just? Where was the light, then, in her darkness? She felt there would always be darkness, if she couldn't face the truth.

At the end of October, she finished her work at the dry-cleaner's and Lew said he'd never been so sorry about anything, there would be a place there for her whenever she wanted it. They both knew it was unlikely she would ever come back, but she kissed his cheek and hugged little Ailie who had come in with Iona to say goodbye.

'Och, hen, I don't know what we're going to do without you,' Iona told her. 'Lew'll be up the wall if I try and help out so we'll have to advertise, eh? Ailie, go get the flowers for Auntie Josie, now!'

'Oh, Iona, you shouldn't have,' Josie murmured, blushing over the handsome carnations Ailie pushed delightedly into her arms.

'A wee thank you,' said Iona, smiling with Matt's eyes. 'That brother of mine's a lucky guy to have you, Josie. You take care now, and put your feet up. Let Matt do the chores.'

'Ha, that'll be the day!' Lew said with a laugh. 'Chores and your brothers, Iona, no' exactly go together!'

'I'm going to miss you both,' Josie told them, 'but I'll see you at Ma's, eh?'

'See you at Ma's!' echoed Iona. 'Listen, did you hear the news? Princess Margaret's no' going to marry that Group Captain. Shame, eh?'

'Well, he is a divorced man,' said Lew, 'I mean, her

270

folks'd never settle for that. Remember that Mrs Simpson and King Edward?'

'Why don't they just run away?' asked Josie. 'I would.'

'So would I!' cried Iona.

But on the way home, Josie wondered. To give up everything for love – was it worth it? Only if love lasted.

Matt surprised her by coming home early one day in late-November and asking her if she'd like to go to a dance?

'Oh, Matt, how can I?'

She was much heavier now and had been given strict instructions by the doctor to rest as much as possible.

'I didn't mean you to dance, thought you could just come and watch. It's a do Ken's organising to raise money for a children's charity. Some time in December.'

'You go, then. I don't mind.'

'I wouldn't want to leave you on your own.'

Josie smiled wryly. As though she wasn't used to that!

'I've told you, I don't mind. Go on, you'll enjoy it.'

'If you're sure? I'll get a ticket, then. I needn't stay long.'

'I expect you'll see Rena there. She'll go anywhere to dance.'

'Well, if I do, I won't dance with her.'

Josie bit her lip. 'I'm sorry I made you promise that, Matt. It was childish of me.'

He gave her a quick glance. 'So, I have your permission to dance with Rena?'

'Yes, why not? She's all right.'

It was true that the idea of Rena as a threat had quite receded from Josie's mind. She and Fay were hardly ever seen, apart from dashing off to work or hurrying back with a parcel of fish and chips, or a loaf of bread and bottle of milk. They got on with their lives, as the rest of the tenants in Piper Street got on with theirs. No one went in for 'dropping in' much, though Josie guessed that she might get to know those with young children rather better after her own

271

baby was born. There was a nice young woman across the way who had a boy a year old. Might ask her over for a cup of tea later on, thought Josie, trying to imagine a life after January the eighteenth, and not really succeeding. Anyway, she was pleased with herself, the way she had handled Matt's dance idea. When he appeared, all spruced up and ready to go on that chill December night, she kissed him goodbye and felt again that she was doing well. Showing maturity and self-control, not a bit of jealousy at all.

It was only when she woke up in her chair after midnight, realising that the range was out and that Matt had not come home, that the old passion began to rise from the depths where she had buried it. She stood up, shivering with the cold, bracing herself to make the effort to get ready for bed.

There was no reason why Matt should be home, she told herself. It was a dance. It would go on late. But, 'I needn't stay long,' he had said. There was only one reason why he should stay, then. Because he was having a good time, had found a good partner, had found Rena Cameron.

Oh, God. Josie shrugged herself into her dressing-gown and with trembling hands filled the kettle to make tea. She pictured Matt dancing with Rena as she had seen them dancing together before. She remembered how she'd felt then, though at the time she'd had nothing to fear. Matt had loved her. How different things were now! She was big and ugly, she had repulsed him in bed, it was almost certain that his love had died. What happened if a man who didn't love his wife danced with another woman all evening? Did they just say goodnight and go home? Or what? What did they do?

Josie drank the tea she'd made, her teeth chattering against the cup, knowing she must somehow calm herself, for the sake of the baby if not for herself, but unable to close her mind to the images burning there.

The outside door slammed. You could always hear that.

272

Always hear when someone came in.

She ran to her own front door and threw it open.

'Matt?' she whispered.

There were two people on the stair, wrapped in each other's arms, the woman dark, the man fair, as Josie could see in the light that shone all night.

'Matt!' she shrieked, and Rena Cameron turned round, her brows bent with irritation.

'What's wrong, Josie?' she asked coldly, and Josie, sagged against her door. She could say nothing. The young man with the fair hair wasn't Matt. She didn't know who he was, and didn't care, as the relief flowed through her veins like wine.

'I'm sorry,' she finally stammered. 'I was just looking for Matt.'

'Well, I don't know where he is!' Rena put her hand on the young man's arm. 'This is a friend of mine – Scott Elder. Scott, this is Josie MacLeod.'

'Hi,' said Scott affably. 'Didny mean to disturb you.'

'That's all right.'

As Josie began to withdraw, Rena called to her.

'Did see Matt at the dance, but he left early.'

'Early?'

'Aye. He had a dance with me and then with Fay, then I didny see him again.'

'Where's Fay now?' cried Josie, her mind racing. Was it Fay, then? Was it Fay she had to fear?

'Och, she's on the stair!' cried Rena. 'Why is everybody out o' their flats tonight?'

'Is that you, Rena? came Fay's voice, and Fay herself appeared, still dressed but with a towel in her hand. 'I was wondering where you were.'

'For God's sake! Can a body no' do what she likes in this day and age?' Rena put her hand on Scott's back and pushed him up the stair. 'Move yourself, Fay, we're coming up for a coffee. Goodnight, Josie!'

'Are you all right, Josie?' Fay asked kindly, peering at

her in the shadows cast by the harsh light on the stair.

'Fine.' Josie laughed lightheadedly. 'I'm just wondering where Matt can be.'

'He's probably gone for a drink with his mates. I'd no' worry.'

'Oh, I'm no' worrying. Goodnight, Fay.'

But when Fay had gone on up the stair, Josie moved stiffly to the front door. She had heard a car stopping. A taxi, mebbe. Matt might have gone somewhere, drunk too much, taken a taxi – he never took taxis. She opened the door, oblivious of the cold night air cutting through her dressing-gown like a knife, and stood looking out into Piper Street. There was a car. Quite a smart one, long and black, or maybe it just looked black under the street lamp. The man who was about to get out of it, though, had fair hair. Yes, that could clearly be seen. And the woman who was leaning from the driving seat, clinging to his hand, had fair hair too. Didn't look much like her brother, did she, Duncan Guthrie's sister?

Chapter Forty-One

'What you have to understand, Josie,' Antonia declared, speaking in a tight, strangulated voice, as though someone were taking the life out of her, 'is that I was only giving Matt a lift.'

They were sitting, the three of them, around the cold range in Josie's living room. Josie was not aware that she had invited Antonia Fearn into the house, but here she was, balanced on the edge of one of the landlord's chairs, her face yellowish-white, her blue eyes defiant.

'So, you see,' she finished, breathing hard, 'this isn't what it looks like.'

Josie turned her head to look at Matt. His arms were folded, his eyes cast down. She wanted to go to him, force him to look up into her face, but she did not move.

'I think it's exactly what it looks like!' she cried, sounding strange and shrill, even to herself. 'You weren't just giving Matt a lift, Antonia. I saw you, I saw you take his hand. You'd been together, hadn't you? I could tell, I could tell!'

For a moment, Antonia was silent.

'I shouldn't have come to the door,' she said at last. 'That was stupid. Why did I drive to the door?'

'Where had you been?' asked Josie. 'Tell me where you'd been. Did you go from the dance to meet her, Matt? Tell me!'

275

He finally raised his heavy-lidded eyes.

'Antonia was at the dance,' he answered in the soft, melodious voice that had charmed Josie from the beginning. She marvelled that it was still the same, when so much else had changed. 'She was going to write a piece about it. A feature, she called it.'

'That's right, for the paper.' Antonia's thin hands fumbled with her bag and she took out a cigarette and lit it. 'You didn't know I was on a Glasgow paper, did you, Josie? Or did I tell you at the christening? That's where I met Matt, don't you remember?'

'And then you met him again,' Josie said drearily. 'But not at that dance. Don't tell me any more.'

But Antonia went on talking, as though she could not stop, as though silence could not be borne.

'I had to go to the technical college – I'd been invited to talk on journalism. I saw Matt coming out of his class one evening and asked him to go for a drink with me. It was quite harmless, Josie, there was nothing wrong in it, nothing wrong, I assure you ...' Her voice trailed away. She bent her head, the cigarette in her hand sending pale blue smoke into her fair hair. When she looked up, her eyes were full of tears.

'What can I say?' she whispered. 'I wish I were dead. What my husband did to me, I've done to you, Josie. I'm not making any excuses. There aren't any. I fell in love, that's all. Like a bloody schoolgirl. Only I'm not a schoolgirl. You can blame me, if you like. Matt would never have thought of it.'

'Wouldn't he?' asked Josie. 'Why, I think you were the answer to a prayer.'

For the first time the blood rushed to Matt's face, but Antonia was shaking her head.

'He would never have asked me. I asked him. I wanted him, because I loved him. That's all I can say. I'm sorry.'

'Don't apologise,' Josie said flatly. 'Everybody loves Matt.'

He got up and stood with his arms folded again, looking at no one.

'Perhaps I'd better go,' Antonia said, grinding out her cigarette on the range. 'But how can I go?' She looked helplessly around her, rubbing her arms and shuddering. 'How cold it is in here! Couldn't you put a fire on, Josie? I'm sure it's not good for you to be cold. Couldn't I make you some coffee or something? Get you a drink?'

From the wreckage of her character, her self-esteem, her assured place in her world, Antonia was trying to salvage all her mother's training in civilised behaviour. Give in to passion, destroy a woman's marriage, feel sick with self-loathing? What about a cup of coffee, then? Or a nice gin and tonic?

'Will you go?' Matt asked her politely. 'Will you leave us alone?'

It did seem very cold in the room after Antonia had gone. Matt went into the bedroom and came back with a blanket that he put round Josie's shoulders.

'Oh, don't!' she cried. 'Don't.'

'I'm going to make you some tea.'

'I don't want any tea.'

'You have to have something.'

She shrugged, and he brought tea on a tray and a tin of biscuits. The first night of her honeymoon came back to her. Eating biscuits under the bedclothes with Matt, giggling like a couple of bairns. As she took a digestive, satisfying surprising hunger, she thought she would surely cry, but she didn't cry. People said when you lost a limb, you didn't feel anything at first. Matt was like a limb, then. Amputated from her, by Antonia's knife. Would she feel anything tomorrow?

'Do you love her?' she asked, drinking her tea.

Matt's eyes widened. He seemed bewildered by her question.

'You know I do not!'

277

'You just used her, was that it?'

'It wasn't like that. She – well, she caught me at a bad time.'

'You're saying what happened was my fault?'

'No, I'm to blame, I'm not making excuses.'

'Sounds to me as though you are. If I hadn't said no to you, you'd have said no to her?'

'Listen, Josie, please listen, it was just one of those things. I never meant it to happen, I hate myself for letting it happen, but it's over, it's all over, it'll never happen again. Can you just remember that?'

'I think I'll go to bed now,' she said, rising and trailing the blanket towards the door. 'Will you sleep there?' She pointed to the couch.

'Don't think I'll sleep,' said Matt.

In the morning, the pain began. A terrible pain around Josie's heart. And now she was seized with ferocious curiosity. She wanted to know everything about Matt's affair with Antonia: where they had made love, how they had made love, whether he had found her good in bed. As good as me, me, me? she wanted to shriek at him. But she said nothing. She set his breakfast before him without a word, and when he caught at her hands, she pulled them away and went to sit opposite him, still without speaking.

'Josie, will you listen to me?' he cried. His dark grey eyes were anguished. 'I don't love Antonia Fearn. OK, I was attracted to her, and when she asked me to her place, I was – well – flattered, I suppose. I mean, Mr Guthrie's sister ...'

'And an attractive woman,' said Josie.

'But I didn't love her,' he said eagerly. 'Don't you see that, Josie? That's what I'm trying to explain. She meant nothing to me, nothing at all. You've no need to worry!'

No need to worry? Oh, God. It seemed to Josie that with every word he spoke, Matt was moving farther away from her. She wanted to put out her hands, hold him, hold on to the Matt she had married, but he was no longer there. Had he ever been there? It was true that other people had seen something different from what she had seen. Had she imagined him, gentleness, beauty, golden aura and all? It seemed to her that he was still handsome, still gentle, but there was no longer any golden aura. That had gone for good.

'Can't you see,' she said at last, 'that if you had loved Antonia, I might have understood better?'

'Better?' he asked blankly. 'That's crazy. You'd never have forgiven me if I'd fallen for somebody else, Josie!'

'I'm not forgiving you now, Matt.'

A look of alarm spread across his features, and she saw with painful satisfaction that she had for once shattered his calm.

'For God's sake, Josie—' he began.

She interrupted. 'You're just what everybody said you were, Matt, only I didn't believe them. Don't let's talk any more.'

He followed her to the bedroom where she was getting ready to go out.

'What are you going to do?' he asked huskily.

'I'm going to the hospital. It's ma ante-natal day.'

'You know what I mean, Josie.'

'I don't know, I can't say.'

'You're not going to leave me?'

She turned her fine, stormy eyes on him. 'I've said I don't know what I'm going to do. Will you excuse me? I have to go for the tram, don't want to be late.'

When Matt came home from work that evening, feeling quite unreal, he found everything in the flat as neat as a pin, his tea all ready and his mother waiting.

'What is it?' he cried, turning white. 'Where's Josie? What's wrong?'

'Now, you're not to worry, Matt,' Agnes began soothingly, 'but Josie's been kept in at the hospital for a wee

279

while. It's her blood pressure, they want her to have complete bed rest.'

'I'll go to her—'

'No, no, sit down, they'll not let you in, it's out o' visiting hours.' Agnes put his plate in front of him. 'Go when you've had your tea, eh?'

He sat down, staring at the food he felt he could not eat.

'Is she very ill?' he asked dully.

'No, no, it's just one o' those things that can happen. Complications. It's no wonder she's not been feeling well, poor lassie. Now eat up, Matt, don't let it get cold.' Agnes moved the salt cellar to and fro. 'The thing is, they might be bringing the baby on. You might be a father sooner than you think.'

Chapter Forty-Two

Josie's baby was born two days later, a fine healthy boy, over five pounds in weight though five weeks early.

'Ma first grandson,' Agnes said softly, visiting Josie one afternoon. 'Och, I'm that proud!'

'I wanted a girl,' said Josie.

Agnes gave her an intelligent look. No one had told her but she didn't need telling, that there was something wrong between Matt and Josie. They were more like a couple of strangers confronting each other than man and wife, and new parents at that. Even the sight of their son seemed to bring no joy, and though Josie looked well and said she felt better than she'd felt in months, there was none of the radiance of the new mother in her face. Oh, what's happened? groaned Agnes. Had some woman been after Matt? Had he not said no? Josie, Josie, you'll have to manage him better than this.

'You're no' saying you don't want the boy?' she asked anxiously. She'd heard of some women turning against their babies, though could never imagine it.

'Of course I want him,' Josie answered, sliding out of bed and tying her dressing-gown round her newly returned waist. She sank into the armchair at her bedside and put back her thick cloud of hair that seemed suddenly to have grown. 'I expect I'll get used to him.'

Agnes sighed and looked around the long ward filled

with new mothers all looking so proud and content as they chatted to their visitors, it made her heart ache. Oh, wait till I see Matt! she thought. But what could she do? She couldn't interfere, had kept her hold on her family by not interfering, letting them sort things out for themselves. Would Matt and Josie be able to sort things out, though? She wasn't too sure.

'I'd better go, pet,' she told Josie, rising. 'Matt'll be along when he's finished work. His flowers are lovely, eh?'

Josie's eyes went to the dark red chrysanthemums by her bed. There were also carnations and mixed bunches from the MacLeods, a basket of fruit from Marie, and a huge bouquet from Lina and Duncan.

'I've done very well,' Josie said obliquely. 'Everyone's been very kind.'

'There's something else,' Agnes said hesitantly. 'You might be having another visitor soon.'

Josie lay back in her chair. 'Who?' she asked without interest.

'I'd better not say, just in case.'

'Why all the mystery?'

'Wait and see.' Agnes kissed Josie's brow. 'It's grand to see you looking so well, pet. Nice to have it over, eh?'

When Agnes had left her, Josie closed her eyes. She really didn't want Matt to visit her, but without a complete and obvious break, would have to make a pretence of being pleased to see him. What we go through, not to lose face, she thought. To have the other women in the ward learning the true state of things between herself and her husband was not to be endured.

'Josie?' a voice said softly.

She opened her eyes, was back for a moment in Ardmore, dreaming that her mother was there, looking at her. Oh, poor Mum, she seemed so anxious, wasn't smiling. She had a bunch of flowers in her hand. Where am I, then? asked Josie.

'Mum?' she whispered.

'Oh, Josie,' said Ellie, and burst into tears.

It seemed it was Agnes who had written to Ellie to give her the news of the baby, a kind little letter that had touched her heart.

'Oh, but why did you no' let me know, Josie?' she cried, laying down her flowers. 'Having a bairn, and no' telling me? And being so bad, and me no' even knowing!'

'Mum, I was going to tell you, I was going to write at Christmas, he wasn't due till January.'

'I could've come over, I could've helped—'

'Mum, you wouldn't even meet me, would you? Why should I think you'd come over and help?'

Ellie lowered her eyes. 'You know how it is for me, Josie. Your dad's no' changed and he's been ill, I was no' keen to cross him.'

'Does he know about the baby?'

'Aye, I told him this time I'd made up ma mind to see you, and he did say he hoped you were all right. He did say that, Josie.'

She laughed. 'Very kind of him, I'm sure.' She leaned forward and took her mother's hands. 'Let's no' talk about him, I just want to look at you, see how you are.'

'There's nothing wrong with me, it's you I'm worried about.'

Mother and daughter studied each other. To Josie's eyes, Ellie seemed thinner and more worn, as though life were gradually wearing her away, but she tactfully made no comment. Ellie thought Josie looked quite surprisingly well, and said so.

'But what are you doing out of bed? she demanded. 'When I had you, I didn't put a foot to the floor for days.'

'Och, they've different ideas now. We all get up, we go to the nursery to feed the babies, we're always on the move.'

'Fancy! Well, I just hope they know what they're doing. Josie, can I see him? Can I see the boy?'

'They'll no' let you into the nursery, but you can see

283

through the glass. I'll take you along, shall I?'

'No, no, you stay where you are. I'll get one o' the nurses to show him to me before I go. But who's he like, Josie? And what's his name?'

'I haven't decided on a name yet,' she answered reluctantly. 'And he doesn't look like anybody.'

Liar, she told herself, he looks like Matt.

'Is everything all right, Josie?' Ellie asked, her gaze still intent on her daughter's face. 'You seem a bit down. No' got these baby-blues you hear about nowadays?'

'No, I feel well, really well.'

'So, how's Matt, then?'

Josie opened her mouth to say, 'He's fine, he's well, he's OK,' or something, anything, to stop her mother looking at her in that suspicious way, but she still had brought no words out when a nurse at the end of the ward rang a bell. It was the end of afternoon visiting time.

'Will you come again, Mum?' Josie asked, hanging on to her mother's hand. 'Will you come to ma flat when I get out of here? Will you come to the christening?'

'You're having the baby christened?'

'Of course. Matt's agreeable.' Josie set her jaw firmly. 'Wouldn't matter if he wasn't.'

Something flickered in Ellie's pale blue eyes, but she only said she would certainly come to the christening, and to see Josie at home.

'Tell me when they let you out, Josie, and I'll come over. And I'll start knitting for the wean soon as I get back. A pram set, mebbe. It's winter, he'll need to be well wrapped up.' Ellie rustled in her bag and took out a package. 'But this is for now.'

'Why, Mum!' Josie unwrapped a small, wooden rattle. Her eyes shone. 'Oh, it's mine! It's the rattle Gran gave me. Oh, Mum, thank you!'

'I thought you'd like it,' Ellie said, blowing her nose. 'I remember ma mother buying that for you, as if it was yesterday.'

'I'll take care of it, Mum, I'll keep it, just like you did.'

'Let the wean have it first.' Ellie looked round. 'Now I want to see ma grandson. Where do I find this nursery?'

Later, when she had fed and changed her son and laid him back in his hospital crib, Josie stood looking down at him. There he lay, as good as gold, snuffling contentedly, the miniature Matt. What damage would he do when he grew up? How many hearts would he break? She took her old rattle from the pocket of her dressing-gown and as the baby opened his eyes, shook it gently. Of course, it was silly to do that, he couldn't see properly yet and with all the noise of roaring babies around him, wouldn't be able to hear either. Yet it seemed to her that he was smiling.

A young nurse came with a pile of clean baby clothes over her arm and leaned over the crib.

'Och, what a charmer, eh?' she cried. 'Talk about bonny!'

'Would you say he was smiling?' asked Josie.

'They say it's wind, but mebbe he is. Looks happy enough.'

'Are you a charmer?' Josie asked, when the nurse had gone on her way. 'Oh, don't be! Don't be a charmer!'

She leaned over and swept the baby up again, laid him over her shoulder, patted his back and pressed her cheek against his. I expect I'll get used to him, she had told Matt's mother. Another lie. She was already used to him. She was going to be used to him for all his life and hers, whether or not he was Matt's son. He couldn't help that, any more than he could help not being a daughter. As she laid him down again and watched his eyelids fluttering in first sleep, she made a promise she would never again compare him with his father. Why, who knew how he would turn out? He might even be like me, thought Josie. On her way back to the ward, it came to her that she too had once broken someone's heart.

Standing at her bed, when she got back to it, was Matt.

285

His face had the same closed expression it had taken on when she told him she couldn't forgive him, but his manner was calm and reasonable. She guessed he was making excuses for her. Women didn't always see things straight when they'd just had babies.

'Hello, Josie,' he said quietly. 'Have you been with the boy?'

'Where else?'

She took off her dressing-gown and got into bed, looking away from Matt but aware that his eyes were warily following her every move.

'I've brought you some tablet,' he told her.

'Oh, good! I'm starving, always am.' Josie tore off the wrapper and bit into the creamy candy. 'Do you want a bit of this?'

'No, thanks. How – how's the baby, then?'

'Thriving. Aren't you going along to see him?'

'Of course I am, wanted to see you first.'

'Well, you've seen me.' Josie lay back, looking down the ward at the mothers returning from the nursery being greeted by their husbands. She put the bar of tablet aside, feeling she had lost her appetite.

'Josie—'

'Yes?'

'What are we going to do? I mean, we have the baby now, we have to think of him.'

She nodded. 'Justin.'

'Justin?' Matt looked aghast. 'You're going to call him Justin? What sort of a name is that?'

'Don't you like it? I've finally decided on it.'

'It's not a Scottish name, it's not a family name.'

'It's a name I want him to have.'

'Why? I don't understand.'

Josie shrugged. Justin meant just, but Matt had never seen the text in her old room, she didn't expect him to understand.

'I had the baby, I choose his name.'

'All right. If that's what you want.'

For some time they were both silent. Matt reached out and took Josie's hand. She let it lie for a moment, then removed it.

'What are we going to do?' he asked again. 'Seemingly, you're never going to love me again.'

'Oh, that's not true, Matt. I think I'll always love you, in a way.' Josie smiled thinly. 'I just don't trust you, that's all.'

His shoulders sagged, he looked away.

'Can't—' He cleared his throat. 'Can't blame you for that.'

'Well, what is it you want, then?'

'You know what I want.'

'Us to be the same as before? We'll never be that.'

'I can't live without you, Josie. I want you to take me back.'

'If things had been different—'

'What things?'

'If I hadn't had the baby – if I'd done ma course—' She moved her head restlessly. 'I could've been independent.'

'You'd rather be on your own?' he asked, and the bewilderment was back in his eyes.

'Why do you find that so hard to believe? Plenty of women manage on their own.'

'You're going to do that? Josie, what about the baby?'

'Oh, you've no need to worry. I'm no' independent, I'll just have to do what other women do. Put up with what I've got. Settle for what's there.' Josie ran her fingers along the hem of her hospital sheet. 'Not what I thought was there.'

'Josie,' Matt said quietly, 'I'm sorry. I'm sorry for what I've done to you. You have to believe me, I didn't think – what I did – was going to wreck our marriage.' He took her hand again. 'It'll never happen again, I promise you.'

She took a breath, asked what had to be asked. 'Has it happened before?'

287

'Before? For God's sake, when would it have happened before?'

'When you were away.'

'Josie, I swear there's never been anything like this before. You have to believe that!'

Did she? Could she? His eyes, limpid, honest, met hers, but hers wavered and fell. She didn't know if she could believe him.

'And it'll never happen again,' he pressed, and bent his head to kiss her hand. 'Say you'll believe that, Josie, please?'

'I want to,' she answered.

He released her hand.

'Better go and see the boy,' he whispered. 'Be right back.'

When he had gone, Josie lay staring out of the ward windows. No one had closed the curtains, she could see the black night sky and the first stars appearing. It was December, would soon be Christmas. Justin's first Christmas. He wouldn't know anything about it, but he would have a stocking and little presents. He would be with both his parents, and that was the best you could say about the situation. They were picking up the pieces, she and Matt. That was what you had to do when something was broken. It might be as good as new, it might not. You'd always wish it hadn't been broken in the first place.

A nurse came along and closed the curtains. The night sky vanished, and with it, the stars.

Part Four

Chapter Forty-Three

Life went on. Josie did what she'd said she would do. Picked up the pieces. Accepted what she had. Sometimes she despised herself for a doormat. Maybe she should have just walked out. She knew she couldn't have done that. Maybe if she'd had her own family to turn to she might have tried it, but she was alone, and she'd had to think of Justin. Justin, who was the light of her life, who'd been joined in June, 1957, by a second light, his sister, Catriona, born for his sake. In their particular circumstances, Josie and Matt would have preferred not to have another child, but Josie, an only child herself, remembered how it had been for her and did not want the same for Justin. If it meant pushing her teacher-training even further away, so be it. Josie didn't see herself ever making it to college, anyway.

Justin was a 'yellow-yin', a true MacLeod, the image of his father, yet with his mother's steady dark-blue eyes that made her think a part of him was hers. As for little Trina, she was her grandmother all over again, and that was not Agnes, but Ellie, who was in raptures as soon as she realised the likeness. Och, she would never be dead, she declared, as long as this one was alive. But as she cuddled her granddaughter, she did not forget to hug her grandson too, for as Agnes did, she adored them both. It suited her very well that Matt should be so often away, for when she came over to visit, that meant she needn't see him. It suited

Matt and Josie, too. It was easier to pretend that everything was the same for them, when they were apart.

Josie never asked about Matt's life away, though she knew he took lodgings near whichever bridge he was working on, sometimes sharing with Ken or other men, sometimes not. In the early days she had schooled herself not to think about him with other women. Now she found it easier not to think of him at all. When he came home, they made the effort to get on. Made love quietly, as a kind of habit, didn't talk about the past. All the pieces of their shattered lives appeared to have fitted nicely into place. Whether they fooled Ma, or Marie, or Ellie, Josie didn't know. Nothing was said, but then having the second baby was an excellent smoke-screen.

In those last years of the 1950s, there was a general feeling in Britain that things were changing for the better. After all, it was a long time since the war, there'd been time to improve housing and living conditions, and unemployment was low. But folk in Glasgow weren't so hopeful. There were plans galore for improvements, and no doubt they would produce results in the sixties, but at present there was still too much sub-standard housing and too little money. Not many in the city's poorer tenements would have agreed with the Prime Minister, Harold Macmillan, when he told the British people in the 1959 election that they'd 'never had it so good'. But the average British person, of course, didn't have to worry about Glasgow's slum clearance, or the decline of shipbuilding. 'Supermac' won his election for the Tories with a handsome majority.

'Och, it'd be enough to drive me to drink,' groaned Ken Pearce. 'If I hadny been driven to it already!'

Earlier than that, though, he'd had something to celebrate, and so had Matt. In September, 1958, they had both been successful in the interviews for the workforce to build the new Forth road bridge. It meant a five-year contract with good wages. Ken said he couldn't believe their luck.

'Not all luck,' Matt commented mildly. 'We've got the experience.'

'No' for a cable bridge, Matt. We'll need retraining.'

This was true, but Matt's point was that men such as himself and Ken had the general experience to show that they could learn the new techniques. Matt had in fact been thinking about the road bridge for years, as his attendance at the fateful evening classes had proved. As soon as he'd heard, in 1956, that it was to be a cable suspension bridge, he had done his best to make himself familiar with the theory of that design. Now he was looking forward to working with its practical application.

'But you won't want to come with me now, will you?' he asked Josie, when he told her about his bridge job. 'I mean, to live in Queensferry?'

'Won't I?' asked Josie.

'There's no need, anyway. I can come home at weekends, like I did before.'

'For five years?' asked Josie. 'You wouldn't want to do that.'

'It's what I do anyway,' he said quietly. 'And it's what Ken's going to do.'

But his wife Millie Pearce's home was not Queensferry.

'I've always thought I would go back,' Josie said slowly. 'I know it's what Mum wants.'

'It's what you want that counts, Josie.'

Their eyes met. There was a time when separation would not have been an option. Now, it seemed, it was the prop of their marriage. Yet Josie was havering. Her old home beckoned, she would be back with the sky and the space she had always loved. As for the old wound of her father's rejection ... was this her chance to make that wound heal?

'I'll go,' she said with decision. 'I think I should.'

Again, her eyes met Matt's. She couldn't tell if he was pleased or not.

'When will we have to leave?'

'Probably not till next summer. They've started work on

clearing the sites on the banks, but they've only just awarded the main contracts.'

'I know that. I told you about Duncan's firm.'

'Aye, what I'm saying is, there'll be a hell of a lot to do before the real work begins.'

'I'll be near Lina again,' Josie murmured, thinking of the changes ahead. 'Duncan's sold that flat he had. They're going to be looking for a place with a garden, for April and the baby.'

Lina's second daughter, Dawn, had been born in the summer of 1958, and Josie and the children had gone down by train to stay with her some weeks after the birth. Lina was fine, but Duncan, though he controlled it well, was on tenterhooks over his firm's application for the contract for the road bridge. Lina, refusing to worry with him, said as soon as he heard that Mer-Civic was successful, he'd be fine.

'But supposing they're not successful?' asked Josie.

'I'm no' even considering it,' Lina answered.

There was tremendous relief, nevertheless, when Duncan came home one August afternoon with a bottle of champagne. The Secretary of State for Scotland had announced the awards of the main contracts for the road bridge. One company would be responsible for the foundations; another, made up of several famous firms, would build the superstructure. Mer-Civic was to be one of the collaborating firms. Duncan would be returning to the Edinburgh office as soon as possible.

'Oh, Duncan, that's wonderful!' Lina had cried, allowing herself, as a nursing mother, just a sip of champagne. 'Josie, do you hear? We're going back to Edinburgh!'

But as Josie smiled and Duncan filled her glass, a tiny frown appeared on Lina's brow.

'You won't be working on the bridge itself, Duncan? You've told them, haven't you, you won't be working on the bridge?'

'I'll be on the site. Can't build a bridge from the drawing-board.'

'But not up high?' pressed Lina. 'You won't be working over the water?'

'If you don't want me to, I won't,' he said shortly. 'But why can't you believe I'd be all right? Haven't I fought my battle long enough?'

'Of course you have,' she said quickly. 'And you've won. It's just me, Duncan, I can't help worrying.'

He kissed her cheek. 'I know, I know, I understand. But, look, this is a celebration and no one's drinking. Come on, Josie, you must join me – drink up!'

'To the road bridge,' she declared, raising her glass. 'And to both of you.'

'To your Matt, too. We need chaps like him. He'll be applying for one of the jobs, won't he?'

'Oh, yes, he'll be applying.'

'And then you'll go back to Queensferry?' asked Lina.

'Who knows?' asked Josie.

Well, she knew now. Come the summer of 1959, she would be going home.

Chapter Forty-Four

On their last night in Piper Street, everyone came round to the flat for a grand farewell party. Agnes and Brandon, Fergus and Gillie, Sandy and Heather, Iona and Lew, and all the children, who now included Fergus's new son, Tim, and Sandy's new son, Hughie. Marie came with Colin, Ken Pearce with Millie, Fay Cameron with most of the neighbours from Number Seventy-two, together with Rena and Scott Elder, who had married in 1957 and moved, but only next door.

Who'd have thought I'd ever miss her? thought Josie, as Rena swept in, holding a bottle in one hand and leading Scott by the other. But Rena had the personality to make folk miss her, just as she made them notice her in the first place and do what she wanted. Why, she'd probably have all the MacLeods rocking and rolling before the evening was out, for though she'd been furious when rock and roll first swept the country and had sworn never to give up her ballroom, in no time she was rocking away as though she'd never heard of the foxtrot. Had even rocked around the clock at her wedding reception, until Scott had dragged her off to catch their train.

Everybody'd brought something to eat or drink. The little kitchen was crammed with sandwiches, pork pies, Ma's fruit cake, Gillie's trifles, Heather's sausage rolls, and Iona was unwrapping her usual bought cake as Sandy tried to slip in his beer without Ma noticing, for she had declared, 'Now we don't want too much drinking tonight, Sandy, Matt and Josie have to leave early in the morning!'

'Och, how can you have a send-off without a wee drop or two,' he'd protested, but he knew there were plenty of bottles about anyway, and when Dad started up on his fiddle and he got out his accordion, Ma'd never notice how many drinks he was having on the side.

The food was disappearing fast, the children were under everyone's feet, the smallest drooping and wailing, the babies already asleep in the bedroom, when Marie took Josie's arm and said, 'Let's make more tea, eh?'

It was an excuse to be together, to say goodbye privately.

'I don't know why I feel like crying,' said Marie, deciding to laugh instead. 'It's no' as if you're going very far, Josie. But, och, I'm going to miss you!'

'Oh, Marie, how about me missing you? You're the sister I never had.' Josie sniffed as they stood waiting for the kettle to come to the boil. 'You will come over to Queensferry, eh?'

'Sure, but you'll be coming back here, anyway.'

'To see Ma and everyone,' Josie murmured.

She already knew that the hardest part of this move would be saying goodbye to Matt's mother. How worried she'd been about meeting her, back in 1954, and how needless those worries had been. Agnes had always seemed to have a particular understanding of Josie, there'd been an affinity between them from the start. More so than between Josie and her own mother, for though Josie did love Ellie, there was no doubt that some of Ellie's ideas did not chime with hers. There had been a new closeness since the birth of the children, and Ellie now visited Josie in Glasgow as she'd never managed to do before. But she was still John Morrow's wife, still owed her first allegiance to him, and there lay the problem. How things would work out when Josie arrived back in Queensferry was a complete unknown. There were times when she wondered if she'd

297

made the right decision to leave Glasgow at all.

At least she and Matt had a place to go in Queensferry, and that was thanks to Ellie. It was she who had arranged for them to take on the tenancy of Mrs Robb's cottage, now that Mrs Robb had moved out to a new house at the end of the town, bought for her by Callum. He was apparently in the money these days and Mrs Robb had become quite grand, Ellie said, which was a joke, really, because all she meant was that Mrs Robb need no longer do other people's housework and could spend all her time in the garden of her new house. But her old cottage would be a godsend to Matt and Josie, for once again Queensferry was to be filled with men looking for accommodation. Not quite on the scale of the days of the rail bridge, when over four thousand men had lived all over the area, some in specially built housing, but even the four hundred required for the road bridge would stretch resources.

'It's a shame you've never been able to get on with your teaching,' said Marie, refilling the milk jug. 'Could you no' get your ma to look after the weans for you?'

'You know the situation, Marie. She's got the boarding house, and then there's ma dad. I couldn't ask her.'

'Aye, it's difficult. That's why Colin and me've decided, no kids.'

'You have to do what's right for you,' Josie said diplomatically.

Since Marie had embarked on training to be a dispensing optician and said she wouldn't have children, there were those in the family, principally Ma, who said she'd live to regret it. But Marie and Colin had plans to start their own business, and maintained they couldn't have everything.

'Aye, you have to settle, eh?' said Marie, as the kettle began to shriek. 'Take what you can get.' Josie, busying herself making the fresh tea, did not answer.

Marie looked at her averted profile for a moment. 'You know, in all these years I've never said anything,' she said softly. 'But now you're going away, leaving us, I'd like to think you were happy.'

'You mean with Matt?' Josie turned to give Marie one of her long, direct looks. 'Are things all right between me and Matt? Yes, they're all right.'

Marie hesitated. 'There was a time when you'd have said more than that.'

'Aye, well, there was a time when I thought he was perfect and you said he wasn't.' Josie shrugged. 'Seems you were right.'

'Oh, God.' Marie bit her lip. 'It's just what me and Ma thought. There was another woman?'

'Is that what Ma said?'

'Josie, Matt's a MacLeod. I mean, he's like ma dad, and Fergus, and a few guys in the family further back, so I've heard. They attract women. Don't always want to, but don't always say no.'

'And their wives are supposed to manage them. Oh, yes, you told me.' Josie shook her head. 'I never did understand what that meant.'

'Just sort them out, give them their rules.'

'It's your fancy woman or me, sort of thing? Where does love come into it, then?'

'Josie, they always love their wives. They do, you have to believe it.'

'Oh, I believe it, I've spent years believing it.' Josie put the teapots on a tray. 'Let's take these in, Marie.'

'Why'd you never talk about it, Josie? It'd have helped, you know, to talk.'

'There was no point, I knew what you'd all say. Just what you've said now.' Josie added the milk jug to her tray. 'Look, it was a long time ago, mebbe I've made too much of it. And ma life could be a lot worse.'

'How d'you mean?'

'You know what I mean. There's women round here end up in hospital on Saturday nights.'

'Come on!' Marie's eyes blazed. 'That's a pretty low

standard to judge ma brother by! And you've got me wrong. I've never said the women in this family should just put up with what the men do. I've got a man of ma own now, a good, decent fella, never looks at another woman. I know how a man should be.'

'Are you two growing the tea-leaves in there?' cried Gillie, putting her head round the kitchen door. 'There's some of us dying of thirst out here, you ken!'

The meal was over, the children had been put temporarily to bed, and the men had piled the furniture round the stair, so that there could be dancing when Brandon and Sandy began to play. But first there were calls for Matt to sing.

'How aboot your Elvis Presley, then?' called Ken, grinning. 'Och, you should hear him, folks, up on the bridges. He's as good as the wireless, so he is!'

'Oh, I love Elvis Presley,' Fay sighed, half closing her eyes. 'When he sings, you think he's singing straight to you ... "Love me tender, love me true ..." Come on, Matt, sing up!'

But Matt said he'd be singing a Scottish ballad, like he always did at family parties. That's what his dad could play, and what his mother liked best.

'Aye, that's true!' Agnes cried robustly. 'All this American wailing – give me a good Scottish song every time!'

So Matt sang the old Scottish airs everyone listening knew so well, and because this was by way of being a farewell, people's eyes moistened, and one or two sniffed and took out hankies, and Rena said had she no' always told everybody, Matt MacLeod should have been on the stage?

'But listen, Josie,' she whispered, when Matt had finished to great applause, 'have you no' got one or two rock 'n' roll records for your gramophone? Just to get the party going, eh?'

'We've no' even got a gramophone, never mind any

records,' Josie answered huskily. 'But Dad's going to play now anyway. He'll get the party going.'

And away they all went, with their reels and jigs, enjoying themselves in the cleared living room as though it were a ballroom. And when Agnes wasn't dancing, she sat with her bright eyes on her family, the yellow heads and the dark heads, and came to rest on Josie's lovely rich brown hair flying from her shoulders as she set to Matt and took his hand to swing across the floor.

Ah, Josie, pet, things'll surely be all right for you, now, thought Agnes. You can take the rough with the smooth if there's love at the end of it. Just as long as there is Matt.

But who knew the truth of things between a man and his wife? Agnes sighed, then smiled, as the music stopped and Lew came over.

'You and me next, Ma,' he told her, breathing hard from the last reel. 'Soon as Dad's had a drink.'

'Aye, and Sandy, too,' said Agnes, who could see him quietly opening another bottle behind his father's back. Oh, but she wouldn't say anything. Let it go, they were all having a good time. And tomorrow Matt and Josie would be gone.

The party was slow to break up, the leavetakings protracted. Dishes were washed and the room tidied, then people kissed goodbye and began to drift away. Sleeping children were carried out for lifts in Lew's van and Colin's car, Rena, Scott and Fay left with the neighbours, promising to keep in touch and singing, 'Will ye no' come back again?' in cracked voices. Marie, winding her arms round Josie, held her tight, then reached up to kiss Matt with a fierce look that made him blink.

'Take care!' she whispered. 'You know what I mean, Matt.'

'Colin's back,' said Brandon, moving to embrace Josie and clap Matt on the back. 'You ready, girls?'

Agnes, one of his 'girls', put her arms round Josie.

301

'Will you see your dad?' she asked quietly.

'Yes, I will,' Josie said bravely. 'I think he should see his grandchildren, whatever he says.'

'Why, he'll no' want to turn the little ones away?' cried Agnes.

'Mebbe not. I don't know.' Josie swallowed hard. 'Oh, Ma, I don't know what to say—'

'Only going to Queensferry,' said Matt cheerfully. 'I used to come back every weekend.'

'But we won't be coming back every weekend,' said Josie. 'There's the difference.'

Colin was swinging his car keys, ready to go. Matt kissed his mother, and she looked into his eyes, as Marie had done.

'You look after Josie and the bairns, Matt, and look after yourself, too. No fooling round on the girders!'

'Forget the girders, Ma,' he said with a laugh. 'This is going to be a different kind of bridge.'

'You can still fall off it, whatever it is.'

'When it's built. We haven't even started yet.'

'Och, take care anyway!' she cried.

They were alone, Josie and Matt, except for Trina asleep in her cot in their room. Justin now slept in the little bed off the kitchen.

'I'm so tired, I could fall into bed just as I am,' said Josie.

Matt gave her his calm gaze. 'How are you feeling? About tomorrow?'

'Seeing Queensferry again? I want to, and I don't want to. Leaving here is the hard thing.'

'Aye, But then there's your dad.'

'After I've seen him, we might just have to keep out of his way.'

'I can do that, all right. Shall I set the alarm? Don't want the van men to find us in bed.'

They lay together, listening to the tick of the alarm clock

302

and Trina snuffling in her sleep. Their last night in Glasgow, was the thought in their minds, and how different was their leavetaking from their arrival, five years before. Maybe it was for the best, that they should have a new beginning, but Josie, turning over, ready for sleep, wondered why anyone should think a new beginning could change an ending. For whatever they had now, she and Matt, it was true that there'd been an ending to what they'd had before.

Chapter Forty-Five

Of course, things had changed. Even in five years a place could change, but it was not time that had changed Josie's home town so much as the coming of another bridge. There was a new atmosphere of excitement, a delighted incredulity that after thirty-five years of talk, the road bridge was about to become reality. Workmen had already cleared buildings from the site, from where the bridge would eventually span out to meet the Mackintosh Rock on the north shore. Everywhere there were men in hard hats and machinery arriving, while passengers in the trains crossing the good old rail bridge looked interestedly down.

'Aye, the place has gone mad,' Ellie told Josie when she came round to Plum Tree Cottage to help her unpack. 'It's bridge fever all over again. of course, there's money flying about – folk are always crazy for that, your dad says, and I'm sure he's right. Just think how much Beryl Tassie's pulling in, wi' that café of hers! And then there's all the lettings and the money spent in pubs, and even Kitty Braid's doing good business, cutting men's hair as well as women's, would you credit?'

'You must be doing good business, too, Mum.'

'Well, I am, but I'm no' letting it go to ma head, that's the thing.'

'I don't think it's just the money that's exciting people,' Josie said reflectively. 'It's being on the map again, it's having folk outside taking an interest. After all, this is something important to the whole of Scotland, you have to think of that.'

Ellie shrugged. 'Mebbe you're right. But let's get on, eh? What'd you like me to do?'

'Could you mind Justin for a bit? Trina's having her nap, but Justin's all at sea. Still doesn't understand why we had to come here.'

'Och, the poor wee laddie! Come to your gran, Justin, come and see this lovely ball! Shall we play with it outside, then?'

Justin's troubled face brightened, as he took his grandmother's hand and agreed to play football with her in Mrs Robb's overgrown garden.

'Can you kick, Gran?' he asked. 'Would you like to be in goal? We could make that tree the goal, eh?'

'Listen to him!' cried Ellie admiringly. 'He's quite the little footballer already!'

'Matt's keen on football,' Josie told her. 'He wasn't home that often in Glasgow, but when he was, he'd play with Justin and the bigger boys in the street.'

'Oh, yes?' Ellie showed no interest. She did not want to talk about Matt and even though he was now living in her own town, had made up her mind to see him as little as possible. It shouldn't be difficult to avoid him, he'd be at work during the day when Ellie would see Josie, and of course neither he nor Josie would be visiting Ardmore.

Josie had turned back into the cottage. She was really quite pleased with it, felt she could make something of it. The landlord had already agreed to let them decorate, and once they'd put some fresh paint about and she'd made new curtains, everything would look fine. Even now, with the furniture they'd recently bought, the place was looking very different from when Mrs Robb had had it, but the nicest thing of all was having a garden! Josie couldn't wait to get out into it, start growing her own vegetables, pick her own fruit, like Mrs Robb. It would be lovely, having their own

305

bathroom (paid for by Callum, Josie remembered) and an extra bedroom, but the best thing would be stepping out of the house on to grass instead of pavement. You never knew how much you missed a garden until you'd lived in Glasgow, thought Josie. Which was not to say that she wasn't missing Glasgow. Here she was, back in her real home, and she was homesick all over again! Josie smiled to herself as she carried on with her unpacking. She knew it was people she was missing this time, not so much a place.

After she'd worked hard for some time, she scrubbed her hands at the kitchen sink and put the kettle on. She'd better make her mother a cup of tea for Ellie would soon have to get back to the boarding-house. Tilly Park, the solid and easygoing young woman who was now the paid help, had been left in charge, but Ellie said she wasn't much good, and of course John Morrow did little or nothing these days. When she thought of her father, Josie's stomach lurched.

'Oh, you've made some tea!' cried Ellie, bustling in with Justin. 'I'm dying for it! Justin, pass your mammie that tin I brought. Some of ma shortbread, Josie.'

'Mum, you've already given me a stew and an apple pie! What next?'

'I knew you'd be too busy to cook today, pet, but looks like you'll soon be straight, with all you've done. Monnie Robb'll have left the place clean, anyway. I miss her now she's a lady of leisure.' Ellie laughed a little waspishly. 'But I still miss you the most, Josie, and that's a fact.'

Josie gave Justin a mug of milk and some biscuits, then ran upstairs and brought down Trina, rosy from her nap.

'Now you can go up and unpack your cars,' she told Justin, and when he'd stomped eagerly away, dandled Trina on her knee and turned to her mother.

'When can I come and see Dad, Mum?'

Ellie paused in the act of biting into a piece of her own shortbread. She swallowed slowly, then took a moment wiping her sugary fingers.

'Well, I think we could leave it a while, Josie. I mean,

306

till you get settled in.'

'Why? It won't make any difference to him whether I'm settled in or not.'

Ellie hesitated. 'To tell you the truth, I don't think he's ready yet.'

Josie gave her mother a long penetrating stare. 'Mum, does he even know I'm here?'

There was a silence. Ellie crumbled the remaining short-bread on her plate.

'He doesn't,' she said at last.

'Oh, Mum! You were going to tell him! You were going to pave the way!'

'Well, I *am* going to do that. When I find the right time.'

'And when will that be? Look, you tell him tonight without fail. You tell him I'm here and I want to see him and I want to show him his grandchildren. Will you do that?'

'Yes, yes, I will.' Ellie poured herself more tea and drank thirstily. 'But it's difficult for me, you know.'

'Mum, it's been five years!'

'Five years for him to dig himself in, Josie. That's the way folk can be. Sometimes, family feuds can drag on for a lifetime.'

'This is no' a family feud.'

'No. Well, I'll do ma best.' Ellie looked round for a clock. 'What's the time? I'd better be getting back.'

Josie checked the watch the MacLeods had given her for her twenty-first birthday. 'It's four o'clock. Oh, Mum, I'm so glad you came today, it's made all the difference!'

'It's going to make all the difference to me, having you back here,' Ellie told her, touching her hand. 'I will tell your dad tonight, I promise. Now, let me just kiss Trina again, and Justin. Tell him his gran's going, Josie, tell him I want to say goodbye.'

When Matt came home from his first day's work, he looked round the cottage in surprise. The furniture was in position, the boxes unpacked, the table set for tea.

'My word, Josie, you've cracked on! I was planning to give you a hand.'

'There's still plenty to do, but I've made a good start. Mum came round to help.'

'Did she?' Matt's face was glum. 'Suppose we can expect to see her pretty often.'

'I don't think you will, ma guess is she wants to keep out of your way. But she's given us a lovely stew for tonight, Matt, and an apple pie and shortbread, you have to give credit where credit's due.'

He only grunted as he washed his hands.

'And when are you seeing your father?'

Josie, peeling potatoes, was casual. 'Mum's going to fix it up for me.'

'You have to have an appointment?' Matt's grey eyes were unusually steely. 'Josie, there's one thing I want to make clear. I won't have Justin upset by your so-called religious dad. OK?'

'Do you think I'd let him upset Justin?' Josie flared. 'What do you take me for?' She glanced at her son who was regarding his parents with a wide-eyed apprehensive stare and slightly shook her head at Matt. 'Don't say any more. Leave it to me.'

'Just remember what I said, then.'

'I've told you, leave it to me.'

Later, when they were sitting down to their first meal in their new home, Josie asked Matt how things had gone for him.

'Fine. All seems a hell of a muddle, but everything's under control.' He whistled a little through his teeth. 'What a job, eh, getting something like this off the drawing-board?'

'What's the bridge going to be like, Matt?'

'One beautiful suspended span. There'll be two towers at each end—' Mat moved the salt and pepper to demonstrate – and another tower in the middle.' He added the mustard

308

pot. 'These'll hold two huge cables to make the deck for the cars. The towers'll have to be supported on piers and for the south one there'll be caissons. You remember there were caissons used for the rail bridge? Great cylinders, a bit like gasometers?'

'Dad told me about them.'

'Well, these caissons'll take the pier for the south side, and the Mackintosh Rock'll take the pier for the north. Then there'll be concrete towers built for the end spans, and anchorages to take the steel cables. A lot of the structures will be made elsewhere, but we'll erect them.' Matt smiled. 'They say the main towers are going to look terrific.'

As he ate heartily of the stew made by his mother-in-law, Josie was apprehensive.

'How can you be sure it'll be safe?'

'Don't worry, it'll be safe all right, but that's the engineers' department. We have to rely on the designers to get their sums right.'

Josie leaned across to Trina in her high chair and wiped her mouth. 'Just hope Duncan doesn't try to go climbing this new bridge, that's all.'

Matt laughed. 'You're like Ma. It'll be years before there's any bridge to climb. What I'm looking forward to is making the cables. Cable-spinning, they call it. That's based on an American system, something new over here. But we'll not be ready for that till next year. Did you say there was an apple pie?'

After tea, the summer evening was still so fine and the children so wide awake, they decided to walk out round the town. Josie wondered if she would see people she knew, but the people they passed were all strangers, and heavens, there were plenty of them!

'Where'd you like to go?' asked Matt.

'Oh, just to the bridge and back. The railway bridge.'

'We'll have to get used to saying that.' He gave Josie a sideways glance. 'Have to go past Ardmore.'

309

'I know. Doesn't matter. I saw it earlier, when we arrived.'

'Hasn't changed much, has it?'

'Curtains need washing.' Josie's voice was trembling. 'Mum did say her help was no' much good.'

'Don't you go volunteering.'

'Me? I'd have to get inside the door first.'

They walked on, Josie noticing that Lina's old home was, as usual, looking in better repair than hers, but she didn't care to look too closely in case she should see Kitty Braid's cold eye staring out.

How bitter-sweet it was to be back, she thought, with every step of the way to the bridge bringing back memories. Of her childhood, of her growing-up, of Matt. She did not want to think of those days when she had run along here, to see if she could see him on the girders. Or when she had met him that ferry-fair day, when they had almost fallen into each other's arms in front of the crowds, but had had to wait until they reached the woods to kiss for the first time. And there, by the bridge, they had kissed again, on the night of Lina's wedding, and a train had gone by and they had talked of marriage. She could remember it all, every detail. Could Matt remember any of it? As he picked up Justin and swung him up to look at the bridge, Josie didn't think so. He showed no sign, anyway. It occurred to her that he had killed something for himself as well as for her, when he had betrayed her. But then she didn't know what else there was in his life, what other secrets he had kept from her.

Justin was enchanted by the great bridge and the trains travelling over it. And the ferry chugging through the water! And the cars waiting to cross! It brought a smile to Josie's face, and Matt's, to see his excitement. Clearly, this new place was proving to have attractions he'd never dreamed about, back in Glasgow. By the time the ferries were gone and the road bridge was built, he would be a big boy. Seven or eight years old. Josie didn't want to think of

310

it, didn't want to look too far ahead. It was better, really, to live from day to day, or as her father might have quoted, 'Sufficient unto the day is the evil thereof'. She didn't want to think of her father, either.

Chapter Forty-Six

During the next few days, Josie constantly expected to see her mother, but Ellie did not appear. Of course, she was very busy, it was difficult for her to get away; Josie understood that and carried on with her work in the cottage and the garden. With two small children under her feet, it wasn't easy, and she was glad to make a break for herself, renewing her acquaintance with old friends. People who'd known her all her life and were delighted to see her back home; Mrs Tassie, at the Queen Margaret Café, who gave her a royal welcome; Patty, now married with a baby girl and living in a small modern house near the harbour, who invited her for coffee.

Patty took particular interest in Lina, who seemed to her to have taken on the glamour of a film star, living such a different kind of life, with money to burn, eh, and lovely clothes, and even a nanny! Yet when she came to the 'Ferry to see her mum, she was just the same Lina as she'd always been, never put on any style, or changed her accent, or anything.

'Och, all these folk doing so well!' Patty exclaimed, as she passed biscuits to the children. 'They say Callum Robb's making money hand over fist, and all set, seemingly, to start his own business. Robb's Tours, he's calling it, and taking out a bank loan that'd be enough to frighten any ordinary guy to death, which he's not – an ordinary guy, I mean. But have you seen the house he's bought for his mum? Well, it's probably on a mortgage, but it's no' a house Ralphie and me could even look at, I'm telling you!'

'We always thought he'd do well,' said Josie. 'Even at school he was a businessman. Used to buy up marbles – fancy glassies, you know – and sell them to other lads at a profit.'

They both laughed, then Patty said hesitantly, 'and Angus has done well, too, so I've heard. Last time we saw Lina, she said he was very highly thought of by that London firm.'

'I'm sure that's true,' Josie said quietly.

'But he's no' married yet.' Patty's look was covert. 'Split up with his girl-friend.'

'That was some time ago. She went to America.'

'Did Lina tell you? What a shame, eh? When he was so keen. There'll be somebody else after him, though, and Callum. What d'you bet?'

'I'll bet you're right.'

Josie knew it was on the tip of Patty's tongue to ask if she ever regretted not marrying Angus, now that he was doing so well, but perhaps she was too fond of Josie to put the question into words. Or perhaps thought Matt so handsome it didn't need asking.

Passing a phone box on the way home, Josie suddenly decided to ring Ardmore; if her father answered, she would just ring off. But it was her mother who said, 'Hello?'

'Mum, it's me, Josie. Why've you no' come round?'

'I'm sorry, pet, I've been that busy – all these bridge men to see to.'

'Have you spoken to Dad yet?'

Silence. Josie, crushed with the two children into the stuffy telephone kiosk, gave an impatient sigh.

'Mum?'

'Not yet, Josie. I did say I'd have to pick ma time. I'll do it today.'

'I wish you would. It's – you know – hanging over ma head.'

313

'This very day, Josie, I promise.'

'And then you'll come round?'

'Soon as I can.'

What is Mum up to? thought Josie, pushing Trina home, with Justin hanging back to jump the flagstones. Is she ever going to speak to Dad? Why don't I just walk round there and speak to him maself? She couldn't face it.

'Mammie, there's a car outside our door!' cried Justin. 'It's a blue one!'

It was a Morris Minor. It was Lina's.

In a red dress with matching scarf, her flaxen hair expertly cut and her make-up immaculate, Lina looked so attractive, so plump and luscious, it seemed no wonder to Josie that Patty was star-struck by her. As for Justin, he was star-struck by her car.

'Oh, look at him, can't wait to drive it, bless him!' cried Lina, following Josie into the cottage with an armful of packages and a bunch of carnations. 'Josie, it's so lovely to see you! And isn't this nice? Mrs Robb's old cottage? I can't believe Callum isn't going to pop out from some-where!'

Josie, hauling in Justin, unstrapping Trina from her pushchair and frantically wondering what she could give Lina to eat, agreed that it was lovely to meet up again. But such a surprise.

'I thought you weren't due till next week, Lina?'

'Och, Duncan was itching to start work so we got our skates on and packed up early. We're staying with Mr and Mrs G. until we find a house. And a nice Scottish nanny!'

'Mrs Guthrie's got April and the baby?'

'Aye, Mum'll no' be pleased, but I just felt I had to have a few hours off. Anyway, she'll be seeing plenty of the girls in the future. Och, is it no' grand to be back, Josie?'

'It is, and grand to see you, Lina. You're as good as a tonic, you really are. Wait, I'll just put the kettle on ...'

'No' for me, Josie, thanks all the same, but Mum's

314

cooking and I'd better no' be late. Just wanted to welcome you back and to leave you these.'

There were toys for the children, chocolates and flowers for Josie, and a crystal fruit-bowl for the house.

'A house-warming present,' said Lina. 'I couldn't think what to get, but I knew you'd have Mrs Robb's garden and all her apples and plums when they're ready, because I remember helping to pick them. In the days when I was no' in disgrace!'

'Oh, Lina ...' Josie was overwhelmed. 'Honestly, you shouldn't have.'

'Come on, we're friends. We're meant to cheer each other up.'

'Do I cheer you up, Lina?'

'Josie, you certainly do.' Lina gave her a last hug. 'Got to get to Mum now. She's up to her eyes in appointments, but still says she misses me.' Lina stopped to kiss Justin and Trina. 'Do you think you always miss your children, however old they are?'

'I'll miss mine,' Josie replied firmly. 'Even when Justin starts full-time school, I'll be crying ma eyes out.'

'Aye, but when they're all at school, think of the fun we can have! Josie, I'll be in touch. Remember me to Matt.'

'And me to Duncan.'

'Wish we could have a blue car like that,' sighed Justin, as the Morris Minor vanished round the street corner.

'Maybe we will, one day,' Josie told him.

She worked well for the rest of the afternoon, buoyed up by Lina's visit, her beauty and her high spirits, her demonstration that you could get through the storms and come out into sunshine. It was only when Josie was taking in her washing and saw her mother unlatching the gate that another cloud came over her own sun.

'Mum, what's wrong?' she cried, throwing the bundle of sheets and pillowcases, small garments and socks, into the basket.

'I'm sorry, Josie!' Ellie cried, her face crumpling. 'Your

315

dad says he doesn't want to see you. Not yet, anyhow. He's sure you'll understand, it wouldn't be right.'

Out came the teapot, on went the kettle as Josie tried to comfort her mother, who had suddenly realised that John Morrow's obduracy was preventing her from having her own grandchildren in her own house, even when they were in the same town. Och, it was unbelievable, not to be borne. But it would have to be borne.

'Stupid old man,' she sniffed, wiping her eyes with her hankie. 'He'll no' listen to the minister, he'll no' listen to me or anyone. He's gone too far, you see, Josie. He'd have to admit he was in the wrong if he turned back now.'

'Never mind, Mum, we're no worse off, are we? In fact, things are better because I'm here now and at least you can come and see me and the children any time.' Josie glanced down at Justin, whose eyes were wide and anxious at the sight of his gran crying. 'You take Trina upstairs, Justin, and play with your lovely new toys that Auntie Lina brought, eh?'

'Lina? Has she been here?' Ellie asked sharply. 'Och, when I think what an easy life she's had compared with you, Josie—'

'Mum, how can you say that? When you think what she went through with poor Duncan!'

'Aye, there was that, but he's better now, and she'll never want for a thing, will she?'

'Don't go on, Mum, I'm quite happy, the way I am. Apart from Dad, I mean.'

'Apart from your dad,' her mother sighed.

It was some time before Josie could bring herself to tell Matt of her father's continued ban on her and her children. When she did, he greeted the news with his usual calm.

'Never thought he'd change his mind, Josie.'

'We thought there was a good chance of it, Matt, because of the children. I mean, being here, right on his doorstep.'

'He'll never change as long as you're married to me.' Matt gave an ironic smile. 'Too bad when you regret that, anyway.'

Josie was silent for a moment. 'I've never said that, Matt.'

'Not in so many words.' He pushed back his chair and stood up. 'Don't need to, I suppose. Mind if I go down the pub a bit? Ken'll be there.'

'No, I don't mind. You haven't seen much of him since we came here.'

She really didn't mind now, being on her own. There was so much to do anyway, getting the children to bed, ironing, mending, and one of these days maybe getting out some of her educational material and reading things up, just in case she could ever take her place at the teacher-training college. She laughed at herself. Should she look out of the window, see if pigs were flying across the lovely sweep of the sky?

Chapter Forty-Seven

While Josie in Queensferry slipped into a quiet routine of looking after house and children, Lina in Edinburgh was finding more exciting things to do. Such as spending money. Buying a fine ground and garden double flat in the West End; choosing extra furniture and curtains, rugs for the polished wooden floors; absolutely up-to-the-minute kitchen units, washing machine, television, and hi-fi equipment.

'Och, do you no' love all this guitar stuff?' she asked Josie, swaying her plump hips to the beat of one of her new records. 'Duncan says it's no' music at all, but I make him listen to it all the same. I mean, I have to keep him young, you know. If it was left to him, he'd never go out, he'd spend all his time at work.'

'Matt's the same. He's just gone on a training course for cable-spinning, I never see him.'

'And he used to be such a lovely dancer, eh? You should get him to take you out more, Josie. Get a sitter and enjoy yourselves. You're only young once, as Mum likes to say.'

Duncan, watching his pretty wife flitting about, looking so radiant, sometimes felt his youth had already left him. It wasn't true, of course, he was some years still from forty, but he'd served in the war and the people Lina seemed to be gathering around her were only children when the war had ended. They could respond to all this rock music and Elvis Presley's groaning, to 'kitchen-sink' drama and novels full of sex. The 1960s had only just begun but the young seemed to be already heralding a new world that was to be theirs, and though Erica said she'd heard it all before, young people had talked exactly the same in the 1920s, Duncan still felt out of step. He was grateful he could go to work every day and concentrate on things that mattered.

He had decided this time not to live on the spot in Queensferry, but to drive in every day from the West End. That way, perhaps once a week, he could get home in time to see the new nanny, a sensible young woman named Noreen, putting the children to bed, and most evenings have a meal with Lina. At the weekends, she liked to drag him out somewhere, to a dinner-dance or the theatre, and he always wanted to go, to please her, for his greatest happiness was to do that, to please Lina. During the dark days of his illness, nothing had upset him more than the thought that he had let her down, taken a pretty butterfly and crushed it with the weight of his depression. She'd been born to be cherished, not to act as support, but she'd come through wonderfully, she'd stood by him, helped him to recover, and now it made his heart lift, to see her so happy. Nothing must happen to spoil that.

But what should happen? It was true, though he rarely admitted it even to himself, that he still didn't care to look towards the old bridge. The cold sweat would be on his brow again, his heart bumping in his chest, but the point was, he had no need to look at the old bridge; certainly would not be working on it. As for the new bridge, Lina had made him promise never to go up on the superstructure, but they were a long way from that yet, and in any case with all its modern safeguards, this bridge was going to be a lot safer during construction than its old rival. The one thing that hadn't changed was the wind. Already, they'd been dogged by gales. If they didn't get calm weather when it came to the cable-spinning, they'd fall well behind schedule. But that was a worry for the future. For now, the erection of the prefabricated bases for the towers was the work in hand, and when the towers themselves were completed, each five hundred feet high, you'd really see the bridge taking shape. Duncan's heart lifted at the thought, almost as much as when he contemplated Lina's happiness. But not quite.

As the bridge progressed, more and more people came to watch what was happening. One of these was John Morrow, who limped off to the site every day, much to Ellie's disgust.

'Aye, he's got the bridge fever, all right. Goes off every chance he gets. Just wasting his time, eh? Josie, have you seen him down there?'

'I have,' Josie told her. 'But I don't think he's ever seen me, and I don't speak to him. I know he wouldn't want it. That's why I don't go to the kirk. He wouldn't want to see me there, either.'

'Now, Josie, that's not true. He would like to think you still went to the kirk. Shall I mention it?'

'No! Don't say anything. We're all right as we are, Mum. Just leave it.'

When Matt could manage it, he and Josie would take the children over to Glasgow for Sunday dinner at Dow Street, and from time to time the MacLeods would pay return visits. It always raised Josie's spirits to be with Ma again, or Marie, especially when she could show them Queensferry and let them see what she meant by open spaces. And they were impressed by the wide sky and the shimmering Forth, the rail bridge – well, of course, they knew what that was like – and the new bridge, progressing. Even the ferries still ploughing away, though their days were numbered, were an attraction, and when the MacLeods saw a sunset, flaming the whole area with scarlet and gold, Ma said it was as good as being abroad, so it

320

was, or else going to the pictures.

'Things no' too bad, are they?' Marie whispered to Josie on a visit in the late spring of 1960; Josie agreed they weren't too bad.

'You and Matt still OK?'

'We're OK. Don't see much of him, really. He's always at work.'

'You've got the kids, though,' Marie said softly. 'And gorgeous they are.'

'Aye, and a telly now. Did you see Princess Margaret's wedding?'

'Princess Margaret's wedding!' Marie snorted. 'Seems like we live other people's lives for 'em these days. Ma always swore she'd never have TV in the house, but there it is, clacking away in the corner.'

'Suppose you've no' got one, then?' asked Josie innocently.

'Sure I have! I'm as hooked as everybody else!'

'Passes the time,' Josie said, laughing.

But it did seem to her sometimes that that was all she was doing with her life these days. Passing the time. What did she expect, though? She had what most women had, or wanted, a home and children. Seemed she wanted something more.

Chapter Forty-Eight

It was late-September, 1961. Josie had done her shopping and was making her way slowly towards the Queen Margaret café. She was looking forward to her little treat, a quiet coffee without the children, for Justin was now at primary school, going off every day, so sweet and solemn, with his piece to eat and his new satchel, while strong-minded little Trina was at playschool. She might look like her grandmother, but Josie was beginning to think she had her grandfather's obstinacy. What battles lay ahead, if that were true!

This part of Queensferry, well away from the site of the new bridge, was as busy as ever, with ferry queues and holiday-makers, who still liked to snap the famous rail bridge. But its neighbour at the other end of town had now acquired its north and south towers, and splendid shining columns they were. The first link, of a stretched cable between them, had been made in July, and actual cable-spinning would begin in November. Catwalks, or footbridges, had already been erected. Matt said it would all be perfectly safe. But there had been an accident earlier in the year, some men had been burned in an explosion inside an onshore shaft. That had shaken everyone. Josie couldn't bear to think about it.

She stopped for a moment to lean on the esplanade rail and looked down at the water, so clearly reflecting the sky it seemed a part of it. This was what she had missed in Glasgow, this was what refreshed her spirit: wide sky, wide water, the wonderful sense of space. Someone said her name.

'Josie?'

She knew the voice. When she turned her eyes, she knew the face.

'Angus!'

He seemed taller. He had certainly put on a little weight, enough to make him look, not older, but more mature. She remembered he had already begun to have that look the last time she'd seen him, and that was a long time ago. How many years was it since he had tied that piece of string around her finger? A lifetime.

'What a pleasant surprise,' he said easily. 'Meeting you.'

She had already removed her gaze from his face, but knew his eyes on her were warmer than when they'd last met. It was a relief to think he was well and truly over his love for her, as he must be, if he was no longer hostile.

'You're here to see your mum?' she asked, matching her tone to his.

'Yes, having a few days' leave. Next week I'm moving to Edinburgh, taking a flat with some other guys.'

Josie's eyes widened. 'You're leaving London?'

'Temporarily. Look, couldn't we go and have a coffee at Mrs Tassie's?' At her dubious expression, he smiled. 'Come on, what's a coffee between friends?'

It was what Mrs Tassie might think it, but Josie shook back her hair and allowed her face to clear into a smile.

'A coffee would be nice,' she told him. 'I was just about to have one.'

Mrs Tassie couldn't get over it. Josie and Angus, together again, if only for a coffee! She served them herself, bustling along with her feather-light scones, butter and jam, while issuing orders to the two unknown waitresses who had replaced Patty and Lina.

323

'You here to see your mam, Angus? That's nice, eh? She really looks forward to you coming. But is it no' grand that Lina's back? And her hubby's better and working on the bridge? What do you think of Josie being back, too?'

When she finally left them, they were both smiling. Dear old Mrs Tassie, so good-hearted but loth to let anyone get a word in. She had broken the ice for them all the same. As they drank their coffee and buttered their scones, they were as relaxed as if taking coffee together was something they did every day. When Angus asked about the children and was told they were at school and playgroup, he raised his eyebrows.

'As old as that already? I don't believe it!'

'We've already been back here two years.' Josie hesitated. 'Seems funny, doesn't it, we've never met before?'

'I'm not here very often, but I've looked for you.'

She made no reply to that. Certainly she hadn't looked for him.

'I was telling you about coming to Edinburgh,' Angus went on. 'Thing is, my firm's seeking to expand. We've a couple of new drugs on the way, and we're thinking about manufacturing in Scotland. I've got the job of organising the feasibility study.' He laughed. 'Naturally I'm biased. I'm going to find in favour, if I possibly can.'

'Would it be in Edinburgh, then?'

'Dunno. Might be Glasgow. Might be the Borders. There's a team coming up next week to work with me on the preliminary survey, then we'll report back.'

'So, it'd be some time before you'd actually be manufacturing?'

'Oh, years. But in the meantime, I'll have some time back home.'

'You still think of Scotland as home?'

'Sure, I do. What Scot doesn't?'

Josie looked at her watch. 'I'd better go, Angus. I have to collect Trina at twelve.'

'It's not even eleven!'

324

'I know, but I want to get ma messages home.' Josie stood up. 'Thanks for the coffee, it's been really nice seeing you.'

'I'll walk along with you,' he said with alacrity. 'Just wait till I pay the bill.'

Returning to the cottage with Angus at her side carrying her shopping, Josie was thinking of how she'd once worried about being seen with Matt, who should have been Angus. And now here she was with Angus, who should have been Matt. That was the way life played its tricks, turned things upside down, inside out. She felt excited and on edge, but saw no one she knew, while Angus, calm as Matt, chatted pleasantly about his brother George, who had taken a job with his father-in-law in Bo'ness, about Bernie, training to be an electrician after National Service, about his own life in London.

'You heard I'd split up with Tammy Harley?' he asked suddenly. 'I suppose Lina keeps you informed?'

'I did hear that. I'm sorry.'

He shrugged. 'One of those things. We didn't want to make it permanent. Lina was always trying to matchmake for me when she was in London. Even got me to go out once or twice with Duncan's sister, but she wasn't for me.'

'Duncan's sister?' Josie put her hand on her own garden gate, which they had now reached. She said casually, 'I knew she was on a London paper now, I didn't know you'd taken her out.'

'Och, she's too nervy. Sets a guy's teeth on edge. Fell out with somebody in Glasgow, and I'm not surprised.' Angus was gazing at Plum Tree cottage, his golden eyes alight. 'Well, here it is, Callum's old home! Fancy you living here, Josie. Aren't you going to ask me in?'

'There isn't time, I have to collect Trina.'

'How far have you to go?'

'Well, it's no' far, but I mustn't be late.'

'Come on, I won't stay long, let me in. I'd like to see the

325

house again. The times Callum and me used to come here, cadging apples or biscuits from his mum!'

Josie was on pins. She didn't want Angus coming into this place she shared with Matt, didn't want him seeing too much into their lives. But it was already too late. He was over the threshold and looking round, his eyes still filled with golden light, his lips parted, caught in the past, yet conscious, Josie knew, of herself, so much in the present. She watched him warily.

'Josie, you've done wonders here,' he said admiringly. 'Callum's poor mother never had a bean in the old days, never could do much, but you've transformed it.'

'I wouldn't say that. All it's had is a coat of paint and some new curtains.'

'And your pictures and your flowers.' Angus turned to look at her. 'Your touch, Josie.'

'I'm glad you like it.' She emptied her shopping bag on to the table. 'But I think I'll have to throw you out now, Angus. Time's getting on.'

He was prowling around, not listening, shaking his head over some old image of himself and Callum.

'He's done really well, you know,' he said, over his shoulder. 'Callum, I mean.'

'People keep saying that.'

'Well, it's true. He's shot up his ladder, all right. Have you heard about Robb's Tours? He could have given Lina anything she wanted, if she'd only had the sense to wait.'

'Lina has everything she wants, Angus. She has Duncan.'

Angus shook his head. 'She was dazzled by Duncan, that's what happened there. If she met Callum now, she'd be dazzled by him, just the same. He was too close to her before. As I was close to you, Josie.'

Josie said nothing. What was there for her to say?

After a moment, Angus came to her and put out his hand to touch her face. 'Josie, will you let me look at you? No, don't move away. I want to see you, really see you.'

'You've seen me already,' she said uneasily.

'You've changed, you know.'

'Yes, grown older. Can't be helped, Angus.'

'No, I don't mean that. You're just as lovely as ever. But there's something different about you. About your eyes.' He stood back, his own eyes grave. 'You've been hurt, haven't you? Matt MacLeod has hurt you. I can see it, there in your face. In your eyes. That fellow's hurt you. Don't deny it.'

'I'm no' going to say anything at all.'

'I told you what he was like, didn't I? But you wouldn't listen. What happened? Another woman? Or, a string of them?'

'Angus, I did ask you to go.'

'I can't go, I can't leave you. I want to know what happened.'

'What's the point? Why should it matter to you?'

'For God's sake, can't you see why it matters to me?' Angus suddenly sat down at Josie's table, pushing away her groceries, Cornflakes, packets of tea and sugar, to rest his head on his hands.

'I thought I was OK,' he muttered. 'How stupid can you get? I'm like an alcoholic who thinks he can take a drink. I said I'd looked for you, but I never did. I always had the sense not to do that. Till today. Then I saw you, looking out over the Forth, and it was so wonderful, it was like going back into the past, and I thought: What the hell, what harm can it do, I'm OK. But I looked into your eyes and I saw you weren't happy ...' He raised his head and saw that Josie's eyes were full of tears.

'Josie!'

He leaped to his feet and put his arms around her, and she didn't push him away. For a long moment they stood together, until he quietly released her and she picked up her bag and her keys.

'It's time to go,' she said in a low voice.

'May I walk with you?'

327

'No, I think, better not.'

'But I will see you again?'

'No, it'd be crazy.'

'Look, you made a mistake, that doesn't mean you can't have another chance—'

'Angus, I have to go.'

She shut and locked the door, and looked at him only briefly. He caught at her hand.

'When does Trina go to the playgroup? What days? Tell me!'

'You're away in Edinburgh next week.'

'But not this week. There are two mornings left. Tell me when I can see you, tell me, Josie!'

'Friday!' she cried. 'Trina goes to playgroup on Friday. You can see me then.'

Of course, she wouldn't let him see her. It had been madness to agree. The terrible thing was that she wanted to see him. As she went swiftly on her way to collect Trina, Josie felt buoyed by an inner delight she knew she shouldn't be feeling and that was baffling, anyway. For what had changed? Angus, for all his new poise and confidence, was still Angus. She'd been relieved to think he no longer loved her. Then, when she had seen him sitting at her table, his shoulders hunched, his flaxen head in his hands, it was as though something had been released in her. A great spring of feeling rose and flowed from her to him and she found herself caught up in a love she had never wanted before. But shamefully wanted now.

She'd half-thought of telling Matt that she'd met Angus and had a coffee with him. That would show it meant nothing. But when Matt came home that evening and sat, exhausted, with his feet stretched out in front of him and his deep-lidded eyes closed, Josie said nothing. It didn't seem the right time to say anything, might stir up trouble perhaps, and Matt was feeling weary. Even at night, when they lay together, she didn't speak, for Matt was soon asleep and then

328

she was able to lie awake and think about Angus. She wished she could see him again, be loved again, as she hadn't been loved for such a long time. But it wasn't possible. She couldn't see him.

On Friday morning he was standing some little distance from the hall where Trina's playgroup was held.

'Hi,' he said softly. 'I've got the car parked round the corner. Shall we go for a drive?'

It was her cue to end what had hardly begun. She opened her mouth to speak, as Angus held the car door for her, but no words came. She got into the passenger seat, and Angus drove away.

Chapter Forty-Nine

The autumn day was beautiful, golden and warm. As they
drove through the countryside where the farmers were
harvesting, Angus said you could almost feel the blackberries ripening.

'Remember when we used to go out on our bikes, black-
berrying? Remember the pies our mums made?'

'Children still go blackberry picking, Angus.'

'Aye, but we had the rationing. For us, they were a
treat.'

Josie was silent. She knew Angus didn't really want to
talk about blackberries.

'Where'd you like to go? I know a good pub where you
can get morning coffee –'

'Angus, this was a mistake. Could you just take me
back?'

He drew into the side of the road and stopped. All was
still, except for the sound of rooks in a clump of tall trees.
Here, even the farmers' tractors were too distant to disturb
them. Angus heaved a deep sigh.

'What's wrong with being with me, Josie? OK, you're
married. But you're not happily married. Haven't you a
right to be happy?'

'I've no right to be here with you, that's all I know.'

'You've every right!' he said fiercely. 'Matt MacLeod
has let you down. You owe him nothing!'

'If I behave like Matt, I'm no better than him, am I?'

'For God's sake, Josie, we haven't even kissed!' Angus suddenly turned her face to his. 'We haven't even kissed,' he repeated quietly, and their mouths met.

Josie couldn't even remember when she had last kissed Angus, but she knew the kiss hadn't been like this one. All his frustrated love was in his lips on hers, all her own longing was responding. When they finally drew apart, Angus's eyes were alight.

'Oh, God, Josie, you don't know how often I've dreamed of being with you again! Never thought it would happen, but now we've found each other again, we mustn't let each other go. Because I can really make you happy. You know that, don't you? With me, there'd be love –' he dropped his voice – 'and trust.'

He was right. With Angus there would be no heartache, no anxiety, no need for jealousy. He was straight and true, as she'd thought she was herself. Yet here she was, with him, and still married to Matt. Here they both were, the straight and the true, playing false.

'Can we go?' she asked.

They were in good time. Angus parked away from the hall and turned to look at Josie. They hadn't spoken on the way back.

'Don't look so troubled,' he said gently. 'Just think of this as being with someone who loves you.'

Comforting words; she wished they could have comforted her.

'Think of yourself for a change,' he pressed, and she saw that his eyes held that soft yearning light she had at one time been so thrilled to see in Matt's. Ah, but it was easy for Angus to look at her like that, to talk to her as he did. He was free.

'I've got to start work on this study next week,' he told her, watching her closely, trying to read her expression. 'I'll have fairly flexible hours, I'll try to see you as soon as I can.'

'I've no' said I can see you again, Angus.'

'But you will, Josie? You will?'

She lowered her head as a middle-aged man walked past the car. Her heart beat fast. Did she know him? He was a stranger and she grew calm again.

'You have to ask yourself where we're going,' she said slowly. 'I can only see a dead end.'

'Let's just meet, discuss the big questions later.' Angus took her hand and held it between his own. 'As soon as I can, I'll bring the car here on a playgroup day. Look out for me. Promise?'

She pulled her hand away and got out of the car. Playgroup day, he had said. So matter-of-factly. On the day her children were out of the way, at school and playgroup, he'd move in. She straightened her shoulders and began to walk down the street, but Angus, so sensitive to her mood, had read her thoughts and was beside her.

'It doesn't have to be this way,' he whispered, taking her hard by the arm. 'We can make it legal. Any time.'

'I have to go!' she cried, and tearing herself free, ran from him to collect her little daughter.

'Did you miss me, Trina? Did you?'

Josie caught her into her arms, but Trina was unimpressed.

'No, Mammie, I didn't miss you. We did colouring in.'

Chapter Fifty

From then on, every time she left Trina at the playgroup, Josie looked round for Angus, but the days passed and he didn't come. She was ashamed to find herself missing him, missing his love that wrapped her in balm. Though they might have no future, how could she turn away from a love so strong and so loyal? Josie thought a great deal about loyalty these days.

Lina had taken to dropping in regularly before her visits to her mother. Sometimes she would bring little dark-eyed Dawn to please Kitty, but April, like Justin, had already started school. She was at St Clare's, where Antonia had been a pupil, and doing very well, Lina said, was going to be clever like Duncan.

'Just as well she's no' got my brains, eh?' Lina asked, laughing. 'Angus is the only clever one in our family. Did I tell you he was in Edinburgh now? Working out new plans for the firm, in case they come north.'

'You did mention it,' Josie answered evenly.

One October morning, Lina suggested they should drive down to the bridge site and see what was happening. Dawn had been left with the nanny, it would be easier to look around without worrying about a three-year-old under their feet.

'To tell you the truth, I'm making myself do this,' Lina told Josie. 'I really hate seeing that new bridge.'

'Lina, why?'

'Well, it's there, that's all. And every time Duncan looks at it, I know he wants to go up it, wants to prove something to himself. That he's OK.'

'But he is OK. Isn't he?'

Lina turned a wary gaze on Josie. 'Callum said he'd never really be better.'

'Callum?' Josie stared. 'When did you see Callum?'

'Och, it was years ago, when I was first in London. He came to ask if we could be friends, he was upset about the way we'd parted.'

'You never told me!'

Lina shrugged. 'Wasn't important, was it?'

Not important? Josie knew Lina had thought it too important to mention. How little one ever knew one's friends, how close they kept their secrets! Never would Lina imagine, for instance, that Josie was seeing Angus again. But Josie hated secrets.

'I don't see that Callum had any right to say that about Duncan,' she said quietly. 'He's no expert, why should he go worrying you? Anyway, Duncan is better, anyone can see that.'

'As long as he stays off that bridge,' said Lina.

Down at the site, with its litter of temporary buildings, cranes and equipment, they stood at a distance and raised their eyes to the bridge where the catwalks were already in position. Although they had wire mesh sides and flooring, handrails and bracing devices for safety, to the women's eyes they seemed precarious.

'Would you go up there?' Lina whispered.

'Not for any money,' Josie answered.

Lina's look was bleak. 'Who'd be a bridge-builder, eh?'

For some time they watched the activity on the site. So many men in hard hats! Josie couldn't pick out Matt, Lina couldn't see Duncan. Josie tried to cheer her.

'Matt said a works foreman has already crossed on the

334

catwalks and was quite all right. Even if Duncan did go up, I'm sure he'd be safe. They've had very few accidents, you know. Andy they say lightning never strikes twice.'

'I don't believe that.' Lina turned away. 'But Matt's never fallen, has he?'

'No, never.'

'He's been lucky.' Lina sighed. 'Och, I suppose I'm worrying about nothing.'

'You are, Lina. Duncan would never take risks, after what he's been through.'

'It's just that I have this feeling he thinks he can't call himself better till he goes up on the bridge – and comes down.' Lina shivered in the October wind. 'I'm frozen, let's have some coffee at your place, Josie, then I'll have to go and see Mum.'

That evening, when the children were in bed, Josie, to make conversation, told Matt she and Lina had been down to the bridge to view progress. She didn't look at him as she spoke, and knew now why he had always seemed to avoid her eyes when he was having his affair with Antonia Fearn.

'What did you think of it?' asked Matt.

'I think it's going to be wonderful, but Lina's worried in case Duncan insists on climbing it.'

'No need to worry, it's safe enough. We've got nets as well as handrails.' Matt yawned and studied the television page in the newspaper. 'Anyway, Mr Guthrie won't go up. He's got plenty to do at ground level.'

'You'd never want to be at ground level, would you?'

'Too right.' Matt, brightening, tossed the paper aside. 'You feel so different up there, you see. You forget what's down here.'

Josie set up her ironing board and began to sort out her laundry. What was there for Matt to forget? Their marriage? She plugged in the iron.

'I just hope you're right about being safe,' she said

335

quietly. 'You'll be working through the winter, there'll be gales and snow.'

'Aye, we're expecting to lose time, but it's a grand system we'll be using. I told you it was American? Invented by a fellow called Roebling. We're the first in Europe to adopt it, that's why we had to go on the training course.'

'What's it do?'

Matt smiled. He seemed pleased at her interest. 'You know that the bridge will be suspended from two great cables? Well, each one is made up of thousands of wires. Cable-spinning is just the way the wires are sent across the bridge and then formed into strands, tensioned and compacted. A lot of it's done by machines, we do the rest.'

'And all up there, so high over the water?' Josie shuddered. 'Matt, I still don't know how you can!'

'I'm looking forward to it. Something different, you see. I mean, think of it – getting thirty thousand miles of wires into those cables! Enough to stretch around the world!'

'And how long will it take you?'

'Depends on the weather. I think they're reckoning on five months or so. We'll be working a two-shift system, eight in the morning till midnight. No meal breaks.'

'And you're looking forward to it?' Josie asked drily.

'Och, we'll be getting hot soup and tea, we'll be OK. And when we're working at night, the bridge'll be lit up. That'll be a sight to see, eh?'

For the first time that evening, Josie allowed her eyes to stay on Matt's face. How happy he looked. Happier than he'd looked in a long time. Thinking about the bridge.

336

Chapter Fifty-One

When Josie eventually saw Angus again, he looked weary. He agreed that he felt under par, had been working flat out in Glasgow, investigating possible sites, studying economic factors, at the same time suffering because he had been unable to contact her.

'It's a kind of hell,' he told her. 'Not being able to pick up the phone, talk to you, say, "Can we meet tonight?" I keep thinking of how things used to be for us.'

'Till I changed them, I suppose you mean,' Josie murmured. 'There's no point thinking like that, Angus.' She looked out from the passenger seat of his car, parked out of sight of the playgroup hall. 'Look, can we go somewhere?'

He switched on the ignition. 'Where'd you like to go?'

'Anywhere out of Queensferry will do.'

They went to a village they knew, a few miles along the Forth, a yachting centre, quiet on weekdays, where they were not likely to meet anyone they knew. There was a pub, a couple of shops, and a distant view of Queensferry and the bridges, if you wanted to climb up through the trees to look. Josie didn't. She felt quite guilty enough, without reminders of bridgeworkers.

'We won't be seen in the trees,' Angus reminded her.

'Oh, I know.' She sighed and gave him her hand as they

climbed up a grassy bank to the sheltering trees. 'I just wish I didn't mind about all this.'

'I wish you didn't too,' Angus groaned. 'We have so little time together, why can't we enjoy what there is?'

There was no one about and he slipped his arms around her. They kissed, gently, then deeply, were beginning to feel passion rising until Josie pulled away.

'It's all the hole and corner stuff, Angus. It's just not me.'

'There is a solution. I told you we could change things. Have you thought about it?'

'You mean divorce?' She shook her head. 'It's no' possible. You've forgotten the children.'

'I haven't forgotten the children! I'd be happy to take them on. I'd love them because they're yours.'

'They're Matt's,' she said flatly. 'And he'd never give them up.'

'Come on, mothers nearly always get custody of young children.'

'Even if the mother's the guilty party?'

'Matt is the guilty party,' Angus said firmly.

Josie looked through the trees to the Forth, at grey water joining grey sky, and massing autumn clouds promising rain. 'I'm no' ready to think about divorce, Angus. It's too soon, we've only just met.'

'Met again,' he corrected. 'When we met on the esplanade, we weren't strangers, were we? We were friends.'

'Had been friends.'

'Friends. Good friends.'

'All right, friends,' she conceded with a smile, and he bent to kiss her.

'I know it's difficult for you,' he said quietly. 'And I'm not going to rush you.'

'It's difficult for you, too, Angus.'

He read what was in her mind. 'Yes, but don't worry, I won't ask you to sleep with me. Not while you're Matt

338

MacLeod's wife. And you wouldn't want to anyway.' His laugh was self-conscious. 'Both children of the kirk, eh? Old teachings die hard.'

'Are you still a kirk-goer, Angus?' she asked nervously.

'No. Gave it up years ago. How about you?'

'I never go. I might see ma dad.'

'He always liked me, in the old days.'

'When you were a kirk-goer. But your mother never liked me.'

'Why are we talking about our parents?' Angus cried. 'So little time, why are we wasting it?'

He began to kiss her hungrily, but it was already time to go. Fleeing before the rain that had suddenly begun to fall, they made for the car, their spirits as low as the sky.

'Oh, God, I'm like you, I hate the way things are for us!' Angus said angrily. 'Can't you see why I want you to be free? We should be married, we shouldn't have to be looking over our shoulders everywhere we go!'

'All we can do is be patient,' Josie answered, combing her wet hair.

'Patient!' Angus laughed shortly. 'You think that's what we should be? OK, I know I said I wouldn't rush you, but the thing is, I could give you so much, Josie. I'm not talking about material things, but I do earn a good salary—'

'This isn't about money.'

'No, as I said before, it's about trust. If you were married to me – well, I won't have to spell it out all over again, do I? You know what I'm offering.'

'Yes, I know.'

'Well, then. Please, darling, think about it.'

He put his key in the ignition. Nothing happened.

Josie dropped her comb. 'What's wrong?'

'Nothing. It's OK.'

He tried the key again. The car remained silent.

'Oh, God, what are we going to do?' Josie's face was white, she was instantly panic-stricken. 'We're miles away from the playgroup, I'll be late, I'll be late picking up Trina!'

339

'You won't, you won't. This is a company car, it's well-maintained, it must be a bit cold, that's all.'

Sweat was starting on Angus's brow, he too was white, when suddenly the engine roared into life and he gave a sigh of relief. 'There, I told you, Josie, it's all right, you see. Nothing to worry about!'

But she was deeply shaken and as they drove back to Queensferry, did not speak. What would she have done if the car had failed to start? Gone to the pub, maybe. Asked to use their telephone. Made some excuse. Got a taxi. Why was she doing this to herself? It was too much, too much.

'Oh, Josie,' Angus murmured, when he drew up as near as he dared to the playgroup. 'Don't punish me. For God's sake, don't say you won't see me again!'

Her heart softening at his anguish, she held his hand.

'I'm so torn, Angus, that's the trouble. I'm pulled all ways, and you can't understand.'

'I do, I do understand. That's why I want us to get our relationship on the right footing. If you could bring yourself to speak to Matt ...'

'I must go.' Josie pulled her hand loose. 'We'll talk when I see you again, shall we?'

'Will you think about what I've said? Will you promise me that?'

'I will, I promise.'

She left the car, pulling a scarf from her pocket to put over her hair, and ran through the rain away from him. For some time he sat on, gazing at the raindrops spattering his windscreen, before driving through the town to call on his mother. She'd said she would make him steak and kidney pudding for his dinner, but he hoped she hadn't had the time. He knew he couldn't eat it.

Later that day, after she had collected Justin from school and was picking late apples from her trees, someone came hurrying to Josie's gate. It was Tilly Park, from Ardmore.

'Oh, Josie!' Tilly's large creased face was full of her bad

340

news. 'Can you come quick? Can you come now?'

'What's happened?' cried Josie, dropping apples in the wet grass. 'Is it ma dad?'

'No, it's your mum. She's fallen doon the stair. Broken something, I couldna say what, the doctor's at the house. Can you come, Josie?'

Chapter Fifty-Two

It was like a bad dream. Scribbling a note for Matt. Persuading Trina to go in her pushchair about which she screamed her resentment, she being too grown-up. She could run fast, she could, she could! Comforting Justin, whose eyes were enormous. What had happened to Gran, then? Was she dead? Why were they going to her house? They never went to her house. What about Grandad? Would he let them in?

Josie, sick with worry, got them all on the road, and while Tilly ran on ahead, went hurrying towards Ardmore as fast as Justin's little legs would allow. There was no time for her to wonder what kind of reception she would get from her father; not when she had to think of Ellie, who must be so shocked and in pain. But, thank God, Tilly had said all the boarders were out. No need to worry about them. Yet.

The house loomed up, its front door standing open, and at its gate, the doctor's car.

'Mammie, I don't want to go in!' wailed Justin. 'I'm no' going in!'

'I'm going in!' cried Trina. 'Let me out, let me out, Mammie, I'm going in!'

'We're all going in,' said Josie.

For a split second, as she rushed the children into the vestibule, Josie was overwhelmed by memories. So many faces, so many voices from the past, all mixing in her mind, in this house where she had not set foot for so many years. But then she was in the hall and there was her poor mother, stretched out under a blanket on the floor, old Dr Ashton kneeling beside her. When he saw Josie, he rose creakily to his feet, dusting his trousers, and greeted her calmly in his precise Edinburgh accent. She knew him well; long ago, he had been her parents' 'panel' doctor and was now head of the National Health practice she herself attended.

'No need to worry,' he told her. 'Your mother tripped on the stair and fell, but she's going to be all right. Very shocked, of course, I believe her left leg is fractured, but I've given her something for the pain. She'll sleep soon.'

'But she'll have to go to hospital?' Josie asked breathlessly.

'Of course, the Infirmary, and I don't want her moved till the ambulance arrives. Don't think me rude, my dear, but could someone take the children? Mustn't knock Mother, must we?'

'I'll take them, Josie,' Tilly whispered. 'I'll go make a cup of tea, eh?'

'Mr Morrow's already away doing that,' said Dr Ashton, 'but by all means join him.'

'Go with Tilly,' Josie whispered to Justin and Trina. 'Now please be good and help Mammie, because Gran's ill. I'll come in a minute.'

'Will Grandad be there?' asked Justin, in alarm. He had always been told that his grandfather was ill and didn't like visitors, that was why they never went to Ardmore. But here they were, in the house, and it wasn't Grandad who was ill but Gran, so what was it all about?

'Just go with Mrs Park,' Josie said so firmly that even Trina took Justin's hand and followed Tilly to the kitchen without a word.

Josie knelt down beside her mother, straightening the pillow someone had put beneath her head. How white she

343

was! As white as the pillow-cover. Her eyelids, however, were struggling to rise.

'Josie?' she whispered. 'You came ... thank God.'

'Don't try to talk, Mum. Save your strength.'

'Aye ... but I want ... I want you to ... look after your dad.'

'Mum.' Josie's eyes flickered. She glanced up at Dr Ashton, but he was already taking his bag.

'I think I hear the ambulance – I'll call your father, Josie.'

Oh, God. Josie found her mother's hand and held it. This was it, then, this was the time. She was to see her father at last.

'Look after your dad,' Ellie was saying, her voice suddenly strong. 'And ma guests. I've men from the bridge, and Mr Warren, a couple from York ...'

Josie was looking over her shoulder, preparing herself.

'Mum, I can't – you must understand –'

'Promise me!' cried Ellie, struggling to sit up. 'Promise me, Josie! I'll no' rest, if you'll no' help me!'

'All right, all right, I will help. I promise.' From the corner of her eye, Josie saw that a white-haired man had come into the hall. 'Just lie down, Mum, the ambulance is here.'

'Aye, lie down, Ellie,' said John Morrow's voice, and Josie, scrambling up from her mother's side, turned to face her father.

'Hello, Dad,' she said bravely.

For a moment, he did not speak. She thought how old he looked, how changed he seemed, from the way she remembered him. Yet his dark-blue eyes on her were as fierce as ever. The moment stretched, the air between them seemed to tremble, full of words, spoken and unspoken.

'Josie,' John Morrow said at last, his voice strained with the effort to speak her name. 'I'm – glad you came.'

Jaunty ambulance men, all unaware, were expertly handling Ellie on to a stretcher, wrapping her again in

344

blankets and removing her to the ambulance, while Dr Ashton fussed along and Kitty Braid from next door came out to see what was going on.

'Anybody going with this lady?' asked one of the ambulance men, his hand on the door.

'Yes, I'm going!' cried John. 'Give me a hand in, will you?'

'Mr Morrow, I wouldn't advise it,' Dr Ashton said firmly. 'You're not up to hanging round in hospital waiting rooms, and there's nothing you can do. Mrs Morrow is already sedated.'

But Ellie's eyes were open and beseeching.

'Josie?' she whispered. 'You promised?'

'I did, Mum, don't worry, I'll look after everything.' Josie kissed her mother's cheek. 'I'll be along to see you tomorrow. Now you just go to sleep.'

'And you can see her tomorrow, too,' Dr Ashton told John, putting his hand on his arm. 'Get someone to drive you in, take it easy. Don't land yourself in hospital as well as your wife.'

John stood back, wilting, as the doors were closed on Ellie and the ambulance roared away. 'I feel bad, no' going with her,' he muttered. 'She should've had someone with her.'

'Ellie'll be all right, John,' Kitty Braid said kindly. 'She wouldn't want you tiring yourself out over at the Royal. You ken well what thae places are like, eh?'

Her green eyes went to Josie and back to John, but she made no comment, only asked if there was anything she could do.

'It's very kind of you, Mrs Braid,' Josie answered. 'I think we'll be all right, thanks.'

'Angus would've been glad to help, but he's had to go back to Edinburgh.' Kitty smiled complacently. 'Got a very responsible job on at the moment.'

'Oh, yes?' Josie took her father's arm, and began to move back into the house. 'Well, we'll see you, Mrs Braid.'

345

'Tell your mum I'll visit her,' called Kitty, her eyes still watchful, as the doctor told John he'd be in touch and drove away. She did not return to her own house until Josie and her father were inside Ardmore and Josie had closed the door.

Chapter Fifty-Three

Panic gripped her when there were just the two of them together in the hall, where Ellie's pillow and the blanket still lay crumpled on the floor. What am I to say to him? wondered Josie. What will he say to me? She released her father's arm and turned to look at him. He looked exhausted, his face yellowish-pale and glistening with sweat. For the first time, she realised how shocked he must be, by her mother's accident and her own reappearance.

'Dad, you'd better go and lie down, this has all been too much for you. I'll bring you some tea, eh?'

'I made some tea,' he muttered. 'Saw the bairns. Grand little lad, your Justin.'

'Do you think so?' Josie asked softly.

'Aye, and Catriona – she's Ellie to the life, eh?' John gave a deep, ragged sigh. 'Och, ma poor Ellie – I wish I'd gone with her, I should've gone, I should never have listened to that Dr Ashton.'

'You come and lie down, Dad. Rest is what you need.'

But on his bed, lying back, her father's eyes entreated Josie as her mother's had done. Their fire was quenched, he seemed a man out of himself. A snowman, melting, thought Josie, yet he had made no apology for the way he had treated her. It had never been his way, of course, to apologise.

'Josie, what'll we do?' he asked. 'There'll be all the

347

folk, wanting their tea. Tilly's no use, your mother says, and I'm no' up to anything – what'll we do?'

She stood looking down at him. So this was how he was going to play it. Talk to her as if the years she'd been banished from his house had never existed, as if she were a girl again, with no godless husband in the background. She was his daughter returned to the fold, she would do what had to be done.

Oh, God, and I will, groaned Josie.

'It's all right,' she told him. 'I promised Mum I'd take care of things. At least, for a while.'

'That's good of you, pet. I knew we could count on you.' John closed his eyes. 'I think I'll sleep for a bit, would do me good, eh? And tomorrow we'll go and see your mother.'

The children, fascinated by the new territory of Gran's house, were behaving badly, running up and down the stairs, rattling the handles of the boarders' bedrooms, while Tilly chased after them, telling them to be quiet, their grandad was sleeping.

'I just want to see ma old room,' Josie murmured. 'Is it let to anyone, d'you know, Tilly?'

'You mean that little place at the top? No, it's no' let, your mum always keeps it free.'

Justin and Trina came tearing up, delighted to be allowed into one room at least, and Trina gave a squeak of excitement at the sight of Josie's old dolls on the narrow, neatly made bed.

'Oh, Mammie, whose are those? Are they yours? Can I have them?'

'They're mine, but you can't have them. They live here.'

'What are they called? Mammie, tell me their names!'

'Teddy's just Teddy, the china one is Shirley, and the rag one is Rita. That little one there came from Spain. I didn't give her a name.'

As Trina danced around the tiny room with the beautiful

348

Shirley, and Justin hugged the others in case they felt left out, Josie's eye was drawn to the old framed text still tacked over her bed, though she distinctly remembered throwing it down.

The Path of the Just is as the Shining Light ... So Mum had put it back. And kept this room, waiting.

Josie walked to the window to look out at the view of the Forth she had loved so much. It was dark now, she couldn't see the outline of the new bridge, waiting to be illuminated for the cable-spinning, but the lights of the railway bridge shone out, blurred by her tears.

'Let's go down,' she said abruptly. 'We've the tea to get, Tilly.'

Ellie had already made cottage pies and individual trifles, so there were only the vegetables to prepare and the table to set.

'See your mum's new fridge?' asked Tilly, showing Josie round. 'Aye, and there's a washing machine in the basement, and a great big telly in the lounge. No' bad, eh?'

'Very good.' Josie was impressed. If her mother hadn't changed the threadbare carpeting or the faded curtains, at least she'd splashed out on things to make life easier or more entertaining. And why not? It cheered Josie to think that Ellie had at last been able to buy the things she wanted.

'Will you be able to stay and give me a hand, Josie?' Tilly asked anxiously. 'Folk'll be coming back now – Mr Warren's already here – they'll be wanting their tea.'

'I promised Mum I'd help, Tilly, but I don't know just how much I can do. I mean, what about the breakfasts?'

She paled. 'Och, I'm no' one for frying bacon and doing kippers! Your mum never lets me do a thing but put the plates out!'

Josie frowned over the problem. The simplest thing would have been to ask the boarders to move elsewhere, though where they would have gone was difficult to say, the town being so full. She couldn't ask them to do that

349

now, anyway. She'd promised her mother to hold the fort, and hold it she'd have to do, for a few days at least.

'Mebbe if I brought the children over, you could take Justin to school while I was doing the breakfasts?' she asked Tilly. 'These bridge men, they don't –' she hesitated, as sharp memories pierced '– don't want it early, do they?'

'No, your mum said she couldna do it and they said they'd manage. I think they work shifts, they're no' always around. Och, there's the doorbell!' Tilly dried her hands. 'I'll see who it is.'

Ringing the bell that had at last been fixed was Matt.

He refused to come in. Josie had to speak to him in the vestibule, where she could see that though his manner was calm, he was concealing one of his rare fits of anger.

'What's going on, Josie? I get back to find there's nobody in, no tea, a note to say that you're down here ...'

'I said in the note that Mum had had an accident, Matt. She's broken her leg, been taken to hospital. I had to come here.'

'To this house?' His grey eyes were wintry. 'Just what are you doing?'

'Mum made me promise to look after things. She was in such a state, Matt, I couldn't refuse.'

'Look after things? And your father too, I suppose? Are you crazy? That old devil who threw you out? Threw us both out?' He ran his hand through his yellow hair. 'I'm not letting you do it, Josie. I may be easygoing, but not that easygoing. You get the children and come home now.'

'I can't, Matt. It wouldn't be right. Even if I hadn't promised Mum, I couldn't just leave things here, could I? I know Dad's behaved badly to us, but he's no' well —'

'He's never well. It doesn't stop him making your life a misery. Get the children, Josie, or I come in and get them myself. We're going home.'

Their eyes locked, neither would give in. Matt had put his hand on Josie's arm to move her from his way, when a

350

voice cried, 'Wait, wait! I want to speak to you!'

It was John Morrow, limping towards them. Matt drew back as his father-in-law fixed his eyes on his face.

'Matt,' John said quietly, 'will you come inside?'

They progressed slowly through the hall where the crazy hat-stand still had to be supported and the circulars for local attractions fluttered from Ellie's notice-board. But John waved them on, towards his own room.

'There's folk coming in all the time, they'll have to be told about Ellie, eh? But I want to talk to you first.'

He sank heavily into a chair by his bed as Josie stood beside him and Matt, rigid and silent, looked down at him.

From upstairs came the sounds of people moving around, opening doors, running water, unaware as yet that anything had happened to their landlady.

John cleared his throat.

'I know what you both think of me. And it's true, I was hard. But I did what I thought was right. You have to understand that.'

If he expected a word of encouragement, he received none. They waited.

'I'd always lived by the Lord,' John went on. 'His word meant everything to me, still does. How could I take a man into ma family who would no' believe? Or accept ma daughter, wanting him. Can you no' see how it was for me?'

'You must try to see how it was for us too, Dad,' Josie answered dispassionately. 'You cut us off. Even the minister said you shouldn't have done that.'

'Aye, he did. But I thought I was right. All along I thought I was right, so what could I do?'

'There's no point in all this,' Matt said strongly. 'I'm going.'

'No, wait, wait!' John put out his hand. 'I want you to stay, Matt. I want you and Josie to be welcome. And the bairns. Will you stay?'

351

Matt have a fleeting smile. 'Very convenient, Mr Morrow. You need Josie. Surprise, surprise, she's forgiven. And even I am forgiven. That's a handy religion you've got, eh? Works as it suits. But we're still going home. Josie, where are the children?'

John struggled to his feet. 'It's no' like that,' he said with dignity. 'I don't blame you for thinking it, but it's no' true. It was seeing Josie again made the difference. I saw her goodness. I thought, If she loves a man and he has made her happy, there must be goodness in him too. "In my Father's house are many mansions, says the Lord." I see that now.' He held out his hand. 'Matt, will you stay?'

Matt's eyes were cast down, he seemed unable to speak. Josie's face was scarlet.

'Matt?' said John again.

Matt gave a long shuddering sigh and put out his hand to take John's.

Ellie's guests, as she liked to call them, had all been given the news that she was in hospital, had expressed their sympathy and eaten their cottage pie. If there was anything they could do? The middle-aged couple from York and Mr Warren, a retired clerk who was boarding for the winter, even offered to do the washing up or make their own beds, while the bridge workers said, nae bother, they'd fit in with whatever was going and could always have their meals at the canteen, just as long as they had a bed for the night, eh? Josie thanked everybody and said there was no need for anyone to help, she and Mrs Park would manage.

'Aye, but at what cost?' Matt muttered, knowing he'd already lost his battle. He raised no further objections. What he wanted to know now was when they could take the children home, for both Justin and Trina had fallen asleep on their grandfather's bed, as soon as they'd been given their tea.

'We'll just have a meal first with Dad,' Josie answered hastily. 'I thought we might as well have something here, if you don't mind?'

'Why should I mind? Looks like we'll be practically living here.'

Josie's eyes widened. 'That's an idea, Matt. I mean, to move in while Mum's in hospital. What do you think?'

'For God's sake, Josie! Just because your dad's speaking to you again, we don't have to live in his pocket, do we?'

'It would only be temporary.' She raised her eyes to his. 'Please think about it, Matt.'

He looked away. 'I know you're happy that he wants us back, but I can't forget what he did to you.'

'Matt, you shook his hand, and I'm very grateful for that, I really am. It does mean a lot to me that Dad's come round, and I think it will to you, once you've got used to it.'

He shrugged. 'OK. What do we do? Where do we sleep? The house is full.'

'We'll fit in somewhere. Let's have our tea and think about it.'

No one was hungry. John said he was too worried about Ellie to eat, Josie was too strung-up, Matt too downcast. But they went through the motions and afterwards Josie put through a call to the hospital, to be told that Mrs Morrow was resting comfortably. X-rays had been taken and her leg was to be set tomorrow, they could visit in the evening.

There, Dad, she's no' too bad,' Josie said comfortingly. 'It'll all be over tomorrow and then we can see her.'

'Aye.' John sat with his head bowed. 'I shouldn've been with her all the same.'

'We've been thinking that it might be easier if we all moved over here till Mum comes back. Then I'd be on the spot to see to things. Is there anywhere we can sleep?'

John's head shot up, his eyes brightening. 'You'd move over here, Josie?'

'If we can fit in somewhere.'

'Sure you can! The folk from York are moving out in a

couple of days, you could have their room, it's the double at the front. And the bairns could have your little room, eh? Why, that's a grand idea, Josie! Och, it'll make all the difference!'

'That's settled then,' she declared, not looking at Matt. 'We'll move in as soon as the room's free, but I'll be over tomorrow to do the breakfasts.'

'Thank you, Josie,' her father said simply. He leaned over and kissed her cheek. 'And thank you too, Matt. I'll no' try to say how I appreciate this.' He rose painfully to his feet. 'Now, I want you to ring for a taxi. Ma treat. Take those bairns home in comfort, eh?'

'A taxi, Dad?' Josie repeated incredulously.

'Aye.' He counted out some coins from his worn leather purse. 'What's money for, then?'

'Seems like the leopard can change its spots,' Matt remarked, when the children, thrilled with their taxi ride to the cottage, were in bed and asleep again. 'Your dad paying for a taxi – what next?'

'He's doing his best to show he's sorry. Matt. It's no' easy to do that.'

'So he's sorry. Means a hell of a lot of work for you, now that he's letting you back in the house.'

'I keep saying, it'll only be temporary.'

'But will it? Broken bones can take a long time to heal. Your mum's not likely to get back to things for some time.'

'We'll just have to see how it goes.' Josie stood up. 'I think I'll have an early night, it's been quite a day.' She glanced at him covertly. 'Thanks again, Matt.'

'For letting you knock yourself up, cleaning, cooking, all that stuff, over at Ardmore?'

'You know what I mean. You shook Dad's hand, you agreed to stay.'

'I'm still not sure why I did.'

'Oh, yes, you are sure.'

'Because your dad thinks I've made you happy?' Matt's

354

mouth twisted. 'Because he thinks we're good people? Well, I suppose he's fifty per cent right.'

Josie turned her head aside, but not before he saw her colour rising.

'I'm going up,' she said, and climbed the stairs.

In bed, before Matt came up, she lay thinking about the confused events of the day, marvelling at the changes a few hours could bring. Had she really been with Angus that morning? It seemed like something from another life. But when Matt came to bed and lay beside her, the colour rose to her face again and burnt like a flame.

Chapter Fifty-Four

Matt was right. Ellie, now in the orthopaedic hospital, made only poor progress as the autumn weeks went by. Though her spirits were sky-high over John's reconciliation with Josie and Matt, her fracture had been a bad one and was slow to heal. There was no prospect of an early return to work.

Josie was worried, not only for her mother, but for herself. While only too willing to help her parents out for a time, she had no wish to end up permanently where she began, as head cook and bottle-washer at Ardmore. Supposing her mother was never able to take up her work again? Matt said her parents should give up the house anyway, but John Morrow's compensation money was too small to live on and they were not yet eligible for the old-age pension. Besides, Ellie's 'guests' provided her main interest, had always been her lifeline; without it, she would surely sink.

There was nothing for Josie to do but to carry on, and hope things would work out for the best. At least the children were happy, living in their mother's old home, looking out of her window at the Forth, playing with her dolls, arranging their own toys in her room, which now held their two small beds. And there was another and surprising bonus to the new circumstances, which was the friendly relationship that was slowly developing between John Morrow and Matt. Josie took particular pleasure in this.

To begin with, Matt was offhand and John was wary, but one evening Matt agreed to satisfy his father-in-law's curiosity about his work. Soon, both were deep in the technical details of bridge-building, the ice between them broken, never to reform. John appeared a different man. In fact, Tilly said she'd never seen him looking so well, for had he no' been starved of his interests all this time, with thae boarders never stopping to give him the time of day? But Josie's Matt was such a sweet fellow, so patient and helpful, eh? His coming to Ardmore was the best thing that could have happened to Mr Morrow. Josie had to conceal her ironic smile.

Bright spots in her life were Lina's visits on her way to her mother's, though Lina at first had been completely shocked by Josie's return to the boarding house, and very disapproving.

'It's grand, I know, that you're all palsy-walsy with your dad again, Josie, but you're going to have to watch your step. It's no' for me to say, but Mrs Tassie always used to think your folks took more from you than they should've done, and here they are, at it again!'

When Josie pointed out that her mother was still in hospital, Lina set her pretty face and said, yes, but it was what happened when Mrs Morrow came out that would be crunch time.

'You just say then that you've done your bit and you can't keep the place going forever. They'll have to pay somebody else if your mum can't manage, somebody better than Tilly Park.'

'That wouldn't be difficult, but I don't see it happening,' Josie answered, laughing.

'Well, be warned, is all I'm saying. Parents like to get their hooks into you, you know.'

'I'd never be like that!' cried Josie.

'I bet that's what everybody says, till their children grow up.'

*

On one gloomy November morning, when the haar hung over the town and foghorns boomed mournfully, Lina brought someone else with her to Ardmore.

'Look who's here!' she cried, and Josie, at the door, had to meet Angus's golden-brown eyes.

'Why, Angus,' she said faintly. 'Haven't seen you – for a while.'

'No,' he said softly.

'I found him going into Mum's,' Lina said, taking off her fur-collared coat with a shudder. 'I said, "Look, this is ridiculous, you come in and talk to Josie," so here he is! Can we go in your lovely warm kitchen, Josie?'

'Of course. I'll put the kettle on. You'll have to excuse the mess.'

'What mess?' Angus stood looking around at the kitchen he had once known so well. 'It's as neat as a pin.'

'Josie was always efficient,' Lina remarked, winding a pink scarf around her neck. 'Children away to school, I suppose?'

'Yes, well, Trina's at playgroup.' Josie did not look at Angus as she switched on the electric kettle. 'Tilly's doing the messages and Dad's down at the bridge site as usual.' She smiled. 'Though what he'll see today with all the mist, I can't think.'

'Is it true Matt's given him a hard hat and shown him all around?'

'Yes, he's as thrilled as a little boy with a train set.' Though pale, Josie believed she was acting well. There would be no reason for Lina to suspect anything, provided Angus stopped staring at her. But then he had always stared at her; nothing so unusual in that. 'Everybody like coffee? It's only instant.'

When she had served the coffee and put out biscuits, she managed to thank Angus politely for the flowers he had sent her mother.

'Mum was so pleased, Angus, it was a lovely thought.'

'I was very sorry to hear of her accident,' he answered,

and Josie, staring hard into her coffee, thought, we might both be on stilts, the way we're acting. She was worried now that Lina would spot something, but then Angus lit a cigarette and began to talk about the Berlin Wall the East Germans had built, and what its significance might be, and Josie relaxed. He too was playing his part.

'Let's no' get on to all that Cold War stuff,' said Lina, also smoking, though she was supposed to have given it up. 'We've got worries enough without that.'

'Why, what worries have you got?' Angus asked curtly.

'Plenty. I'm no' going into them now.'

'Snap, then.' Angus suddenly leaped to his feet. 'Josie, it's been nice seeing you again, but I think we ought to be going. Mustn't keep Mum waiting, Lina.'

'See what I mean, about the hooks?' she asked, coolly blowing smoke. 'OK, OK, I'm coming. Where did I put my coat?'

'Hooks?' asked Angus.

'Just something we were talking about the other day.' Lina gave Josie a hug. 'Now, you look after yourself, Josie, and remember what I said.'

'You don't need to remind me. If you're looking for your coat, I think it's in the hall.'

As Lina left them, Angus instantly seized Josie's hand and pressed it hard. His eyes on hers were dark with meaning, his lips silently framing the words, 'Next week?'

She could not reply. Lina was back, snuggling into the fur of her collar, taking Angus's arm.

'Goodbye, Josie, take care!'

They were running into the clinging mist, Lina turning to smile, Angus not. Moisture glittering on her splendid hair, Josie stood at the door of Ardmore until they had disappeared. Two beautiful friends. Why shouldn't she keep them both?

Chapter Fifty-Five

'Next week,' Angus had mouthed, which meant a week from that day, another playgroup day. Josie hadn't said she would meet him, but she knew she would see him. Though Tilly took Justin to school while Josie fried the bacon and eggs, Josie always managed to take Trina to playgroup herself, for then the breakfasts were over and Tilly could get on with the washing up. One week after Angus had made his silent assignation, Josie, wearing a navy raincoat and a hat she called a tam, saw him in his usual place, waiting for her by his car.

He pulled off his tweed cap when she came up, and opened the car door, but she noticed he didn't smile. There was something different about him, something hard and resolute. He had the air of a man who had made up his mind.

'Angus, I can't go with you,' she said quickly. 'I've no time for drives any more, I'm sorry.'

He set his mouth grimly. 'Where are you going now, then?'

'Back home, once I've got the messages.'

'I'll walk with you to the shops.'

'No, how can you? Look, things are difficult for me at the moment, I'm no' as free as I was—'

'Free!' He smiled. 'When were you ever free? But there's no point in arguing, I'm going with you, and that's all there is to it. We have to talk.'

'We can't exactly talk in the shops, Angus.'

'No. Let's walk towards the bridge, then. You could do the messages afterwards.'

'I'm no' going to the Queen Margaret,' Josie said sharply. It had been risky enough letting Beryl Tassie see them together that first time. It was sheer luck she didn't appear to have mentioned it to Lina.

'We'll just walk,' Angus told her.

The morning was clear for November, but grey and chill, the sort of day Josie felt for the men on the bridge, so cold and numbing as it must be up there. Cable-spinning was due to start soon, and then the poor fellows wouldn't even have proper meal breaks; Angus was fortunate, he worked in very different conditions. But as she glanced at him, striding some distance from her along the pavement, his cap jammed back on his flaxen hair, it seemed to her that he didn't look well. He might have taken some inner stand, but he was still like a man labouring under a huge and intolerable burden. It didn't take much intelligence to guess what it was.

They passed Ardmore and Seafields. Was John Morrow looking out? Was Kitty Braid? No, they would both be otherwise occupied at that time of the morning, John with his newspaper, Kitty with her clients. Anyway, why shouldn't the two of them walk together, Josie and Angus, two old friends? It was the look on their faces that would give them away.

Here were the Sealscraig Rocks and then the long straight line of the esplanade stretching towards the old bridge, but it seemed they were not going as far as that, for Angus abruptly stopped. He leaned over the rail, looking down at the weed-covered rocks below and the little stretches of gritty sand, while Josie stood waiting for him to speak. He turned his head to meet her eyes.

'Josie, I want us to become lovers.' He raised his hand as her lips parted. 'I know I said I didn't want that, while you

361

were still married, but I've changed my mind. I want you now.'

The wind was strong here, tugging and chewing, and Josie made great play of settling her tam more firmly and turning up her coat collar.

'You haven't asked what I want,' she said, finally.

'No, because I know you'd rather let things drift. I can understand that, you've got a lot on your mind, but the thing is, I've reached the stage where I can't go on. I mean, the way we are. It's affecting my work, I can't concentrate on what I have to do, and it's important, very important. Something's got to be done, that's the way I see it.'

'Even if we were lovers, the situation'd be the same. I mean, what would change?'

'Everything! It'd mean you were committed. Committed to me. Committed to asking for a divorce, getting us settled.' Angus took Josie's gloved hands. 'Isn't that true?'

'I've explained why I can't ask for a divorce.'

'And I told you, you'd get the children. Look, come to me, Josie, let's find a way. Make a solemn commitment. Then we'd know where we were.' He released her hands. 'I'd know where I was, anyway.'

Josie looked away from him, out over the Forth to Fife. She felt it was she who was carrying a burden now, a great weight of guilt over her heart that would never lift.

'I can't, Angus. I can't do what you want.'

He made her look at him, turning her with gentle hands towards him.

'Why not?'

She shook her head.

'All right.' Angus straightened his shoulders. 'Answer me this, then. Do you love me? Just say yes or no.'

She tried to speak. He stopped her.

'I don't want you to say you're very fond of me, or that you care for me, or that you'll always be my friend. Do you love me, yes or no?'

Do you love me, yes or no? Even if you didn't want to, it

was a question you could always answer. Josie knew what she must say.

'Angus, you're right to want the truth. The thing is, I don't love anyone now, the way you want me to love you.'

The words hung in the wind. The truth. His answer. But he hadn't wanted the truth.

'I wish,' he said at last, 'I could say the same. I wish I didn't love anyone.'

Without warning, she burst into tears. 'There's no point in saying I'm sorry, is there? Some things you can't say sorry for.'

'Don't blame yourself. I knew what I was risking.'

She shook her head. She would not hide from herself what she had done. Used Angus, as Matt had used Antonia. It was true that Matt had not felt anything for Antonia, whereas she had felt something for Angus – oh, yes, she had, and she clung on to that – but in her heart she'd always known she'd never go to him. She'd taken his love for temporary comfort and let him believe she wanted so much more. Wanted what he wanted, in fact. How could she have done that? She couldn't say, but she knew she would have it to face for the rest of her life. There would always be that secret she would have to keep, that knowledge of herself. And the knowledge of Angus's pain.

'You'd better go for your messages,' he said quietly. 'I'll walk on.'

'Where? Where will you go?'

'I don't mind. Maybe the Hawes.'

'They won't be open yet. Not for alcohol.'

'You read my mind.' He shrugged. 'I'll wait. I need a drink.'

So do I, thought Josie. But she had to do the messages.

'Why, Josie, have you been crying?' Tilly asked, when Josie arrived back at Ardmore with the groceries and Trina.

'It's the wind,' said Josie.

Matt was late home that evening, though he'd said he'd be

363

back for his tea. It wasn't until Josie had said goodnight to the children and was on her way downstairs, that she met him coming up. He looked exhausted, said he'd been held up.

'I'd like a bath. Is it free?'

'It is.' She followed him into their bedroom where he was unbuttoning his shirt. 'Are you all right, Matt? You look a bit down.'

He slid his grey eyes over her face.

'I saw you and Angus Braid today.'

'Oh.' Josie sank onto a chair.

She should have guessed things would work out this way. Lower your guard for an instant, and you never got away with it. Always before, when she'd been with Angus, she'd worried about being seen. Had looked over her shoulder, kept her head down, and said, 'Drive on, drive on,' so that they would not be seen walking together. But when they were saying goodbye, she'd forgotten all about being seen. Other people hadn't existed for that time. And that was the time Matt had seen them.

'We were just talking,' she said faintly.

'You were crying.'

'How did you see us?'

'I was driving past with another guy. We'd been over to a store. Does it matter?' In his unbuttoned shirt, Matt sat down on the edge of the bed. 'How long have you been seeing him?' he asked quietly.

'Not long. We only met a few times, just for drives.'

'You were in his car?'

'Look, it's not the way you think!'

They were both silent, thinking of those words that had been said before.

'We were saying goodbye,' Josie went on, doggedly. 'There was no future in it.'

'What does that mean?'

'Well, Angus wanted me to marry him, he wanted me to ask for a divorce.'

364

Matt's face seemed to close, all expression vanishing as though wiped away by his hand. 'That would have been a future.'

'I didn't want it.'

'Because of the children? We could've worked something out.'

'Worked something out?' Josie was on her feet, glassily staring. 'What are you saying? You want a divorce?'

'No. It's just that we haven't been too happy these past years, have we? If you wanted to be with Angus, I wouldn't blame you.'

Her eyes swept over him, his blank face still so handsome, his serene eyes, his yellow hair lying on his brow. What he was feeling she had no idea. Did he mind about Angus? Or not? Would he really be content if she left him?

'And the children? Would you let me take them?'

He stood up, taking off his shirt and throwing it down. 'Like I said, we could work something out. If you want that.'

'I don't want it!'

'All right, let's leave it then.' Matt ran his hands over his face. 'God, I'm tired! Better have that bath and get to bed.'

'Don't you want something to eat? I've kept the beef.'

'OK, but I must get some rest. We start cable-spinning tomorrow, remember.'

Chapter Fifty-Six

People came from all over the area to see the new bridge lit up, once the work on the cables had started, and they were not disappointed. It was as good as Blackpool, they said, as good as Christmas, though some, seeing the new bridge for the first time, were surprised that it should be so different from the rail bridge. Of course, the famous humps of the rail bridge had been everyone's image of the Forth Bridge for half a century. Now, here was another bridge, incomplete, yet lean, streamlined, leaping like a greyhound across the dark waters of the Forth! It was a grand sight, and would be a grand achievement, so everyone agreed.

Everyone except perhaps Ellie Morrow, now home from hospital, her leg newly out of plaster. She had been taken in her wheelchair to see the bridge in all its illuminated splendour, but had only said, 'Yes, well, it's very nice, but what's a bridge, eh? It's just a way of getting from A to B, why all the excitement?'

'Come on, Mum, you must see that it's a wonderful piece of work,' Josie protested. 'When you think of all that has to go into it. Everything has to fit, they have to get it right.'

'Och, it's just another place for men to risk their lives,' Ellie muttered. 'That's what they like doing, seems to me. Look at your dad!'

But if she was not impressed with the bridge, Ellie was

delighted that John had taken Josie back into his heart, and even welcomed Matt MacLeod, though she was still astonished over that. She would never understand it, she declared, not till her dying day, though she had to admit that Matt was quite different from what she'd at first thought.

'Aye, I mebbe misjudged him, Josie. He seems a good enough lad. Very nice with your dad and the bairns, and works hard and all. Thing is, he's made you happy, and that's what counts, eh?'

'Yes,' answered Josie, washing dried fruit for the Christmas cake. 'That's what counts.'

'So, even though he's no' a professional man, you made a good choice,' Ellie went on, leaning over to help herself to a currant or two. 'You tell him to take care up there on that bridge, mind. Thae winter gales are something to watch.'

'He doesn't need telling, Mum. Do you think you should go and have your rest now?'

'Aye, will you bring me a cup of tea?'

When she was lying on her bed, a pillow at her back and cup of tea to hand, Ellie gave a contented sigh.

'Och, what'd I do without you, Josie? What a blessing you've been to your dad and me, pet.'

'That's all right, Mum. You drink your tea and have a nice nap, while I do the cake.'

'To think I'm no' doing ma own cake this year,' Ellie sighed, sipping her tea. 'Or the puddings, eh? Still, it's a weight off ma mind that you know what to do, Josie.'

'Just have a rest, Mum,' said Josie, sidling towards the door.

'I was worried at first, about you leaving Monnie Robb's cottage,' Ellie's voice inexorably continued. 'But seemingly that fellow Ken Pearce has taken it on, your dad was saying. Sharing it with some mates, and all doing their own cooking!'

'Men are more capable than you think.'

'Aye, well, just as long as you're no' out of pocket,' Ellie murmured, her eyes closing at last.

'Out of pocket?' Josie tiptoed away. 'I'd say we were in credit.'

In credit financially, maybe, she reflected back in the kitchen, chopping cherries and nuts, creaming butter and sugar. But in other respects? The letting of the cottage to Ken seemed to have closed another door on her own life. She was more firmly set than ever into Ardmore, Matt too, especially now that he had charmed her mother as well as her father. Angus came into her mind. Her escape route. No, he had never really been that. All along his way out had been blocked, and she wouldn't even think of it now. Or poor Angus himself. That pain was too bad. Lina had said he'd chosen a site in Glasgow for his firm's new venture, but that he'd made it clear to Kitty he would never work in Scotland himself. Because of me, thought Josie, her eyes filling with tears. He has become an exile because of me.

The children came running into the kitchen, anxious not to miss any tastings, and Josie gave them some of the nuts and fruits but said they were not to scrape out her bowl, it wasn't good for them to eat uncooked mixture.

'Oh, why?' cried Justin. 'I like it uncooked!'

'So do I,' chimed Trina. 'Please, Mammie, could we no' have just a wee taste, then?'

As she gave in and the two of them happily set to, scraping out the mixing bowl, Josie felt the better for her children's presence, yet knew they were not an answer to what ailed her. With the cake in the oven and the children away to play, she drew the curtains on the black November night. The wind was rising, she could hear it rattling down the pipe of the kitchen range, howling round the side of the house. She thought of Matt and the others on the bridge, working the midnight shift, and hoped things weren't too bad for them up there. Said a little prayer, in fact.

368

Chapter Fifty-Seven

Whenever Duncan looked up at the bridge during the cable-spinning, he saw himself on it. Striding the catwalk beneath the endless tramways that sent the wires from anchorage to anchorage, checking with the men who were compacting and positioning, disregarding the winds and the cold. Never, of course, looking down. At night, when the bridge was lit up and the waters of the Forth by contrast were inky black, his spirits faltered; he did not see himself on the bridge at night. But daytime was another matter, and as the work progressed without incident, he began to feel he could make it. Yes, by day. Whatever Lina thought. A man couldn't organise his life to save his wife anxiety. Besides, she needn't know.

Lina herself came over to see the bridge one evening in December. Said, yes, it was wonderful, but oh, she was so cold! In spite of her fur-collared coat, fur hat, boots and mitts, she said she couldn't endure the frosty air and if Duncan didn't mind, would hurry straight back to her mother's for a hot drink.

'And you were born in this part of the world?' he marvelled, smiling down at the glimpse of her face showing beneath the fur hat. 'Anyone would think you'd spent your life on the Riviera!'

'Fat chance.' Lina took his arm. 'Come on, it's your night off, Duncan, let's get out of this cold.'

369

'What about sparing a thought for the chaps up there? Any idea what it's like?'

Lina shivered. 'I'm just glad you're not with them.'

He made no reply.

'Come on.' She tugged his arm and they moved away, threading slowly through the knots of people who had come, braving the cold, to see the bridge. A tall man in a long dark overcoat stepped aside to let them pass, looked at them, and halted.

'Lina?'

'Heavens, fancy meeting you!' She gave her high little laugh, and shot Duncan a quick glance. 'Duncan, this is an old friend, Callum Robb. Callum, my husband, Duncan Guthrie.'

Callum Robb. Duncan, his dark gaze riveted on the other man's face, put out his hand. In that light, it wasn't possible to see Callum Robb's features clearly, but Duncan could tell that he was strong and confident, a man of some presence, though quite young. There was money behind him, and the power to make it. That was what gave him his particular strength, but Duncan knew he would have others. This man would be able to go up on the bridge, would be able to look down. Callum Robb would never have a nightmare in his life.

'It's strange we've never met.' Duncan released Callum's hand, but kept Lina's arm in his. 'But then you're based in London, I believe?'

'That's right.' Callum's eyes were moving between Duncan and Lina, lingering on Lina. 'Just up for a short break, thought I'd see the new bridge. Not before time they got it off the drawing board, eh?'

'No, it's very much needed.'

'Yet they're trying to make us all pay tolls?' Callum shook his head. 'I knew there'd be a catch.'

'No decision has yet been made on tolls,' Duncan said stiffly.

'No, but we know what it'll be, don't we? Still, that's

370

nothing to do with you. Listen, why don't we all go for a drink? Get thawed out?'

'We were just going round to Mum's,' Lina said uneasily.

'Come on, let me buy you both a whisky, you look as though you need it.'

Although highly uncomfortable at the idea of drinking with a man who had once loved his wife, Duncan allowed himself and Lina to be dragooned into the saloon bar of the nearest pub. He refused a whisky, however, said a beer would do, and Lina, loosening her coat and removing her hat, sat staring at Callum over a gin and tonic.

'You're looking prosperous,' she told him. 'Robb's Tours must be doing well.'

'It is. Very.' Callum drank some whisky and waved a hand at the curtained windows of the bar. 'Look outside, see that frost? Folk want to get away, right? Well, more and more of 'em are travelling Robb's Tours. It's like, as they say, taking sweeties from a baby.'

'Don't underestimate yourself,' Duncan said coldly. 'No business succeeds if the boss doesn't know how to run it.'

'Suppose I always knew how to run things, ever since I was a kid at school.' Callum smiled. 'The good old days, eh, Lina?'

'My good days are now,' she returned, sliding her eyes towards Duncan, who got to his feet, saying he would get refills.

'Oh, not for me,' Callum protested.

'I insist.'

'Doesn't want to be beholden to me, even for a drink,' Callum said in a low voice, as Duncan made his way to the bar.

'He's just being polite.' Lina's large, limpid eyes were troubled. 'Why did you have to do this, Callum? Can't you see how embarrassing it is?'

371

'I wanted the chance to speak to you, that's all. To say that what I said before still stands, OK?'

'What? What did you say?'

'You know. That if you ever needed me, I'd be there.'

'Callum, I appreciate the thought, but why should I need you? You can see that Duncan's better. He's fine, we're very happy.'

'Has he been up that bridge?' Callum asked softly.

'No, he does other work, he doesn't have to be on the bridge.'

'A bridge engineer who doesn't go on the bridge?' Callum's mouth twisted. 'He's not better, Lina.'

'For God's sake, Callum – he's coming.'

'One whisky,' said Duncan, setting a glass before Callum. 'Two tonics, for Lina and me.'

'Tonics? Come on, that's no way to keep me company!' Callum cried.

'We have to go back to Edinburgh and I like to keep a clear head when I'm driving,' Duncan answered smoothly. 'Especially if there's ice about.'

'And one gin's enough for me,' said Lina cheerfully. She stood up, carefully replacing her fur hat over her flaxen hair, conscious that both men were watching her. 'It was very nice seeing you again, Callum. Thanks for the drinks.'

'You're going?' He had risen to his feet.

'We'd better not be late,' Duncan murmured. 'I've an early start in the morning.'

'And we've still got to look in on Mum.' Lina held out her hand. 'Goodbye, then. Take care.'

After a moment's pause, Callum shook Lina's hand, but Duncan, murmuring a cool goodbye, did not offer his hand again. Callum was left standing by the table on which were three full glasses, dark red colour staining his cheekbones. His eyes were fixed on Lina, or rather her fur hat, all he could see, going out of the door. But suddenly she was back, her great eyes meeting his with a look he couldn't fathom – pity, maybe, or else regret. He tried to grasp her

372

hand, hold her just for a little longer, but the fur hat was shaking from side to side.

'Callum, I'm sorry.'

His hazel eyes flashed. 'You remember what I said.'

'I will.'

Duncan, a tall, dark thundercloud, was between them.

'Lina, are you coming?'

His hand under her elbow, Duncan steered her purposefully away and Callum watched them go. He snatched up his whisky and drank it off, coughing only slightly, then he too left the pub.

Lina and Duncan did not visit Kitty, who had after all not been expecting them. Lina said she was too tired and too nervy after meeting Callum, she just wanted to go home, but Duncan was not prepared to let her off the hook.

'What was the idea of going back to speak to him like that?' he asked sharply, as they drove away from Queensferry. 'Were you trying to encourage him, or what?'

'Of course I wasn't encouraging him! What a thing to say!'

'It's obvious he's still in love with you. Isn't that enough for you?'

'Why are you talking like this? I went back because I felt bad, if you must know. We didn't treat him very well, did we?'

'We had a drink with him. What else were we supposed to do? If he had any idea how to behave, he wouldn't have made himself known to us, he'd have kept out of our way.'

Lina's face reddened with anger. 'Oh, well, he doesn't know how to behave, does he? Didn't go to a good school or anything. Just like me!'

'Lina, don't try to make something out of nothing. I'm not running Callum Robb down, he's done very well, I'd be the first to admit it. But you don't need to go to a public school to care about other people's feelings.'

Lina laughed. 'You expect Callum to care about your

373

feelings? That's a bit hard, considering what you did to him.'

'There were two of us involved,' Duncan answered quietly. 'If you remember.'

The rare coolness between them lasted until they went to bed, when Duncan slipped off Lina's nightdress and held her close.

'Did you make the right choice, Lina? Now you've seen him again, you don't regret marrying me?'

There was a moment of suspense as she hesitated.

'Lina! For God's sake—'

'Duncan, you don't have to ask me, you know I only want you.'

He let her go and relaxed. 'Well, it's not been any bed of roses, being married to me. You might have done better with him.'

'Why don't you say his name, Duncan?'

He shrugged in the darkness. 'Makes him seem more real, giving him a name.'

'I tell you, you're the one I want,' Lina whispered, twining herself around him. 'I feel sorry for Callum, I wish he'd find someone of his own, but that's as far as it goes.'

It was what Duncan wanted to hear, he should have been satisfied, but even when they'd made love and tired themselves with passion, his thoughts still returned to Callum Robb. Lina was sleeping, her face turned away, no conscience troubling her now. Why should it? She'd a right to marry as she chose. It was only seeing Robb again, still alone, still so obviously in love, that had upset her. If she didn't see him again, she could forget him again. But Duncan couldn't forget him. Though he had said nothing, Duncan knew Robb would be aware of his own past history and would very likely despise him for it. Despise him for all that he had put Lina through, and might put her through again. For of course it was true. Duncan himself knew he walked on shifting sands, never knowing when he might sink.

To hell with it! He slipped out of bed quietly, so as not to wake Lina, and flung on his dressing-gown. There were cigarettes in the pocket, a lighter on the tallboy. Soon he was smoking, trying to calm his churning thoughts. But Lina had woken, after all.

'Duncan, can't you sleep? What's the matter?' She snapped on the bedside light and came to him, tying her own dressing-gown around her, sliding on to his knee. 'You're no' still worrying about Callum, are you?'

'No. Yes. I suppose I am.'

'What does that mean?' She took his cigarette and drew on it.

'You didn't answer me straight away. When I asked – you know what I asked.'

'I told you I wanted you.'

'You took your time.'

She put his cigarette back between his lips. 'It's no' what you think. I was remembering something I never told you. Tonight wasn't the first time I've seen Callum since our marriage.'

Duncan sat very still. After a moment, he quietly lifted Lina from his knee and stood up.

'You're right, you never told me.'

'It was only once, Duncan, a long time ago.'

'When?'

'When we were in London. Callum met me in the park, I had April in the pram.'

'Met you by accident, I suppose?'

'No.' Lina was tying and retying the cord of her dressing-gown. 'He'd been looking out for me. He just wanted to say he was sorry we'd parted on such bad terms, and we should be a bit more – you know – civilised.'

'Civilised!' Duncan stubbed out his cigarette with great force, and laughed. 'The last thing he would like to be is civilised.'

'That's all there was to it, Duncan. We just walked back through the park and we said goodbye. We parted friends, and we felt better.' Lina was suddenly defiant. 'I'm not sorry about it because I think we did the right thing. I mean, where was the harm?'

'No harm at all. So why didn't you tell me about it?'

'I – I didn't think it was important.'

'You've just said it was. It made you feel better. You'd done the right thing. So why not tell me?'

'No' important to you, I meant.'

'You think what's important to you isn't important to me?'

'Och, I'm no good at this!' She burst into tears. 'I thought you'd go on, the way you're going on now, that's all it was. I'm sorry, Duncan, I didn't want to upset you.'

He put his arms around her and kissed her gently.

'Come on, let's go back to bed. I know it didn't mean anything, I won't go on. It's just upset us both, I think, seeing him again. Callum. There, I've said his name.'

Lina gave a watery little smile and willingly snuggled back into sleep, but Duncan was again lying awake. There were times to tell and times not to tell, it seemed, and he'd been right to think he needn't tell Lina what he intended. Tomorrow. Whatever the weather. Tomorrow, it was.

Chapter Fifty-Eight

The morning was perfect, cold and clear, with very little wind; at least at ground level. It would be different on the bridge. Duncan had decided to go up with the first shift rather than alone. Safety in numbers. His smile was grim. Everyone was alone on the bridge.

Amongst the men was Matt MacLeod. Duncan managed to speak to him.

'I thought you were working the midnight shift, Matt?'

'Not this week, Mr Guthrie.'

Matt's limpid gaze rested on Duncan's face, but he said nothing. No one said anything. Neither the cable-spinners, nor the engineers. Everyone knew that Duncan did not work on the bridge, everyone knew why, but the fact that he was now up there, on the catwalk, brought no comment. It was as though no one wanted to be the first to speak, no one wanted to say the word that might upset him.

What am I? thought Duncan. A piece of Dresden china or a bridge engineer? Well, this was make or break time. Either he proved he was fully recovered or he cracked. Like the china. And how easy it would be to crack, to break, up here in the sky, the wind roaring in his ears, the machinery for the carrying of the wires rattling overhead, the cold piercing his very being.

To his right was his old enemy, the railway bridge, but he would not look at that. Nor would he look down. Even without looking down, he could sense how far he was now from the Forth below. Even without seeing distant land, dolls' houses, tiny craft, he could feel his vulnerability. It was all there, laid out for him, on the catwalk stretching out, undulating away, miles and miles of it, towards the opposite shore. In fact, there could only be one mile, but that didn't seem possible. No, what there was, was infinity. Or as good as. That one mile of catwalk stretching to the north was infinity for him. For he could not move.

All around him, the spinning process that was controlled from the south shore was continuing, the endless tramway carrying the spinning wheels travelling on, the men in position, ready for their own particular jobs of stranding and compacting the wires when there were enough. No one looked at Duncan, standing so still, his face glistening with sweat, his eyes below the brim of his hard hat blank as a sleepwalker's.

He knew he must break the spell, drag his gaze from the metal path he could not take, but when he slowly turned his head, he saw what he had vowed he would not see. The railway bridge. Scene of nightmare, of disaster, source of all his troubles. All the old fears came back, joining with the new, and he heard the laughs of the briggers again as they went leaping over girders, he heard their cries as they fell, as he had fallen, and a sickness rose in his throat, wringing more sweat from his brow, sending him reeling. It came to him then, as he had perhaps always known, and had certainly feared, that he would not get off this bridge alive.

A hand was on his arm. Matt MacLeod's voice said, 'Are you all right, Mr Guthrie?'

All right? Duncan forced his eyes to focus on Matt's handsome, concerned face. It was Matt who had helped to rescue him after his fall from the railway bridge, he had always been grateful for that. But Matt could not rescue him now.

Duncan took a gasp of air, he felt the sickness recede.

'I – can't – move, Matt. I've – lost – my nerve.'

'No, you haven't.' Matt, as Duncan had known he would be, was unruffled. 'You've not been up for a while, it's strange to you. Just hang on, you'll be OK.'

'I can't move, I tell you. I can't go back or forward.'

'Aye, happens to us all. Doesn't last, you'll see. What you do, you just put one foot forward, then another …'

'I can't I can't!'

'Will you take my arm, then? Will you walk with me?'

'No, no!' Duncan was aware now of men looking up from their tasks to stare; of one of his colleagues, an engineer named Dick Berwick, coming towards him. He felt consumed by shame at his situation, at the same time marvelling that he could care, when he was under sentence of death, what other men thought. Yet he did care. He had come up here to restore his faith in his own courage, to let everyone see he had not been beaten. And now that they were seeing something very different, he minded out of all reason. Why not let go? he asked himself. Why struggle on, when the burden had become too much? Lina's lovely face swam before his eyes, his daughters' trusting little hands reached out to him, but they faded and Callum Robb was smiling. 'I've always known how to run things, since I was a kid at school …' Let him bloody run things! thought Duncan. I give in, I give in!

'Just walk with me,' Matt was saying imperturbably. 'One step and then another. Come on, Mr Guthrie, you can do it.'

'For God's sake, if you're trying to save my life again, call me Duncan!'

'Anything you say. Just let's get to the north tower, eh? One step and then another.'

'I can't take your arm, Matt, I don't want to do that.'

'Follow me, then, Duncan. Just follow me.'

And Duncan, like a child learning to walk, lifted one foot and put it down, lifted the other and put it down, and followed Matt's steady tread along the catwalk, as Dick Berwick fell back to let him go and the men watched in silence.

The wind had grown stronger, just as it had when it took

379

him from the railway bridge. Now it was gusting, sending the catwalk trembling and swaying, but the men, back at work hammering wires into circular form, positioning them into frames, seemed not to notice. Duncan knew that when the gales got too strong, work would stop, they'd already lost many hours for that reason, but work was not stopping now, these men could cope as he could not. Matt turned round to look at him and shouted something lost on the wind. Duncan shook his head and Matt, tunnelling his voice through his cupped hands, cried, 'Tea's up, soon!'

Tea? They could think of tea? Duncan closed his eyes, then opened them again, as the catwalk shifted beneath his feet and his heart met his mouth. How far now to the north shore? Infinity still.

It was only gradually that it dawned on him that he was going to make it. One step and then another and the steel column of the north tower was coming nearer. He was not looking up at the sky or down at the water, he was seeing nothing but Matt's hard hat and broad back in front of him, he was feeling nothing but Matt's dynamism forcing him on. Was the north shore coming nearer? He couldn't believe it. Something in him was rising and fluttering, some hope that he had not lost everything, might even have won a little. If he could complete this one mile aloft, could say he'd done it, he might just be able to live with himself, meet the eyes of the men who came up here every day ...

'Know something?' shouted Matt, turning back to face him. 'We're nearly there. Aye, you're going to make it!'

Duncan could scarcely raise his eyes to the nearness of the north shore. His head felt heavy as a cannonball, his knees were sagging. He would have liked to sink to the metal floor of the catwalk and cry, 'Thank God, thank God!' But even at such a time, it wasn't in his nature to say those words aloud, especially as Matt was leaning back against the side mesh, his hat pushed from his brow, smiling as though there had been no danger, no fear.

'Know something else?' he cried, into the wind. 'We're

not going off. You haven't finished, Duncan.'

'What the hell are you talking about?'

'We're turning round, we're walking back.'

'Walking back? Are you crazy?' Duncan put his hand across his cold wet brow. 'I couldn't do that, Matt, I couldn't go back.'

'It's the only way, Duncan. It's the way to beat this thing forever. Once you've done it – gone back – you'll be free.' Matt grinned. 'You'll be running up and down this bridge like a spiderman. Trust me. I've seen it happen, I know.'

Duncan was hesitating, longing to be safe, yet knowing that if he went down now, he would never come back. Thanks to Matt, he would have got himself off the bridge, but would he have gained anything? He might feel able to live with himself, but he would never work again, as he wanted to work. One more effort, though, one more mile, and he might, as Matt said, be free. Matt had known men like him before, he had seen them bound by their fear, and he had seen them released. One more effort, one more mile.

'I'll do it!' he cried, and saw Matt raise his hand. A moment later, a gust of wind, flaring violently across the bridge, drove Matt's hat from his brow, and as he swore and leaned to catch it, sent him flailing over the side mesh. And down.

Immediately, mysteriously, fear for himself left Duncan. He who had been too terrified to look up and down or even to walk on the bridge without Matt's help, now ran to the side of the catwalk.

'Matt MacLeod's over!' he cried, to the men running with him. 'Start rescue procedures! Call the shore!'

Then, icily calm, he himself looked down.

He could see Matt below, caught in the safety net, where the wind was tugging his yellow hair. Some distance away, his hard hat bobbed on the surface of the water. But Matt himself was not moving.

381

Chapter Fifty-Nine

'He's not dead,' Duncan told Josie. 'But he may be hurt.
We don't know. He's been taken to the Royal.'

They were standing in the hall of Ardmore, where Josie
was twisting her sugary hands – she had been making
meringues for the boarders' tea – and Duncan, ashen-faced,
was trying to make her sit down.

'No, I'm OK. Just tell me what happened?'

He told her, stumbling over his words, as the horror
increased in retrospect, and she listened carefully, still
moving her hands together.

'It's what happened to you,' she said, when he finished.
'I'm sorry.'

'For God's sake, don't think about me! Listen, I have my
car outside, I want to take you to the hospital.' He looked
round desperately. 'Is there someone who can look after
things here?'

'There's Tilly, and mebbe Mum – will you wait for me,
Duncan?'

'Take all the time you want, Josie. I'll be in the car.' He
suddenly put his arms around her and held her for a
moment. 'Ken Pearce is with me. I'm taking him to the
hospital, too.'

'Ken? Yes, he's Matt's friend.'

'He wanted to be the one who told you what had
happened.' Duncan ran his hand across his dry lips. 'But I

said it should be me. Matt had been helping me, you see, Josie. Without him, I'd – look, I'll wait for you.'

She went slowly up the stairs, to fetch her coat and bag. She felt numb, frozen. Matt had had an accident, Matt was on his way to hospital, it wasn't known how badly he was hurt. At one time the news would have meant the end of the world for her. She would have been whirling out of control, crazy with fear that she might lose him. But she had already lost him, or at least they had both lost their love. So what should she feel now?

At the turn of the stair, she stopped. Here, long ago, she had looked up and found him waiting. He had stretched out his arms and she had gone to him. It had been the most perfect moment of her life. The most perfect moment, when she had realised that he loved her ... She swayed a little, remembering, and a fine sharp needle of pain pierced her heart. Oh, Matt ... They had had so much, they had gone so wrong. He had betrayed her, but then it was easy to betray, she knew that now. You had to be strong to be true, and people weren't strong, that was the thing. They were weak, they depended on each other. Great tears began to course down her face as she took her coat and bag from her room, but she didn't know whether they were for Matt or herself.

'Josie, what's happened?' cried her mother, on crutches at the foot of the stairs. 'It's no' your dad, is it?'

'No, it's Matt, Mum. He's had an accident, I have to go to the hospital. Duncan Guthrie's taking me.' Josie clutched her mother to her for a frantic moment. 'Can you manage? Tilly can do most of it, can't she? If you could just supervise?'

'Of course I can manage!' Ellie cried. 'I can sit at the table and do the lot. Oh, but poor Matt! Josie, how bad is it?'

'I don't know yet. He fell from the bridge.'

'Fell from the bridge?' Her mother sagged. 'Och, it's history repeating itself, eh? A damned bridge taking another man!'

383

'Don't talk like that, Mum. We don't know, you see, we don't know ...' Josie was buttoning on her coat, running to the door. 'Will you remind Tilly to pick up Justin? She's bringing Trina back when she's done the messages. And there's some bacon and cabbage for the dinner ...'

'Just go, just go!' Ellie cried.

But when the door had banged on Josie, she sat down and burst into tears. It was too much, this was. All happening again. Too much. And where was John, anyway? He'd gone down to the site as usual, but he should have been back by now. Did he know about Matt? Had he seen the accident happen? As soon as Tilly came back, Ellie decided she would send her out to look for him, she'd give her the money for a taxi to bring him back, shouldn't cost more than a shilling or two, and in the meantime she'd better get herself to the kitchen and start doing the tatties. Why was it that whatever happened, you had to think of food?

Matt was still in Casualty, a nurse told Josie, but X-rays had been completed and he would soon be on his way up to a ward. He was conscious and very cheerful, she added, smiling, and Josie's spirits rose.

'He'll no' be too bad, if he's conscious?' she whispered, when she and Duncan, followed by Ken found seats in the waiting-room.

'Och, he'll be fine,' Ken said heartily. So heartily Josie looked at him with suspicion.

'You think there's something wrong? Something serious?'

'No, no! I'm no' saying that!'

Josie glanced at Duncan, whose dark gaze was fixed on the scarred, well-polished linoleum at his feet. 'What do you think, Duncan?'

'Josie, I've no idea. If the nurse says he's conscious and cheerful, well, that's good.'

'I think there's something you're no' telling me. If you know something, you should tell me. I need to know.'

384

Duncan and Ken exchanged glanced. Duncan cleared his throat.

'All we know is that when he was being lifted into the ambulance, Matt said – he couldn't feel his legs. Now, Josie, don't look like that! It needn't mean anything. That's why we didn't tell you. What was the point in worrying you, when there might be no need?'

Josie looked around the waiting-room, at the despondent faces of the people on the benches, the dogeared magazines, the notices on the distempered walls – No Smoking – Please Give Blood – Would You Like to Help the WVS – and she saw none of it.

'It's like Mum said,' she murmured, half to herself. 'History repeats itself. The bridge has taken Matt, just like the rail bridge took ma dad.'

'Josie, Matt's going to be all right!' Duncan said urgently. He clasped her hands in his. 'He's going to get through this, I promise you!'

'You call it living, without the use of your legs?' She pulled her hands free. 'Some people could manage but no' Matt. All he cares about is being up on a bridge. You should understand that, Duncan, are you no' the same?'

He bit his lip and returned his gaze to the linoleum. Ken leaned forward and patted Josie's arm.

'Why'd we no' go and get a bite to eat in the canteen? Don't know about you, but I'm starving!'

It seemed a very good idea. Saved talking, saved thinking, and the tomato soup and ham rolls in the hospital canteen were surprisingly good – not that they really had any appetite. When they returned to the waiting room, it was to be told that Mr MacLeod had been taken to his ward. They could see him if they liked, shouldn't stay too long.

His bed was at the top of a long ward that smelled like all hospital wards of disinfectant and sick humanity. There was a bandage round his brow, and his face, though it appeared tanned against the white pillows, had a greyish tinge. When Josie bent over and kissed him with nervous warmth, carefully avoiding the bandage, his eyes flashed a little. With surprise, she thought. Maybe he hadn't expected her to kiss him.

'It's good to see you,' he murmured. 'Good to see you all.'

'See you've got your bed near the nurses,' Ken said, trying to joke. 'They'll have their eye on you, eh? Better do what you're told, Matt.'

'Don't I always?'

Duncan, never one for chit-chat, asked gravely, 'And how are you feeling now, Matt?'

He shrugged. 'I'm OK. Black and blue, got a few cuts, but I'll live.'

He's not saying anything about his legs, thought Josie, but he doesn't know that I know.

'Point is, how are you, Mr Guthrie?' Matt was asking smoothly.

'I thought it was to be Duncan? Well, you're never going to believe this, but I'm all right.' Duncan shook his head. 'I'm absolutely all right. I don't know how it happened but I'm myself again. I can work on the bridge any time I like.' His voice faltered. 'And I'm thanking God for it, Matt. And you.'

'You don't need to thank me, Duncan.'

'I'd never have made it without you.'

'I didn't do anything, you did it yourself. That's the way it has to be.' Matt's heavy eyelids trembled, and Duncan, with a glance at Ken, said they should go.

'Josie, we'll wait for you outside?'

'I won't be a minute,' she said huskily. 'Mustn't tire you, Matt.'

'You won't tire me, Josie. Thanks for coming.'

'Did you think I wouldn't?'

'Didn't know if you could get away.'

'I'd have come, whatever happened.'

386

He smiled faintly, and asked about the children. They hadn't been too upset about him, had they? Hadn't been frightened?

'I haven't even seen them, Matt. Mum'll take them from school, she'll be good with them. She's pretty upset herself, and so will Dad be, but I haven't seen him either.'

'How about my folks?'

'Oh, heavens!' Josie coloured richly. 'Oh, how could I have forgotten? Matt, I'm sorry, I'll phone tonight, soon as I get home. I'll phone Iona at Lew's, that'll be best.'

'You needn't say much.'

'Oh, I won't. I won't worry them.' She hesitated. 'Look, Matt, mebbe I'd better tell you, I know about your legs.'

He lowered his eyes.

'Are they – still the same?'

He nodded.

'What do the doctors say?'

'They're waiting to see the X-rays.'

'Surely they could have said something?'

'Like to be sure, I suppose.'

Josie gave him her long direct gaze that he knew so well.

'When they are sure – if it's no' good news – I want you to know that I'll do all I can. I mean, whatever happens, we'll go through it together.'

Matt's eyes were now closed. He made no reply.

'Matt?' Josie whispered. 'Won't you look at me?'

He shook his head and she was appalled to see tears sliding down his cheeks. She had never seen him cry before, or any man, but Matt was so serene, so tranquil of spirit, his tears were totally unnerving, she could find no comfort for him. But he reached out his hand and she took it and held it, and so they were sitting when the doctors came to them.

Dr John Calder, Dr Lorna Mason. They had youthful, bright faces, they smiled easily, but neither Josie nor Matt could act well enough to smile back.

'Just been taking a look at your X-rays, Mr MacLeod,'

said Dr Calder. 'Thought I'd let you know as soon as possible – they show no permanent damage to your spine at all.'

No permanent damage. The sweetest words in the world, yet it was as though Matt and Josie had been given bad news. They appeared stunned, they could not speak.

'Obviously, you're wondering why your legs aren't functioning,' Dr Calder went on. 'With a fall such as yours, there can be that kind of symptom. You gave your spinal cord a pretty bad jolt, remember. But you'll find it's temporary.'

'You can rest assured,' Dr Mason put in firmly, 'you are not going to be in a wheelchair.'

'Thank you,' said Matt in a deep strange voice that didn't seem his. His drenched grey eyes were filled with light, his whole face against his pillow was luminous, as though the doctors had pressed a switch and brought him alive.

Can they no' see they're dealing in miracles? thought Josie, as they appeared to notice no change in Matt, only chatted for a few moments about his treatment, as though they were discussing the weather. When they finally moved off down the ward, these two messengers of the gods, in flapping white coats with biros in the pockets, Josie and Matt turned their eyes to each other.

'I'm so happy for you,' Josie whispered.

'I was a bit of a fool just then, eh?' Matt asked lightly. 'A great jessie.'

'Oh, come on!'

'Don't think I've cried since Ma left me my first day at school. I was ashamed of myself then.'

'Matt, it's no disgrace to shed a few tears. Men should cry, they should be allowed to cry.'

'I'm not crying now,' he said softly. 'Josie, I'll never forget what you were willing to do for me. That's what the tears were for. I couldn't believe you'd want to stay by me like that.'

'I meant it, Matt.' She bent her face to his and kissed him gently on the lips.

*

388

'It's strange, the way things work out,' Duncan said, driving Josie towards Ardmore. They had left Ken at Mrs Robb's cottage after he and Josie had hugged each other fiercely in their incredulous relief.

'I mean,' Duncan went on, 'this morning I thought today would be one of the worst days of my life, on a par with when I fell myself from the rail bridge. Now, it's one of the happiest. Matt's going to be all right, and so am I.'

'I feel the same,' Josie answered. 'In fact, I can't believe the things that have happened on this one day. I feel I've lived through a lifetime.'

But the day was not yet over. When they arrived at the house, they saw two cars parked there they hadn't expected to see. One was Lina's blue Morris, the other was Dr Ashton's Rover. Josie's eyes met Duncan's.

'The doctor's car ... Oh, it's no' the children, is?'

She ran to the front door, but before she could open it, Lina appeared and flung her arms round her.

'Is it Justin?' cried Josie. 'Is it Trina?'

'No, no, the children are fine. It's your dad, Josie. He's gone.'

'Gone?' She had wild pictures of her father packing a bag and departing. 'Gone where?'

'You know.' Lina's golden eyes were fearful. 'Oh, I wish it wasn't me had to tell you! He's dead. A coronary, the doctor said. Seemingly he was told about Matt at the site. When he came home, he didn't feel well—'

'I must go to Mum,' said Josie.

389

Chapter Sixty

'Would you like to see him?' asked Ellie. 'He's very peaceful.' She gave a quivering smile. 'More peaceful than he ever was in life, ma poor John.'

Dr Ashton looked up from the death certificate he was signing. 'Yes, go with your mother, Josie. It will help you, to see your father.'

'Of course I want to see him,' said Josie.

She looked exhausted, all her euphoria gone, but there was still a kind of resolute beauty in her face as she steeled herself for yet another ordeal. Lina touched her hand and said Josie needn't worry about the children, Kitty was looking after them next door. It was Kitty who had phoned Lina to tell her about Matt; that was why Lina had come over, to help. Oh, yes, she was wearing an apron, Josie noticed, quite a strange sight on her these days. Then she wondered how she could notice something like that, on her way to see her dad.

He was lying in the room he had shared for more than twenty years with her mother, this man who had meant so much to her; who had cast her away and taken her back, who had always somehow commanded her love, though she had once sought not to believe that. While Ellie sobbed into her handkerchief, Josie sombrely studied her father's face. Already, she thought, he was beginning to change in death. His nose – surely that had not been so sharp? His closed eyes were sunken, his mouth a falling line. But it was true, he looked peaceful. Wherever he was, all would be clear to him now.

She dropped to her knees and bent her head at his bedside, thanking God that they had made their peace before this death. The forgiveness she'd thought would be too hard had been easy, the bitterness had died, reconciliation was sweet. Now she need remember nothing else.

'They're taking him to the Chapel of Rest,' Ellie whispered, as Josie scrambled to her feet. 'But I'll no' go to see him, it'll no' be him there. Folk say they do them up so they look like nobody.'

'We'll say goodbye here, then.'

'Aye.' Ellie wiped her eyes. 'He was a good man, you know, Josie.'

'I know, Mum.'

'I'm no' saying he wasn't difficult. There were times when I used to wish him in Jericho! Aye, but he always thought he was doing the right thing, you have to remember that. You will remember it, Josie?'

'Yes, Mum.'

'And he even took to your Matt in the end, eh?' Ellie drew in her breath sharply. 'Why, Josie, I've never even asked you how he is!'

'He's going to be all right. No need to worry.'

'Thank God for that.'

It was hard, making the last goodbye. There would be the funeral, of course, but they would not see John Morrow then. This was their only chance to be with him, just the three of them, as the little family they'd once been. Both Ellie and Josie wept as they kissed John's cold brow, then went back and kissed him again.

'I knew as soon as he didn't come home this morning that something was wrong,' Ellie murmured. 'I was going to send Tilly out to look for him, then he came in with his face all grey and he said your Matt had fallen and it had given him such a turn. "Bed for you," I told him, and when he just went along and lay down, I knew there was something to worry about, because he'd never have done that without arguing. So I thought I'd get the doctor. But even before I got to the phone, he'd gone, Josie. Just slipped away.'

Josie put her hand on her mother's arm. 'Come on, Mum, you need to rest.'

'You'll see the minister, Josie? He's coming this evening. You tell him I want a really good send-off for your dad. There was never anybody worked for the kirk like ma John.'

'I'm sure he knows that, Mum.'

'And then there's the undertakers.' Ellie's voice shook. 'You'll see to them and all, Josie?'

'I'll see to everything, Mum. You just lie down.'

As she couldn't sleep upstairs, a bed had been made up for Ellie in the dining room. Just for once, the boarders could have their meal from a trolley in the lounge, and though she was upset about that, Ellie went quite meekly to her bed, with a cup of tea and a couple of pills left for her by the doctor. It was a relief to Josie to have her settled, though when she went back to the kitchen where Tilly had fresh tea waiting, Lina told her she should be lying down herself, she looked exhausted. Everything was organised for the meal that night. Why, Josie had done most of it herself that morning. Made meringues as well!

'I made meringues?' Josie repeated. 'Was that this morning? I can't believe it.'

She felt a sudden longing to see her children. When Kitty, full of sympathy, brought them round, Josie clung to them, taking sad comfort from their smooth, rosy faces, their lovely youth and freshness. All was over for her father, but for her children everything in the world was new.

'Your dad's going to be all right,' she told them, stroking back their hair, looking long into their solemn eyes. 'He'll be quite better soon, and then he'll come home.'

'Grandad's no' better,' said Justin. 'He's gone.'

'He's gone to heaven,' declared Trina. 'Where the good people go. Was Grandad good, Mammie?'

'Yes,' Josie answered. 'Very good.'

The five guests in residence at the time were subdued by the latest sadness to strike Ardmore. These were long-term boarders, all bridge-workers except for Mr Warren, the retired clerk, who felt not only a natural sympathy for the family but anxiety about their own future. Would the place keep going? Would Josie be able to manage? She had surely enough to think about, with what had happened to Matt. Mr Warren, who had a special soft spot for Ellie, kept offering to help with the tea, until politely told by Kitty to sit down and relax, it was in hand.

'As for you, Josie,' she said briskly, 'you'd best away to your bed, you look fit to drop. We'll take care of everything here.'

'I can't rest yet.' said Josie bleakly. 'The undertakers are coming.'

Much later, after Kitty and Tilly had departed and the minister had called to arrange a date for the funeral, the undertakers came and went, discreetly taking John Morrow's body with them. Then Josie made her call to Iona, soft-pedalling her news, before lying down in the little room next to her children; somehow, that night, she couldn't face sleeping alone in her own double bed. Meanwhile, Duncan drove Lina home.

He knew he was in trouble. She hadn't looked at him all evening. In the car, he said tentatively, 'Lina—'

'It's no use talking, Duncan, there's nothing you can say. You went up that bridge and I can't forgive you.'

'For God's sake, it wasn't exactly a crime! It was something I just had to do, that's all.'

'Something you had to do!' She turned her flashing eyes from the road ahead to his fine profile. 'You mean risk

393

your life? Risk going back to what you were? You didn't give a damn about me and the girls, did you? What would have happened if you'd fallen again?'

'It was Matt who fell,' he said quietly. 'After he'd helped me. I should have thought you'd be worrying about him.'

'I am worrying about him! That's the whole point, can you no' see?' Her voice thickened with tears. 'But it could have been you, Duncan. You went up there and risked everything, without even telling me.'

'It paid off,' he said stubbornly. 'I'm well, I'm myself again, and I'll never regret doing it. Except for what happened to Matt.'

'You weren't to blame for that, there's no need to blame yourself.'

'I feel bad, all the same.'

They drove in silence for some time, Lina dabbing at her tears, Duncan giving long exhausted sighs.

'Look, I'm sorry I didn't tell what I was planning to do, Lina, but I wanted to save you worry. Anyway – you haven't always told me things.'

He head came up sharply, her eyes glittering. 'What do you mean? What have I no' told you?'

'About meeting Callum Robb.'

'That was years ago! And it meant nothing!'

'Didn't tell me, though.' He gave a grim smile. 'Not that I care about Callum Robb. He's not going to get what he wants now.'

'What he wants?' Lina repeated warily. 'What are you talking about?'

'I'm talking about him waiting to step into my shoes. Oh, don't look shocked – you know that's been in his mind. If anything had happened to me, he'd have been there, wouldn't he? Taking my place?'

'Duncan, that's a terrible thing to say!'

'A terrible thing to want,' he answered softly.

*

Josie had looked in on the children before going to bed. Trina was serenely asleep, Shirley seated close by in state, but Justin was moving restlessly, his teddy clutched to his thin little chest. Josie kissed his brow and his eyes flew open.

'Mum?'

'It's all right, Justin, I'm next door, you go to sleep.'

'Dad's OK, isn't he? He's no' going to be like grandad?'

'He's quite all right. I told you, he'll be coming home soon.'

'Those men took Grandad away, didn't they? In a box?'

Josie shivered. 'You shouldn't have been watching, Justin, you shouldn't have been out of bed.'

'I couldn't go to sleep, I got up and went to the stair and I was the men, I saw them carrying a box and I knew they'd got Grandad.' Justin flung his arms round Josie's neck. 'And I was scared, Mum, I was so scared!'

'It wasn't really Grandad, Justin. You know we all have a body and we all have a spirit. You can't see the spirit, but it's what makes us people. When we die, the spirit leaves us and goes to heaven, it's only the body that's left, and that's no' really us. So don't worry about the box, darling, it's no' Grandad in there.'

He seemed comforted and when she had tucked him in and fitted in Teddy beside him, said he thought he could go to sleep.

'But leave the light, Mum!'

'I always leave the light, Justin pet.'

Aching in mind and body, Josie lay sleepless. She had known she would not sleep, the events of the day held her too fast, there could be no escape. In a way, she didn't even want oblivion. Awake, her father was with her, and so of course was Matt. He was all around her. This had been his room when he had first stayed at Ardmore. It was in this bed that he had lain and thought of her, next door. And, oh, God, she had thought of him!

She twisted from side to side in the cold sheets Lina had helped her to put on the bed. They'd changed the sheets on her father's bed, too, so that it would be ready for her mother next day. Poor Mum, who hadn't even woken when the undertakers had come for her husband's body. How would she cope when it really sank in that she had lost John? How would it be for me, Josie asked herself again, if I lost Matt?

She remembered the pain on the stair, the needle in her heart. But that had been for the past. She didn't know about the future. Her eyes were closing, her head on the pillow was heavy. Perhaps she would sleep after all. There were tears on her face as she drifted away, tears for her father and for Matt, who had himself wept that day.

Chapter Sixty-One

The funeral was everything Ellie had wanted. The kirk packed with people who had known and respected John, everyone singing his favourite hymns, a fine eulogy from the minister, stressing all his achievements. And no one daring to look sideways at Josie, no one choosing to recall her estrangement from her father or that it had been her father's fault. All that was in the past, as would have been made very plain if only poor Matt had been able to attend the funeral. But, of course, he was still in hospital, not yet walking, Josie said, though expected to any day. He would have come to John's funeral if he could, atheist or no atheist, and how proud Ellie would have been to see him! How happy it would have made John, if he could have looked down and seen the unbeliever praying for him after all! But it was not to be. At least everyone else was there who could be there. Even Matt's relations from Glasgow who'd never even met John, though they'd been glad to hear of his reconciliation with Josie and their son. Even Mr Guthrie. Even Angus Braid.

The wind from the Forth chilled the mourners to the bone as John Morrow's body was laid to rest in the graveyard, but Josie felt only a hollowness in her being. Death was something the living could surely never accept. They pretended they did. They said life must go on. But all the time they were as empty as she inside, trying to make the connection between the man they had known and what was in the box, as Justin called it, being buried. Her father's spirit had gone to heaven, she had told her son, but as the earth fell over his coffin and the watching people turned away to leave him, did she really believe that? Matt didn't believe it. If Matt had died on that bridge, in his view he would have died forever. 'I am the Resurrection and the Life,' said the mighty words of the burial service, but there would have been no resurrection for Matt. And now Josie felt chilled by something colder than the wind that gripped her at her father's grave. Now she knew what losing meant. Now she knew she could not have faced it. She could not have faced losing Matt for ever.

Back at the house, the warmth and comfort after the cold wind, the table piled with food, the glasses of port, the cups of tea, all seemed to give the lie to her idea that the living could not accept death. Yes, here was life truly going on. George Braid laughing with Matt's brothers and Iona raising sleepy eyes to Bernie's admiring face, Mrs Tassie dandling Patty's new baby, Agnes cuddling Trina, Kitty Braid passing a plate of ham to Brandon, Marie and Lina deep in talk as Duncan filled glasses. Even Ellie, accepting one of Tilly's potted meat sandwiches from Mr Warren, was looking flushed and proud at the grand turnout for her John, and her own hospitality.

Perhaps it's only me, thought Josie. Perhaps I'm the only one who can't accept death.

'Hallo, Josie,' Angus said quietly.

He seemed very tall in his dark suit, and he had gone thin again. His collar was loose around his neck, there was no fullness to his face.

'It was good of you to come,' said Josie. She knew she too looked thin in her black dress, and now that the wind-whipped colour in her cheeks had faded, was pale again. 'Have you found something to eat?'

He shook his head. 'I wanted to speak to you outside the kirk, but there were too many people.'

'Yes, a good crowd. Mum's thrilled.'

'I wanted to say how sorry I was about your dad. And also about Matt.'

'Thank you, Angus.'

'How is Matt?'

'They say he's going to be all right.'

'I'm glad.' His eyes were steady on her face. 'I've finished my work up here, made a decision on a site.'

'Yes, Lina told me,' she replied politely. 'Glasgow, isn't it?'

'Yes, we think we've found just the place.'

'But you won't be moving up?'

'No.' He smiled briefly. 'I'm going to America. A temporary assignment. Then I'll probably be based in London again.'

She remembered who was in America. 'I hope all goes well for you, Angus. You know I mean that, don't you?'

'Yes, I do.' A sudden spasm at his mouth gave the lie to his calmness. 'I suppose it just wasn't meant, eh? For us to be together. Not in our stars.'

'I want you to be happy!' she cried.

'So's you can be happy too? Well, I'll do my best.' He bent his head and kissed her on the cheek. 'Goodbye, Josie. Don't forget me.'

'I'll never do that, Angus.'

'And don't feel guilty. I told you before, I knew what I was doing.'

Why did his words only make her feel worse? thought Josie, as she watched his bright head move away from her for the last time. Guilt was like love, you couldn't stop feeling it to order. She looked round dazedly to find Marie at her side.

'Now why don't you take a break?' Marie asked gently. 'You look worn out.'

'Doesn't make me feel any better, telling me that.'

399

'Well, just sit down and let me bring you some tea. Or something stronger, if you've got it.'

'Something stronger?' Josie smiled tiredly. 'We're lucky Mum's even allowed us port. But when have I drunk port?'

'Tea it is,' said Marie cheerfully, as she steered Josie towards a chair.

'Now, tell me how you are,' she ordered, stirring sugar into Josie's tea. 'It's been hell, eh?'

'You could say that, but I'm managing. We all are.' Josie drank her tea and sat back, sighing, in her chair. 'It was good of you folk to come over from Glasgow, you know. Mum's really grateful.'

'We didn't know your dad, but we all wanted to come, because of you.'

'I appreciate that. And you're a lifeline, Marie, you always were.'

'I wish I could just wave a wand and get you on a cruise somewhere, you and Matt.'

'If I'd a wand to wave it wouldn't be for a cruise.'

Marie's bright gaze dropped. 'No.' She heaved a deep sigh. 'He's still no' walking, Josie.'

'It will come, they said so.'

'Aye, but when? I think he's beginning to wonder if they're right.'

Josie set her cup on the floor beside her chair. 'They must be right, Marie, it's their job to be right.'

'Just have to be patient, then?'

'I haven't been able to see him for a couple of days. How is he, Marie? How's he feeling?'

'Typical Matt. Never lets you know.'

The memory of his tears made Josie lower her eyes. He had not been able to prevent her knowing his feelings then.

'I'll go to him when this is over,' she said in a low voice. 'Duncan and Lina can give me a lift, and Mum's got Mrs Robb and Tilly to help.'

'I think it'll do him all the good in the world to see you,

400

Josie. He's told us, you know, what you offered. Said it meant so much, though he'd never take you up on it.'

'He won't have to,' Josie murmured. 'He's going to be all right.'

'Sure he is,' Marie agreed.

Matt wasn't in his bed when Josie arrived. She had changed from her black clothes, not wanting to depress people in the hospital, and her face, flushed from hurrying, and her lovely hair, hanging rich and free, made the eyes of the men in the ward follow her as she went searching for her husband.

'Mr MacLeod?' repeated a nurse. 'He's still in the dayroom. Probably waiting for someone to push him back.'

He was in his dressing-gown in a wheelchair. Two other patients were watching television in the corner but Matt was turned away, his eyes on his newly pale, soft hands.

'Matt?' said Josie, coming to him.

He looked up and at the light that came into his eyes, her heart stirred and sang.

'Josie! Och, it's good to see you! Never thought you'd come today, not with the funeral and everything.'

'I wanted to see how you were. Got a lift with Duncan and Lina.'

'So you'll have to go back on your own? Josie, you shouldn't have bothered.'

'Duncan's driving me back. I told him he needn't, but he insisted. He said he wouldn't come in when I was here, he'll look in tomorrow, but he'll wait for me in the car-park.'

'That fellow.' Matt shook his head in wonder. 'Have you ever known anyone like him?'

'It's because of you, Matt, he'll do anything for you. Because of what you did for him.'

'Hell, I didn't do anything.' Matt took Josie's hand. 'How was it, then, the funeral?'

'Oh, it went off well. The church was packed, every-body'd turned out.'

'Folk thought a lot of him, eh? Well, I suppose he was a good man. In his way.' Matt smiled wryly. 'Did what he thought was right.'

'Made mistakes. Like the rest of us.'

'You mean me?'

'I said us.'

Their eyes met. Matt's were the first to fall.

'Bit late now, to change anything.'

'No, it's not!' Josie leaned forward. 'It's never too late to do anything, if you want it enough.'

Matt glanced at the men watching television. 'Why don't you take me back to the ward, Josie? We can talk there.'

Josie had never pushed the wheelchair before and was cut to the heart as she pushed it now. Matt, so strong, so fearless, used to working high in the sky, had become like a child, dependent on her, sitting quietly in the chair, his yellow head below her eyes, his hands folded on his lap. She felt she couldn't bear it, yet swallowed her anguish, for it was Matt who must bear it, not she. When they reached his bed, she knew panic, for how was she to get him into it? But it seemed he had already become adept at swinging himself from chair to lowered mattress, grinning at her as he did so, pleased that he could do as much unaided. She busied herself straightening his bedclothes, so that he would not read whatever was in her face, but he read it anyway.

'It's OK, Josie, I'm getting used to it. Don't fret for me.'

'They promised!' she cried. 'They promised you'd be all right!'

'Well, I still might be.'

'Might?'

'Takes time.'

'Time ... you're so patient, Matt, aren't you?'

'Think so?'

Josie pulled up a chair to the bedside. 'What are they doing then, to help you? They can't just give up!'

'They're not giving up. They're doing what they can. It's

402

possible I might be transferred to another hospital, they'll see how I go.'

Josie was silent, oblivious of all the activity of the ward, nurses and visitors coming and going, people laughing and talking.

'At least I've lost my bandage,' Matt said cheerfully. He pushed aside his hair to show a healing scar on his brow. 'Something's getting better, anyway.'

'Oh, Matt.' Josie bent her head over his hand. 'Do you think we can? I mean, change things? Go back to what we had?'

He pulled his hand away. 'Let's not talk about that now.'

'Why not? Why shouldn't we?'

'Things have changed anyway. I'm not the same as I was.'

'But, Matt, you will be, you'll be just the same as you were. You said so yourself.'

'I said might, not will.' His eyes rested on her eager face. 'There's a difference.'

'I told you once, whatever happened, we'd go through it together,' Josie said steadily. 'I'm going to say that again because things have changed for me, too. Changed back, whether you can see that or not.' She put her face close to his. 'I love you, Matt, just as I used to do.'

He lay back against his pillows. He said nothing.

'Don't you believe me?' she whispered. 'Do you think I'm just saying it?'

'I think we shouldn't talk about love now, Josie. It's like the doctors said, I have to see how I get on.'

'It doesn't matter how you get on! We'll still have a marriage, a life together!'

He shrugged. 'Maybe.'

'What do you mean, maybe?'

'They said to give it time. Let's do that.'

The bell was ringing for the end of visiting. Josie drew away, her face a mask. Should she make him say what was in his mind, make him say he loved her? He did love her,

403

didn't he? There had been that light in his eyes when he saw her. Maybe it didn't mean as much as she'd thought. She felt something of a fool, offering love after all these years, after what had happened between them, offering – and receiving nothing in return.

'I'll come tomorrow,' she said stiffly, and kissed him on the cheek. 'Now, I'd better hurry, Duncan will be waiting.'

At the door of the ward she looked back, but a nurse was shaking a thermometer by Matt's bed and she couldn't see whether he was watching her or not.

Chapter Sixty-Two

One thing Josie had given no thought to was her father's
will. Why should she? He would have had nothing to leave.
She was therefore astonished to learn that he had left a total
of seven hundred and fifty pounds, excluding money set
aside for his funeral. Five hundred pounds would go to her
mother, and – Josie couldn't believe it – two hundred and
fifty pounds was to come to her.

'Why, I didn't know Dad had anything!' she cried, when
her mother told her the contents of the will. 'Where did he
get this money from?'

'Did you no' think he'd have insurance?' asked Ellie.
'Five hundred came from that, and he saved the rest. He
never smoked or drank, remember, didn't go out much.'

'That's true,' said Josie, thinking, Poor Mum, what a
life. 'Well, I'm thrilled. I've never had any money of ma
own before, I'll keep it for a rainy day.' Which might not
be too far away.

'You could buy a little car,' her mother said casually.
'Second-hand, of course. I looked in the paper, you can get
a nice fifties car for a hundred and something. Then you'd
still have a bit left.'

'You've been looking at car sales? What's come over
you? What would I want with a car?'

'You could drive to your job.'

Josie stared. Had her mother gone a little...?

405

'What are you talking about, Mum? I have no job.'

'Listen, Josie.' Ellie leaned forward, her reading glasses wobbling on the end of her fine nose. 'I've been thinking about you. And worrying. I don't want you to end up like me. I don't want history repeating itself.'

Josie lowered her eyes. There was no need for her mother to spell out her fears. They were the same as Josie's. The parallels were staring them in the face. A man damaged for life by a bridge. A woman making a living, cooking, cleaning, going round, and round, following the pattern, turning the wheel.

'I always wanted you to have something better than me,' Ellie was murmuring. 'One time, I used to think you could make a good marriage – I mean, to somebody like Mr Guthrie.'

'Yes, Mum,' Josie sighed. Where was the point of all this?

'But I know now I was wrong to want that. Women should make their own way, eh? No' be dependent on a man, 'cos look what happens to men. Even Mr Guthrie. So I've been thinking, why don't you try for that teaching course you wanted to do?'

Josie's head shot up. 'Teaching course? Whatever's made you think of that?'

'I'm telling you, I want you to have a better life than mine. I don't want you running this place, working all hours, never having time off, doing the messages, thinking of meals. If you've got to be the breadwinner, I want you to have a professional job. And I'm sorry now I didn't think of it before.'

'Mum, there's nothing I'd like better.' Josie gave a weary smile. 'But just how could I go off on a teaching course? With the children to look after, the work here, and Matt – ' her voice faltered '– mebbe in a wheelchair. It's just no' possible.'

'It is possible, Josie. Monnie Robb's willing to come back to Ardmore. She's knocking round that house Callum bought her like a pea in a drum, and when she's done her gardening, what else does she have to do? Now, she wouldn't want much in wages, and we'd still have Tilly. I'm sure we could run the house without you and bring the bairns home from school, 'specially as I'm getting better every day. Come on, it's worth thinking about, eh?'

'There's Matt,' Josie said slowly. 'We don't know about him.'

'No. You'd have to see what he thought.'

'And how he is.'

'Aye.'

They were silent for a time, then Josie sprang up and folded her mother's thin frame in her arms.

'Thanks,' she said quietly. 'Thanks, Mum. You don't know what this means to me.'

'Be careful, you're knocking ma glasses.' Ellie sniffed and stood up. 'Have you noticed how I'm walking these days, Josie? If Matt has to have ma room on the ground floor, I reckon I could go upstairs. Och, it's the Lord's will how things work out, eh?'

Haven't worked out yet, thought Josie, but her heart was beating like wings in her breast as she cleared the kitchen, set out her baking board, flour and sugar, eggs and apples. Eve's Pudding, that would be nice and filling on a cold December day. Folk always wanted a hot pudding on a day like this, especially with custard. Two hundred and fifty pounds kept going through her head like a litany. Enough to buy a car and have a bit over. Yes, Mum was right. And then if she did get to Moray House for teacher-training and did qualify, she could spread the net to find a job. Could be a professional at last, doing what she wanted.

'Josie,' came her mother's voice. 'There's a telephone call for you.'

'Who is it?' asked Josie, alerted to anxiety by the peculiar tone of Ellie's voice.

'It's the hospital.'

*

'I told you sensation would come back, and it has!' said Dr Calder, grinning widely. 'Matt here got the first tingles in his toes last evening, bawled for the nurse, bawled for me, and from then on we haven't been able to tie him down. Wants to do a Highland Fling up Princes Street, eh, Matt?'

'No, the road bridge,' said Matt, his eyes on Josie.

He was sitting in a chair by his bed. He was wearing a dark blue shirt and grey trousers and looked as bright and shining as a new penny, as golden as he had looked in the old days, when Josie had thought he carried a special kind or radiance wherever he went.

'Come on,' the doctor urged. 'Do your party piece, Matt. Stand up, take a step.'

I'm going to disgrace maself, thought Josie. I'm going to break down. But why shouldn't I? This is so wonderful, this is unbelievable. Oh, Matt, Matt...

He slowly rose to his feet, watched covertly by the other patients and their visitors. Someone gave a weak cheer, and Matt grinned and bowed his yellow head. He seemed strangely tall to Josie, as though he had grown while he was in hospital, but it was only because she hadn't seen him on his feet for so long.

'Take a step, Matt,' said Dr Calder. 'Just one or two will do. We don't want him to do too much, Mrs MacLeod, the muscles have to be built up and he's still going to need physiotherapy.'

Matt obediently took a step towards Josie, and the ward wit gave another cheer. Dr Calder laughed and pulled the curtain round the bed. 'Sorry about the noises off – there you are, a bit of privacy, eh?'

Josie cleared her throat, staring, charmed, at Matt, who took another step and then sat down.

'I don't know what to say, Doctor. You were right... you were absolutely right!'

'I know you were worried,' he said easily, 'and I don't blame you. As I explained before, a jolt to the spine can do damage to nerves that isn't always easy to isolate. Usually

408

it clears, but it takes its time. You have to be patient.' He put his hand on Matt's shoulder. 'As this fellow has been.'

'He's a patient man,' said Josie.

'Helps, always helps. Well – I'll leave you for the moment.' Dr Calder shook Josie's hand and looked for a moment into her face. 'It's been a difficult time for you,' he said gently. 'But it's over now.'

And then Josie did break down.

For some time they sat together, she and Matt, on the edge of his bed, trembling with a joy they could not express. Then they began to kiss, gently, in the privacy of the curtain.

'What will folk be thinking?' Josie whispered.

'To hell with what they're thinking. This is my chance to be alone with you.'

'I wish you'd phoned me last night, to tell me the news.'

'Didn't dare. In case it wasn't real, in case I'd dreamed it.' Matt shivered a little and played with Josie's beautiful hair, running the strands through his fingers. 'Sometimes I did dream I could walk again, and when I woke up and found I couldn't – it was pretty hard to take.'

'It's over now, Matt, it's over.'

'Aye, well, that's why I didn't phone you. Wanted to be sure.' He smiled. 'Had a terrible night. Kept waking up and feeling my legs, getting out of bed to make sure they still worked. Then the night nurses kept coming up and offering me tea. Tea! I didn't need any tea, didn't even need a drink. I was drunk already!'

'How long will you have to stay in, do you think?' she asked. 'You will be home for Christmas?'

'You bet. They won't see me for dust!'

'Were you serious just then, about going back on the bridge?'

He looked at her in surprise. 'Of course I was serious. It's my life, Josie. I'm a bridge man, it's where I belong.'

'I keep thinking of Duncan.'

'I'm different from Duncan. Anyway, he's all right now. We'll be up there together.'

'If it's what you want,' she said, sighing.

'It's one of the things I want.' He kissed her long and passionately. 'Shall I say I love you now?'

'Why wouldn't you way it before?'

'You know why. I wasn't going to let you tie yourself to a fellow who couldn't walk.'

'Matt, I am tied to you, whatever happens. And that's what I want.'

A shadow crossed his face and he let her go from his arms.

'I don't know why. After what happened. I was such a bloody fool—'

'I told you, we both made mistakes.'

'I certainly did. But there were no other women, you know, when we were apart.' He looked at her sombrely. 'Mebbe, when I went away, you used to think—'

Josie looked down. She didn't want to remember what she'd thought when he went away, or how she'd pushed the thought from her mind, so that finally she hadn't thought of him at all.

'You might have forgiven me Antonia Fearn,' he said quietly, 'if you hadn't thought there were others.'

'Let's no' talk about it.'

'There never were any others, Josie. I never was a womaniser.'

She raised her eyes. 'I know, Matt.'

'Until I changed everything.'

'Things must have changed back. I love you, Matt.'

'Oh, Josie.'

He held out his arms in the old way and she went to them. It was almost as if they had come full circle, back to the meeting on the stairs at Ardmore, back to the start of their love. But that love was different now. They had renewed it. Strengthened it. They had weathered their storms, they had come through to the sun.

Finally, Josie pulled herself away from Matt's clasp.

'Think I'd better open the curtain now,' she said breathlessly. 'Before Sister tells us off.'

'Ah, do you have to?'

'I want to give you some news anyway.'

'Good news, I hope. Only good news is allowed today.'

'I think it's good news.' She told him of her little legacy and her mother's idea that she should do the teaching course. 'What do you think, Matt?'

He pulled her back for one last kiss. 'I think two hundred and fifty pounds is a nice little nest-egg. You put it in the bank because I'm thinking it's time I tried to buy an old banger myself. Now's the time, when I can earn good money.'

'And the teaching?' she asked, a little anxiously.

'Och, Josie, you know you don't have to ask me about that. It's what I want for you, something better than wasting yourself at Ardmore.'

'I just want you to be happy about it.'

'I am.' Matt's handsome face was serious. 'Oh, God, I am, Josie. Happier than I've ever been. About everything.'

'I will open the curtain now,' she said quietly. 'Then I'll find the doctors.' Her smile returned, wide and generous. 'Ask them when you can come home.'

Epilogue

It was Friday, 4 September 1964, the day of the royal opening of the Forth road bridge. And there was a haar.

'Oh, I can't believe it!' cried Josie, standing with Matt early in the morning at their bedroom window in Ardmore. It showed the estuary masked in a blanket of unmoving grey. No hint of bridges, no ships, no signs of life. 'It's too cruel, today of all days!'

'It's got time to clear,' he muttered. 'The Queen's not due till eleven.'

'And if it doesn't clear, nobody'll see a thing!'

'Aye, there'll be a hundred thousand folk out there who might as well have stayed at home.'

They listened for a movement to the foghorns booming from the unseen naval ships gathered for the celebrations, then turned away. It was time to wash and dress. There were already sounds of moment from the rest of the house; Matt's family, who had come over from Glasgow the night before, were surfacing. How wonderful it was, thought Josie, hastily making their bed in the first floor back, the best room of the house, that she could now put everyone up. That was because Ardmore was no longer a guesthouse. For two years now it had been a private house, owned by Matt and Josie – with help, of course, from a building society.

There were still times when Josie felt she was dreaming all the changes that had come about since her father's death. It was not so incredible she should at last be training to become a teacher in Edinburgh, hoping to qualify next year, for she'd always had that goal in mind. But that she and Matt should own Ardmore, and that Ardmore should no longer have boarders – surely such a thing was from the world of fantasy! Yet it had happened. All thanks were due again to Ellie, for when her landlord died and his daughter put the house on the market, it had been Ellie who had suggested she lend Matt and Josie the deposit.

'Now what do I want with money?' she'd asked, tossing her head in another of her grand gestures. 'I've got your

415

dad's five hundred, I've got a bit put by of ma own, and all I'll do is leave it to you when I go, Josie. So why not take it now, at the time you need it?'

When Josie had pointed out that she was training as a teacher, she could no longer run a guest-house, Ellie had cried triumphantly that Ardmore needn't be a guest-house. Matt was earning, Josie would be earning, they didn't need the income as Ellie had needed it. It'd be a big house for Josie and Matt, aye, but they had a family, they could put Matt's folks up, they could spread themselves.

'And I do like space,' Josie had said thoughtfully. 'But what about you, Mum?'

'All taken care of. I'll move in with Monnie. She's asked me to, and I want to. Going to be sixty soon, Josie, time to be slowing down.'

'Not you, Mum!'

'Monnie and me'll still look out for the bairns, though. You'll have no need to keep on Tilly, she'll easily find something else.' Ellie had sniffed. 'Never does under the beds anyway! But we'll still come in and give you a hand, nae bother. What do you say?'

'You always seem to be asking me what I say,' Josie answered, laughing with a catch in her voice. 'I say it's wonderful. Perfect. If Matt agrees.'

'He'll agree. Always does what you want, Josie.'

'I can't imagine Ardmore without boarders,' she said slowly. 'What about Mr Warren, Mum?'

'Mr Warren? Don't worry about him. He's coming over to lodge with Monnie.'

'You'll both be with Monnie?' Josie raised her eyebrows, and Ellie flushed a little.

'She's got three lovely bedrooms, Josie, we'll all be very comfortable.'

'And Mr Warren's always had a soft spot for you, Mum.'

'He's a good friend, that's true.' Ellie's eyes filled suddenly with tears. 'But I'm no' forgetting your dad,

416

Josie. I'll no' be marrying again, no need to think that.'

'Mum, you do just what you want. Anything you do'll be fine with me.'

'Right, then let's see the lawyer and get our offer in, eh? For Ardmore.'

And so it had come about that Matt and Josie became householders, and Matt, whenever he had time, was already making improvements, painting, pointing, tiling, doing whatever repair came to hand. Trina had Josie's old room to herself, Justin had the room next door, while Matt and Josie gave themselves the best bedroom, leaving the rest of the rooms available for Agnes and Brandon, now retired, or any of the MacLeod family, to come over whenever they liked.

For the opening of the bridge, they'd all wanted to come, though Marie's Colin and Iona's Lew couldn't leave their businesses, and Matt's brothers said while there was still work on the Clyde they'd better no' skive off. Ken had proved right to worry, the future for Glasgow's shipbuilding was bleak, but today wasn't the time to brood on that. Josie was 'specially pleased that Marie, now a qualified optician and seven months pregnant, had driven herself over for the celebrations.

'What an idiot, eh?' she'd said when she'd given Josie her news, rolling her bright eyes. 'Fallen at last!'

'And a good thing too!' cried her mother.

'Och, will you look at the weather!' the MacLeods cried, at breakfast in the big kitchen. 'Isn't it enough to make you weep?'

'Could still clear,' said Josie, swathed in a large apron, frying bacon and eggs at the stove where she had cooked for Matt and Ken so long ago. 'Who wants fried bread?'

At the chorus of voices calling for the whole works, eggs, bacon, fried bread, tomatoes as well, she laughed.

'So, that's Ma and Dad, Gillie and Heather, Marie and

417

Iona, Polly, Shona, Midge, Tim, Hughie, Ailie, Matt, Justin, Trina and me. Might as well be cooking for the boarders again, eh?'

'Thank God you're not,' said Matt.

They had to finish breakfast quickly, clear up and be on their way, for they had to be early in their places. Justin and Trina, with the other pupils of their primary school, had been given special standing room in the royal reception area. They should have a wonderful view of the Queen, mist or no mist, but what anyone else would see was doubtful. Matt was to be on the bridge, with the workmen and their families, but Josie had elected to join the crowds already gathering at the south side, with Matt's family, her mother, Monnie Robb and Mr Warren.

'Be sure to wear something warm!' she cried, as everyone scattered to get ready. 'That haar is like a wet blanket.'

'Wet blanket is right,' sighed Iona.

'Come on, it's got time to clear,' said Marie.

'Why does everyone keep saying that?' asked Heather, 'From what I've heard, this stuff could last all day.'

'Aye, we're way behind schedule with the opening because of this kind of weather, not to mention snow, frost and gales,' Matt said cheerfully. 'But I'm an optimist, I say we'll see the sun today.'

And he was right. Just before eleven o'clock, when the Queen was due to arrive from Dalmeny where she'd spent the night in the royal train, the first glimpse of the road bridge began to appear through the fog. Everyone held their breath, until with wonderful theatrical effect, the rest of the clinging greyness rolled back like a curtain and the sun shone over the Forth. A great cheer went up, for the Queen, the sun, and the new bridge. As the royal party stepped up on to the dais, the pipes and drums sounded, bells and hooters rang across the water, and the ceremony began.

'Can you see what she's wearing?' whispered Ellie.

418

'Och, I wish I was a foot taller!'

'Blue coat,' said Mr Warren, who did have the advantage of a few more inches. 'Blue hat, shiny brooch.'

'Sapphires and diamonds,' sighed Iona. 'She often wears that brooch. And pearls.'

'And the Duke is wearing a grey suit and carrying a brown hat,' observed Brandon. 'If anyone's interested.'

There were speeches and a prayer from the Queensferry minister. The Lord Provost asked that the men who had died during the making of the bridge should be remembered. Compared with the toll the rail bridge had exacted, there had been very few fatal accidents, but a chill went through the crowd as they thought of the families grieving that day. Josie bent her head, thanking God for Matt's deliverance. She wished she could have seen Duncan and Lina, but they had seats elsewhere. It was Marie who felt for and pressed her hand.

The Queen's speech was short and clear, ending with her official declaration that the road bridge was now open. As a twenty-one-gun salute thundered out from eight of the ships in the Forth, flags were raised, the crowd cheered, presentations were made, and then the royal cars began to move slowly towards the bridge for the crossing to the north.

'Matt will see the Queen now,' said Agnes, dabbing her eyes. 'Oh, thank God, it's all gone well.'

They knew she hadn't meant just the opening ceremony.

Afterwards they all agreed they had never seen a finer sight than the completed, streamlined bridge spanning the glassy waters of the Forth, towers and cables glittering in the sun, while its senior neighbour, the rail bridge, seemed to stand aloof, still famous, still loved. But what of the ferries? Centuries on from an older queen's journeys, a contemporary queen was to make the ferry's last trip, when Queen Elizabeth II was brought back from North Queensferry. And the waiting crowds, though many had cursed the queues in the past, shed a few tears as the ferry came in and docked for the last time.

'Och, it's so sad,' Josie murmured to Lina, who had found her in the crowd. They watched the Queen leave the ferry for the car that would take her to lunch in Edinburgh. 'I can't believe we'll never travel on the ferries again. Remember how we used to watch them coming in from Mrs Tassie's?'

'Aye, I do.' Lina gave a little sniff, then brightened. 'Talking of Mrs Tassie, she's got a gold mine going in the café today. Queues nearly to the Sealscraig Rocks! I've a good mind to nip in and put ma apron on again, to give her a hand!'

'Have you seen Patty?' asked Josie, laughing at the idea of the elegant Lina back as a waitress.

'Oh, yes, she's here somewhere.' Lina hesitated. 'And did you know Angus was here too? With Tammy?'

Angus had married Tammy Harley the year before in London. Josie had met his bride when he brought her home to see Kitty, and had thought her very sweet and clever.

'A bit like you to look at,' Matt had observed.

'A lot like you,' said Ellie. 'Poor Angus, eh?'

But Josie was relieved to think he was happy.

'Another piece of news,' Lina said casually. 'Callum Robb's engaged.'

'I had heard that,' Josie admitted. 'To some girl in New York, apparently.'

'I don't know, everybody seems to be getting hitched.' Lina shrugged. 'There's our Bernie, buying a ring for that girl he met when he was doing his National Service – imagine! And Antonia's just written to Duncan's folks to say she got married last Saturday in a register office to some chap from Oxford. Never said a word to anybody. Let's hope this one lasts, eh?'

'Let's hope so,' agreed Josie, smiling and at ease. 'Here's Duncan, looking for you.'

'Yes, there's a party of us going to have lunch together in Edinburgh. Not with the Queen in the Assembly Rooms,

420

I might add!' Lina waved her hand. 'Over here, Duncan!'

He stooped to kiss Josie's cheek. 'Wonderful day,' he said quietly.

She nodded, reading his thoughts. 'Matt's still up on the bridge, showing the family the views.'

'He'll be going out celebrating with the lads tonight, I expect?'

She laughed. 'If I let him.'

'Well, don't forget, we're taking you out for a celebration ourselves – as soon as you're free.'

'We'll look forward to it!' cried Josie, watching Lina and Duncan disappear into the crowds.

The streets of Queensferry were filled with people enjoying the warm sunshine as Josie and Matt led a tired straggle of MacLeods back to Ardmore. Ellie and Mr Warren had already gone back to Monnie Robb's house for a light lunch and a lie down.

'And I wouldn't mind putting me feet up maself,' sighed Agnes.

'Me, too,' said Marie, 'But when I've had a bite to eat, I think I'll drive maself home. Got to tell Colin everything he's missed.'

'Fancy you driving around, and in the family way!' Agnes exclaimed. 'And isn't it wonderful you can afford the car!'

'Good for Marie, I say,' said Gillie.

'Amen to that,' agreed Agnes. 'I'm not criticising.'

'Even I've got a car,' said Josie. 'Well, Matt has, and I'm going to drive it. I've passed ma test.'

'Know something, Aggie?' asked Brandon. 'We were born too soon.'

'You don't mind me going out with the lads?' Matt asked Josie that evening.

He was changing his shirt in the bedroom, Josie was combing her hair at her mirror. Downstairs the older children were twisting to a Beatles record on the radio, while

Brandon groaned and played snap with the younger ones, wishing he'd brought his fiddle over. In the kitchen, Agnes and the 'girls' were preparing a meal, with much giggling and sampling of the drinks Matt had set out for them. Everyone was feeling pleasantly relaxed. A good job had been done, the celebrations had gone well.

'Of course I don't mind,' Josie answered. 'You fellows should be together to celebrate, it's your special day. Or night.' She stood up. 'I'd better go down, sort that lot out, eh?'

'Had a good day?' he asked.

'Oh, yes! Just wish ma dad could have been here to see the Queen open the bridge. He'd have liked that.'

'He would.'

'Think I'll put some flowers on the grave tomorrow.'

'We could all go with you, if you like.' Matt hesitated. 'Listen, Josie, I've been meaning to talk to you. My job's finished here, I should be looking out for something else. But would you rather I didn't? I could stay put. Mebbe find something local.'

'You go for what you do best,' she said firmly. 'You're a bridge man. You need to work on bridges. You know I understand.'

'You won't mind if I have to travel again?'

'I've already said.' She gave him a long straight look from her dark-blue eyes, and his met hers in understanding.

'Thanks, then,' he said softly. He put on a tie and swept back his still thick hair. 'Mebbe we could all do some travelling some time? We're not doing too badly these days. We could take one of those package tours abroad, eh?'

'Robb's?' she asked, her face lighting up. 'Why, Matt, do you think we could?'

'Aye. See those faraway places you used to talk about.' He laughed. 'Well, Spain anyway.'

They both laughed and briefly kissed, then Josie said she really was going down to see what those girls were up to in her kitchen. Yet on the way past Trina's room she paused

422

for a moment and went in. Summer was only just over, the evening was still light as she looked around the room that had been hers. Here were her old dolls, still in position on Trina's bed; here the window where she had loved to stand to look out at the Forth. Two bridges to see now, if you twisted your head either way. And pinned to the wall still was her old text.

'The Path of the Just is as the Shining Light.'

There had been some sad times in this room, but happy ones, too. That was the best you could expect, maybe, in this life, a little of each. Of course, you only wanted happy times for your children. Josie looked up at the text. She had not been much of a kirk-goer since her return to Queensferry, but she still had a feeling for the old ways, the old words. She said a little prayer, that her children, all the children, might tread the path of the shining light. Though she could never define it, she was sure she knew what it was.

She'd thought Matt had gone, but he was waiting for her on the stairs when she came out of her old room.

'Remember?' he asked, holding out his arms.

She laughed. 'Oh, Matt, I'm on ma way down!'

But she slid into his arms, anyway.